RACHEL STEIN. The beautiful young American immigrant who returns to Jerusalem to rebuild her life and find the terrorist who murdered her fiancee.

JIBRIL ABU ALIM. The new generation, ruthless inheritor of the Presidency of the State of Palestine who will stop at nothing to return Jerusalem, Jaffa and Haifa to the Palestinian people.

MEIR TAL. The red-bearded, zealous Israeli settler who is a prime suspect in a diabolical assassination plot which could change the future of Jerusalem.

YIGAL RAMON. The Chief of Israel's General Security Service Jerusalem Bureau, who suspects Rachel Stein holds the key to finding the group plotting to execute the deadly plan hidden in...

THE JERUSALEM CONSPIRACY.

"Riveting from beginning to end... terrifyingly plausible."
                                   — M. Friedman

"Gripping... foreboding... The believable characters and .... *on the edge of my s* .... ston

D1500725

— THE — JERUSALEM CONSPIRACY

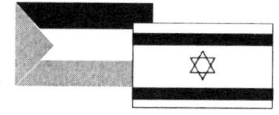

CHARLES SAMUEL

THE JERUSALEM CONSPIRACY is a work of fiction.
Names, characters, places, and incidents are either the product of
the author's imagination or are used ficticiously. Any resemblance
to actual persons, living or dead, or locales is entirely coincidental.

THE JERUSALEM CONSPIRACY
Published by
Providence House
POB 43294
Jerusalem, Israel, 91431

Providence House softcover edition / January 1996

ISBN 965-222-688-2

Printed in Jerusalem.

For Chana

— THE — JERUSALEM CONSPIRACY

One

The Peugeot station wagon slipped off the main high-way onto the dirt road. A man and woman sat in the front seat. A passenger sat in the back seat; keeping watch out the rear window to make sure they weren't being followed. The car bobbed up and down, following the hard-packed dirt and gravel surface for a few kilometers. At an unmarked hill they turned left and continued to zigzag for another half-kilometer following the tire tracks that indicated they had found the right route. The terrain looked more like the surface of the moon than a traditional desert. Gray, rocky foothills almost hugged each other, limiting the driver's vision to barely one hundred meters in any direction.

In a sheltered area hidden between two small barren mounds, the dusty car stopped; the occupants silently got out. The men were wearing blue jeans, T-shirts, and running shoes. The woman had on a dark skirt and loose-fitting blouse. Her thick eye make-up and long, red fingernails seemed out of place in the desert.

The passenger opened the hatch of the station wagon, removed two large green duffel bags and carried them to where the driver and the woman were waiting. Glancing at the couple, he sensed their relationship had already developed well beyond the operation they were rehearsing. He frowned, then quickly looked away, not wanting the driver to see his disapproval. It was wrong to have such a beautiful woman involved, for many reasons, yet he was in no position to protest. The driver knealt down, unzipped one of the bags and pulled out three M-16 rifles. The black handrests of the semi-automatic weapons glimmered in the late afternoon sunlight.

At the same time, the passenger unzipped the second duffel bag and pulled out a large cardboard placard on a wooden post — a grinning portrait of the overconfident president of Palestine, Jibril Abu Alim. He ran fifty paces straight ahead of the small group into the lengthening shadows, and pounded the post into the hard dirt with a large rock. He returned, and the driver handed him a rifle, motioning him to take his position on the hill behind and to the left. The woman quickly paced off sixty meters to the right. Her long, wavy, black hair was lifted by the warm desert breeze as she jogged.

The driver took his position, and paused to glance up at the blue sky. He thought he heard a sound in the distance. He quickly brought his index finger to his lips demanding quiet. The thick desert air pressed silently against his eardrums. Nothing. He took a deep breathe and sensed a wisp of moisture; the long hot summer was over. He loved this desert. It was so peaceful. Then anger welled up inside him as he realized how much violence there would have to be before peace would finally come to the land. The driver slowly lifted the M-16 to his shoulder and snapped the lock to automatic. He aimed, waited a moment and nodded. The desert silence exploded with the roar of automatic weapon fire and the signpost flew out of the ground.

The passenger ran to retrieve the target and brought it back to the car; the other two were ready with the engine running. He threw his M-16 into the open duffel bag in the trunk, zipped it up and slammed down the hatch. He slid into the back seat and shut the door as the Peugeot roared away, shooting out loose stones and gravel from under the spinning tires. He pulled out the placard and pushed it over the front seat so they could all see it. The driver smiled: Abu Alim's face was blown away.

Two

"Excuse me dear," said a plump elderly woman with silver-gray hair carrying an oversized handbag, "but I believe you're in my seat... and I asked specifically for an aisle seat because I have a weak bladder." Rachel still lost in a daydream, laid her book in her lap and stared absently up at the lady standing beside her.

"Nu?" she persisted, "it says right here on my boarding pass '21-C.' Should I call the stewardess? Stewardess! Stewardess!"

"No, no, it's fine. I'm sure I'm the one in the wrong seat," Rachel said unbuckling her seat belt. "I'm sorry. I'm a little distracted, and I didn't check my seat number." Rachel opened her purse to look for her own boarding pass and momentarily panicked when she didn't feel her gun. Then she remembered that the check-in attendant insisted she put the handgun in her checked baggage — "airline regulations."

"Yes, here it is," said Rachel. "You're right, I'm 21-B." She slipped her slender frame into the middle seat, and the old lady wedged herself in beside her.

"No need to be nervous, dear. First trip to Israel?" She didn't wait for a response. "I always travel El Al. They never have any security problems. Pooh, pooh, pooh. We're in good hands — don't worry."

Rachel forced a smile and picked up her book. "Thanks," she said, hoping the book would be an effective escape from the endless verbal onslaught she expected.

"My granddaughter's getting married in Jerusalem. The King David Hotel, no less. If you're not busy Thursday afternoon you just *have* to come to the wedding. He's an Israeli boy. A few of my friends say to watch out that he's not marrying her just to get a Green Card. Some of them do that, you know." Rachel smiled and nodded, then retreated back into her daydream as the lady chattered on. The woman could not know the change her words had made in Rachel's heartbeat.

"That's where they're going to build it," said Ari pointing to the barren windswept hill, "our new home." Rachel looked up into Ari's dark brown eyes; in them she saw a mixture of purposefulness, intensity and caring. Those eyes promised her a future that no house in the Judean desert ever could.

"Look, look at it. Isn't it beautiful? The prophet Amos walked through these hills. Abraham and Sarah drove their flocks across this land." Ari was lost in an age long past.

Rachel turned to look; it took her breath away. "What did I ever do to deserve all of this?" she asked Ari. "Not only is it the promise of the promised land come true," she continued with emotion, "but it's my own dream and our dream come true as well."

Every day since her Bat Mitzvah she had prayed fervently that the God of Abraham, Isaac, and Jacob would bring the Jewish people back from the four corners of the earth, back to the land of her people. "It's not just a national home," she remembered her father explaining to her as a little girl, "but Eretz Yisrael *— the Land — belongs to the Almighty Himself. He has entrusted it to the Jewish people to build a model nation on it based on the values of our Holy Torah."*

As a teenager, Rachel had joined the protests outside the Soviet embassy in Toronto to free Soviet Jewry. She was a precocious child who was fearless when it came to standing up for the rights of her people. She spent her summers at a religious Zionist camp in upstate New York and became fluent in Hebrew. After high school, she spent a year at a women's seminary in Jerusalem. It was during that year that she met Ari, who was also a yeshiva student.

"When they finish building our new subdivision of Ma'alot Yair, there will be more than seven hundred families — that's over three thousand people. Not bad for a "settlement." There was always a tone of pride in Ari's voice when he talked about Ma'alot Yair. His family was involved in its inception shortly after the 1967 Six-Day War. In those days it really was a settlement of mobile homes placed east of the ceasefire line in empty, disputed territory between Israel and Jordan. Today, as the Israeli's and Palestinians were negotiaing its future status as part of the Oslo Accords, it was a bustling village with mediterranean style villas, manicured gardens, schools and public parks.

"Oh! I almost forgot," she exclaimed, reaching into her purse, "your engagement present!" Ari smiled at his bride-to-be. The contrast of his white teeth against his olive skin was dazzling. He took the package from Rachel's slender fingers. "I hope you

*like it," she said filling the silence as he unwrapped
the gift. Out here on the barren hill tops far away
from the noise of the city you could almost touch the
stillness.*

"So, do you think they're all like that?" asked the lady.
"By the way, my name is Klein, Milly Klein. Nice to meet
you."

Rachel snapped out of her dream knowing Mrs. Klein
was unaware that she had totally tuned her out. "Are all
whom like what?" Rachel asked, her mind still lingering on
Ari.

"Are all Israeli boys just out to marry American girls so
they can get a Green Card and leave Israel? You know, I
belong to a Hadassah women's group, and we helped build
that country. It's terrible that all those young Israeli people
are leaving just to make a little more money in America."

"I was once engaged to an Israeli boy," said Rachel
quietly.

"We must have raised hundreds of millions of dollars
since 1948 to build hospitals, factories, and schools," Mrs.
Klein chattered on, "and this is the thanks we get? They
really think life is better in America...?" Mrs. Klein stopped
mid-sentence and turned to Rachel as if seeing her for the
first time. "What do you mean "once engaged?" Is everything all right, dear? Here, let me give you an orange; you
don't look so well. A skinny thing like you." She reached
into her overstuffed handbag and pulled out a piece of fruit.
"Let me peel it for you, dear."

*"It's exactly what I wanted!" laughed Ari. "A
gold Shabbat watch. But you didn't have to spend so
much on me. It must be so expensive. We could have
used the money buy something for the apartment."
Ari was always practical and thinking ahead. You
had to be, to survive in the Middle East.*

"Don't be so up tight," said Rachel, brushing back her windblown auburn hair. "This watch belonged to my grandfather. It was the only thing left from Austria, and my grandmother brought it with her to Canada after the war. She gave it to me to give to you. She's hoping that some day we'll name a son after my zaidie, and the watch will be passed down to him."

"Rachel, I love you," Ari said. His voice reflected the growing bond between them. He looked deeply into Rachel's light brown eyes that matched her hair. The delicately sculptured features of her face and smooth complexion required no make-up. She had the kind of beauty that might go unnoticed at first glance, but became more attractive each time Ari looked at her. There was a purity in her face that allowed her spirit to shine through. "The watch is beautiful, Rachel, but I'm not going to wear it while I'm on reserve duty. It might get lost or broken while I'm on maneuvers."

"Well, at least try it on," she insisted disappointedly. Ari strapped the watch to his wrist.

"It really is exquisite," she said, "but I have to admit it looks a little silly with your army uniform."

"Well, I'm certainly not going to scratch it up before the wedding." He took off the watch, put it back into the case, and slipped it into his shirt pocket. "Let's go, or we'll be late for our meeting with the caterer."

They got into the white Subaru and sped off down a one-lane road past a number of small Arab villages. Rachel was always tense traveling down this back road leading from the settlement of Ma'alot Yair to the main road to Jerusalem. Even during *daylight hours there was a sense of quiet foreboding. During the last few months a number of Israeli cars had been stoned by Palestinians nearby, and a Molotov cocktail had damaged a settler's vehicle. Luckily no one had been hurt in those incidents. Rachel clutched her handbag as they chatted about the details of the wedding.*

Ari made a sharp right turn when they reached the Jerusalem junction just outside Bethlehem. A hundred meters after the turn they heard a loud thud as a large boulder smashed into the roof of the Subaru. Rachel let out a scream; she felt a lump in her throat and her heart was pounding heavily. Ari instinctively swerved the car and sped up to avoid any more rocks that might be thrown at the car. His front left tire struck a large, sharp stone in the middle of the road. The tire began to lose air, pulling the vehicle to the right. He yanked the steering wheel to the left against the tug of the flat tire. He continued driving for a few hundred meters down the road until he felt they were out of danger.

"Are you all right?" he asked Rachel.

Even though stoning had become commonplace, it was terrifying to experience. Thousands of incidents had taken place since the beginning of the Intifada; the six year violent uprising of the Palestinians against the Israeli occupation of the disputed territories. A rock crashing through the windshield of a car traveling ninety kilometers per hour, could be lethal. Rachel gathered her wits. "I'm okay," she answered quietly.

The car came to a stop near some Arab-owned shops. "I'm going into that furniture store to call for help. I don't want to be changing the tire out in the open, by myself on this road," Ari said. "I'll be back in a minute. Don't leave the car." He turned quickly away.

Tears welled up in Rachel's eyes. For years this nightmare had repeated itself over and over in her imagination. She felt as if she were lost in a trance that she couldn't get out of.

"Are you sure you're all right dear?" asked Mrs. Klein. "He didn't hurt you did he? You know how rotten men can be. Don't worry, sweetie, a beautiful thing like you, they'll be lining up after you. So what happened — did he break it off?"

Rachel swallowed hard. Over the years she had learned to hold back, to reveal information only when necessary. "No, it's nothing like that," she said quietly. "Let's just say it wasn't meant to be."

It all happened so fast. Ari ran across the street with his hand pressed against the pistol tucked under his belt. He glanced back at Rachel and disappeared through the open doorway. Suddenly, a beige station wagon screeched up to the curb in front of the store. A man with a red kefiyah wrapped around his face jumped out of the car. Rachel gasped, "Oh my God! Ari!"

The Palestinian ran into the store. Seconds later, an old man came running out, waving his hands wildly and yelling in Arabic.

Rachel was frantic. Should she get out of the car? Stay inside? Drive away? She slid into the driver's seat and clamped her hands onto the steering wheel. Moments later the Palestinian came running out of the store stooped over, clutching his left hand, dripping blood. The station wagon started

moving even before he could get in. He lunged for the
door and fell into the passenger seat just as the car
sped away.

Even now, Rachel still couldn't bring herself to talk about Ari's murder. She was told by the army authorities that he had put up a valiant struggle, but that didn't help her find meaning in his senseless death. "Why Ari?" she kept asking herself. The Prime Minister had said, "This was an act of the enemies of the peace process." How did the Prime Minister know that? Maybe this was an act against the Jews. After all, before the Palestinian slaughtered her fiancé, did he ask Ari if he was for or against the peace process?

Rachel's initial anger and confusion had evolved into a sadness that permeated her every action, but her tradition taught her that everything happens for a reason; Events, big or small, good or bad, were opportunities to exercise one's free will, to choose greatness or to give up in defeat. Rachel had decided that it was time to stop mourning and start growing. She was on her way to tie up the loose ends of the past and start building a future. Her grandmother in Toronto had persuaded her to go back to Israel and continue pursuing her dreams. Rachel wanted her own family. She wanted to be part of building the State of Israel, and she wanted the terrorist who murdered Ari brought to justice.

"Don't worry dear, time brings wounds and heals them," said Mrs. Klein quoting a favorite Yiddish proverb. Rachel was a jumble of emotions. She was excited about coming back to Israel, yet it was tempered by the churning in her stomach that she felt everytime she replayed the attack in her mind. Her anxiety was compounded by not having the gun she had been carrying since Ari's murder. The innocent twinkle in Mrs. Klein's eyes had a calming effect on Rachel. She even reminded her a little of her own grandmother. It might not be so terrible to spend the remaining ten hours next to her. It might even be therapeutic.

"You know, my *bubbie* says that all the time," said Rachel, thoughtfully. "Maybe I will have some of that orange after all. Is it a Jaffa?"

Three

Yigal Ramon picked up the bullet-riddled poster lying on the large conference table in front of him. "Whoever did this, is certainly not a friend of the new president of Palestine," he said dryly.

The operations room of the *Shabak* Jerusalem branch was quiet as the two officers standing beside the table waited for their boss, Yigal, to continue. *Shabak,* also known as the *Shin Bet,* is a Hebrew acronym for General Security Services, the Israeli version of the American FBI. "What kind of weapon was used?" He fingered the holes that had eradicated Jibril Abu Alim's portrait.

"An M-16," answered one of the officers.

"And where exactly did you find this poster?"

"About one kilometer north of the Ma'alot Yair settlement."

Yigal looked up at the men standing around the table. They looked like two plainclothes security men at an El Al check in counter. Both were in their early thirties and just under six feet tall — fit but not muscular. Udi Harel was blond with deep brown eyes and severe good looks. Amiram

Barr was dark and mediterranean looking. Yigal spoke quietly, "Was he a Jew or an Arab?"

Silence.

"*Nu*? What's the identity of our assassin-in-training?"

Udi cleared his throat. "We're not exactly sure, Yigal. But based on the bullet casings we found, there was more than one M-16 fired. It looks like there were three people in the group, unless one of them fired two M-16s."

Yigal took off his glasses and rubbed his forehead. He explored his receding and thinning hairline with his right index finger. Middle age was catching up with Yigal, further exasperated by a small paunch developing around his midsection. His men knew this gesture meant he did not feel in control. "Do you have any ideas?" Yigal asked pensively.

"There's a good chance they're part of a new Jewish underground," said Amiram. "The Arabs usually carry AK-47s. Although there have been a number of our soldiers who had their M-16s stolen in the last few months."

The term 'Arab' was back in common use since the establishment of the Palestinian State, referring to Israeli Arabs. The government did not want to confuse them with their cousins across the border, although the Israeli Arabs continued to call themselves Palestinians.

Yigal drummed his fingers on the table distractedly. "Do the Palestinians know about this yet?"

"We don't think so."

"Good," he said standing up. "Keep it quiet. If they find out they'll milk it for all it's worth. They'll claim it's an Israeli government conspiracy and bring the UN down on us. For all we know it could just be a few Jewish settlement kids out having fun." Yigal handed the shot-up poster to Amiram. "Just find out who's doing this — and fast — before the media get onto it," he ordered.

"Yigal," said Udi. "Rachel Stein is back."

Yigal stopped, and stared at Udi. His eyes narrowed. "Since when?"

"Four days."

"That's all I need now," said Yigal throwing up his hands. He opened the door and turned back, exasperated, to face Udi. "Find out what she's up to. I want a full report by the end of the week."

Four

The taxi pulled up to the King David Hotel and the uniformed doorman opened the door of the Mercedes cab. Rachel stepped out, grasping the bottom of her long wool skirt to keep the wind from catching it. As she looked up at the majestic hotel entrance, Rachel wasn't sure if her hand embroidered sweater and matching black skirt were formal enough for a wedding at the King David. She pushed her hand against the wood and brass revolving door and entered into a forgotten era of Israel's history.

During the British Mandate for Palestine, the posh Edwardian hotel served as military headquarters for the British Military Forces. In those days, Palestinian meant "Jew." The Arabs refused to have their British identity papers stamped with the word 'Palestinian,' — they were part of the Arab Nation and the artificial borders drawn up by the victorious allies at the end of World War I meant nothing to them but an insult.

"How quickly people forget," thought Rachel as she strolled elegantly through the lobby.

In those pre-1948 days, murderous Arab terror attacks increased against the Jews. The British refused to intervene.

The *Irgun* Jewish resistance forces under the leadership of Menachem Begin mounted a campaign against the British military to persuade them to either stop the Arab terrorism or leave the country.

As a teenager, Rachel's mother lived in New York. She used to help Rachel's grandfather smuggle guns to Begin's forces in Palestine. She would sit on wooden crates in the back of the trucks carrying arms to ships waiting in the harbor. The crates were marked 'used clothing.' The fact that there was a young girl sitting on the crates helped distract the customs agents.

"Well look at *you*, dear. You look beautiful!"

Before Rachel could react, she felt a wet kiss on her cheek — the kind that left a big smudge of red lipstick. It was planted there by Mrs. Klein. *"Mazel Tov!* Congratulations!"

"Mazel Tov!" said Rachel. "I really *feel* good too. It's great to be dressed up and at a wedding. For the last four days I've been unpacking all my things that have been in storage."

"Come, let me introduce you to the bride!" said Mrs. Klein, pulling Rachel by the hand.

They walked down the hallway next to the front desk and entered the King David 'Reading Room.' Dozens of guests were milling around with crystal glasses of white wine in their hands.

Mrs. Klein continued to drag Rachel through the crowd. Suddenly, sitting regally in front of the them in a high-backed white bamboo chair was Mrs. Klein's granddaughter. She looked like a queen sitting on the platform surrounded by bouquets of white flowers. Three little girls were sitting at her feet in white satin dresses.

"Rachel, this is my granddaughter Ilana," beamed Mrs. Klein.

A lump formed in Rachel's throat. She reached out and shook Ilana's hand. *"Mazel Tov*, may you...," she began reciting a traditional blessing in Hebrew, but it was too much. The tears welled up in Rachel's eyes and she turned to run out of the room thinking of her own wedding that never took place. She ran all the way to the sidewalk in front of the hotel and stopped to compose herself. She hoped she hadn't embarrassed poor Mrs. Klein.

Rachel looked up and down King David Street to get her bearings. The Klein wedding was only her first stop this afternoon. She hadn't planned to stay very long anyway. The next appointment on her itinerary was unscheduled. It was going to be even more difficult than the wedding. Rachel had been putting it off since her arrival.

She was glad she didn't need a cab to get to the next address. The walk would give her a chance to calm down. She set off down King David Street and turned right at the first intersection. She walked down the hill, not noticing the white Ford Sierra that had pulled over to the curb behind her.

The driver of the car was startled when Rachel stopped in her tracks. She looked up and directly across from her was Jaffa Gate and the ancient walls surrounding the Old City of Jerusalem. A feeling of comfort overwhelmed her. She felt at home.

She hurried down the hill, and at the "T" intersection at the bottom she turned right. She reprimanded herself for not having visited the Western Wall yet.

The road turned into a path, and Rachel entered Yemin Moshe. She passed a few tourists who had come to the re-furbished neighborhood to visit some of the art galleries. Most of the renovated hundred-year-old homes were owned by wealthy English-speaking immigrants, or upscale Israelis.

Rachel continued down the stone walkway past the beautiful gardens until she reached number 59 Montefiore

Street. She nervously pressed the buzzer under a sign that read, "LEAH TAL — SCULPTURE."

A tall man in his thirties opened the door. He was holding a cordless phone to his ear. "Hi. You here to volunteer?" he asked.

"No," said Rachel, a little confused.

"Just a minute Itzik, there's someone at the door" he said into the phone. He turned his attention to Rachel and forced a smile. "Hi. If you are looking to buy some sculpture, I'm sorry but there's nothing here. All of Mrs. Tal's work is at the gallery on Jaffa Road."

"Even though I love her work, I'm not buying today. Actually I'm an old friend of Leah's. Is she home?" asked Rachel.

"Well why didn't you say so! Come on in... She's in the Dining Room," he said with a flourish opening up the wooden door.

Rachel entered the house cautiously while the man continued to give orders to Itzik. She was surprised to see so many people buzzing around the home that had always been a quiet haven from the bustle of Israeli life.

Leah stood at the dining room table also talking on the phone. She was dressed as elegantly as ever in a tailored suit. Her silver hair tinged with some of her natural brown from her youth gave her an air of sophistication commensurate with her sixty worldly years. Two teenage boys wearing knitted skullcaps called 'kipahs' on their heads were stuffing envelopes at a makeshift card table in the living room. Leah made a hand motion to another middle-aged woman sitting at the table typing on a laptop computer. Rachel's form caught the corner of Leah's eye and she dropped the handset with a shout, "Rachel!"

Rachel ran into her arms and got a giant bear hug. She felt like a little girl.

"When did you get here? Why didn't you call me? How are you?"

"I arrived Monday," answered Rachel tearfully. "I was going to say I didn't call because I wanted to surprise you, but the real reason is that I was afraid to call. I didn't know how I would react on the phone. I'm glad I waited to see you in person."

Leah hugged her again and said, "I'm glad you're finally ready to confront Ari's memory. I'm just starting to get back to normal myself." The two women looked at each other knowing there would be lot's of time to talk about Ari. Now wasn't the time.

Everyone in the room stopped to look at the unannounced guest. Leah gave Rachel another hug and then grasped her firmly by both shoulders and turned her to face the people in the room. "Everybody, I want you to meet Rachel Stein. She's my...," Leah paused. "She was my son Ari's fiancée."

Five

"What's going on here, Leah? I left this place and it was the home of a nice old *Bubbie*. Now it looks like head-quarters for an election campaign," Rachel said with a laugh.

Leah put her arm around Rachel's waist and guided her around the maze of placards and posters piled up around the large living room. "Come, let's go into the studio where it's quiet and we can talk over a cup of coffee. I'll explain every-thing."

Rachel flopped down into the worn leather easy chair in the corner of the studio. She loved the smell of clay in this room. Leah perched herself on her sculpting stool and started to explain.

"It all started just a few months ago," she began. "I never thought I'd get involved in politics, but after Abu Alim won the Palestinian presidential elections, things started to get unbearable. People in the movement call him *Abu Alimut*."

"Cute," said Rachel with a sneer, "*Father of Violence*."

"Exactly," continued Leah. "Even though the PLO's dream of getting the Palestinians their own state, and a launching pad for their 1974 "salami plan" to dismantle the

State of Israel piece by piece came true, it wasn't enough for the Palestinian in the street."

"Why not?" asked Rachel sipping her coffee, "I thought that was the kind of "Piece" they were negotiating for all along."

"That's true," agreed Leah, "but the fact that the old PLO leadership backed down in the negotiations and allowed Jerusalem to remain in Israel's hands was enough to get them labeled as traitors. Under international pressure they couldn't delay having open democratic elections any longer, and the old leadership lost.

"The Palestinians looked at Abu Alim as a no-nonsense right winger who will follow through on his commitment to annex Jerusalem and the remainder of the disputed territories captured during the 1967 Six Day War that are still in our hands.

"But that's not our biggest problem. He's running with a minority government. The Islamic Fundamentalist party, is the loyal opposition along with about a dozen radical splinter terrorist groups. It's only Divine intervention that kept the Moslem terrorists from joining together and making one party. Had they done so, they would have won."

"What a frightening thought. What about the next elections?" asked Rachel.

"Next elections? Who's thinking about the next elections? We've got to deal with the threat today," said Leah. "You see, to stay alive, literally and politically, he has to appease the Moslem terrorist parties. The extremists feel he has made too many concessions to the Zionists. They will assassinate him unless he gives them some freedom to act and continue their holy war against Israel until all of the land of Palestine, including Tel Aviv and Haifa, is liberated."

"What does that mean?"

"That means the Extradition Treaty, and the Hot Pursuit of Terrorists Agreement signed between our Government and the Palestinians are not worth the paper they're written on. Now, *Islamic* terrorists cross the border, murder Jews and run back across the border right under the noses of the Palestinian Border Patrols.

"When the army starts chasing them, they get stopped at the Border by the Palestinians who tell us it's under their jurisdiction to pursue the terrorists and bring them to justice. What a joke! If they so much as lift a finger against *the* Islamic fundamentalists, Abu Alim is dead. The next night the same terrorists are at it again under the watchful eye of the Palestinian 'Police.'"

There was a knock at the studio door and a head poked its way in, "Sorry to interrupt, Leah, but it's Meir on the phone. He says it's urgent." It was the same tall man with the chestnut colored hair who had answered the door.

"Thanks Marc," said Leah taking the cordless phone from his hand.

Marc walked into the room to wait for Leah's instructions. "This is a great time to be coming to Israel," he said to Rachel. "How long are you here for?"

"Actually, I live here. I have an apartment in Rehavia. I guess you could say I've been on an extended trip to Canada."

"Great! If you're as close to Leah as it looks, then we'll probably be seeing a lot of each other," he said with a smile.

Leah handed the phone back to Marc. "Take the keys to the Van and pick up Meir at the printer's before seven, otherwise we won't have the new posters for the demonstration tonight."

"Demonstration?" thought Rachel. Leah really had changed.

"So, where were we?" asked Leah, focusing her attention back on Rachel.

"I thought we were going to catch up on old times," complained Rachel. "Like... How are Meir and Shoshana? How's your sculpture selling? Did Yoni take his first steps yet? Instead, we're talking about politics and demonstrations."

"There'll be lots of time for catching up on family matters on *Shabbat*. In the meantime, if we don't get going, we'll be late for the demonstration. It's six-thirty already, and we have some stops to make on the way. Did you eat yet?"

Rachel shook her head. She wished she had stayed for some of the hors d'oeuvres at the wedding.

"No matter, we'll grab a *falafel* on the way." Leah took Rachel's arm and led her back to the living room where the frenzy of activity had seemed to pick up. "Bye everybody," called out Leah as they walked out the door. "We'll see you later at Zion Square."

Six

The Ben Yehuda pedestrian mall was filled with the sounds of young people laughing and street musicians performing. Tourists gazed at jewelry shop windows, and Israeli soldiers on leave flirted with their girlfriends at outdoor cafes.

The throng of people celebrating this perennial summer Jerusalem ritual paid no attention the Jeeps gathering at the foot of the pedestrian mall next to Zion Square.

Leah and Rachel blended into the crowd strolling down Ben Yehuda Street. "Why don't we have any signs?" asked Rachel.

"Don't worry, there will be plenty of placards. Marc is on his way with the new signs, and the *Mercaz HaMa'avak*, who co-ordinate the activities of all the grass roots groups, have been distributing material all day to the neighborhood committees," explained Leah. "It's still early, and I like to stand back and watch things develop, trying to anticipate the instructions the police have been given. Whether they are planning on inciting the crowd to violence or not."

"The police incite the demonstrators?" asked Rachel in disbelief.

"Sometimes," said Leah matter-of-factly. "The government is losing control of the situation and is terrified of a grass roots movement against them. They'll even plant plain clothes police in the crowd pretending to be demonstrators. They incite the crowd to break the law by encouraging them to get off the sidewalk and stop traffic. That gives the police the excuse to declare an illegal demonstration and start beating and arresting people... especially the organizers. The same thing happened a lot in the huge anti-government rallies in the wake of the signing of the declaration of principles. The goal is to eliminate the leadership of the anti-government groups and to intimidate the general population from coming out to further demonstrations for fear of being beaten."

They reached Zion Square and watched the police set up blue metal barricades around the sparsely occupied square that was regularly used for artisans to sell their handcrafted earrings and broaches. The barricades were to keep the demonstrators, who were yet to arrive, off Jaffa Road. A group of young yeshiva students appeared carrying a large Israeli flag mounted on a broomstick. They took up a strategic position against the barrier closest to the street. The police eyed them suspiciously as three more Border Patrol vehicles arrived and parked on a side street.

"Why is the government so afraid of some grandmothers and yeshiva students?" asked Rachel.

"It's not just us, it's whom we represent. Over sixty five percent of the people are against the policies of this government. If a tired old lady like me has become an activist, when I should be playing with my grandson, you know the government has crossed a red line. They know it too, but they don't know how to get out of the hole they've dug themselves into. So they're fighting like a caged cat with the people they're supposed to be protecting."

"I've decided to quit my job," said Ari, dropping a bombshell.

Rachel was taken by surprise. "But you just got a promotion, and that will entitle us to a larger home on the army base."

Don't worry Rachel, I'll be able to get a fine job and we'll be able to afford a new apartment," said Ari. "There's a big demand for electronics engineers in the communications field in private industry."

"But I thought you loved your job, what happened? You and Udi have so much fun together. Did you have an argument with your boss Yigal?" Rachel was confused.

Ari shook his head trying to think of a 'safe' way to explain to Rachel what was bothering him. She thought Ari was working on developing top secret communications equipment.

"It's not Udi or Yigal. I'm going to miss them both very much," he said slowly. "It's just that I can't in good conscience work for the army anymore based on how things have developed lately."

"How so?"

"The IDF is no longer solely concerned with the security of the citizens of Israel. It has become the political pawn of the Prime Minister."

Ari looked into Rachel's eyes. He hated to speak about the Israel Defence Forces this way, but he loved her dearly and wanted to share everything with her. But for her own safety he held back.

"Ever since the extreme right wing movements were branded, 'terrorist organizations,'" he went on, "the army has been sent on a witch hunt to pick up as many Jewish activists in the territories as they can.

Instead of hunting down real Arab terrorists who are plotting to kill us, our Jewish soldiers are rounding up Jewish citizens to show the world how even-handed we are."

"But some of the settlers really are dangerous," said Rachel.

"Sure, they are. And they probably should be locked up," he agreed. "But this goes beyond picking up a few extremists. The government is testing the waters to see how the public reacts to using the army this way. Mark my words, they will eventually send in soldiers to forceably transfer Jews from their homes in the territories. Then it will get much worse."

Ari was saying what many people in the country were feeling but were afraid to admit.

"When my grandchildren ask me, 'What did you do Zaida, when the government pit soldiers against Jews?, I don't want to have to answer, 'I was working for that same government and army.'"

"God will never let it come to that," said Rachel.

Ari stared at her and didn't answer.

Rachel watched the police and border patrolmen in army fatigues take up positions around Zion Square. She thought about Ari who never lived to see the first part of his "prophecy" come true when the army evacuated Jewish settlements to make way for the Palestinian State. She hoped tonight she wouldn't witness the second phase of his "prophecy" come true as well.

"If only we hadn't let the left wing in coalition with the radical left to stay in power we wouldn't be in this mess," said Rachel.

"Listen, after the government railroaded the Palestinian State through the Knesset, depending on the support of the

Arab parties, the right-wing were shell-shocked for months. They all started blaming each other for allowing it to happen. It's a wonder civil war didn't break out amongst the right. You really expected them to unite together for the elections?" asked Leah.

"I guess not, but to splinter the vote among so many right-wing and religious factions so that Yossi Shiloni could come to power with only 42 out of 120 seats in the Knesset is beyond comprehension," said Rachel shaking her head. "If only the old timers in the left hadn't handed over the reigns to the next generation. They never would have gotten voted back in after lying to the people for so long about the deal with the PLO."

"They weren't stupid. They knew they'd never win again either. They wanted to end their political careers with what they felt was a victory. They figured by handing over the reigns to Yossi Shiloni, if they lost it could be blamed on Shiloni, and not on themselves."

The crowds began to arrive at the square and started shouting slogans. Immediately, the foreign TV crews switched on their equipment and started filming the demonstrators. Israel TV had a mobile trailer parked nearby with a satellite dish ready to broadcast the events live on the evening news.

"Things are starting to heat up," said Leah. "It's twenty minutes to eight. Let's move into the crowd. We like to time things so that there is a good image for the opening of the eight o'clock news."

The women crossed the street, and Leah started to greet some of the regulars and the leaders of some of the groups who had shown up.

The diversity of people and signs that she saw surprised Rachel. Things had changed a lot since she had been gone. Before she left for Canada, almost all the people attending these kinds of demonstrations were observant, primarily religious Zionists, and members of the settler movement. There was a temporary moratorium on large anti-government demonstrations following the Rabin assassasination, but eventually they resumed. Tonight she saw a cross section of the nation. The black hats of the ultra-orthodox community peppered the mass of demonstrators and there were as many men without head coverings as there were with *kipot*.

The signs called out, *"Stop the Leftist Coercion," "Police State," "Yossi Go Home!" "The Palestinians Want Jerusalem and Tel-Aviv," "Stop the Killing of Innocent Jews," "Alim means Violence."*

The square overflowed onto Ben Yehuda, as a steady stream of angry citizens continued to flow from all directions. People got off the public Egged buses waving placards and Israeli flags.

"There are more people than even we expected," said Leah. "I guess they're reacting to the terrorists who murdered Rivka Weinstock yesterday. The army was chasing the terrorists when they slipped over the border. Alim said we should trust him to capture them."

"I guess the people don't trust him," said Rachel in an understatement.

The demonstrators were shouting louder now as more people arrived. The senior police officers were on their walkie-talkies calling in reinforcements. A few minutes later, eight mounted policemen arrived on huge brown horses. A sergeant sent a group of cadets hurriedly across the road and made frantic hand signals to the border patrol pressed against the metal barricades holding the crowd back.

"It's not good," said Leah solemnly, "the police are getting nervous."

A foreign TV correspondent who recognized Leah as the head of *Kol Ha'am*, pulled her away for an interview.

Kol Ha'am, was a Hebrew play on words. It literally meant, "Voice of the Nation," but it was a homonym for "All the Nation," as well.

Some teenagers carrying torches shoved Rachel to the left. She noticed them handing out plastic bags to the people in the crowd. A boy handed her one. "Take it," he said in a whisper, "if the horses start to charge, throw some of the pepper in their noses. It stops them in their tracks."

The crowd got louder and angrier when they saw the horses approach. There was no more room in the square, so people started congregating on the other side of Jaffa Road which irritated the police. The demonstration permit only specified Zion Square.

When the water cannons pulled up, loud shouts of "BOO!" rang through the crowd. The group started chanting "Police State, Police State."

One minute to eight and the camera lights flicked on the Israel TV reporter. A group of teenagers broke through the barriers and sat down on Jaffa Road stopping traffic. The police raced after them and dragged them by the limbs into the awaiting paddy wagons. More demonstrators started pushing the barriers forward and two mounted policemen swung around to confront them.

Rachel felt a hand clamp down on her shoulder, and turned, ready to smack whomever had touched her.

"Rachel! Quick, let's get out of her, there's going to be trouble."

Rachel turned to see a familiar round freckled face framed by an unmistakable short-cropped red headfull of curls. "Devorah?! What are you doing here?"

"Isn't everyone who cares about this country here tonight? Come on, let's get out of here."

Devorah dragged Rachel through the crowd and ran with her up the *Ben Yehuda* mall just as the water cannons started firing at the demonstrators. People were trampled not only by the horses but by each other in the ensuing riot. It was all recorded live on the evening news and broadcast uncensored throughout the world on CNN. The next morning the official government reports would acknowledge eighteen seriously injured including two police officers.

Seven

Udi hated coming to meetings with Yigal with only partial answers. It made him feel like a schoolboy who was caught not doing his homework. Whenever the short briefings took place in Yigal's sparsely furnished office, it was like being sent to the principal.

"So where do we stand with the alleged assassination plot?" he asked glancing at the one-page brief Amiram had just handed him.

"We haven't gotten much farther, other than reports of automatic weapons fire yesterday in the hills near Ma'alot Yair," answered Amiram. "No one has officially reported the incident; not the Army, Arabs or Settlers, so we're assuming it's our friends out on target practice again. We have some men scouring the area for bullet casings or another poster."

"That's it?" asked Yigal impatiently.

"Well we have a few thoughts," added Udi, trying to give the impression of progress. "Either they're Jewish kids just having some fun, they're sloppy amateurs...," he paused for drama, "or they're deliberately trying to draw attention to themselves."

Yigal looked up from the brief and stared at Udi like he had just landed on earth from another planet.

"We know it's stretching it a little," he stammered, wanting to crawl under the desk. "But why wouldn't they use silencers, and why would they leave one of the placards lying around for someone to find? It's the kind of stupid macho act that some *Islamic* terrorists might do in order to taunt us."

"Mummph," Yigal was semi-impressed with Udi's 'save.'

Yigal rubbed his eyes and ran both his hands through his unkempt hair. He was thinking. Udi would rather be unclogging a sewage pipe than be sitting in the chair opposite Yigal when he was thinking.

"Get me some hard information by Tuesday. Dismissed." The two officers got up to leave. "Udi, wait a minute," said Yigal curtly. Amiram was glad to be able to escape and shot a wink of encouragement to his colleague as he left the room.

Udi was still standing as Yigal addressed him in a warmer tone, "So what's Rachel up to?"

"Yigal," said Udi impatiently, "it's only been twenty-four hours!" Udi wasn't afraid to show a little *chutzpah* in front of Yigal when he knew he had firm ground to stand on.

"I realize that," he snapped back indignantly taking the high ground. "Where has she been?"

Udi pulled a small orange notebook out of his breast pocket. This time he was prepared, and he read confidently.

```
Wednesday 5:35 PM she left her
flat and entered a waiting taxi.
5:47 she arrived at the King David
Hotel. 5:55 she left the King David
and proceeded on foot to number 59
Montefiore Street in Yemin Moshe,
```

Leah Tal's home, the head of *Kol Ha'am*. Ari Tal's mother.

Yigal narrowed his eyes as Udi continued his report.

At 6:30 she and Tal departed by automobile and parked in the underground car park at the City Tower. They proceeded to a *falafel* stand on King George Street, and after eating, continued down the Ben Yehuda Mall to Zion Square where they took part in the demonstration. I lost track of her in the pandemonium when the riots broke out.

Yigal rubbed his forehead. "You know that they're going to appoint a government inquiry into that bloody riot. And Shiloni's going to try to dump it on us. 'The *Shabak* should have had intelligence information that such an event could happen,' they'll say. Our illustrious Prime Minister will 'reluctantly' agree with the commission and heads will roll. He'll do anything to hold onto power.'"

Udi agreed with his boss, but it was uncomfortable to hear a senior officer of *Shabak* talking out loud that way about the Prime Minister.

"Who did she meet at the King David?" asked Yigal.

"I don't know. She was in and out of there too quickly."

"Well find out who it was! Maybe that will give us a hint into what she's doing back here. We can't afford to have her snooping around. Who knows what Ari told her before he died?"

Eight

Rachel loved Friday mornings in Jerusalem. The city was abuzz with people rushing to get their last minute errands done before the shops began shutting down at 1:00 p.m. for *Shabbat*. She loved the energy. There was a party atmosphere in the air for her.

She picked up her car keys and headed toward the front door of the apartment. As she reached for the doorknob she stopped and looked down at the keys in her hand and remembered that this was Jerusalem and not Toronto. Why take the car on such a beautiful morning? It would be more of a nuisance running her errands than a help. You really didn't need one in Jerusalem. Even though the city received an inordinate amount of attention in the press giving the impression of a cosmopolitan city, Rachel felt she was in a small town whenever she strolled the tree-lined streets. There was always someone you bumped into that you knew.

Rachel stepped out of her apartment building and began walking up Ramban Street in Rehavia. The sun was shining and the sky was a glorious desert blue. The fresh November air engulfed her. She felt invigorated in contrast to the terror she felt at the riots the night before. That was the real opportunity and the true meaning of Jerusalem; It was a place to help one return, renew and rejoice.

A burst of colors filled the sidewalk in front of her. Buckets of pre-wrapped roses, carnations, orange lilies and many exotic flowers grown in hothouses were on display. On Fridays, vendors hawked their floral wares all around the country to passing motorists stopped at traffic lights. It didn't matter whether you were religious or secular. Fresh cut flowers were a tradition for many at the Friday night Sabbath table.

A bell chimed as Rachel entered the small flower shop. She surveyed the brilliant array of flowers and picked out a dozen white roses. They were Leah's favorites. Rachel paid. The bareheaded shopkeeper handed her the bouquet and wished her a *Shabbat Shalom*."

Rachel smiled and felt a warm glow inside. Over the years she had been gone, she had forgotten what it was like to live in a city whose rhythm followed hers.

She lifted her shoulder bag and placed the bouquet into a plastic carrying bag and continued down the sidewalk in the direction of King George Street. She ducked into a small grocery store where some locals were buying their last-minute purchases for the weekend. As is typical, every available square centimeter was used to display products of every kind. She squeezed past an elderly man at the front check-out counter who was putting four large braided *Challah* loaves into his plastic carrying bag. More customers blocked her way as she moved to the back of the store to the wine section. As she passed, they all smiled and said, *"Shabbat Shalom."*

Rachel looked over the dozens of labels of wine available. It was traditional to bring wine, flowers or chocolates as a gift to someone's home to whom you were invited for *Shabbat*. Rachel decided to bring all three. After all, this was a special *Shabbat*. She would be having a reunion with Leah, her son Meir, his wife Shoshana and their children.

Rachel had a hard time making her mind up between a sweet red wine for *Kiddush*, or a dry red one for drinking with dinner. In the end, she opted for the *Kiddush* wine and picked up a bottle of *Hashmonaim Atik*. The woman beside her said, "The *Malachi* is better, and it's a little cheaper too."

Rachel had also forgotten how irritating, yet comforting it was to have strangers mixing into her private affairs. Every Jew in Israel felt a closeness of family even if they disagreed and argued with each other constantly — which is what happens in most families. It wasn't uncommon in Israel to find bus passengers scolding other passengers for not getting up for a pregnant or elderly woman. People would jump up out of their seats automatically to help a woman off the bus with a baby stroller. Frequently passengers would interrupt conversations on the bus and throw in their two-cents, especially if the talk centered on politics.

Rachel smiled at the lady, and thanked her, saying, "*Todah*." She put down the *Hashmonaim* and picked up the *Malachi*, assuming the woman knew what she was talking about. Judaism wasn't just a religion or a nation. For Rachel, being Jewish was primarily being part of one big family.

On the way back to the check-out, she picked up a box of pralines and some 'bubbles' for the children. Rachel stuffed her purchases into her blue plastic carrier, hoisted her bag over her shoulder and continued walking up Ramban Street.

Rachel's happy pre-*Shabbat* mood was broken when she reached France Square, opposite the Kings Hotel at the intersection of King George and Ramban Streets. She had enough of demonstrations for her first week back in Israel and was hoping *Shabbat* would provide a welcome spiritual break. But there, filling the square, were about fifty silent women dressed in black T-shirts holding placards. *"Stop the oppression of Israeli Arabs!" "Autonomy for Nazareth," "East Jerusalem belongs to the Palestinians."*

Rachel felt anger welling up from the pit of her stomach. For years these women stood there every Friday morning demanding the end of the military occupation of the territories. It was ironic that these self-proclaimed defenders of human-rights were dressed in 'black.' They shed crocodile tears whenever Palestinian rights were violated, yet they were never heard from when Jews were slaughtered. They disbanded temporarily when the Palestinian State was finally created. They had succeeded in handing over the Jewish heartland and biblical homeland to the most cold-blooded murderous enemies of the Jews since the Nazis. Now more Jews were being murdered daily by the Arabs and these women insisted on defending the right to hand another slice of the country to the enemy.

Outraged taxi drivers and other motorists honked their horns and shouted obscenities at them. To their credit, the demonstrators maintained their silent vigil and didn't respond.

Rachel tried to hold back as she walked in front of them but gave in and asked one of the young women sporting a short haircut, "Do you shed a tear for Rivka Weinstock and all the hundreds of other Jews who were murdered by Arabs?"

After being attacked verbally the whole morning by furious passersby, she exploded, "Nazi! All you settlers are fascists. You don't understand anything about the value of life."

Rachel felt like taking the woman's placard and smacking her with it. She thought to herself that it was this self hating attitude that had brought the country to this state. But then she thought back to how Ari always responded when they drove past this intersection on Friday mornings on the way to his mother's.

"It's not their fault. What do you expect from them?" he said trying to calm Rachel's temper. *"They went through the secular Israeli school system and on to university where they were indoctrinated to despise religion. They were fed a steady diet of Secular Humanism and Moral Relativism."*

"But with all those brains, you'd think they'd be able to read some history books to see who we're dealing with. The PLO are murderers. How can they trust them when Fatah are still carrying out terror attacks? Are these women suicidal?" Rachel refused to give an inch.

"If you don't believe in God. All you have left to believe in, is Man. And if the only man around is a murderous terrorist who has committed crimes against humanity, then you believe in him as well," said Ari calmly. *"We, the orthodox Jews are to blame. We know better. We didn't protest when they received no meaningful Jewish education. As long as our own children had good religious schools, we let them assimilate western secular values to fill the void in their lives. Now we're all suffering. Our job is not to blame them, but to begin communicating and educating them."*

Rachel didn't feel like educating the woman who had just called her a Nazi. She felt like strangling her. Rachel's grandfather had been burned in Aushwitz. The only thing she had left from him was his gold watch. He had handed it to her grandmother as the Gestapo soldiers dragged him away while the black-shirted Nazi supporters looked on.

But this woman standing opposite Rachel in the black shirt was a Jew. An ignorant Jew. Part of the family. It was

Rachel's job to educate her. Rachel stared at the woman with the short cropped hair. The rage in Rachel's eyes melted into sorrow for what this woman was missing in her life. The woman felt uncomfortable and turned away to avoid Rachel's gaze.

"*Shabbat Shalom*," said Rachel quietly, and she continued down the sidewalk on her way to meet her friends and greet the Sabbath together — as family.

Rachel turned to catch one last glimpse of the women protesting. She wished she had the nerve to run back and invite the woman to join them for *Shabbat*. If Ari had been with her, she was sure he would have done it.

Nine

Everyone else in the office, except for the security men, had left for the day. The secretary started to arrange the paper files lying in front of her workstation.

She looked at her watch. There was one more important task to finish before she could leave for the day. She glanced over her shoulder at the guard standing by the door. He shot back an impatient look. Even though he liked watching her long black hair bounce as she worked, he was hoping she would leave already so he could lock up and find a cozy couch to catch up on his sleep with nobody looking on.

She hesitated for a moment with him in the room, but carried on, realizing there was nothing to fear because he didn't understand English anyway.

She nervously grabbed the 'mouse' on her computer, taking care not to crack any of her long red nails. She opened a new document in the word processing window and began translating from the hand-written note she had been given earlier that day. As she typed her short but shocking message she chose to use the transliterated Hebrew name 'Shimshon' instead of the anglicized version 'Samson.' She felt it would have more impact even though she hadn't been informed of the exact meaning of the cryptic fax.

With the mouse, she selected 'FAXcard' from the print options menu, and clicked 'OK.' She didn't want to create any paper evidence so she decided to send the fax electronically.

The built-in fax program prompted her for the phone number that the message was to be sent to. Before entering the information, she double clicked on the 'User Options' button. A window showing the owner of the program's company name and fax number appeared on the screen. This is the information that would appear on the top line of the fax as it was received on the other end. She carefully typed spaces over the name and number, thereby making the 'sender' anonymous.

After typing in the receiver's phone number, she clicked the 'Send Now' button. The PC dialed the fax number and the secretary listened anxiously as the familiar screeches of the two fax machines "handshaking" came over the PC speaker. Less than a minute later she received a "Fax Transmission Completed" message on her screen. She reset the Sender Name and Fax number, and exited the word processing program being careful not to save the message she had sent.

She left the machine on, like every other night, so that it could receive any incoming faxes. She picked up her bag and walked quickly out of the room past the guard who had already dozed off in his chair. He snorted slightly as her perfume tickled his nose.

Ten

"White roses! My favorite," said Leah giving Rachel a hug. "I'm so happy you're spending your first *Shabbat* back in Jerusalem with us."

"Who could pass up the opportunity to welcome the *Shabbat* in Yemin Moshe?" Rachel winked at Leah letting her know that she would have been spending this *Shabbat* with Leah even if she lived next to the old Central Bus Station in Tel Aviv.

"Come, let me help you with your things," said Leah taking Rachel's overnight bag. "You'll be staying in Meir's old room. Meir and Shoshana will be in the guest room and the kids are going to sleep on mattresses in the studio."

An invitation for *Shabbat* dinner in Jerusalem at a religious home assumed you would be sleeping over. Driving is forbidden on the Sabbath. Even though Rachel lived within walking distance, she preferred to stay the whole twenty-four hours and join the Tal's in all three festive meals.

"What can I do to help?" asked Rachel looking around the room. She was amazed how the headquarters of *Kol Ha'am* had been transformed into a typical Israeli living/dining room so quickly. The only evidence was a pile of neatly stacked over-sized posters in the corner of the room.

"How about setting the table? You still remember where everything is don't you?" asked Leah.

"Sure," said Rachel walking over to the oak dining room hutch that Leah had brought with her from 'the old country,' America. She opened the top drawer and pulled out a neatly folded white linen table cloth. "How many are we tonight?" she called out to Leah who had gone into the kitchen to check the turkey roasting in the oven.

"Well," answered Leah coming back into the room wiping her hands in a dishtowel, "you and I are two. Meir, Shoshana and the two kids make six, and Marc makes seven."

"Who is this 'Marc' anyway?" asked Rachel as she started placing the crystal wine goblets on the table.

"His name is Marc Goodman. He's wonderful. I never would have been able to start *Kol Ha'am* without him. I met him at an evening class given by Rabbi Steinberg at Ellen and Benny Kahn's apartment in David's Village. Marc is a *neighbor* of the Kahns." She emphasized the word neighbor, baiting Rachel.

"He has an apartment in David's Village? Not bad. Is he single?" smiled Rachel anticipating Leah's next comment. David's Village was a luxury condominium development next to Yemin Moshe. Most of the occupants were wealthy immigrants who could afford the starting prices of $950,000 for a two-bedroom apartment.

"He was an investment fund manager on Wall Street," said Leah. "Two years ago he made three brilliant deals in a row and made millions in commissions. He retired at age 35, fed up with the values of Wall Street, and came to Jerusalem to study Torah. He's been learning every morning at a Yeshiva in the Old City." Leah opened the glass door of the hutch and took out the crystal wine decanter and handed it to Rachel adding with a twinkle in her eye, "And yes, he's single."

They both laughed.

"But I didn't invite him because you were coming. Marc doesn't like spending *Shabbat* alone, but he prefers not to sleep over at other people's homes. So he tries to spend *Shabbat* with people who are in walking distance. He has a few friends in the Old City. It's not appropriate for him to be here with me alone, so he usually joins us when Meir's family comes for *Shabbat*." The explanation seemed plausible to Rachel, although the idea of it being a 'set up' didn't bother her either. Few people knew Rachel as well as Leah, and Rachel trusted her to pre-screen a blind date for her.

The phone rang and Leah went back to the kitchen to answer it. Rachel continued folding the linen napkins, arranging them in a fan in the wine goblets. She liked the extra touches that helped make *Shabbat* so special. She felt a swell of joy dwelling on the fact that as an observant Jew this wasn't a rare occurrence. *Shabbat*, and it's formal dinner party with guests, wine and song came once each week.

"That was Meir on the car phone," said Leah bringing in two large braided *Challahs* and the *Challah* knife. "He said they might be a little late. There are extra army checkpoints and they are checking every single car with 'settlers' in them. The line ups are huge. It seems they are anticipating another attack by Arab terrorists dressed up as Jews. They've been cutting their hair short and growing their beards long. When they put on a knitted *kipah* and *tzitzis* it's almost impossible to distinguish them from Jews. It gives them the ability to walk around with Uzis and M-16s without drawing attention unless, of course, they open their mouths and start talking."

The anger stirred again in Rachel. One thing she had always liked about being in Israel was that you knew who your enemy was. In downtown Manhattan you never knew who wanted to hurt you. It could be a depressed computer programmer to go on a shooting spree in a Macdonalds restaurant, or a drug addict to pounce on you and rip your purse away. Now that the Arabs were dressing up as Jews, she felt the same sense of fear of 'not knowing' whom to take a second glance at or steer clear of on the sidewalk.

"Here's a vase for the roses," said Leah. It was already filled with water. Rachel tore open the plastic wrapper of the bouquet and arranged the flowers in the vase. She placed them in the center of the table next to the silver candlesticks putting the finishing touch on the *Shabbat* table. Rachel stepped back to admire her 'masterpiece.' The crystal and silver sparkled in the late afternoon light. The wine in the crystal decanter glowed ruby red, like a jewel in the crown waiting for the approaching Sabbath queen.

With the protection of *Shabbat*, there was no need to think about Arabs, or terrorists. Rachel thought of the times she, as a little girl, used to help her grandmother set the *Shabbat* table. Her *Bubbie* would say, quoting the Sages, "'More than the Jewish people have kept the Sabbath, the Sabbath has kept the Jews,' You must set the table with love *Racheleh*."

It was twenty-four hours to get out of the day-to-day mundane rut that pits man against man in a struggle for power. Time to focus on God as the King of kings who has a plan for history, and a special covenant with the Jewish people whose role it is to help bring about that ultimate goal. Rachel reminded herself that *Shabbat* was the 'sign' of that covenant.

Eleven

The noisy tourists filed their way down the giant staircase toward the Western Wall Plaza. Half way down the staircase, Israeli soldiers on reserve duty checked the visitors' bags as they moved through the metal detectors. It created a bottleneck for the 'locals' who were on their way to the *Kotel* for the Friday evening prayers.

Meir and Rachel each held one of eight-year-old Sarah's hands as the trio scampered down the stairs. It was getting late. One of the soldiers was checking the purse of a grandmotherly type wearing Reeboks. "Oh Selma," she called out loudly to her companion in a New York nasal drone, "it's such a thrill to have an *Israeli* army protecting us." The soldier, rolled his eyes at his fellow reservist. "*Shabbat Shalom*," he said in his best Israeli accent and waved her on not wanting to disappoint her by revealing that he remembered Mrs. Klein as a kid growing up in Brooklyn.

Meir nodded to the soldiers and said, "*Shabbat Shalom*," as they rushed passed the checkpoint. The group of tourists were patiently waiting their turns to be inspected.

"Hey, Mrs. Klein, *Mazel Tov* again on the wedding, and *Shabbat Shalom!*" called out Rachel as they hurried down the staircase. Jerusalem really is a small town, thought Rachel.

The soldiers answered back to Meir, *"Shabbat Shalom,"* and continued checking the tourists. Just like at the El Al security counter, the soldiers knew who to stop and who not to stop just by looking in their eyes. They checked the Jewish tourists coming down to the Wall primarily as a public relations measure. It made people like Mrs. Klein feel more secure which was good for tourism.

"Sarah, you go with Auntie Rachel while I go and *daven* in the men's section," instructed Meir. All the Tal's considered Rachel part of the family even though her wedding with Ari never took place. "It's a good thing that Imma and Yoni stayed with *Savta* Leah. We would never have made it in time," he hurried passed a group of German tourists who were gathering at the chain separating the public plaza from the designated prayer area in front of the Wall. They, along with thousands of others, had come to observe the Jews welcoming their Sabbath at the holiest place to the Jewish people.

Rachel walked reverently up to the ancient Wall, absently squeezing Sarah's little hand a bit too strongly. She reached out and delicately touched the stone and then leaned her head against the smooth slab. It felt cool and calming against her forehead. It was here that three thousand years of history came crashing into the present and provided hope for the future. She thought about the future without Ari and tears filled her eyes.

"Are you okay Auntie Rachel?" asked Sarah.

"I'm fine Sarah. I was just thinking about your Uncle Ari and it made me sad," said Rachel looking into the concerned eyes of the little girl.

"My teacher says that the Western Wall continues to stand because the poor people built it. Everyone had to contribute to build the Temple. This part was built by the ones who had no money to donate. They did it with their own hands, out of their love for *HaShem*." Sarah, like most religious Jews used the term '*HaShem*,' meaning 'the Name,' to refer to God in conversation.

Sarah continued to talk, trying to make Rachel feel better. "The Talmud says that the Second Temple was destroyed because Jews hated each other for no reason. Everyone wanted things done their own way, and anyone who disagreed they hated."

"That happens often when people want to listen to themselves, instead of listening to what *HaShem* wants from the world. People sometimes pretend to be God," said Rachel.

"I guess it's hard to pretend to be God when you're so poor," said Sarah.

Just then a loud chorus of singing flowed over from the men's section. They were singing "*Lecha Dodi*," the traditional song sung by congregations all over the world, enjoining all Jews to greet the Sabbath Bride. The melody echoed off the ancient wall and rose skyward. At the last stanza, the group singing turned and faced the startled tourists watching them. Tradition says that the spirit of *Shabbat* rushes in from the West toward the site of the Temple.

> *Enter in peace, O crown of her Husband,*
> *Even in joy and good cheer,*
> *Among the faithful of the treasured nation,*
> *Come enter, O bride! Come enter O bride!*

The worshippers bowed, and turned back to face the Wall. It was at this point in the service that *Shabbat* officially began.

Rachel followed along in her white leather-bound *siddur*. Ari had given it to her. It is the traditional present a groom gives to his bride. She felt his presence with her at the

Wall. Rachel also felt the prayers of the millions of Jews around the world flying past her shoulders and into the cracks between the stones in the Wall before her. She felt the tears of hope of the millions of her ancestors who throughout the ages prayed for the return to Jerusalem and peace unto Israel. Rachel felt at one with her people. She felt she had come home.

Twelve

"We're back!" called out Sarah as she bolted through the door. She had run ahead when they reached the entrance to Yemin Moshe. The adults had taken a little longer because the return journey from the Western Wall was primarily uphill until you reached the exit from the Old City at Jaffa Gate. Shoshana gave her daughter a hug and a kiss on the forehead. Moments later her husband, Rachel, and Marc whom they had run into at the Wall, came into the house a little out of breath from the brisk walk.

Meir Tal was short and stocky. Some might call him pudgy. His curly red hair and big bushy red beard matched his personality. He was quick-witted, and high strung. His sense of humor and penchant for action made him fun to be with. Meir wasn't a philosopher, but he had razor sharp street smarts. When he knew something was true, he would throw his whole being into it. It was this passion and zeal for life that had attracted Shoshana to him when they had met at a Bnei Akiva religious Zionist youth group rally in Jerusalem twelve years before.

Meir was born the same year that Leah and Irving Rosenthal made Aliyah from New York. They arrived in the spurt of immigration from America that took place in the euphoria after the Six Day War in 1967. Irving had the family name shortened to "Tal" so that their firstborn would have a full "Israeli" name. Meir's little brother Ari came into the world eighteen months later.

Growing up, the inseparable boys were as different as night and day, not only in stature but in personality as well. One thing they shared was their unflinching love and passion for their People, their Land and their Torah. The 'Tal Boys' represented the cream of the Zionist dream. They were serious Yeshiva students, and respected officers in their elite reserve units in the Israel Defense Forces.

There was no question that Meir would move to a settlement when he married Shoshana. Everyone assumed it. It was part of fulfilling the biblical prophecy of returning to the Land. His little brother had planned to follow Meir to Ma'alot Yair so their future children could grow up together as next-door cousins.

Following Ari's murder, and the government actions that preceded and followed it, Meir underwent a profound change. He, like most other Jewish settlers felt abandoned by his own government. They had become outcasts. "Obstacles to peace." When they demanded more security from the Army after the promised increase of terror took place that took his own brother's life, the Prime Minister labeled the settlers, "Crybabies." Further protests fell on deaf ears, and when they started to protect themselves, the government began finding excuses to revoke gun licenses and placing settler leaders under administrative detention.

The love and pride of the State of Israel he was weaned on turned sour. Meir and his friends began losing respect for the values of the secular State and replaced it with an increased trust in God and loyalty to His Torah.

"Come Yoni, it's time for your *bracha*," said Meir calling to his son to receive a special Sabbath blessing. Yoni's eyes lit up as he toddled to his Abba. Even though he couldn't speak full sentences yet, Yoni understood clearly what his father meant. He stood calmly, faced his father, grabbed onto his knees and lowered his head. Meir placed his hands on the little boy's head and recited the traditional Hebrew blessing,

> *May God make you like Ephraim and Menashe;*
> *May God bless you and keep you,*
> *May God bring the light of His countenance to you,*
>   *and be gracious to you.*
> *May God turn his countenance to you*
>   *and establish peace for you.*

Meir kissed Yoni on the head and then blessed Sarah who was waiting patiently 'in line' behind Yoni. In their family, the Tal's chose to bless the children from youngest to eldest. Meir then walked over to his mother Leah who blessed him. It is traditional for all parents to bless their children with peace on *Shabbat*, no matter what their age.

Everyone joined in singing "*Shalom Aleichem,*" "Peace be unto You" and "*Eshet Chayil,*" "Woman of Valor" before moving to the table for the recital of *Kiddush*.

This was always the most difficult part of the evening. Irving, as the head of the house, had always been the one to recite the blessings over the wine and bread. Since his fatal car accident the previous year, and following Ari's murder before that, there were no men left in the house to conduct the ceremony. When Leah was alone, she recited it herself. Whenever Meir and his family came to visit, he conducted the ceremony. Everyone glanced uneasily at the two empty chairs of the absent Tal men as he recited the blessings.

"Hey Imma, this *Challah* is great. I couldn't have chosen better myself at the bakery," joked Meir knowing that his mother had lovingly baked the *Challah* as she always did. He was trying to break the tension in the room as he handed the tray of *Challah* to Shoshana.

"How does the national president of *Kol Ha'am*, find time to bake her own *Challahs*?" asked Shoshana, getting up to help Leah serve the chicken soup. "I have only two children to look after, and it's been months since I've found time to bake *Challah*."

"What would be the point of leading a movement to bring Jewish values back to the Jewish State if I became too busy to fulfill the wonderful *mitzvah* of baking my own *Challah*?" she said as she ladled out a second *matzo* ball for Meir. "The day I have to stop baking my own *Challah* will be the day I retire as head of *Kol Ha'am*. If it ever comes to that, Marc can take over." She looked over at Marc handing him his bowl of soup and crinkled her nose, "Why aren't you running this thing anyway? It was at least half your idea."

"Your Hebrew is better," said Marc dryly as he took the soup from Leah and gently placed it on his dinner plate.

"What are you talking about?" jumped in Meir, "I took Imma out for ice-cream last week, and the girl who took her order brought her a slice of pizza!"

Sarah burst out laughing. "Abba, stop it. You made the chicken soup go up my nose!"

"Just how did *Kol Ha'am* get started?" Rachel asked Marc trying to save her friend any further embarrassment. "Leah says she met you at a class at the Kahn's apartment," she said to Marc.

Marc turned to look at Rachel. Her dark eyes focusing directly on him and waiting for an answer caught him off guard. In the candlelight, with her hair tied up in a bun she looked especially attractive. Normally in this situation, he would have cracked a joke, following Meir's lead. For a moment he held himself back, worrying about what kind of impression he would make if he wasn't funny. His face flushed slightly as he put his soup spoon down. He hoped no one noticed.

"That's right," said Marc, "Rabbi Steinberg spoke that evening about how the Jewish people should react when being threatened with war over *Eretz Yisrael*, the biblical land of Israel."

"I can't imagine why anyone would be interested in that topic," said Shoshana tongue in cheek.

"He used the example of Jacob returning to the Land of Israel after spending years working in Laban's house in order to marry Leah and Rachel."

"LEAH! RACHEL!" called out Yoni pointing to his grandmother and aunt.

"Jacob was trying to come home in peace to the Land that he inherited from his father Isaac. There waiting for him was his evil brother Esau with four hundred armed soldiers ready to kill him. Esau had regretted selling his birthright to Jacob and wanted to take it back by force.

"Threatened with a war over the Land, Jacob set the precedent for all Jews to follow. He readied himself for war by doing three things. Do you know what they were Sarah?" It was traditional to involve the children at the *Shabbat* table in the Torah conversation.

The little girl paused before answering, "He divided his camp in two so that if there was a war, half the Jews would survive. He sent gifts to his brother hoping he would change his mind. And finally, he prayed to *HaShem* to save him."

"Perfect," said Marc. Meir and Shoshana beamed with pride. He continued, "And what we learn from this said the Rabbi, is that neither action without prayer, nor prayer without action will be enough to win God's victories. We Jews must take our faith, and put it into action. It helps us see how real we are in terms of our relationship with God. In the end, the miracle of the victory comes from the Almighty. But without us taking the action we aren't partners with Him in earning our own perfection in the world by harnessing evil and bringing an increase of good to humanity."

Leah turned to further explain to Rachel, "I had been spending a lot of time alone praying to God to make some sense out of Ari's and Irving's deaths." Leah looked down at her soup and slowly stirred it. "The Rabbi's words shocked me into reality. I realized that if I didn't start doing something to change the circumstances that had caused the two tragedies, then I wasn't acting like a Jew. I decided to take all of that energy and try to fix things as much as I could."

Marc echoed her feelings. "We spent a lot of time talking about what we could do that wasn't already being done by other people trying to slow down the leftist government's rush to give in to the PLO," he continued. "As former Americans, we thought we could bring a different approach to the growing anti-government movement. I wasn't sure if we could really make a difference. I never did anything like this, but we had to try."

"I remember being at those mass rallies with Ari outside the Prime Minister's office just before and after the Declaration of Principles was signed on the White House lawn in September of 1993," said Rachel. "If 100,000 people couldn't get the government's attention, what did you think you could do that would work any better?"

"Rachel, don't be so naive," said Meir. "Don't you know that Ima is a crack shot? With her American 'know how' the Chairman of the PLO couldn't stand a chance."

"Meir, that's not funny. Don't joke about things like that. Especially after the Rabin assassination. Somebody might start taking you seriously. And especially at the *Shabbat* table," scolded Shoshana.

"You're right," he agreed, "let's sing a song and bring out the next course. All this talk of Americans is reminding me of the delicious turkey waiting to make its contribution to the *Shabbat* meal."

Thirteen

The rest of *Shabbat* passed without incident. It was indeed a respite from the intensity of the upheaval going on in Israeli society. Meir spent some time catching up on his *Daf Yomi* Talmud lesson that he attended every morning at 5:00 a.m. before daily prayers. The sessions each morning were sort of a mental aerobics for him. They also helped start off the day on a 'holy' foot and set the tone for all of his actions at work the rest of the day.

Rachel used the time to catch up on her sleep and finally get over her jet lag. It was difficult to imagine she had been back in Israel for less than a week. Leah had used the opportunity to read to her grandchildren and go for a walk in Liberty Bell Park with them. Shoshana took pleasure in the fact that she was a guest for all the meals.

Leah felt a knot in her stomach as Meir and Shoshana began packing up their suitcases and loading up the car for their trip home. She hated it when they drove home at night on the dark roads leading back to Ma'alot Yair. Leah flicked on the radio in the kitchen to catch the seven o'clock news report to hear if there had been any unrest over the weekend. She hated turning on the first news report after *Shabbat*. She prayed that there had been no terrorist attacks. She held her breath unnoticed by anyone else as the female news anchor came over the air. Over the years Leah had learned how to tell if a tragedy had occurred simply by the tone of voice that the newscaster used to introduce him- or herself.

She breathed a sigh of relief when the main headlines were foreign stories. Leah didn't even bother listening to the report after that. She turned off the radio and started to return to the family in the living room when the phone rang.

"*Shavuah Tov*," she answered, greeting the caller with a wish for a good week.

"*Shavuah Tov*, Leah, this is Itzik. We just found out Moshe Porat is speaking at the Renaissance Hotel to a Philadelphia Jewish Federation group tonight at 8:30. Gotta run, *Lehitraot*."

Leah looked at her watch. There wasn't much time. She quickly made three calls that activated the main branches in the *Kol Ha'am* phone network. Each of those would in turn call their own three contacts and so on down the chain. In the seventy minutes that remained before the Police Minister arrived at the hotel for his speech, it was probable that up to two hundred people would be there waiting to protest the police responsibility for the injuries at the demonstration the previous Thursday evening.

The pyramid phone network was one of the "American-style" activism techniques that Leah and Marc had introduced to the Israel scene. The government had a hard time coping with this thorn in its side. Even when they cut off one of the activists phone lines in the chain, it was no problem the patch it up by putting someone else in their place. The net result was that the government Ministers could not speak anywhere in public without being greeted by a group of angry protesters. They kept speaking engagements secret until the last minute, but it still didn't help, as the right wing groups had 'informers' everywhere.

Leah found it amusing to see the Ministers pull up to the hotels and be rushed into back entrances like fugitives in their own country. It was embarrassing, which was exactly the tactic that was being used. It angered and irritated the government, and in response, they often made outrageously stupid remarks in the press that lowered them even further in the eyes of the public. In the long run, public opinion would swing so much against them that in the next national elections no amount of splintering would keep the Right from forming the government.

Leah walked back into the living room. "It looks like we don't have to look for something entertaining to do this Saturday night, Rachel. We've got a date with the Police Minister at the Renaissance Hotel. He's speaking to a Jewish group at 8:30."

Meir picked up Yoni who had already fallen asleep on the couch. "I'm sorry we're going to have to miss the party. He's one of my favorites too. But we've got to get the kids to sleep. Besides, we're going to have a very busy week before Abu Alim makes his historic visit to the Temple Mount."

"Thank you Imma for a wonderful *Shabbat*," said Shoshana giving her mother-in-law a peck on the cheek. "We'll call and leave a message on your machine when we get home. It looks like you're going be out on the town tonight." Meir and Shoshana walked into the cool night air, each carrying one of the dozing children.

"If we hurry, we can still get most of these dishes done and still be on time," said Leah to Rachel. She was a stickler for order, and she wanted the house to be neat for the volunteers the next morning. "I'll start washing, and you call Marc and let him know about the demonstration. Maybe he'll whip together an appropriate sign or two to take along." Rachel surprised herself by being happy to have an excuse to speak to Marc.

Fourteen

The leg of the trip from Jerusalem to Bethlehem passed without incident. The children slept quietly in the back seat of Meir's blue Subaru station wagon. Meir and Shoshana both sat quietly with their thoughts. Meir was reviewing ideas and suggestions to bring up at the next meeting of the *Mercaz HaMa'avak*.

Shoshana was silently praying for this drawn out nightmare to be over already. She was tired of feeling the panic in her chest each time the children's school bus was five minutes late coming home in the afternoon. She was tired of sending her children off to school in the morning not knowing if they would return home safely. She was tired of being afraid to take her children shopping with her for fear of being stoned, firebombed or shot at along the way. She was tired of listening to the government officials blame her for being a victim.

Meir slowed down as they approached the army checkpoint. Large tin coffee cans stuffed with kerosene-soaked rags burned a bright yellow giving the area an eerie glow. He proceeded with caution because during these tense times, frightened soldiers had been known to fire acciden-

tally at Jewish vehicles. Especially since the Arabs had been
stealing cars with Israeli plates and anti-government bumper
stickers on them so that you'd think they were settlers.

The car in front of them was pulled over, and the soldier used his flashlight to wave Meir over to the curb as well.
It looked like they were searching for something or someone.
He couldn't tell if they were searching for Arab terrorists, or
if they were looking for a settler who had a warrant against
him for administrative detention.

Meir picked up the car phone and dialed. "Hello
Imma?" he said, "I'm glad I caught you before you left.
Don't forget to take the camcorder and the still camera. If the
police get out of hand, at least you'll have a record of it. And
if they take away one camera, you might be able to smuggle
out the second one." Meir resented having to give mental
energy to fight his own government. 'Don't we have enough
enemies?' he thought.

"I'm more concerned about you. Are you home yet?"
asked Leah, like a good Jewish grandmother.

"We're fine. Just being held up at a checkpoint. The
kids are asleep in the back of the car."

"Just be careful, they might have a tip-off that there are
terrorists on the road."

"Not to worry," he said in Hebrew, "I've got my Uzi
and a pistol. If any Arab even looks the wrong way at your
grandchildren..."

"Meir!" interrupted Shoshana. "Stop it. They can put
you under arrest just for talking like that. It's bad enough
they have our home phone tapped. But you're on a car
phone. How difficult is it for a scanner to pick up your conversation?"

Meir looked at Shoshana with a frown. Of course she
was right, but he had long ago given up being worried about
being listened to. He assumed all his conversations were be-

ing monitored, as were his mother's. But if he was constantly paranoid about every word he spoke, life would be unbearable. If they wanted to pick him up, they didn't need a telephone conversation as an excuse. Since they lived in what was still technically over the Green Line in disputed territory, they were under jurisdiction of the Israeli Military government. They could arrest anyone without cause under its anti-terrorism mandate. "Imma, have a wonderful time tonight. It's a beautiful evening. I wish I could be there with you. *Laila Tov*." He put the hand set back in its cradle beside the gearshift, and smiled at Shoshana.

After showing the soldier his driver's license, ownership and car registration, they were on their way again. Apparently the Army was on the lookout for a stolen car similar to their own.

A few kilometers later, Meir slowed to turn left off the main highway onto the road to Ma'alot Yair. As he braked, a Peugeot station wagon came hurtling down the highway straight at him and made a hard right turn onto the Ma'alot Yair road barely missing the front left headlight of Meir's car. 'They should know better,' thought Meir as he noticed the driver was wearing a *kipah* and his wife was sitting beside him.

"What was that?" asked Shoshana. The jolt of Meir jamming on the brakes woke her up.

"Some maniac. If he had been going in the other direction I would have said he's probably on his way to the hospital with his wife to deliver a baby. Why would he be in such a hurry to get to Ma'alot Yair?" Meir assumed they were on their way to the Jewish settlement.

"Maybe she has to go to the bathroom," said Shoshana, always trying fulfill the *mitzvah* of judging everyone favorably. "There aren't any gas stations along this road you know."

They both laughed as they continued on their way home.

Fifteen

"*Medinah Mishtarah, Medinah Mishtarah.*" The crowd was chanting "Police State, Police State." "Democracy is dead," shouted an American immigrant into a mobile television camera.

Leah felt a smug sense of pride as the group of about one hundred fifty people waved placards and Israeli flags at the news cameras. Her phone network worked. They had beaten the Police Minister in the race to the hotel, and had a group large enough to merit a "video byte" on the eleven o'clock news.

Leah moved through the crowd like a mother hen tending to her brood. Most of the people out tonight were women. They came out to identify with Rivka Weinstock who had been murdered on Wednesday night. Most of their husbands stayed home to baby-sit and do the post-*Shabbat* washing up. It was difficult to find baby-sitters Saturday night.

The group gathered opposite the main driveway leading up to the hotel entrance. Security was tight and the police didn't allow the demonstrators into the hotel lobby. Technically, a group larger than fifty people required a permit. For now at least, they let the group protest as long as it didn't get violent. The Chief of Police was a little "gun shy" after the riot Thursday night. There were some reporters even in the leftist press who had blamed the riot on an over-reaction of the police and a show of too much force.

Tourists arriving back at the hotel after a day of sight-seeing turned to look at the angry crowd not knowing what the demonstration was about. One stopped to ask Rachel what was happening. "We're fighting for our people," she said quietly. The tourist continued on into the hotel with a shrug and a puzzled look still on his face.

"Hi Rachel, still looking for trouble?"

Rachel turned to see who had recognized her in the dark. "Devorah! Are you a season ticket holder or some-thing?"

Rachel was glad to see Devorah again. After the riot, they didn't do much more than exchange pleasantries. Rachel had been too upset to accept Devorah's invitation for a cup of coffee on Ben Yehuda. They traded phone numbers and agreed to be in touch during the week. This was one of those Jerusalem coincidences that had made telephones un-necessary in the city before they became widely available. In Jerusalem, if you needed to speak to someone, somehow you 'accidentally' bumped into them during the day.

Devorah had been part of the gang of Israeli friends that Ari had gone to Hebrew University with. She had grown up on a religious *kibbutz* that her parents had helped found. Devorah was a passionate Zionist and in general was against the policies of the leftist government, but felt, unlike some of her friends, that the struggle to keep *all* the Land at *all* costs was wrong. The main goal was to build a Jewish State under Jewish Law in the Land. For that you needed Jews to be alive, not dead. So she always made sure to let people know that under certain circumstances she would be willing to trade some land if it meant Jewish lives would be saved. On this point Rachel wholeheartedly agreed with her. What they disagreed on were the intentions of the Palestinians once they got their State. Rachel felt that Palestine would become a launching pad for a war to 'push the Jews into the sea.' Devorah felt that even if that was the case, which it might not be, the IDF would be able to protect the Jewish population.

At university Devorah met and married Ari's friend Moshe even before she graduated. They moved to Ma'ale Adumim, a bedroom town east of Jerusalem. It was eventually annexed to metropolitan Jerusalem as part of the concessions the Palestinians made when they got their State. This helped complete a ring of Jewish settlement around the eastern part of the city that the Arabs claimed belonged to them. This was also one of the concessions that had branded the previous Palestinian leadership as traitors and was what Abu Alim was trying to rectify.

After the massacre in which 29 Arabs were gunned down in the Machpelah Cave in Hebron, Devorah had become active in the demonstrations against the government. The cave was the traditional burial site of Abraham and Sarah, Isaac and Rebecca, and Jacob and Leah. It also served as a Jewish synagogue as well as a Moslem Mosque. When the Arab worshippers were murdered by a Jew, she was outraged that things had gotten so bad, and she was afraid of the situation deteriorating into a civil war. Through Meir, she made contact with Leah and put herself on the *Kol Ha'am* phone network. She explained to Rachel that she was three people down in the phone call chain from Leah when she got the call tonight.

"Do you really think the police plant people in the crowd to incite them to break the law?" asked Rachel.

"I know a lot of people who have been arrested. I've also been to most of the demonstrations," said Devorah.

"Eventually you get to know the 'regulars,' but so do the police. They take photographs and video tapes. If you stick around to the end of the demonstrations sometimes you'll see some of the 'new faces' who were 'arrested,' sitting in the back of the paddy wagons having a cup of coffee joking with the police. None of the people I know personally who were arrested ever got offered a cup of coffee."

Marc, who had been distributing signs, came over to say hello. He knew Devorah from previous demonstrations and planning meetings. "It's after nine already," he said looking at his watch. "They must have taken Porat around to the back entrance to keep him from having to confront us."

"Does that mean we leave?" asked Rachel still getting used to the idea that there was a science to demonstrating. Every time she had been to a protest in the past with Ari, it was simply as a participant. Now she was part of the organizers.

"No, not yet," said Marc. "We'll stick around for a while and maybe catch him on the way out. We have to give it our best shot." He winked at Rachel, and then immediately wished he hadn't. Was he making it too obvious that he liked her? He turned and walked back to a small group that Leah was talking to.

"The Police Minister isn't the one we should be giving our best shot to. We sure could use a couple of well placed shots in the direction of Abu Alim," said Rachel to Devorah. "That's probably the quickest way to put an end to all of this. It's going to happen sooner or later. Either by one of them or one of us."

"Rachel, I'm surprised at you. When did you get so tough?" asked Devorah. She regretted having asked the question as soon as it left her lips and wished she could take it back.

Rachel looked at her friend. The silence made them uncomfortable as they both thought of Ari.

"I guess it's from spending time with Meir and Leah. In
America you get lulled into a stupor and think, 'Oh maybe
things will work out. Let's give it a try.' But after being back
here for just a few days, I've been shocked back into the
reality that this is the Middle-east, not the Mid-west."

"You're right," said Devorah. "The Americans keep assuming the Arabs are going to act like some labor union in
Detroit and keep to their collective bargain. The only thing
that Detroit and Dahaishe have in common are murderers,
and a large Arab population."

A couple of plainclothes security men walked quickly
out of the main hotel entrance. They were pressing their ear-
phones deeper into their ears, straining to hear instructions
coming from an unseen source. The walkie-talkie in the hand
of the young police cadet standing in the road next to Rachel
clattered to life. A senior police officer came running down
the hotel driveway and barked some orders and made some
frantic hand motions to the border police lining the
driveway.

Rachel sensed something was about to happen, and
butterflies filled her stomach. The people around her started
chanting louder. The young policeman in front of Rachel
started to 'herd' the group farther back onto the sidewalk
away from the street. There weren't any barriers set up for
this spontaneous 'illegal' demonstration. The crowd instinctively started pressing forward in the opposite direction.

The policeman started to look frantic. He was tired, and
frustrated. This morning he had been on duty in east Jerusalem where a group of young Arabs had gone on a rampage
down Salah-e-Din street near Damascus Gate. He had been
bruised trying to push a masked rioter into the paddy wagon.
Later in the day he and his company had been shuttled to the

Western Wall Plaza to guard the Jewish worshippers. Now he was here protecting his boss from his friends and neighbors. In fact, had he not been on duty, he would probably be on the sidewalk demonstrating with them. He was angry that he had to be there, and stood helpless feeling empathy for the people calling him 'traitor' and 'quisling.'

The officer in charge shouted at him to move the crowd back farther. He turned and faced him with a tired blank stare. The officer turning red with anger pushed the cadet aside and grabbing both ends of his riot stick with a fist shoved Rachel back with his full body weight. She would have been knocked off her feet had there not been a wall of humanity three people thick behind her. "Hey!" she shouted at the officer. "You're not allowed to touch me. It's against the law. I'm going to report you. Besides I'm an American citizen."

The officer's face glowed even redder. He reached up to his breast pocket and defiantly, and illegally, snapped his name tag off his blue shirt. "Go back to where you came from, you don't belong here. You're not one of us," he snapped at her and walked away shouting some more orders into his walkie-talkie.

Marc came rushing over to Rachel. "Don't touch him," he whispered. "that's exactly what he wants, so he can lock you up for the night and justify his pushing you if you lodge a formal complaint." Marc looked at the anger in Rachel's eyes. Concerned she might do something rash he added, "When Porat's car drives buy, don't go near the car. If you touch it they can consider it an attack. These guys are tired enough and frustrated enough that they might use their weapons."

Rachel decided that she wasn't going to let the Police Minister leave without giving him a piece of her mind. Just then, the Minister's black Chevrolet began moving down the driveway toward the road the demonstrators were standing on. The chauffeur made a sharp left turn and the passenger side of the car faced directly in front of Rachel. The crowd started moving and shouting along in the direction of the slow moving car. Some of the protesters had spilled onto the road in front of the 'limousine' hampering its progress.

The police started pushing and kicking the crowd to keep them away from the car and clear a path for it to escape. Rachel bent over and stared at the Police Minister in the eyes. From deep inside of her a shriek exploded, "Anti-Semite!" She felt someone fall against her knocking her into the car window. The Minister jumped back in his seat. Rachel felt her foot slip off the curb and her ankle caved under her body as she fell to the ground. The momentum of the crowd forced a few other people to trip and fall on top of her as she stretched out her arms to break her fall to the pavement.

Moments later the car was gone and people began untangling themselves from each other and from the twisted placards. Rachel breathed in the fresh evening air as the people around her stood up. But tears came to her eyes as a sharp pain shot up her arm.

"Come, let me help you up," said Devorah grabbing hold of Rachel's hand.

"No! Don't touch me!" pleaded Rachel holding on to her wrist.

"What happened?" asked Leah who had pushed her way through the crowd.

"It's my wrist. I think it's broken." Rachel was a jumble of emotions. She didn't know what to be more upset about; her arm, the Police, the Minister, the Arabs, the Government. She wished Ari were here to help her sort out her feelings. Rachel started to sob.

"It's all right," said the police cadet kneeling down beside her. "I've called an ambulance. They'll be here any minute."

Sixteen

"Meir, would you please get Yoni a drink of water?" Shoshana stopped typing at her computer and looked at her watch. It was 10:30 p.m. You could set your watch by Yoni's crying. For the last few weeks he had been waking up every night. She made a mental note to take Yoni to the doctor for a "strep" test tomorrow morning.

Meir finished reading the section of Talmud he was preparing for the next morning's lesson. He got up from his chair next to the dining room table and walked to the kitchen lost in the argument on the laws of damages that the Talmud was dealing with. It was a difficult section of Talmud to follow and he hated to break his concentration, but he didn't want to take Shoshana from her work. She was compiling a digest of the daily headlines in the newspapers and translating them into English to be faxed to Jewish leaders in North America in a campaign to sway public opinion to sympathize with the right wing settlers.

He took a plastic cup from the kitchen cupboard and turned on the faucet. Yoni's crying got louder but he didn't hear him, being lost in the world of the Talmud. The water spilled out over the top of cup and splashed on his hand, waking him from his trance. As he reached for a dishtowel, the door buzzer rang out with a simultaneous pounding of fists on the door.

"Who could be in such a panic at this hour of the night?" he thought. He reached instinctively for his gun, hoping it wasn't neighbors coming to rouse reinforcements against a terrorist attack.

He put his eye to the peephole and saw four soldiers standing on the porch. His heart sank, hoping that they weren't coming to tell him that something had happened to his mother and Rachel. He was the next of kin. He opened the door slowly and the soldiers burst into the room.

"Meir Tal?" said one of them curtly.

"Yes," he answered cautiously.

"And Shoshana Tal?" he continued.

"She's upstairs."

"Well get her now. We're going to take a ride to military headquarters." The soldiers accompanying the man talking gripped their Uzis tightly.

"What for? Do you have a warrant? What's this all about?" asked Meir in total astonishment.

"You can ask all the questions you like when we get to headquarters," he snapped back heartlessly.

"What's all the noise?" asked Shoshana coming into the room.

"Lets go!" said the officer adamantly. "And bring your guns."

"But we have two children sleeping here. You want us to leave them all alone?" Shoshana wasn't asking a question, she was making a statement. "Meir, you go along and find out what this is all about. I'll stay here with Sarah and Yoni." She took the cup of water from Meir's hand and started to go to give Yoni his drink.

"Both of you. Now. We have explicit orders."

"This is crazy," shouted Meir. "At least give me a minute to go and get a neighbor to come and stay with the children." He knew there was no point in arguing. They didn't need a warrant. They could pick up anyone, at anytime and hold them for up to 48 hours. The officer nodded to one of the soldiers holding an Uzi to follow Meir on his mission to rouse a neighbor. Within minutes they were back with Menachem from next door. He was already in his pajamas and bathrobe. He knew enough not to ask any questions. He just hoped Meir and Shoshana would be back before the children woke up. He didn't want to have to tell them that soldiers had come in the night and taken away their Imma and Abba.

The officer placed Shoshana in the passenger seat and Meir in the back of the van so they wouldn't be able to talk to each other. He was to make sure that they couldn't exchange any words from the time they arrived at the Tal home and the time he delivered them to the investigators at headquarters.

Meir was thankful they hadn't handcuffed them and that the children had been asleep. He thought that maybe this was a punishment from God for not sympathizing enough with the Soviet refuseniks during the eighties. He suddenly realized the terror they must have felt living under the threat of being picked up and arrested at any moment simply for having opinions contrary to the Communist government. He resolved to write a letter of apology to Natan Sharansky and Yosef Mendelevitch when he got home. Meir always felt that by trying to learn the message in everything and making some positive change in his life as a result, he was certain to be better off for it even if he was wrong about the lesson.

The van sped down the road and arrived at a small army base surrounded by barbed wire. Tents were scattered throughout the camp that served as sleeping accommodations for the soldiers as well as a large dining area. A half dozen

caravans were used as barracks for officers and administrative buildings. A guard waved the van through the main
gate and the driver stopped in front of a beige mobile home
badly in need of a coat of paint.

The soldiers took Meir and Shoshana inside and led
them to two separate rooms that looked like small offices.
The base was so small, that there were no formal interrogation rooms.

"*Shavuah Tov*, Meir, I understand you were at your
mother's house for *Shabbat*." It was Amnon Tamar, the head
of the base. Meir knew the pudgy, middle-aged career officer
from countless meetings when the Settler Committee from
Ma'alot Yair met with him to discuss improving the security
situation in the area.

"*Shalom*, Amnon," he tried to be pleasant, hoping this
would be over soon. "What's the emergency that you have to
drag me *and* my wife out in the middle of the night?"

Tamar sat down, clasped his stubby fingers together
and lay them down on his bulging tummy. The buttons were
pulling at his shirt. He wore pants with the same waist size
that he had when he was married. They didn't fit around his
waist so he buttoned them up under his girth. "What time did
you leave Jerusalem?" he asked.

Meir realized he wasn't going to get any information
from Amnon. He felt bad his wife had to be put through all
of this as well. Meir looked at Amnon with a frown, "Around
eight o'clock, I guess."

"Aha," said Tamar making a note on the pad of paper
on the cluttered desk in front of him. "And what time did you
get home?"

"A little before nine. We got stopped at that checkpoint
near Bethlehem which slowed us down. I remember turning
on the news right after putting the kids to sleep." Meir was
getting impatient.

"Did anything happen out of the ordinary after you passed the checkpoint," asked Amnon.

Meir tried to think if anything had happened, but was distracted by trying to figure out what Amnon could be getting at. "No. Nothing."

"Meir, when was the last time you fired your guns?"

Meir looked at Amnon with disdain. "You can't be serious. You picked us up in the night to question us about that incident in Hebron last month?" The previous month an unidentified settler had gotten out of his car in the middle of a rain of rocks being pelted on him by a group of Palestinian youths. He shot at them and fatally wounded one. The settler hadn't stayed around for fear that he would be jailed for using his weapon in a 'non-life-threatening situation.'

"Just answer the question," said Amnon stonily.

"I fired the Baretta two months ago at target practice, and last week I fired the Uzi at the firing range before we went out on guard duty at the settlement." There was a rotation system at Ma'alot Yair, like at all other settlements where the men took turns during the night taking guard duty to provide extra security. Approximately twice each month, every adult male received a three hour shift.

"Do you have any other guns?"

"What do *you* think? I only have a license for the Baretta. The Uzi is on loan from the army."

Amnon didn't like that Meir hadn't answered his question directly.

"We're going to have to take your guns for ballistics testing. I understand you brought them with you." said Amnon dryly.

"But the Hebron incident involved a Glilon, not an Uzi," complained Meir. "And ballistics testing can take up to two weeks. You can't leave me without a gun for that long when the Prime Minister is promising more terror attacks."

"I'm not talking about the Hebron incident. There was an attack tonight near the Ma'alot Yair junction. Two Arabs were killed and one survived. It was a drive-by shooting. It happened just after 8:30 p.m. The survivor said it was settlers in a station wagon. He noticed the driver had a knitted *kipah*," Amnon paused for effect. "And there was a woman in the passenger seat."

Meir looked at Amnon in astonishment. "You really think Shoshana and I would go on a shooting spree with two sleeping kids in the back seat?"

Amnon looked at him with disdain. "I don't think anything anymore. And don't worry about not having a gun for the next two weeks. You'll probably be locked up for a good portion of it until we get the ballistics report back. And as for your kids, if your wife's story isn't too incriminating, we'll let her go home to take care of them tonight. In the meantime you can start making yourself feel at home."

Seventeen

The emergency room at Hadassah Ein Kerem hospital was bustling with the typical Saturday night rush. Each night, the hospitals in the city took turns being duty hospitals for different emergencies. Tonight, Bikur Cholim was on duty for births, and Hadassah was on duty for emergency room. Saturday night was busier than usual because all the minor playground bumps and bruises that didn't warrant breaking the Sabbath for were brought to the duty hospital at night for X-rays 'just in case.' Since a large portion of the city population was religious Jews, there were quite a few boisterous boys and girls waiting in line for the X-ray machine in front of Rachel.

Marc came back from the registration desk with Rachel's identity card and sat down in the empty orange plastic chair beside her. Leah had decided to let Marc go alone with Rachel in the ambulance. She would be in good hands, and besides, emergency rooms gave Leah nightmares.

"How's your arm?" Marc asked, handing to Rachel the blue plastic folder holding her papers.

Rachel was sitting with her head tilted back against the wall with her eyes closed. She was trying to mentally block out the pandemonium of noise the children were making in the emergency room waiting area. Some were crying while others were shouting with laughter, happy to have an excuse to stay up late. A television set was blaring in the corner of the room. She opened her eyes and looked at Marc, glad to have some company. "*Baruch HaShem*," she said calmly with a small smile.

"*Baruch HaShem, good*? or *Baruch HaShem bad*?" he asked trying to make her laugh. Normally the non-committal "*Baruch HaShem*," meaning "Blessed is God" perplexed him. He understood why religious Jews responded that way, but it didn't inform the inquirer how the person was really feeling. It only indicated that the one with the illness knew that everything happened for a reason, and that God is the source of all blessing. Whether something positive or negative happened in one's life, it was always in one's best interest as an opportunity for growth.

Rachel's smile broadened. She liked Marc's sense of humor. "*Baruch HaShem*, pretty good," she admitted. "If it's broken at all, it's only a slight fracture." She had a lot of experience with sprains and fractures from her Tomboy days at summer camp in northern Ontario.

The police cadet came back from the hospital administration office scribbling notes on a pad of forms. "You think you'll be all right?" he asked Rachel with genuine concern. She reminded him of his sister.

"*Baruch HaShem,*" she answered automatically. Then she glanced at Marc with a smile and added, "*Hakol Beseder*," indicating everything was okay.

"I've taken care of all the paperwork here. I've got your information. I'm going to go down to the Russian Compound to fill out my full report that I'm sure my boss is eagerly awaiting. I'll call the hospital later to find out the results of the X-rays. If there's any problem, here's a card with my number on it at the office. I also wrote down my boss's name and badge number if you decide to file a complaint against him for shoving you. But I don't recommend it. *Refuah Sheleimah,*" he said wishing her a full recovery as he handed her the card and walked out of the emergency room.

Rachel took the card and slipped it into her bag past her handgun. She was relieved that it was her left arm that was injured and not her shooting arm. Rachel snapped the bag shut quickly hoping Marc hadn't noticed the gun. She didn't want to spook him while she was trying to make a good impression. She didn't want to have to explain that she had decided to carry a gun since Ari was murdered. "At least there are still some good cops left," she said cheerfully to Marc.

"A kid like him is in a 'no win' situation. I feel bad for him. He probably won't last long on the police force," said Marc. "His boss will start noticing his sympathy towards our side and he'll be either fired or banished to some menial office job and he'll quit. Then, depressed, he'll probably go on a trip to America because he can't find a job and end up driving a cab in New York, like a million other former Israelis."

A nurse walked into the waiting room and called out the name of the next person in line for the X-ray machine. Marc glanced at his watch. It was already ten o'clock and there were still five more people ahead of them. He started to feel the frustration rising in his throat that he always felt when he had to spend countless hours waiting in lines in Government institutions. Usually he brought a book along to read. Then he realized the extra wait would mean another hour talking with Rachel and his frustration vanished faster than it had arrived.

Rachel always had a difficult time with people who had anything bad to say about Israel. There was a biblical prohibition against speaking slander about the Land of Israel. In fact, the Jewish people ended up spending forty years in the desert because the spies Moses sent, had brought back a slanderous report about the Land of Israel. Some religious Jews like Marc were careful to make a distinction between what they said about the God-given Land of Israel and the secular socialist society of the modern State of Israel. She tried to keep from saying anything bad about the State in order not to fall into the trap of defaming the Land, although she did succumb at times as well. Rachel didn't want to offend Marc but she decided to say something. "If you're so cynical about Israel and Israelis, what made you want to live here?"

Marc sat up a little straighter in the uncomfortable plastic "bucket" seat and asked, "Do you want the long version, or the short version?"

"The long version. It looks like we've got some time on our hands," she said rubbing her sore wrist. Besides, she really was happy to have the opportunity of getting to know more about him.

Marc took a deep breath, and with an impish grin that forced two deep dimples in his cheeks he began, "Well, it all started many years ago in Brooklyn. You see, I was born a poor child, in a ramshackle tin shack under the Brooklyn Bridge... "

"Oh stop it!" said Rachel with a laugh. She felt like smacking him with her good hand, but held herself back remembering the custom of not touching.

"Okay, okay. So we weren't so poor."

"Marc!" she protested. "Come on, seriously."

"All right. We weren't so poor *and* we didn't live in a shack. But I did grow up in Brooklyn. My family wasn't so observant. I guess the Jewish Federation was sort of a religion for my parents. My father who was in the clothing business, was always involved in some fundraising campaign for the Jewish community or on a solidarity mission to Israel. We drove to the Orthodox *shule* on Yom Kippur, but we fasted all day."

"You *drove* to the *Orthodox* synagogue?" asked Rachel incredulously.

"Sure. A lot of families did. My grandfather was a poor immigrant from Poland. He was meticulous in his observance of the Sabbath. My father went with him to services at an Orthodox *shule* on the Lower East Side. To survive in the New country, it was important for my Dad to become 'Americanized.' They sent him to public schools, and so began the great assimilation of American Jewry. Judaism was no longer the focal point of one's life, it became something you painted onto your American identity.

"When we moved to Brooklyn, and were no longer in walking distance of the synagogue, we drove to the Orthodox *shule* on the High Holydays even though it was "prohibited," because that's were my Dad felt most comfortable. We parked the car a block away, and walked the rest so as not to offend any of the congregants. He expressed his spirituality that way, even though we really weren't observant. Are you sure you still want the long version?"

Rachel nodded. "Sure, go on." She was always fascinated to hear the stories of people who chose to become Orthodox who didn't grow up that way. The man sitting next to her was wearing a *kippah* on his head, and hadn't grown up with one. Somewhere in his story there was going to be a fascinating turn of events.

"When my grandfather passed away, so did most of the religion that was left in the family. First it was the pepperoni pizza. And then it was the Chinese food every Sunday night.

When we brought it into the house my mother was careful to keep the non-kosher food on paper plates. For some reason she still kept separate dairy and meat dishes while we were eating "spareribs" on the disposable dishes. And somehow I didn't consider it odd or hypocritical. It was just our way of being Jewish."

A young boy and his mother came out of the X-ray room and the nurse called out two more names. Marc glanced back down at his watch. "Hey, we're not making bad time."

"*Nu*? Finish your story already, before I have to go in," said Rachel.

"Well to make a long story, medium, I graduated from University with a degree in Computer Science. I liked numbers and got a job as a stock broker. The Market was like one big puzzle for me, waiting to be cracked. I made enough money in commissions that first year to earn myself an extended vacation. Not because I was so smart. I didn't really know what I was doing back then, but I happened to be around the right people at the right time. I quit my job and spent a summer cycling through the Grand Canyon. With the Fall arriving, I decided to go to Israel for the first time and visit a high school friend for the High Holydays who had gone to Yeshiva instead of joining me at University. That's when I first ran into Rabbi Steinberg."

"Hurry up Marc, or we'll be late for our appointment with Rabbi Steinberg. We can't keep the Rosh Yeshiva waiting!" David grabbed his friend by the elbow and pulled him down the narrow street of the Jewish Quarter of the Old City of Jerusalem.

"He's only a Rabbi!" cried out Marc. "What's the big deal? Nobody's dying or getting married are

they? How much of a rush to be on time could he be?"

The two twenty-three year olds hurried up a narrow staircase and into a residential apartment that served as the Yeshiva offices. David nodded at the secretary seated behind a small brown melamine desk in the waiting area outside of the Rabbi's office. Trying to catch his breath, David knocked hesitantly at the door. There was a buzz, and the door opened.

Marc slowly followed his friend into the room, surprised by what he saw. He expected a dark oak office, filled with large tomes behind the glass doors of floor-to-ceiling bookshelves and a huge desk with a big leather chair. Sort of like the offices of the Rabbis back home. Instead, he saw a sparsely furnished room. The Rabbi sported the stereotypical long white beard and wore a black suit and a black Homberg hat. He was seated behind a modest melamine desk to match the secretary's out front. A small bookshelf housed sets of reference-sized copies of the Talmud and other Hebrew books that Marc didn't recognize.

"Come in, Come in," the Rabbi rose from his chair and motioned the young men to take a seat in the two empty chairs facing his desk. Before David had a chance to sit down, Rabbi Steinberg gave him a big bear hug. Marc hadn't realized the two were so close. He hoped they weren't plotting some conspiracy against him. The Rabbi sat down and looked at Marc straight in the eyes, "So David tells me you're old highschool buddies?"

Marc felt the Rabbi's eyes piercing into him much more powerfully than he had anticipated. He knew that David and the Rabbi were going to try to get him to stick around and study at the Yeshiva for a while, especially since he was between jobs and had some time on his hands. He had prepared himself accordingly and decided to not beat around the bush in an attempt to get the upper hand of the discussion.

"Yes, we've been close for quite a long time," acknowledged Marc. "It's great to be together with him here in Israel and I'm so happy for him that he's enjoying his studies here at the Yeshiva. In fact I respect him for what he is doing and his committment to Judaism." Marc put up a tough exterior, but inside he was unsure of himself facing the distinguished looking Rabbi.

David shot a smile at Rabbi Steinberg. He had told the Rosh Yeshiva that his friend was a great guy. Marc's quick mind and innate ability at problem solving would make him a natural in the Sea of the Talmud.

"But to be perfectly honest Rabbi," said Marc leaning forward and lowering his voice as if about to reveal a secret, "God doesn't expect me to keep the commandments."

In his years in this business, Rabbi Steinberg thought he had heard it all. Often he had to hold himself back from giving "boilerplate" responses to "boilerplate" statements. But this was a first. "Son, you have gotten my attention," admitted the Rabbi, "Tell me how you know such a thing."

David turned red with embarassment. "Well," said Marc confidently leaning forward on the desk, "last month I was riding on my ten-speed bicycle through the Grand Canyon. The view was breathtaking. The wind was streaming through my hair and I was in awe of the beauty that God had put *in the world. The fact that I was driving on a winding road along the face of a cliff made the experience even more thrilling. Then all of a sudden a big Mac truck came barrelling down the highway from behind me. I tried to pull over to the shoulder of the highway to avoid the suction effect as he passed me but I was too close to the edge of the cliff. So the vacuum sucked me dangerously close to the side of the truck as it came alongside me. When end of the truck pulled clear of me, the break in the vacuum whipped me back in the opposite direction and threw me over the cliff."*

Marc waited for the looks of disbelief in the listeners' faces that he had seen in everyone to whom he had told the story in the last month.

"But if that's true, how come you're still alive?" asked David suspiciously.

"Well like I said, God really loves me. You see I started to freefall and about twenty feet down the two hundred foot drop, I crashed into a large bush that was jutting out of the face of the cliff. I thought I was a gonner, but God had reached out His Hand and caught me like an outfielder would snag a fly ball."

Marc paused for a moment while the Rabbi shook his head in amazement.

"And you know what Rabbi," continued Marc, "I don't keep any *Mitzvahs. I don't keep* Shabbat. *I eat cheeseburgers. I'm not religious. And in spite of all that, God performed a miracle to keep me alive. Like I said, He obviously doesn't expect me to keep the commandments. Otherwise why would He keep me alive to be telling you the story?"*

Rabbi Steinberg took off his eyeglasses and thought for a moment. Then he leaned forward,

Charles Samuel

looked Marc in the eye, and in a whisper asked, "Did you ever stop to think about who sent the truck in the first place?"

Eighteen

The group of radio and television reporters jockeyed for position at the steps to the entrance of the President's official residence in Jericho. Inside, Abu Alim and his advisors were huddled together selecting the best strategy for responding to that evening's shooting near the Ma'alot Yair road.

Two hours had already passed since the incident. The inner circle of Palestinian leadership shouted at each other from their usual positions at the briefing table in the "Green Room" that served as Alim's office.

"You must act outraged that it took the Israelis so long to inform us of the slaughter of our Palestinian brethren on their territory," advised Rajai Ahmed, the Minister of Defense.

"We must demand that UN forces finally be brought into Jerusalem and the other parts of the pre-1967 occupied territories that were not returned to us. The safety of our nationals must be protected," shouted Tawfiq Shaban, the Minister of Interior.

"Abu Alim, now is the right opportunity to suggest that we convene an International Conference to discuss the future of the remaining territories and the status of Jerusalem. They keep boasting that all religions have free access to their holy sites. We can claim that in fact Moslems have no access at all if they are afraid to travel their own streets for fear of their lives." The Foreign Minister was naturally a little calmer than the others.

Abu Alim had his hands tightly clasped resting on the oak table. He surveyed the motley crew of 'former' terrorists before him. The previous Palestinian President had presented an argument for using the title "Secretary" favored by the American government rather than the "Minister" labels used in the parliamentary system. The idea was to make Palestine appear more democratic and find empathy in the eyes of the American public who traditionally identified with the more western Israelis. A smirk came to his face. His Ministers looked, and acted nothing like their American counterparts.

"Gentlemen," said Abu Alim. He barked the word at them like a master would to his dogs. "We must all agree that when the press interviews any of us about this incident, our first words must be an expression of sympathy and sorrow to the bereaved families. Remember, this was the previous Israeli Prime Minister's fatal flaw. Whenever a Jew was killed by us, his first words were always about how this was an attack against his policies. His people eventually came to hate him for it."

The group of leaders looked at each other red-faced. "Of course, Mr. President, that goes without saying," stammered Shaban.

Abu Alim frowned. He didn't really like his Minister of Interior. He needed him for political reasons. He came from one of the more prominent clans in Hebron. "And forget the territories. Every statement, every word, uttered by any of us over the next week leading up to my triumphant appearance at the *Al Aksa* mosque, must relate to *Al Quds*, the Holy City.

The battle is for Jerusalem. When that is won, the rest will come along with it."

The Ministers nodded in unison. Abu Alim frowned again. He hated "yes" men. You never knew if they really respected you for your ideas, but it was the price to pay to be the dictator in a democracy.

"Come, let us not delay any longer," said Abu Alim rising from his oversized leather armchair. "We don't want to irritate the media when we have so much world sympathy on our side."

The President of Palestine quickly moved towards the front door. When he made his decisions he acted immediately. Those around him found it a troubling habit, especially the Palestine Secret Service. The Ministers scrambled to fall in line behind their leader and the Secret Service men rushed to the door ahead of their leader. The wide double doors swung open and Abu Alim emerged from behind a wave of body guards. He smiled as the bright video lights switched on and the reporters began fawning before him, "Mr. President, Mr. President!"

Nineteen

"I can't believe that 'cliff story' really happened to you. It's too good to be true," protested Rachel with a laugh. "But then again, it's too good for someone to have made it up either. Tell me, what happened next?"

The nurse came out of the X-ray room and called out Rachel's name. Rachel turned to Marc and said, "Don't forget where you were, I don't want to miss a detail." She got up and crossed the waiting area toward the entrance to the X-ray room. Out of the corner of her eye she recognized Abu Alim's face on the television screen. The eleven o'clock news had come on and he was being interviewed. She paused for a moment to watch as the camera zoomed in to a close up of the President of Palestine. A bodyguard standing directly behind him reached up to adjust his earphone. As he turned to look at something that caught his attention off to the left of the TV screen, a flash of light reflected off the bodyguard's wrist. Rachel's heart skipped a beat as she strained to look at the small detail in the top right corner of the screen. "It can't be," she thought to herself, just as the camera switched to a wide angle shot. "It's just my imagination," she muttered as she continued on her way to have the X-ray camera examine her own left wrist.

Marc got up and walked toward the television so he could hear the news broadcast. The few plastic seats nearby were occupied by a nurse and a couple of orderlies who were taking a break after the wave of post-*Shabbat* patients had subsided. Marc stood and subconsciously folded his arms expecting not to like what he was about to hear coming out of Abu Alim's mouth. One of the orderlies leaned forward to turn up the volume.

"I first want to express my extreme sorrow and condolences to the families of our murdered Palestinian brethren, and wish a full and speedy recovery to the third victim. This was a shameless act of cowardice by fanatic settlers and once again shows how little they value human life."

Marc gritted his teeth. This was the man who sent PLO terrorists to plant bombs in supermarkets. He had ordered suspected collaborators to stab Jews to clear their own names and to be accepted as members of *Fatah*, the PLO military faction.

Abu Alim struck a statesmanlike pose and continued calmly, "This is another example of how our Palestinian brethren are not being protected by the Israelis. How is it possible that these murderers could have committed such an act with an Israeli Army checkpoint so close by? Could the soldiers have possibly turned a blind eye? These are questions that must be answered."

Marc felt the blood beating in his temples. He preferred the old Arafat days. Had he been still around as leader, he would have immediately declared the attack an Israeli conspiracy and that some of the bullets fired had been by soldiers assisting the attackers. As a result no one took Arafat's statements too seriously. But Alim was much smoother. Instead of making outrageous accusations he subtly asked questions instead. It planted seeds of doubt and made him seem more moderate, when in fact he was much more blood-thirsty and dangerous than Arafat.

Abu Alim was born in 1948 in a refugee camp near Bethlehem. The Jordanians told his parents during the Israeli War of Independence to temporarily flee their homes east-ward while the Jews were pushed into the sea. In a few days they would be able to return to their home and plunder the booty left behind by the dead Jews. By all laws of war and statistics, that is exactly what should have happened when the five invading Arab armies attacked the newborn State of Israel the day after it was declared. But through a miracle the Israelis won. After the cease-fire, the Jordanian king found himself with tens of thousands of unwanted Arabs on his side of the cease-fire line. The King built them refugee camps rather than integrating them into Jordanian society preferring to keep Abu Alim's family and myriads like them in squalor as political pawns.

For nineteen years, Alim's teachers taught him to hate the Israelis for causing him to live in such poverty. After all it was because of them, that his parents lost their home. The teachers conveniently 'forgot' to teach him about the United Nations partition plan dividing the British Mandate in Pales-tine into a State for the Jews and a State for the Arabs. They also forgot to teach him that the five Arab countries initiated the war.

In April of 1964, as a sixteen year old, he sneaked his way into the Ambassador Hotel in east Jerusalem to attend the official founding of the Palestine Liberation Organization. At that time, all of the West Bank, Gaza Strip and East Jerusalem were in Arab hands. He was awestruck when a young man in his thirties took notice of him, put his arm around his shoulders and took him out to the patio in front of the hotel. The man pointed to the west, toward the

Mediterranean Sea. "One day, not only will the Alim home be returned to its rightful owners, my little brother, but also Jaffa, Haifa and Tel Aviv will become part of the Arab homeland," promised the young man with the wild eyes. His name was Yasir Arafat - a rising star in the fledgling liberation movement.

Abu Alim attached himself to Arafat, learning everything he could from him. Arafat shared everything with the boy, so Alim wasn't surprised when the Arabs planned another war to push the Jews into the sea. It was part of the "master plan." What everyone was surprised by was the Israelis' pre-emptive lightning strike that devastated the Arab world's honor in just six days. They thought that the Jews would stick to the silly western 'gentlemanly' principles and never initiate a strike. In any event, the cease-fire left Abu Alim back in the squalor of his refugee camp, only this time as an orphan under the control of the Israeli Army. His parents were killed when they were caught in the cross-fire between Israeli and Jordanian soldiers. The war also left him separated from his beloved Arafat whom he and others called Abu Amar, his nom de guerre.

During the years of Israeli control, Jibril Abu Alim became one of the PLO's key players in the territories. He helped plan and co-ordinate numerous terror attacks on both sides of the Green Line although he was never directly connected to actual murders. Others went to jail for that. That was why even though he was imprisoned for being an Intifada leader in 1989, he was able to be among those released during the Peace Talks of 1994. He had "no blood on his hands." Which simply meant the Israeli courts hadn't been able to pin any of the murders he was responsible for, directly on him. Upon his release, he immediately took a senior position in Arafat's 'police' force.

Abu Alim belonged to the young generation who only knew the refugee camps. He was weaned on hatred for the Jews. Where the old timers often fought for their own aggrandizement and power, Alim fought because it was in his bones. He didn't care what the world thought of him like some of his predecesors did. The people on the street accepted Arafat as the President of Palestine, but eventually viewed him as an anachronism. In Abu Alim, they found a kindred spirit. He knew exactly what to say to the people. He empathized with them and the Palestinians felt it. It's no wonder that they discarded the PLO old guard, and crowned Abu Alim their leader the first chance they got.

Abu Alim was going to take back his parent's home, Jerusalem, Jaffa and all the rest of the land that the Jews had taken from his People. That's what the Palestinians wanted. Abu Alim would deliver.

* * *

"Mr. President, how do you think this will affect the Israelis' hesitation about allowing you to visit the Temple Mount in Jerusalem on Friday?" called out the CNN reporter.

Abu Alim smiled, wondering if one of his aides had prompted the reporter to ask the question. Then he immediately forced a stern and concerned look on his face. "Everyone knows that the Israelis pride themselves on the open and democratic nature of their country. They guarantee access to all the holy sites to people of all religions. There is no question in my mind that the Prime Minister would never prevent me from praying at Al Aksa for these innocent souls who were so cruelly murdered by some fanatics." Abu Alim had prepared every word carefully to use this opportunity to guarantee that he would be in Jerusalem, at Al Aksa this week. Everything depended on it.

Marc felt like kicking in the television screen. He said out loud, "You lying, sick, murdering, cynical..."

"Hey Marc," said Rachel coming out of the X-ray room, "What's going on?" Her left arm was slung in a sling.

"Two Arabs were murdered in a drive-by shooting near the Ma'alot Yair road. They think it might have been settlers. Abu Alim is milking it for all it's worth to pressure Shiloni to let him come to Jerusalem this week. He doesn't give a hang about the dead Arabs. He's ordered a lot more than two Palestinians killed for collaborating with the Israelis during the Intifada. Now he's pretending to the world what a warm compassionate human being he is."

Rachel looked at the screen, and the image of Alim surrounded by the shouting reporters. He was basking in the attention, the fame and the power like a poor little kid from a refugee camp who had kissed a frog and turned into a prince. "He certainly doesn't look like somebody who is mourning the loss of his Arab brothers. In fact, if you didn't hear what he was saying, you might even say he looked happy."

The nurse came out of the X-ray room holding an oversize manila envelope with the image of Rachel's arm. "The doctor says it's not broken. It's just a bad sprain. A few days in the sling and it should be fine."

"*Baruch HaShem!*" said Rachel and Marc at the same time and they burst into laughter. The nurse thought they were acting a little strangely. She handed Rachel the envelope and wished her a speedy recovery.

"Come, I'll drop you at home in a cab," said Marc picking up Rachel's bag for her and taking the envelope. We can celebrate tomorrow. It's late and you need to rest."

Rachel was beaming as they walked out into the cool, fresh air of the Jerusalem night. She could see why Leah respected Marc so much.

Twenty

Udi Harel rushed down the hallway grasping tightly onto two beige cardboard filefolders. He called out *"Boker Tov!"* with a big smile wishing everyone in his path a good morning. Udi was so excited, he forgot to stop and knock before walking into Yigal's office. It was going to be a great week. He had two breakthroughs and it was only Sunday morning.

"You're away from the office for one day and you forget to knock?" grumbled Yigal. He was still sipping his first cup of coffee. You *never* talked to Yigal until after his first cup of coffee. "I wonder what you'd forget if Israel ever moved to a two-day weekend."

Udi slapped the files onto Yigal's desk. "Do you want the good news, or the good news?"

Yigal looked up and sneered at Udi. He hated people who were in a good mood before 9:00 a.m. "Stop being so happy and just tell me what you've got." Yigal reached forward and opened the top filefolder.

"Meir Tal has been picked up in connection with the murder of those two Arabs last night near the Ma'alot Yair road. The surviving Arab said he thought the attackers were a 'settler couple' in a station wagon," said Udi excitedly.

"That's what you're so excited about?" said Yigal, slightly deflating Udi's enthusiasm.

Udi hated it when Yigal made judgments before he could get his whole story out. Udi could never pack enough words into a sentence to make his point fast enough with Yigal, but he pressed on. "A few minutes before the attack, Meir Tal called his mother. We've been monitoring both Leah Tal's home phone and Meir's car phone for months."

Yigal rolled his eyes. He hated it when people being monitored phoned each other. It was such a waste of department funds to have two employees listen to the same conversation. He scribbled a note for himself to speak to the communications people. Was there a way to automatically cut off one of the eavesdropper's lines so she could move on to monitoring another conversation and avoid the duplicated effort?

Udi continued with his report and flipped through the type-written pages trying to highlight only the key points for Yigal. "Listen to this," he said reading from the report.

LEAH: Just be careful, they might have a tip-off that there are terrorists on the road.

MEIR: Not to worry, I've got my Uzi and a pistol. If any Arab even looks the wrong way at your grandchildren...

SHOSHANA (faintly in the background): Meir! Stop it. They can put you under arrest just for talking like that. It's bad enough they have our home phone tapped. But you're on a car phone. How difficult is it

for a scanner to pick up your
conversation?

"They've locked up Meir while his guns are undergo-
ing ballistics testing," added Udi.

Yigal looked up from the paper he had been reading
along with Udi. "While they're at it, have them check his
guns against the casings we found on the hill near the shot-up
poster of Abu Alim," said Yigal dryly, taking another sip
from his coffee mug.

Udi felt relieved now that Yigal was on his wavelength.
He relaxed a bit, and trying to score a few points with his
boss, he added, "I've already put in that request."

"Good," said Yigal trying to downplay the fact that he
had been pre-empted by his agent. He closed the file and
placed it face down on the right side of his desk as if turning
a page in a book and opened the second beige folder. "Now
what's the other good news?"

"Rachel Stein," answered Udi, a little disappointed that
he didn't get any praise for anticipating his boss's instructions. "Two things. First, I ran the list of guests checked into
the King David Hotel on the day Rachel visited, through our
computer. It seems that the millionaire Harry Waxman was
there at the time. He's being investigated by the FBI on suspicion that he was making illegal donations to right-wing
settler groups in the territories. She might have had a rendez-
vous to pick up some cash from him. We're still checking it
out. The second thing that happened was too good to be true.
If I was religious, I'd say God was on our side."

"*Nu?*, get to the point," grunted Yigal scanning the
pages.

Udi scolded himself for lapsing into a babble and
snapped into 'agent mode.' "Well, you know that every

Sunday morning I get faxed reports from all of our informers in the settler, and anti-government groups."

"*Nu? Tachlis*," said Yigal, urging Udi to get to the point. He hated being told information he already knew. Udi squirmed a little in his chair. Every time his boss used the Yiddish expression, it was a sign that he was losing patience.

Udi continued, speaking a little faster. "Well, Devorah Eisenstadt, our informer in *Kol Ha'am* says she ran into Rachel twice since she's arrived. It turns out they're old friends. Now in addition to following her, and tapping her phone, we've got someone who can get information out of Rachel that she'd never say over a telephone line." Udi paused to watch Yigal's reaction, hoping his mood would perk up.

"Can we trust this Eisenstadt woman to inform on her old friend?" asked Yigal.

"Well, we brought her in after the *Machpelah* Massacre in Hebron. Even though she's against the government's concessions to the Palestinians, she is terrified about the damage that could be done to Israel if there is another major terror attack committed by Jews. That's why she's co-operating with us. She only reports information she thinks might be related to the formation of a Jewish underground, or an impending terror attack by Jews."

Yigal paused to think. Udi could tell he was asking himself the same question that Udi had been pondering since reading Devorah Eisenstadt's report. "If we tell her that we suspect Rachel might be back to carry out a revenge attack for Ari's murder, it might gain her total commitment to the investigation, but it might also backfire on us. Without revealing to her all the facts of the case, Eisenstadt might think we're over-reacting. Here, if you look at her report on page three, she's reporting about Rachel because she thinks Rachel has inside information about Meir Tal, not because she suspects Rachel."

Yigal silently read from the page in the folder. It was more like a letter than a professional report. After all, the author wasn't a trained agent, she was an informer. Buried in the middle of Eisenstadt's report he found the relevant sections.

> On Thursday night, I ran into Rachel Stein at the demonstration at Zion Square. She was there with Leah Tal. Rachel was engaged to her son Ari Tal who was murdered in a terrorist attack.

Yigal smiled. He found it humorous that his informer was telling him about one of his own agents. Even though Rachel and possibly even Devorah knew that Ari had worked with a 'Yigal' and an 'Udi,' they had never met them. Devorah knew Udi by his cover name 'Yoram.' After Udi brought the Eisenstadt woman in, he only communicated with her by telephone and the fax machine with the built-in scrambler that the 'Communications Department' had provided her.

> I wouldn't have reported it, except that I ran into her again Saturday night at the demonstration outside the Renaissance Hotel. Before Rachel knew I was there, I overheard her say to a tourist, 'We're fighting for our people.' She told me that she had spent Shabbat with Leah, Meir and Shoshana Tal. 'Fighting' words aren't usually part of the vocabulary of the Rachel I know. Then she asked me about the police planting people in the crowds to incite them to break the law. She was really angry about that.

We started talking about the peace process and the government's policies and that's when I really got concerned. Rachel said, 'We sure could use a couple of well placed shots in the direction of Abu Alim. That's probably the quickest way to put an end to all of this. It's going to happen sooner or later. Either by one of them or one of us.'

Many people will jokingly say the same thing. But there was fire in her eyes when she said it. When I challenged her on it, she said, 'I guess it's from spending time with Meir and Leah.' I can't imagine Rachel being able to do such a thing, but I don't think it's beyond Meir. He hasn't been the same person since his brother was murdered.

Afterwards, Rachel got into a shouting match with the police and she attacked the Police Minister's car. She injured her arm in the incident and was taken by ambulance to the hospital.

Yigal put the papers down. He got up from his chair and walked over to the credenza by the wall and poured a second mug of coffee from the coffee-maker sitting on top of it. Deep in thought, he didn't bother to offer Udi a cup.

Udi broke the silence. "Should we tell Eisenstadt about the 'Shimshon File'?"

Yigal took a sip from his mug while still standing beside the credenza. It gave him time to think before answering. A copy of the Shimshon File had been printed from Ari's terminal just before he quit his job.

Twenty One

The phone rang, startling Rachel out of her dream. Her face was buried in her pillow and she instinctively reached out with her left hand to grab the receiver and felt a sharp stab of pain shoot up her arm from her wrist. It took her a moment to orient herself and recall what had happened the night before. She rolled over onto her back and reached out with her good arm to pick up the phone. "Hullo?" she said softly trying to clear the sleep out of her voice.

"I'm sorry. I woke you up," apologized Leah. "I figured you'd be up already, and I wanted to find out how your arm is."

Rachel opened her eyes and looked at the clock on the night table beside the phone. It was just past nine o'clock. "*Baruch HaShem*, it's only a sprain. And thanks for calling, I wanted to get up early. I can't believe it's nine o'clock already."

"Listen, I'll speak to you later after you have a chance to wake up. I'm glad you're all right. Bye, and take care of yourself." Leah figured the news about Meir's arrest could wait until later. Rachel was probably still upset about the previous night's events.

"Good-bye. I love you," said Rachel hanging up the phone. She sat up in bed and recited the *"Modeh Ani"* blessing which were normally the first words she spoke every morning. Since she was a child, Rachel had without fail recited the blessing thanking the Living King, for restoring her soul to her body each day. Sometimes she said it mindlessly out of rote, but today she said it with devotion thanking God for keeping her alive and healthy, and giving her the opportunity to grow and serve Him. As she washed and dressed, she thought about Marc's bicycle story, and wondered why God thought it was necessary to have her knocked down at the demonstration and hurt her arm. Was she using her arm to do something she shouldn't be doing? Was it a message that she shouldn't be going to demonstrations? Without coming up with an immediate answer, she decided to ask Marc later if he had any insights. It would also be a good excuse to hear more of his story.

After reciting the remainder of the morning blessings and prayers, she left the apartment to buy some fresh rolls, cottage cheese and fruit yogurt for breakfast. Israel had the creamiest cottage cheese. She loved it mixed up with the fruit yogurt. It was one of the few high-cholesterol indulgences she allowed herself.

At the corner *Makolet*, she asked Moshe, the owner of the grocery store standing at the cash register, to put her purchase on her account. Even though she had been back less than a week he trusted her. That's the way it was done in Israel. Everyone was on the honor system when it came to the local *Makolet*. "And add a *Press* to the bill as well," she called out picking up the newspaper. Even though she was fluent enough to read the Hebrew dailies, she preferred to read the English paper over breakfast when her brain was still 'warming up.' She didn't bother to check the sum Moshe wrote down on her index card in the cardboard box holding his customers' accounts. Rachel trusted him also.

"*Refuah Sheleimah*," he said, looking at the sling on her arm. "Feel better."

Rachel hurried home, appreciating the cool overcast morning. At this time of year, the weather hiccuped each day between hot and cool during the short spasm between summer and winter.

As she opened the door of the apartment, the nutty aroma of fresh dripped coffee made her even hungrier for breakfast. Rachel was glad she remembered to put the coffee on before she left for the *Makolet*. She poured herself a mug, and sat down at the kitchenette table with her breakfast and newspaper. Rachel loved this special time alone in the morning. Although she felt she was ready to trade it in for the pandemonium of rushing a husband and a bunch of noisy kids off to work and school in the morning.

The front page was devoted primarily to the murder of the Arabs the night before. A five-column photograph of the two bodies being wheeled away on stretchers in body bags was topped with the headline, "Settlers Suspected in Drive-by Shooting." Rachel turned the page, and her heart skipped a beat like it had the night before when she saw a photograph of Abu Alim surrounded by his entourage being interviewed.

Rachel ignored the caption and the article and leaned forward squinting at the picture. By 'coincidence' the photograph had been taken at the same moment she had looked at the television screen. Perhaps the gold flash on the screen occurred when the *Press* photographer took this picture. In the black and white photo, the gold was replaced by a thin strip of light gray crossing the wrist of the body guard.

Rachel's nose was almost touching the newspaper. She trembled, "It really does look like my grandfather's watch."

The phone in the kitchen rang, and made Rachel jump. She didn't feel like talking to any well wishers. Too many thoughts were running through her head. "Hello?" she said abruptly.

"Rachel, are you okay? This is Devorah."

"Thank God, I'm fine. It's only a sprain," said Rachel impatiently. She glanced down at the picture again, her head spinning. She didn't have time for chit-chat. "Do you watch the news on television?" she asked.

Devorah thought that the question wasn't so strange to be asking a religious Jew. Many chose not to have a television in the home because eighty percent of the time was spent dwelling on sex and violence. What was strange was that the question came in place of the anticipated description of Rachel's injury. "Yes, as a matter of fact we do have a TV," she answered cautiously. Perhaps there was something in particular that Rachel wanted to watch.

"Have you ever noticed if Abu Alim always has the same bodyguards around him when he appears in public?" asked Rachel nervously.

Rachel's question set off an alarm throughout Devorah's body. She tried to remain as calm as possible and answered innocently, "I dunno. Why would you want to know something like that?"

"Oh, never mind, it was something I was just curious about. Listen, I'd love to talk, but I've got a million things to do this morning. I'll have to speak to you later."

Devorah hung up the phone so confused she forgot to say good-bye. After a moment to gather her wits, she picked up the phone and dialed the special number that 'Yoram' had given her in case of emergency.

Rachel didn't want to tell Devorah that one of the reasons she had come back to Israel was to find Ari's murderer and bring him to justice. The police had closed the investigation even though Rachel had insisted that the missing gold watch could serve as valuable evidence in tracking down the terrorist. The police claimed that even if they did find some-one with a similar watch there was no way to prove it was the one in Ari's possession at the time of the murder. Rachel wanted the watch back. She promised her grandmother that the one to wear it would be the father of a baby boy named after her grandfather.

Rachel grabbed her car keys and quickly headed out the door. She had to get to the *Jerusalem Press* as quickly as possible and obtain a copy of the original photograph. When she reached her designated parking place behind the apart-ment building she froze and let out a scream.

She ran back to her apartment, picked up the phone and shaking, began dialing Leah's number. After the first three digits she hung up, put the receiver down on the table and took her address book out of her purse. Rachel nervously leafed through the pages until she found the right page. She punched the number onto the dialing pad and clumsily picked up the receiver with her good hand. She waited for six rings until a voice on the other end answered.

"Marc? It's Rachel," she said sobbing. "Can you come over right away? Someone slashed the tires on my car."

Twenty Two

"That cursed Shimshon File," said Yigal slamming down his mug, splashing the contents onto the papers on his desk. Udi grabbed a handful of tissues and began brushing off the brown liquid from the pages he had so carefully prepared for his boss. "I wish that idiot Yossi Shiloni had never come up with the lunatic idea in the first place." Yigal was shouting.

"But it was precisely those lunatic ideas that found him so much favor in the government's eyes. They indirectly became the cause of him becoming the Prime Minister," said Udi.

"Don't remind me," snorted Yigal. He walked to the credenza to refill his mug while Udi wiped up the mess.

When the Olso Declaration of Principles was being negotiated with the Palestinians, the Israeli Foreign Ministry was looking for creative and legal ways to evacuate Jews from the territories and give east Jerusalem to the Palestinians as the capital of their Palestinian State. Bold creative strategies were needed to implement the plan that went against forty-five years of Israeli public opinion. According to the Foreign Ministry, 'progress' was paramount, the consequences were secondary. It was the antithesis of what the "Security and Intelligence Communities" stood for, and was the reason why Yigal despised the Foreign Ministry so much. They were willing to take unnecessary risks with the country, assuming that Yigal and people like him would clean up the ensuing mess. Yigal hated cleaning up messes.

The Foreign Minister had turned to his brilliant whiz kid Yossi Shiloni to formulate position papers on every possible scenario from 'Confiscating all the settlers' weapons,' to 'Evacuating the Jews from Hebron.' At the time, Yigal and his team had specific orders to fully cooperate with Shiloni and provide him with a detailed analysis of the security implications of the position papers. Yigal reluctantly went along with the silliness, even though it took precious time from his dealing with the terrorist threat in the country. But the most outrageous request of all was the Shimshon Plan.

Shiloni's most difficult challenge of all was to figure out a way to manipulate Israeli public opinion so that the Jews would be willing to give east Jerusalem and the Temple Mount to the Palestinians as the capital of the Palestinian State. The extreme left factions in the government naively thought that if Arafat got Jerusalem, he would give up on the dream to liberate Jaffa and Haifa as well.

A quick and dramatic change in Israeli public opinion, reasoned Shiloni at the time, would only come about by a quick and dramatic event. He racked his brains for months trying to come up with a scenario, but nothing seemed to work.

Then, on Purim of 1994, a Jewish doctor from Kiryat Arba gave Yossi the answer, when he shot twenty-nine Palestinian worshippers in the Cave of the Patriarchs in Hebron. The ensuing world outcry was enormous. Shiloni pushed for seizing the opportunity to evacuate all the Jews from Hebron and declaring it a Palestinian city. It would have worked if not for the government hawks' stubborn insistence to sticking to the letter of the Declaration of Principles that promised no Jewish settlements would be uprooted during the interim period. They feared civil war if the Jews would be transferred. Shiloni disagreed, counting on the religious principles of the settlers to keep them from shooting at their fellow Jews.

Shiloni lost the argument, but he now had his idea on how to give back Jerusalem. He didn't need to change Israeli public opinion. His plan would so outrage the world, that Israel would have to give back Jerusalem under the threat of UN sanctions and an international military force greater than the one arrayed against Saddam Hussein during the Gulf War.

Yigal recalled vividly the day he first read those ugly words of Shiloni's request:

```
    Please advise as to the feasi-
bility of Israeli agents, dressed as
settlers, committing a massacre of
Palestinian worshippers at the Al
Aksa mosque on the Temple Mount.
They must not be captured by Pales-
tinians, Wakf Security, Israeli Po-
lice or IDF Soldiers who might be in
the vicinity.
```

Yigal's hands shook the day he read those words, and his hands began to shake again today. "That maniac Shiloni. If only I had thrown the idiotic plan straight back into his face. That's what I should have done," said Yigal mumbling to himself.

"Sir?" asked Udi, not hearing what Yigal had said.

"No Jew in their right mind would ever, for one instant, think of carrying out a plan like that, even if a lunatic like

Shiloni thought it up. It's one thing for a lone gunman to commit an atrocity at Hebron, but that a Jewish *government* would commit mass murder of innocent Arab worshippers in order to give away the Temple Mount to non-Jews?"

Udi winced as Yigal spoke.

"You know Udi," said Yigal calming himself down, "Ari didn't quit because Shiloni was considering such a diabolical plot. He told me he quit because I bothered to answer Shiloni's request seriously and show how the plan could be carried out successfully."

There was a quick knock at the door, and Amiram came in. "A phone call just came in," said Amiram to Udi. "I thought it was important enough to interrupt your meeting because it has to do with what you're talking about."

"How did you know we were talking about the Shimshon File?" asked Udi.

"Shimshon File?" echoed Amiram a little confused. "No, it was Eisenstadt on the phone. She just had a conversation with Rachel Stein. Rachel started asking about Abu Alim's bodyguards. She wanted to know if he always had the same set of guards whenever he appears in public."

Yigal immediately switched modes and began handing out orders. "We have to find out if Rachel or Meir have seen the Shimshon File. For the moment we have to assume that it was Ari who printed out a copy of the report before he quit, even though he knew it would be traced back to his terminal."

"He must have figured, what has he got to lose? He was quitting anyway," said Amiram.

"You're right, but he also knew that the information in that file was so explosive it was something our Prime Minister might give an order to get it back 'at all costs,'" said Udi trying to defend his friend.

"It doesn't matter for now. If Rachel and Meir got hold of the file, they probably would assume that we were the ones who eliminated Ari, even though we know that's not true," said Yigal. "To avenge his murder, they could carry out the attack on the Al Aksa mosque, escape, and then leak the Shimshon File to the press. The *Shabak* would get blamed for the attack, and the Shiloni government would fall in the ensuing scandal. The Right-Wing would take over the government for at least the next twenty-five years, and no more land, especially Jerusalem would be ceded to the Palestinians."

"They'd get everything they're after, including avenging Ari's murder," said an astonished Udi.

"Exactly," said Yigal, "and we'll all be in jail with our 'friend' Yossi Shiloni. Not to mention having a Jihad of all Islam nations against us." Yigal got up, walked around his desk and stood next to his two agents. "Try to get the Eisenstadt woman to find out how much Rachel knows without telling her about the Shimshon File. Also interrogate Meir Tal and find out if he knows about it. And keep close tabs on Rachel Stein."

There was another knock at the door and Motti Nir, the chief of the communications department walked in without waiting for an answer. He handed Yigal a piece of paper and said, "We received this fax Friday afternoon. We've been spending the time since trying to trace it's origin and determine if it's genuine or just a prank. We're coming up with a bunch of dead ends, so I thought you should see it. Especially in light of what appeared in this morning's paper about Abu Alim wanting to come to the Al Aksa mosque this Friday."

Yigal looked down at the short fax addressed to him and read,

Dear Yigal,

If you don't eliminate Abu Alim
and stop this nightmare, I will rise
again to bring down the temple of
the Philistines upon the Philistine
King and his worshippers.

Shimshon the Judge

Yigal blanched. He cursed Yossi Shiloni for cynically naming the plan after the Biblical figure Samson. The analogy was clear. The Palestinians and their 'king' Abu Alim, would die at their own 'temple,' Al Aksa, at the hands of Jews unless the *Shabak* eliminated Alim first.

He turned to the two men without revealing the contents of the fax or letting them know that the sender had known his real name. "Move fast," he ordered, "we haven't got much time." If Abu Alim had his way, he would unwittingly be at the Al Aksa mosque in five days not only to pray to his God, but to die as a Palestinian martyr.

Twenty Three

"Well, I guess we'd better call the Police," said Marc, looking sympathetically at the four flat tires of Rachel's white Mitsubishi Lancer. He thought about the day he had his car stripped in downtown Manhattan a few years earlier. "Don't worry, the tires will be replaced before you know it." He did his best not to reveal his own fears about the slashing to Rachel.

Rachel was glad Marc arrived so quickly and had taken charge. She felt violated and vulnerable. They walked back into her apartment. "It's not the tires that I'm worried about. It's just terrifying not knowing who did this to me, and why they did it," she said. Rachel walked over to the coffee maker and felt the glass pitcher. It was still hot. "Can I pour you a cup of coffee?" She felt almost back to normal now that Marc was here.

"Sure, I'd love one," said Marc cheerfully trying to make Rachel feel like nothing out of the ordinary had happened that morning. He picked up the phone and dialed 100 and reported the tire slashing. Technically it wasn't an emergency, but he couldn't be bothered looking up the Police

Investigations Department phone number. Especially after how the police acted last night.

Rachel came out of the kitchen carrying a tray with a plate of cookies and two mugs of coffee. "What did they say?" asked Rachel putting the tray down on the coffee table in front of the couch.

"They'll send somebody over immediately. That could mean by noon Tuesday. They also wanted to know if your car had been depressed or acting suicidal lately."

Rachel laughed. She sat down and picked up a cup of coffee. "Do you think it could have been Arabs who did it?"

"In this part of town?" said Marc incredulously. Rehavia was a mixture of upwardly mobile orthodox and upwardly mobile secular Israelis. "With all those anti-government bumper stickers plastered all over your car, it was probably just one of the kids of a neighborhood leftist having some fun."

The theory seemed plausible to Rachel and she relaxed a little as they chatted and sipped their coffee waiting for the police arrive. In a few minutes, to their surprise, the doorbell rang and two uniformed policemen appeared at the door. They went through the motions of filling out the report, knowing that it was hopeless. They'd never find the slasher, but they knew the car owner needed these reports to file claims with their insurance companies. They were gone in a minute after handing Rachel a copy of their hand-written report.

Marc got up hesitantly to go, now that his job was complete. He moved slowly to the door not wanting to leave, but a bit embarrassed to say so. He wasn't sure if she really liked him yet.

Rachel broke the temporary uneasy silence. "If you don't have to be anywhere in a rush, perhaps you can give me a ride to the *Jerusalem Press*. That's where I was going when I discovered what happened to my car."

He felt that if he told her he was planning to study at the Yeshiva all morning, she would have insisted he go. Marc smiled, "Sure. I'd love to give you a ride. But don't they sell newspapers at the local *Makolet?*"

"Stop being so silly. I'll tell you why I have to go there once we're in the car," said Rachel, placing the empty mugs back on the tray and carrying it into the kitchen.

They left and got into Marc's Volvo that was parked at the curb beside the entrance to the building. Along the way, Rachel told him about her grandfather and his gold watch. She recounted the events of Ari's murder and how the watch had never been recovered. The terrorist was never apprehended and the Arab shopkeeper claimed no knowledge of the watch. By the time she told him how she had noticed the flash of gold on the TV screen the night before, and shown him the photograph in this morning's newspaper, they had already arrived at the parking lot of the *Jerusalem Press*. Marc had been so enthralled by the story that he had a hard time keeping his eye on the traffic in front of him, let alone notice the white Ford Sierra that had been following them a few cars behind.

"We'd like to speak to the head of your photo archive," said Marc to the receptionist at the main entrance to the building that looked more like a warehouse than the headquarters of the world famous English-language daily. Marc was happy to be at a place where he didn't have to apologize for speaking his mother tongue.

A few minutes later, a white-haired elderly gentleman came shuffling into the waiting room. "*Shalom*, I'm Isaac Abramson, can I help you?" he was speaking to Marc. He and Rachel were the only one's there other than the receptionist.

"We're from *Kol Ha'am*, and we're doing some research for some demonstration posters we're preparing," explained Marc, stretching out his hand to shake Abramson's. "We wonder if you could help us out with some recent, or older photographs of Abu Alim that might have appeared in your paper."

"Come on in!" said Abramson enthusiastically, "Whatever I can do to help get that lousy *mamzer*." Abramson was happy he could help them openly. He remembered the old days, when the paper was owned by the left. Then, he would have had to sneak this nice young couple into the building. Now, things were different since the new owners took over. In fact the government was constantly complaining about the anti-government editorials, and right-wing slant to the paper. Abramson laughed off the attacks. It was ironic to him that if you simply told the truth, you would be attacked for being 'right.'

Twenty Four

Sunday 12:05 p.m.

"You've got a visitor," said Amnon Tamar, unlocking the door to Meir's cell. Meir got up from the cot he had been sitting on in the tiny room without answering Tamar. He wondered who his visitor could be. Was it Shoshana back with his *tallis* and *tefillin*? They told him they were letting her go home to be with the children but they didn't let him speak to her before she left. Meir hoped she had noticed that he left his phylacteries and prayer shawl at home the night before, not anticipating they would hold him overnight. He needed them for his morning prayers. As he walked out of the cell in front of Tamar, Meir glanced down at his watch. It was past noon already.

"I have instructions not to hand-cuff you, so don't try anything funny," warned Tamar, as they walked down a narrow corridor to the interrogation room. There had been an international campaign against the Israeli government's anti-democratic actions for the past few years. It was bad enough they were holding Meir without charges. The authorities wanted to make sure there was no hint of mistreatment while he was under detention. As they walked down the hallway,

Meir hoped it was a lawyer who would help get him out of here as quickly as possible.

The armed guard accompanying Meir and Amnon opened the door to the interrogation room. Amnon Tamar motioned to Meir to enter first. A man in civilian clothes was sitting behind the single desk in the otherwise barren room. A naked light bulb hung from the ceiling, not so much because it was an interrogation room, but simply because Israelis weren't strict about hanging light fixtures. In many homes it was common to see a naked light bulb hanging from the ceiling of a bedroom or bathroom.

"Major Tamar, I'd like to speak with Mr. Tal alone please," said the man. Tamar nodded, and awkwardly backed his huge bulk out of the doorway. The guard closed the door and took up his position outside. Meir narrowed his eyes, trying to size up the man, who was about his age, on the other side of the desk. What was a civilian doing interrogating him on an army base? He obviously wasn't a military lawyer or he would have been in uniform. It wasn't a lawyer for his defense. Shoshana would have called someone from Krausz and Wurtzman. As an activist during the past few years, Meir had often needed legal advice and by now knew everyone in the firm. 'No, he isn't a lawyer,' he thought, 'he must be *Shabak*.'

"My name is Yoram," said the man getting up from his chair to shake Meir's hand.

"And I'm Menachem Begin," said Meir sarcastically, making a point that it was obvious the *Shabak* agent's real name wasn't 'Yoram.' Meir plunked himself down in the wooden chair facing the desk. He didn't shake the man's hand, leaving him red-faced, standing with an outstretched hand grasping at air.

Udi sat down, trying to maintain his cool. His strategy for getting information out of Meir was to be the 'good cop.'

Udi figured there were plenty of 'bad cops' around to make life miserable for Meir. Meir might respond to him if he could gain his trust. Things had already started off on the wrong foot. Udi's mind raced as he looked across the desk at the pudgy little man with arms folded tightly across his chest. Something dramatic had to be done to diffuse the tension in the room and open Meir up. There wasn't much time to lose, it was already Sunday afternoon. There were only four days left to find the group who were plotting to carry out the Shimshon Plan. Udi leaned forward, and in a serious tone said calmly, "I don't believe you had anything at all to do with the shooting of those Arabs last night."

Meir paused for a second and then sprang from his chair with a cynical smile, "Great, that makes two of us. I guess that means I can go now." He startled Udi by reaching across the desk and shaking his hand vigorously. "Hey, you didn't happen to bring a *tallis* and *tefillin* with you? I still haven't *davened* yet this morning. Maybe I can borrow yours before I leave?" asked Meir, taking another jab at the obviously secular *Shabak* agent. For a moment, Meir thought about his childhood when he looked up to all Israeli military and security personnel as his protectors. He tried to remember exactly when things had changed and why. He couldn't remember. All he knew was that today, anyone connected with the army who was clean-shaven without a *kipah* was an enemy, or at least considered 'unfriendly' until proven otherwise. Meir wanted to blame someone for this splitting of the nation, but there was no one person responsible.

"Meir, please sit down," said Udi, "you know I have no authority around here to release you. As much as I'd like to, only someone in the Army, the Minister of Defense, or the Prime Minister can do that — and I'm none of the above."

"Well you certainly fooled me. I thought you were Yossi Shiloni. You certainly look like him, although a little younger." Now it was Meir's turn to lean forward on the desk. "But if you're none of the above, then who exactly are you, and why should I answer any of your questions? They haven't even let me talk to my wife, let alone a lawyer." Meir was certain that Udi knew he suspected he was a *Shabak* agent. He wanted Udi to squirm a little and admit it. Meir stared him straight in the eyes.

The fire in Meir's eyes made Udi uncomfortable. He stood up to avoid the accusing gaze, placed his hands in his pockets and turned his back to Meir and looked out the window. He paused to think of a way to change the tone of the conversation. In the distance, outside the front gate of the army base he noticed a group of teenagers and a few adults shouting and waving placards. *"Medinat Mishtara, Police State!"* *"Let Meir Tal go home to his family!"* *"Big Brother is Watching US."* Udi felt a sense of frustration well up inside him. He was tired of chasing his own people. He would much rather be hunting down Arab terrorist cells, but the Jewish fanatics had to be stopped before they led the country into an all out war with the Arab nations. Udi desperately needed Meir's cooperation. He racked his brain to find some common ground they might share to win over the red-headed settler with the wiry beard sitting behind him. Then, it came to him. He turned to face Meir and said slowly, "I'm *Shabak*, I used to work with your brother Ari."

Meir sat for a moment in shock and then got up to shake Udi's hand. "Pleased to meet you," he said cautiously, "I'm *speechless.*"

Twenty Five

The charcoal gray Chevrolet stopped in the line of cars waiting impatiently at the red traffic signal. The restless noon-time rush hour drivers began honking even before the light changed to green. "Shall I put the siren on?" asked the chauffeur to his boss who was sitting in the back seat hidden from the outside world by darkly-tinted bullet proof glass windows.

Yigal sighed, "No, don't bother." He was happy to have the extra few minutes to gather his thoughts before the meeting. He had made this ride many times before. Most Israelis would relish the idea of meeting with the Prime Minister. Yigal hated the thought. Not meeting the Prime Minister, that is, but meeting with this particular Prime Minister, Yossi Shiloni. Had it not been for Shiloni's unbridled ambition to please his superiors, he never would have come up with the Shimshon Plan in the first place. And Yigal wouldn't have to be making this trip to the Prime Minister's office.

Yigal had wanted to wait until he had more information before informing Shiloni about the fax he received, but the security Cabinet was meeting right now as it did every Sun-

day morning. On the agenda was the issue of allowing Abu
Alim to pray on the Temple Mount on Friday. The Prime
Minister had to be made aware of the terrorist plan before
any decisions were made and announcements made to the
press. The cabinet was under tremendous world pressure to
agree to Alim's request, especially after the terror attack last
night against the Arabs.

Yigal hadn't informed anyone, even his immediate su-
perior, the head of *Shabak*, about the fax. He didn't want to
call ahead to the Prime Minister either. The issue was too
sensitive. When he arrived at the Prime Minister's office, he
would call the Prime Minister out of the cabinet meeting. As
the traffic began to move, he scribbled a note, that he was
sure Yossi Shiloni would not be happy to see, but would
guarantee to pull the Prime Minister out of the meeting.

Just as the Chevrolet approached the guard post at the
fence leading to the Prime Minister's Office, the car phone
rang. Yigal picked it up, frustrated that his thoughts about
how to conduct the meeting with Shiloni were being interrupted.

"This is Amiram," said the voice on the other end of
the scrambled telephone line. "I've come up with some important information, that I thought you would want to know
before I got a chance to report in writing."

"*Nu?*" said Yigal impatiently. It bothered him when
people wasted time explaining why they were going to say
what they were going to say anyway. Just say it.

"I've been following Rachel Stein this morning. She
went to the *Jerusalem Press* with Marc Goodman." Amiram
paused, waiting for Yigal to respond. When confronted by
silence on the other end of the line, he continued. "I sent my
partner on to tail them while I went in to talk with the people
at the newspaper. They met with the head of the photo archives. He said they were looking for photographs of Abu

Alim for some demonstration posters they were preparing. They ordered copies of about a dozen pictures from a file of about thirty or so that they have at the *Press*.

"So? What's so significant about that? They're both working with *Kol Ha'am*, and their specialty is anti-Shiloni and anti-Alim posters. Actually, some of them are pretty good," added Yigal.

"I looked at all the pictures they ordered. They didn't take any that were of Alim alone. All the photographs are of him at public events or press conferences where he's surrounded by bodyguards. Not very good poster material. It seemed suspicious."

"Find out what they're up to and keep in touch by phone," ordered Yigal, not commenting on Amiram's analysis.

Yigal hung up the phone without saying good-bye. The car had pulled up to the entrance to the new Prime Minister's wing of the drab office building rather than the main entrance. It was faster that way. He got out of the car and tucked a small briefcase under his arm containing the fateful fax. A sunglassed security man opened the glass and metal door. The guard nodded in recognition of the familiar face, as Yigal quickly strode past him.

Twenty Six

"I haven't been here for years," called out Rachel getting out of the passenger side of Marc's parked Volvo, "I forgot how breathtaking it was." Marc got out of the car carrying the two plastic bags of groceries filled with the picnic lunch they had purchased at a local *Makolet*. They walked from the parking area towards the curved stone patio of the Haas Promenade overlooking the Old City of Jerusalem. It was a special spot favored by tourists, especially Jewish Federation groups who were often brought here directly from the airport for their first glimpse of the city.

"After everything that's happened in the last few days, I thought a picnic here with this view would help us relax," said Marc placing the groceries down on a stone park bench. "It's a favorite spot of mine." He didn't let Rachel know that of the few women he had dated since he arrived in Israel, he had brought them all here at least once. It was an especially romantic spot particularly at night, when the Old City Walls were illuminated and the lights of the city glittered like stars in a panorama.

Rachel looked at Marc and smiled, hoping he was using the Promenade as many young men did to make an impression on their girlfriends. "Whenever I'm up here I always feel connected to history," she said sitting down beside Marc on the bench. "Someone once told me that this is traditionally the place where Abraham lifted his eyes and first saw Mount Moriah on his way to do the binding of Isaac. From here we're about three days walking journey from Hebron behind us to the south. If you're coming from that direction like it says in the Bible, then this is the first place you can see the Temple Mount."

Rachel caught herself being a tour guide, stopped talking and turned to smile at Marc. Her mother always told her, that if you want to make an impression on a boy, let him do the talking and let him talk about himself. Men have such weak egos, they'll think you're wonderful and a fabulous conversationalist. "Enough ancient history," she said, "I'm more interested in hearing the rest of Marc Goodman's history. You told me how you fell off a cliff, and how you met Rabbi Steinberg, but you still haven't told me why you eventually decided to live in Israel."

Marc appreciated the way Rachel made it so easy to spend time with her. If there was ever a lull in the conversation, she always found a way to break the tension and smooth things over. As an introvert, he was constantly amazed by people who could make small talk any time, any place and with anyone. In business, he could fake being an extrovert, but he was uncomfortable in social situations. It was a skill he looked forward to learning from someone like Rachel someday.

Marc reached into one of the bags, pulled out a couple of apples and handed one to Rachel. "Here. You'd better take this to munch on, so that you don't faint from hunger while I finish the story. I remember you said you wanted the long version."

Rachel took the apple and laughed. She loved the way Marc made her laugh. She realized she hadn't smiled this much in years.

"Well, when Rabbi Steinberg asked me who did I think sent the truck in the first place," said Marc picking up right were he left off, "he threw me totally for a loop. I realized that if there was a God who could save me, there was a God who could try to get my attention as well. The Rabbi explained that I was not alone in wanting God to be a senile old grandfather who gives you candy no matter how good or bad you are. He reminded me that we Jews pray to *Avinu Malkeinu*, Our Father, our King. A good father showers you with blessings if you are making responsible decisions in life. If you're messing up, he might slap you around a little to get you to wake up."

Rachel nodded. This Father metaphor had helped her deal with physical ailments in the past, but she still hadn't been able to come to terms with a loving Father who would take away a life like Ari's.

"I decided to stay and study at the Yeshiva for a few months to become literate in Judaism. I realized I knew nothing, and felt incompetent. I was fascinated by the intellectual approach and the deep philosophy. I was a tough customer and forced the Rabbis to give me rational explanations for everything from 'angels' to the 'age of the universe.' I didn't expect to get the answers that I got and eventually I boxed myself into an intellectual corner. Once I learned what the authentic Jewish concepts were concerning God, Revelation, Torah, Miracles and Redemption, it made sense to me that there was a God who gave the Torah to the Jewish people at Sinai. And that He gave the Jews the Land of Israel to become a Torah nation." Marc paused to reflect on the excitement of those first days of discovery of his heritage.

"And, so..." said Rachel munching on the apple, encouraging him to continue. She loved listening to Marc. He was so rational. Like Ari had been. Rachel considered herself more intuitive, more of a feeler than a thinker. It was comforting to know there were people who had worked out the issues critically. It made her more confident about her own lifestyle, even though she hadn't personally worked out all the answers. Experiencing first hand the family and communal values in the Torah communities she had lived in were good enough for her.

"Like I said. I worked out that it was true, but emotionally I wasn't ready to deal with the lifestyle changes. So I took off back to New York with the excuse that I had to get a job to pay off my student loans."

A busload of tourists pulled up to the Promenade and it disgorged its contents of about forty people with their guide on the patio beside them. Marc frowned. He remembered another reason why this place was more romantic at night — no noisy tour groups. He continued telling his story trying to ignore the tour guide's loud melodramatic explanations in broken English. "I went back to America and got a job as a stockbroker. I made contact with some families in New York that my friend David suggested. In my own time, and at my own pace, I became observant. Coming back to Israel was always in the back of my mind, but I was so busy following the markets and making deals, I had no time for a social life, let alone plan on making Aliyah. The few women I met were nice, but none of them were serious about coming to live in Israel. So I stopped dating and put all my energies into my job. If it hadn't been for *Shabbat* I would have become a seven-day-a-week animal like some of the driven young guys on Wall Street. Then, all of a sudden, I had a string of big deals, and the commissions were enormous. The money just fell out of the sky. One day, Rabbi Steinberg was in town on a fundraising trip, and was happy for the Yeshiva to be the beneficiary of some of my good fortune. He reminded me that the same One who could snag a falling cyclist out of the air, could drop a few millions out of the sky as well. In an instant, I realized the message. Not all messages have to be painful. I was being given the opportunity to learn a lesson about how to relate to money. I asked myself, 'Am I living to make money, or making money in order to live?' That same day I quit my job and booked a flight to Israel."

Rachel looked at Marc with tears in her eyes. She has been searching for someone with Marc's strength. She wanted someone like him to trust, and to take care of. She thought that Ari was the only one in the world like that.

Now it was Marc's turn to break the tense silence. "How about some *pita* and *humus*?" he said reaching into the bag.

"But we don't have any water to wash with before breaking bread," said Rachel with a sniff.

"Wait, I've got a Jerry can full of water in the trunk of my car. I'll be back in a minute."

Rachel watched Marc jog past the group of tourists to the Volvo. He opened the trunk and bent over to retrieve the Jerry can. Neither Rachel nor Marc noticed the shadowy figure standing in the shade of an olive tree near Marc's car.

The swarthy young man momentarily glanced at Marc who was in easy reach, but passed him over. The yellow license plates on Marc's Volvo indicated he was an Israeli citizen. Today's instructions were specifically for an attack against a tourist. That was why this place was chosen. It was a favorite of tourists, yet provided an escape route down the hill into the Arab village below. Like a wolf stalking a herd of sheep he scanned the group for its weakest members. He spotted an old woman wearing an orange hat with the travel agent's insignia, sitting on a bench a few meters behind the group. 'She can't run away so easily if she's sitting down,' he thought to himself. He bent over as if to tie his shoe, and slipped out a large kitchen knife that was strapped to his leg.

As he sprang out of the shadow of the tree, terror struck Rachel's heart as she saw the knife-wielding Arab running toward Marc's bent over figure. She reached down to grab her handgun out of her purse. "NO!" she screamed, realizing she had left her purse in the car. "NO! NO! NO! Marc!"

Marc turned to see why Rachel was shouting, just as the Arab ran by him toward the woman sitting on the bench. He froze as he saw the terrorist running toward the old lady shouting, *'Allahu Akhbar!'* Before any one of the crowd of tourists could turn around in response to the Arab's battle cry of 'Allah is Great,' three shots rang out. The terrorist dropped to the pavement dying instantly before he reached his target.

People started screaming and running in all directions thinking the shots were part of the terror attack. The tour guide shouted at everyone to lie down on the ground. Children were crying. In spite of the screaming, people slowly began to realize that no more shots were being fired and there were no more attackers with knives. Those nearest the old woman began to calm her down. Rachel pushed through the crowd gathered around the dead terrorist trying to find Marc. Thank God it didn't happen again, she thought.

In the pandemonium no one noticed the marksman who had fired the shots, get into his white Ford and drive away. He didn't want to explain to the police and reporters who he was and why he was there.

Twenty Seven

Yossi Shiloni crumpled the note into a ball and stuffed it into his suit-jacket pocket. The few words scribbled by Yigal on the piece of paper just handed to him by the Parliamentary aide seared at his stomach like an ulcer.

"The Shimshon Plan." To Shiloni it had almost been a joke. But in those heady days just after the signing of the Declaration of Principles on the White House lawn, he and the small group of 'golden boys' in the Justice and Foreign ministries felt they were invincible. Anything was possible. They had been the architects of the secret negotiations in Norway between Israel and the PLO. At that time, the government had given them free reign to let their imaginations run, and explore all the possibilities — even some of the impossibilities.

The Middle-East became a game board where they played out the scenarios. At their disposal were all the resources of the nation. The self-imposed time limit of the Declaration of Principles created a frantic pace for the negotiations. The side who came best prepared, so went the theory, would have the upper hand in the bargaining. Shiloni let his imagination go wild, and one of his brainstorms was the

Shimshon Plan — a way to get east Jerusalem back in the hands of the Arabs without having to fight a war.

Shiloni never expected it to be taken seriously. Even he found it outrageous, yet he enjoyed the power of forcing others to take it seriously. But in the Middle-East, the unexpected becomes tomorrow's headlines. He didn't expect to become Prime Minister so quickly either. It wasn't his turn. Yet here he was sitting at the Cabinet table deciding the fate of Jerusalem. He looked around the room at his senior Cabinet members, the IDF Chief of Staff and the Chief of Police. He winced. This wasn't how he dreamed it would be. These men with their open shirt collars, shouting at each other and munching on the regal spread of food laid out on the huge wooden conference table, reminded him more of a giant poker game than a group of statesmen deciding the future of their nation. 'Why did there have to be all this food?' he thought. It was so... so Jewish. Just looking at the spread gave him heartburn.

He thought back to the days when he was a little boy, and his mother would take him on the thirty minute bus ride from Rehovot to Tel-Aviv. She always packed a big bag of fruit, sandwiches and drinks to take along. It was only thirty minutes! And he had just eaten lunch.

'Why did they have to have all this food at 10:00 a.m. for a one-hour meeting?' he asked himself with disgust. 'Didn't they all just eat? Couldn't they last an hour without eating something? They certainly didn't do this in the White House.'

Shiloni got up without a word while the Police Minister was shouting something at the Chief of Staff. The men around the table paused momentarily to look at the Prime Minister, who made a hand motion for them to continue. They all resumed squawking at each other, assuming he was being called away on a personal matter.

Yigal Ramon was waiting outside the Cabinet Room door when the Prime Minister came out. Shiloni whisked passed Yigal and nodded at him to follow him into his office. The two didn't exchange a word. As Yigal followed Shiloni, he shook his head slowly from side to side, as if saying to himself 'I can't believe this guy.' The Prime Minister was wearing an immaculately tailored gray herring-bone suit and polished black oxfords. His hair had been perfectly groomed that morning as it was every day by his private barber. In fact, Shiloni had sent his barber and tailor for one month of training by the White House staff. Shiloni wanted to import to Israel some of the honor that the Americans showed the Presidency. Yigal figured it was just a way for Shiloni to get some respect for his external appearance, since he was lacking in years and in experience. Yigal had read 'Dress for Success' during a short stint as Israel military attaché in London years ago. For all his brilliance, Yigal found Shiloni mundanely predictable.

The two men entered the Prime Minister's private office, and Shiloni took up his position of power in the large leather armchair positioned behind the oversized wooden desk. Finally he looked Yigal in the eye who had taken a seat on the opposite side of the desk. "What's this all about? I thought this Shimshon Plan died along with that agent of yours a few years back," said Shiloni. He knew Ari Tal had quit the *Shabak* over the issue, but Yigal never told him about the copy of the files that had been printed from his computer terminal. Erroneously, the Prime Minister had thought that when Ari died, the only person willing to make an issue over the plan was dead.

"Here, look at this," said Yigal handing Shiloni the fax that was addressed to him. Yigal used the time while Shiloni was reading to formulate how he was going to explain why he had kept the existence of the stolen copy of the Shimshon File a secret for all these years.

Shiloni read each word slowly,

```
Dear Yigal,

    If you don't eliminate Abu Alim
and stop this nightmare, I will rise
again to bring down the temple of
the Philistines upon the Philistine
King and his worshippers.

                  Shimshon the Judge
```

He slowly re-read the fax before handing the piece of paper back to Yigal. "This is what you pulled me out of a Cabinet meeting for?" he asked condescendingly. "I get hundreds of letters like this from crackpots every day. This guy sounds like he's one of those crazy Messianic settler fanatics."

Yigal spoke slowly, like a doctor speaking to a patient who was denying the biopsy results confirming a malignancy. "On its own this fax could be harmless, but taken in context we must take this threat very seriously. First of all, the author used my real name. It could have been a lucky guess, that there was someone at *Shabak* called 'Yigal.' But then, how did they know the fax number for our incoming intelligence? Thirdly, there is the allusion to the Shimshon Plan." Yigal watched Shiloni's body language for a response. Like Yigal, Shiloni liked to think before he spoke.

Shiloni folded his arms defensively and leaned back in his chair, not wanting to believe this skeleton was really coming out of the closet to haunt him. "If it's not a crackpot, then you seem to be describing an inside job," said the Prime Minister taking the attack.

Yigal frowned. He desperately wanted to win his point without having to reveal the existence of the missing computer printout. "There have been some serious developments in the last week or so, indicating there is a newly formed underground planning to carry out the Shimshon Plan, or at least attempting to assassinate Abu Alim," explained Yigal. "We picked up a poster of Abu Alim that had been used for target practice near Ma'alot Yair. Then there was the drive-by shooting of the Arabs in the same vicinity last night. Then there's the fax."

Shiloni leaned forward on his desk. "Do you have any idea who these people might be?"

"Well, Meir Tal, the brother of my agent who quit over the Shimshon Plan, was picked up late last night on suspicion that he committed the drive-by shooting. We have some wire taps incriminating him," said Yigal. He deliberately omitted the fact that Meir's kids were in the car at the time, and that the information in the wiretaps was circumstantial at best. He didn't have any hard evidence yet, but that might not be necessary to get the Prime Minister to follow Yigal's instructions. "Rachel Stein, the murdered agent's fiancée, arrived in Israel last week as well. She made a suspicious four-minute visit to the King David Hotel last Thursday at the same time Henry Waxman was in the hotel."

Shiloni took a Havana cigar out of a carved wooden box inlaid with ivory sitting on the corner of his desk. He licked the tip and placed the cigar in his mouth. He reached into his jacket pocket searching for his gold lighter. His hand found Yigal's note crumpled in his pocket. Shiloni fished it out and placed it in the crystal ashtray on the desk. Then he stuffed his hand back into the pocket to retrieve the lighter. He put the flame to the end of the cigar, sucked strongly and puffed until the tip was glowing. Satisfied it was lit, he lowered the lighter to the note in the ashtray and delicately touched the flame to the corner of the paper. It flared up and in a moment it was a small pile of gray ash. Shiloni stared blankly at the ashes hoping this whole episode would disappear in a puff of smoke like the piece of paper. "Is that it?" he asked Yigal without looking at him.

"Well, Stein was snooping around the *Jerusalem Press* this morning with a rich American. They ordered copies of all the photographs the paper had of Abu Alim appearing in public places." Yigal stopped talking. He had given Shiloni all the information necessary for him to draw the conclusions without having to explain the missing report. If the disgruntled Ari had told anyone about the Shimshon Plan, it would have been his fiancée or his brother. He wouldn't have needed any papers to explain the idea to them. They even had a motive — not only were they right-wing settlers actively involved in the anti-government protest movement, but they could be planning these acts in revenge for Ari's murder.

Shiloni leaned back in his chair, put his hands behind his head and drew silently on the cigar. A puff of blue smoke enveloped both him and Yigal. Yigal grimaced at the nauseating sweet smell of the cigar smoke. His wife would kill him if he came home with this stench on his clothes. "What do you suggest we do?" asked Shiloni, breaking the silence.

"Well, one thing's for certain. We can't have Abu Alim up on the Temple Mount this Friday. Everything points to that being the day of the attack, if there is going to be one," said Yigal matter-of-factly, assuming Shiloni would agree with him.

Shiloni pinched the cigar between his right index and middle fingers and pulled it away from his lips. He leaned forward menacingly and stared Yigal in the eye. "Corporal Ramon," he said impatiently, "if we know the plan, because *we* devised it..." Shiloni emphasized the 'we' to remind Yigal of his own share in the plan, and therefore his responsibility to take care of the problem, "... and we also have the chief suspects either under arrest or under surveillance, then why shouldn't I let Abu Alim on the Temple Mount? There should be no problem stopping the attack. At the same time we'll show the world how liberal and understanding we are by letting that crazy Arab up there to put on his show."

Yigal's palms began to sweat. It was time for him to pull out his trump card. There was nothing that Shiloni could do to him, except make him feel very uncomfortable, because both Yigal's and Shiloni's names were on the missing report. "Yossi," said Yigal quietly, "there's one more thing. Before Ari Tal died, a copy of the Shimshon File was printed out from his computer terminal. Any one of a number of people could have it. If they succeed in even partially carrying out the plan and the report is leaked to the press, the world will pin the whole massacre back on the *Shabak*. You and I will be held personally responsible for the attack."

Shiloni stared for a moment at Yigal, absorbing the enormity of what he was saying. He stamped out his cigar and reached for the 'green phone' on the credenza behind his desk.

Twenty Eight

Meir Tal stared at the *Shabak* agent standing next to the window of the interrogation room trying to determine if he was friend or foe. Why did he tell Meir that he knew Ari? Was it a trick to gain his confidence? Did he really know his brother?

Meir's head was swirling with thoughts. His quick wit was useless now. What he needed most was to stay calm and not be careless. If the man looking out the window really was a friend, he could be a tremendous help in solving the mystery of Ari's murder and bringing the terrorist to justice.

The sun beat down mercilessly as the two young men fought for match point in their one-on-one basketball game. The net had been torn away from the orange metal loop by some local kids. The year-old cement playing surface was already starting to buckle under the pounding heat of the Judean desert sun. Ari broke away from Meir whose hand had been delicately touching the back of his T-shirt. Ari spun and lobbed a jump shot. The ball bounced off the cracked paint of the backboard and clanked through the naked hoop.

Ari picked up his unfinished bottle of mineral water and gulped it down. After only half an hour in the sun, the liquid was much hotter than luke warm.

Meir finished his bottle too. "How come God gave you the tall, skinny, basketball genes, and I got stuck with the short, round ones that are only good for making people chuckle?" complained Meir. The brothers laughed and shook hands. They sat down to catch their breath under a lone fig tree outside the chainlink fence surrounding the Ma'alot Yair basketball court.

"I've been offered a job with Shabak," announced Ari, "What do you think Meir, should I check it out?" Ari treasured his special relationship with his brother. He could share anything with him and get a totally different approach than he would come up with himself. Ari trusted Meir with his darkest secrets.

"Are they nuts?" laughed Meir, "hiring a religious guy?! How can you be religious and work for the Shabak? I can just see it. You've been following some suspicious Arab for three days. You're in the middle of the highway, when suddenly you realize it's almost Shabbat, so you pull over to the edge of the highway, stop the car and start walking so as not to break Shabbat. 'So long Ahmed! Shabbat Shalom."

"Come on Meir," complained Ari, "be serioius. You know there have been religious agents in the Shabak, as well as in the Mossad and in senior positions in the Army. We've both been in situations like that on our Miluim reserve duty. Whenever there's a situation of life and death, all the Sabbath laws get pushed aside. Even in a doubtful security

situation, the military commander's orders are considered to have the status of Jewish law."

"Sure, we survive for three to four weeks a year on reserve duty. But that's a lot different than putting yourself in the situation of having to break Shabbat all the time as part of your full-time job," countered Meir. It was out of character for him to be the practical brother.

Ari stood up, and plucked a ripe fig from the tree. It was already late August and the lush fruit was beginning to turn purple. He made a blessing and split the fig open to make sure it didn't house any bugs before biting into it and savoring its moisture. Ari spotted another one, snapped it from the branch and offered it to his brother. "They're not dumb, Meir. After all they're part of the intelligence community. They even brought up the subject at the interview, and said they were specifically looking for someone observant who understood the religious. It's sad, but often they have to deal with security threats from our community. Every once in a while, someone just loses it, and decides to take things into his own hands."

Meir looked at Ari in disbelief. "You mean you would actually consider turning in an observant Jew to the authorities?"

Ari reached up while sitting cross-legged and plucked a low-hanging fig leaf. He rested his elbows on his knees and began to tear the leaf into neat strips. This was exactly why he had picked Meir, and only Meir, to discuss the idea of joining the Shabak. Everything with Meir was straight and to the point. Ari wanted to be confronted by his brother, it would help keep him honest about the decision he needed to

*make. He looked at Meir solemnly, "I've given it a
lot of thought. And I've bounced back and forth
between the pros and the cons. They're going to be
watching our community anyway. Better that I should
be there, than someone else who we don't know. If I
set a good example, it might help change their
attitudes about religious people. Besides, I have my
red lines. I can always leave, if things get out of
hand."*

*Meir could see his brother had already made up
his mind. All he could do was throw in one last
warning. "Just remember Ari, they might make it
easy to get in, but it's not always so easy to get out."
He leaned over and gave his brother a big bear hug
and added, "I don't want to ever hear any more of
this, no matter what you decide. It's not safe for you
to share information like this, even with your big
brother."*

Tears came to Meir's eyes as he realized he would
never again have the wonderful feeling of giving his little
brother a hug, or losing to him in a basketball game. He
didn't know if it was good or bad that he had held Ari to his
promise not to share any information about his *Shabak* activities. Perhaps if he knew more, it might help him use
'Yoram' to find Ari's murderer. Then again, if he had more
information it might help incriminate himself and keep him
in prison.

Meir looked at Udi who had sat down again, and decided to put him to the test, "What was my brother's favorite
soft drink?"

Udi was taken by surprise, but he quickly realized what
Meir was doing. It was years since Ari had died. Udi shut his
eyes and tried to project a picture on the back of his eyelids
of the last time they sat together in the 'company' cafeteria.

Then it came to him. "Kinley," he said, restraining himself. He felt like he had just won a prize on a TV game show. Usually the men at *Shabak* preferred the caffeine in one of the popular colas. Ari had preferred the orange-flavored drink favored by kids.

"Why did you tell me you knew my brother? Isn't that against *Shabak* rules?"

"I want to help you. It's the least I can do for Ari, even though he's gone. But I need you to trust me. You have to tell me everything you know in order for me to convince the people above me to let you go," explained Udi.

Meir shifted in his seat. "Listen, this whole thing is absurd. I didn't shoot anybody. My two kids were sleeping in the back seat and my wife was in the car! What do you take me for?"

"Perhaps you shot back in self defense, trying to protect your family. Did the Arabs throw any rocks at you while you were driving by?" said Udi, trying to sympathize with Meir.

"I suppose you're next going to ask me if I've stopped beating my wife. Are the hidden tape recorders running?" Meir looked around the room as if trying to find the tell-tale sign of a microphone. "Do you here me out there? We didn't drive by any Arabs. I didn't shoot any Arabs." He shifted his gaze back to Udi and said, "I thought you said you were here to help me. I might as well just shut up until they've checked my guns. As soon as they find out the bullets weren't fired from them, they'll have to let me go anyway." Meir stood up to leave the room and return to his cell, ending the interrogation.

Udi began to panic inside. The last thing he wanted was to report back to Yigal with no progress. Time was running out. He watched Meir walk slowly to the door. Udi figured he had nothing to lose, he might as well take a risk. "Wait," he said, "please sit down. I need your help. Our country needs your help."

Meir stopped and turned back to look at Udi. The sincerity and urgency in the *Shabak* agent's voice was unnerving. He wondered if a similar plea had been used with Ari to persuade him to join their ranks. The words 'Our country needs your help' were mesmerizing. He walked back to his chair and sat down waiting for Udi to continue.

Udi paused to chose his words carefully, he didn't want to alienate Meir again. "We have reason to believe that there is a plan to assassinate Abu Alim."

"So what else is new? There are probably a dozen rival factions, including those in his own *Fatah* who would blow him away in a second, if they could get away with it. If not for you guys in *Shabak* and in military intelligence protecting him, Alim would probably have been dead long ago."

Udi smiled for a moment, realizing how right Meir was, but not being able to admit it. He personally had been involved in two operations to stifle Islamic fundamentalist plots to kill the President of Palestine. "This time it's different," he said gravely. "we have reason to believe it is a plot of a new Jewish underground."

Udi paused to gauge Meir's reaction to the accusation of a Jewish underground. Meir sat poker-faced. His body language revealed nothing, not a twitch of discomfort. Silence filled the room for an agonizing few seconds. Udi resisted the temptation to speak. In negotiations, the first to speak always loses.

Meir looked at the man sitting across from him, still trying to figure out if he was a friend or not. If he really wanted to help him, Meir could afford to be straight with him. If he was out to get him, then it didn't really matter what he said either. They could ruin his life if they wanted to, even if he maintained silence. Meir decided to play along and be himself. An impish grin crossed his face and he said, "Well if the Arabs can't get their act together to rid themselves of that evil son of *Amalek*, then I guess our boys will have to do the work for them."

"Do you know who murdered those Arabs near the Ma'alot Yair junction last night? The murderer may be part of the assassination team. Based on the location of the attack, there's a good chance he's one of your neighbors."

"Even if I knew who it was, do you actually expect me to hand over a Jew to you? To be tried in a secular court that doesn't follow Jewish law?" Meir thought back to cases where the Israeli legal system had handed down harsher judgments than those demanded by the Torah, or found people guilty of crimes based on evidence that would not have been sufficient according to Jewish standards. He also thought back to the days of the British Mandate in Palestine, when the labor-Zionist *Palmach* military wing handed fellow Jewish freedom fighters in the rival *Irgun* over to the British who hanged them for treason.

"You don't understand, Meir. If we don't catch them, and there is even an unsuccessful assassination attempt, it could mean an all out *Jihad* from the Arab world. Millions of Jewish lives would be at stake."

Meir rolled his eyes. He couldn't take Udi's melodrama seriously. "What are you talking about? At least half the Arab world would love to see Abu Alim dead. And, if they want to go to war with us, they don't need an assassination as an excuse. Did Nasser need an excuse other than simply to destroy the Jewish State when he decided to go on a war of annihilation against us in 1967? Did Sadat need an excuse to initiate a war to destroy us on Yom Kippur of 1973?"

Udi frowned.

"And if the Arabs didn't launch a *Jihad* after 29 Moslem worshippers were gunned down by a Jew at the Cave of the Patriarchs, then a simple assassination won't provoke them into a war either, unless they were planning to attack us anyway."

Udi resisted the temptation to reveal to Meir that in this case, even more Moslems would be killed at an even holier Islamic site. There was no way to equate the significance of the Machpelah Cave to the Mosques on the Temple Mount. Even Meir would have to admit it, but Udi wanted to see if Meir would volunteer any knowledge of the Shimshon plan. He decided to draw Meir out on the subject of the Hebron massacre. "I still can't understand how a Jew could slaughter innocent Moslem worshippers... Especially a religious Jew..." said Udi, baiting Meir.

Meir looked at Udi cautiously and scratched his beard. He knew he was being dragged into a discussion he didn't want to have. No one wants to hear a rationalization of a massacre. In the pit of his own stomach Meir was abhorred by the image of the dead bodies strewn about the stone floor of the Yitzchak Hall. What was to be gained by defending the doctor who had done the shooting? Perhaps the truth, thought Meir.

"Are you just asking, or do you really want to know?" asked Meir. "Because if you're just asking, I'll tell you want you want to hear — 'he must have been mentally deranged,' or 'he was a religious Messianic fanatic,' you know, all the excuses you guys made up so as not to have to confront reality. If you've got the guts, and you're really interested in understanding what could motivate an intelligent, otherwise sensitive doctor to do such a thing, I'll tell you that instead."

Udi shifted in his seat. He always felt nauseous whenever he met someone who supported the Hebron Massacre. He felt like changing the subject, but he was here to get information about Meir Tal, and his friends. "I really want to know."

"Well, let me first ask *you* a question. If you could go back in time to 1936, and assassinate Adolph Hitler, *yemach shemo*, and save six million Jewish lives, would you do it?"

Udi thought of the lesser ranking enemies of Israel whom he had helped eliminate when far fewer lives were at stake. *"Nu?"* he said, acknowledging the obvious, and indicating to Meir to continue.

"And if the only way for you to kill him, was to set off a bomb while he was delivering a speech in a German church, taking out 29 innocent worshippers along with him?"

Udi looked down at his folded hands resting on the desk and began clicking one thumbnail against the other.

"Let's assume Hitler himself didn't arrive for the speech at the Church. And assume that at the Church, for weeks the Priest had been delivering sermons inciting the congregants to 'Slaughter the Jews.' Now if you were certain that if you blew up the Church anyway, and killed the 29 people, that it would put an end to Hitler's political rise to power, thereby saving six-million Jewish lives, would you still do it?" Meir's face was reddening and his voice was pressing louder.

Udi squirmed in his seat. *He* was supposed to be doing the interrogating. How had he let the conversation get out of control? "Enough. I get your point," he said sharply, trying to put an end to Meir's tirade.

"It's not enough," shouted Meir. He stood up while the veins were pulsating in his temples, "You said you really wanted to know!"

The door opened and the guard posted outside peeked into the room to see what all the noise was about. Udi silently nodded to him, indicating everything was all right, and the guard shut the door.

The interruption helped Meir gather his wits. He sat down and continued more quietly, but still spoke through gritted teeth. "You see, to paraphrase Bernard Shaw, we've established that *even you* could have committed the Hebron Massacre. All we're negotiating now, are the circumstances under which you would do it. The person who committed the attack was, for years, the doctor of Kiryat Arba and Hebron. He was the first one on the scene after many, many stabbings and shootings of his friends and neighbors. His hands were drenched in Jewish blood as he desperately tried to bandage the victims before the ambulances arrived. Only weeks before the Hebron attack, he held the heads of his good friend and his son in his hands, who were slaughtered in a drive-by shooting. Like most of us, the good doctor tended to believe the statements of Arafat, rather than those of the Israeli government. The government kept backtracking on their promises. Arafat never once changed his tune. He said he was using the peace process as a way to implement the 1974 plan of stages, whereby a Palestinian State would be set up in the West Bank and Gaza as a launching pad to destroy the rest of Israel and it's four and a half million Jewish citizens. After the signing of the Declaration of Principles in Washington, even people in his own *Fatah* faction were involved in 21 terror attacks against Israelis, including the murder of Chaim Mizrahi."

Udi felt like asking Meir to stop his monologue. Instead, he got up from his seat and turned to look out the window to avoid being in Meir's direct line of fire. He noticed the group protesting for Meir's release had gotten much larger.

Meir pressed on. "Imagine that a large portion of four million Jewish lives will be destroyed if a Palestinian State is created and taken over by Islamic fundamentalists. Imagine that your own government is handing the most bloodthirsty murderer of Jews since Adolph Hitler, a state on a silver platter. Imagine that no amount of legal protesting, mass demonstrations, or petitions have any effect on budging your government from its suicidal policies. Add to that, the admission of the government, that the Islamic extremists are the real threat, and that if they get control, it will mean war. In fact, that is why the secular leftist government was dealing with the 'secular' PLO. Then the polls tell you that Arafat is weak and is afraid of the Islamic fundamentalists. The conclusion you come to is to get the Palestinians to pull out of the process because the Israelis continue to negotiate even though Jews are being murdered daily by Palestinians.

"And how do you get the Palestinians to pull out? Well, when the Islamic fundamentalists want to get Israel to pull out of the talks, they murder Jews. Their logic tells them, that in the face of terror, the Jews should pull out. After all, if the same atrocities were committed against them by Jews, they would have enough self respect to pull out, assuming the Jews weren't sincere.

"Do you get it yet?" asked Meir trying to get Udi to look at him. "You have to enrage the Islamic terrorists so much, that they force the PLO out of the talks. And how do you do that? You kill as many Moslem worshippers as you can while they are praying at a Moslem holy site. Now I ask you, 'Mr. Yoram,' would you kill 29 worshippers at a mosque, where for months they had been preaching '*Itbach al Yahud*, Slaughter the Jews,' in order to stop the modern day Hitler from achieving his first stated goal in the destruction of the State of Israel?"

Udi turned and looked at Meir. He cleared his throat, as if to speak, but chose to think some more before responding. He felt numb. Not so much by the horror that there might have been some logic behind the Hebron massacre, nor by the fact that the man sitting across from him looked like he might be able to commit a similar act, and there were probably dozens, if not hundreds of other people just like him. Udi had always thought that the battle the settlers had with the government was over returning holy land that was promised to the Jews in the Bible. For the first time, he came face to face with the fact that what was really motivating them was the saving of Jewish lives. Hundreds of thousands if not millions of Jewish lives. After the Holocaust, the picture painted by Meir was no longer impossible. Udi was numbed by the clash between his emotions, which felt the revulsion of the massacre, and his intellect which had been ever so slightly penetrated by Meir's logic. Udi was sweating because he realized that in the past, his superiors had used similar logic to convince him to execute people when the stakes were much, much less.

Udi walked to the door and opened it, leaving Meir's question hanging in the air. 'Will you do it Udi?' The question rebounded in his head as he remembered the times Yigal had asked him to eliminate an enemy. Such assignments were never ordered. Agents were asked to volunteer, based on their understanding of the logic of the situation. "We'll continue our talk another time," he said solemnly, nodding to the guard to take Meir back to his cell.

Meir got up feeling a mixture of disgust and triumph. Before walking out the door, he stopped and confronted Udi one last time, "If you're my friend, tell me who murdered my brother."

Meir's question hit Udi like a lightning bolt on a clear day. His shoulders twitched before being able to speak, giving Meir his answer before any words came out of Udi's mouth. He had guessed all along that *Shabak* had known who the murderer was. The question was why had they covered it up all these years?

Udi didn't want to lie, Meir was too sharp, and he would catch him on it. Then, thankfully, the words popped into his head, "I'll help you find out who did it. I promise."

Twenty Nine

Jibril Abu Alim gazed with glee at the wall of television screens opposite his desk in his private office. Joining him in the 'Green Room' was Nasser Rajoub, Palestinian Foreign Minister, and Alim's closest adviser. Together, they were surveying the mid-day news reports. Built into the wall was a large forty-inch screen tuned into Palestine State Television. On either side of the large screen were two columns of three, smaller twenty inch monitors. The column farthest to the left, was broadcasting the American networks — ABC, NBC and CBS. The next column was the world networks, CNN, Worldnet, and BBC. On the right side of the wall were Jordan, Egypt, Syria, Iraq, Iran and at the bottom right, Israel Television. Although there were dozens of other frequencies being monitored regularly by his Palestine Security Service, he liked to have these dozen foreign stations available in his office. They were his favorites.

Abu Alim leaned back in his black leather office chair and put his feet up on the desk, toying with the remote control in his right hand. As a child, growing up in the poverty of the refugee camp, his family could not afford decent food, let alone a television set. And even if they had been able to own one, who had time to watch? In fact, as a young boy, he didn't even have the luxury to be a child. He was forced to grow up before he was a teenager. At eight he was hurling rocks at passing cars with yellow Israeli plates. By eleven he had seriously wounded his first Israeli soldier. His official entry into manhood came at seventeen when he killed his first Israeli, and was admitted into the Fatah Hawks. Young Jibril never had toys, nor time to play. Ironically, now that he was reaching middle age, with the responsibilities of a nation on his shoulders, he finally had time to be a child and play with his television sets, personal computers, cellular phones and other electronic gadgets provided to him by his security services.

The President particularly enjoyed the news broadcasts when he was the center of attention. At this moment, his trim figure filled two screens as his interview about the terror attack from the previous night was being rebroadcast. His thumb punched a button on the remote control that activated the volume on the CNN monitor. His strongly-accented English filled the room, *'... the Prime Minister would never prevent me from praying at Al Aksa for these innocent souls who were so cruelly murdered by some...'* The sound of his voice was interrupted by the loud ringing of the telephone on the corner of Abu Alim's desk.

Nasser Rajoub jumped in his chair, and the adrenaline began to flow through his body as a result of being startled by the loud ringing of the 'Green Phone.' He looked at the President, expecting him to pick up the direct line connected to the office of the Prime Minister of Israel. It had been a 'fail-safe' tool connecting the Palestinians and Israelis ever since Israeli undercover agents mistakenly shot six armed senior *Fatah* men in Gaza during the Olso negotiations. Since 'red' was the color used for the 'hot line' to Washington, the PLO Chairman had suggested 'green.' It was a color the Arabs believed kept the evil eye away. The front door of many Arab homes was painted green, or blue, for just this reason.

Abu Alim ignored the ringing and continued to watch himself on the monitor. Rajoub stared curiously at his leader, wondering why the President let the call from Yossi Shiloni's office go unanswered. Abu Alim punched another button to activate Jordan television as the telephone nagged out its tenth ring. The President looked down at the phone with disgust as he imagined who was at the other end. He had been expecting the call all morning. Then he glanced up at his Foreign Minister and a sadistic grin crossed his face. A smiled cross Rajoub's face as well, as he realized what his boss was doing. 'Let the Jew sweat,' he thought to himself. After all, if Jerusalem initiated the call, it meant the Israeli's had something to panic about.

Abu Alim pressed the 'mute button' on the remote control and nodded for Nasser Rajoub to pick up the phone. Rajoub pressed the 'speaker button' so that Abu Alim could listen in to his conversation. "Yes?" said Rajoub in his best English.

"My dear Jibril, this is Yossi," said the voice over the loudspeaker stating the obvious. It sounded like someone who was troubled, overcompensating by being too friendly.

"I'm sorry, the President is busy. This is the Foreign Minister speaking," said Rajoub as sternly as he could. 'Let him sweat,' he thought. Abu Alim smiled in approval.

"I must speak to the President immediately. It is of the utmost importance," demanded Shiloni, assuming Rajoub would put Abu Alim on the line.

"Concerning what?"

Shiloni began losing patience and felt like insulting the man at the other end of the phone. If it wasn't important he wouldn't be using this silly 'Green Phone.' He hated it when what he termed, 'these backward shanty town dwellers' exaggerated their self importance as soon as they got a 'title.' The Prime Minister looked at Yigal, glad that he couldn't hear how he was being insulted by the Palestinian. Shiloni took a deep drag on his cigar and said as calmly as he could, "It's about his request to visit the Temple Mount this Friday."

"Ah... *Al Aksa*," said Rajoub correcting the Israeli, with a subtle dig. He never used any terms that might refer to Jewish historical rights over Jerusalem. The Al Aksa Mosque and the Golden Dome of Omar were originally built in the 8th century, precisely on the site of the ancient Temple of Solomon. It was just as much a demonstration of political sovereignty as a religious act.

Abu Alim reached across the desk to pick up the handset and placed it to his ear. "Yossi, I'm so happy to hear from you. I hope you have some good news for me about my visit. The news reports say that you've been in a cabinet meeting all morning discussing the issue."

Shiloni glanced nervously at Yigal thinking carefully about his words. He hated having to be polite with this terrorist, especially in front of Yigal. "Some very serious information has just come to my attention. We believe that there is a group planning your assassination. The attack could very well take place on Friday, if you visit Jerusalem."

Abu Alim burst out into a loud cackle of laughter. "You've been in a meeting for three hours and that's the best excuse you can come up with to keep me out of *Al Quds*." He used the Arabic term for Jerusalem, meaning 'The Holy.' "And you say there is 'a group' planning my assassination? You mean *groups*. After all, I personally know of three groups plotting my death. Really, now Yossi. I know you are under a lot of pressure, but certainly you can do better than that."

Shiloni pursed his lips and drummed his fingers on the desk. He despised melodrama, and didn't like people playing games with him. "Jibril, this is serious. It looks like it's a new Jewish underground. Trained Israeli reservists. They aren't your average teenage Islamic fundamentalists using outdated weapons and homemade bombs."

Abu Alim winked at Rajoub. "Listen, Yossi. Even if I chose to believe you about this assassination plot, which I'm not sure I do. What are you going to tell the world? Public sympathy is on our side. My religious freedom is being denied. I want to pray for some innocent brethren who were gunned down in cold blood. What are you going to tell the world? That there are some bloodthirsty Jews who are out to kill me while I'm praying at my national shrine? That will be great for *your* image." Abu Alim knew how to hit Shiloni in his soft spots.

Shiloni sighed. "It will do worse for my image if they actually do shoot you. But then you won't be in such great shape either." The formality lessened and the cynicism increased as Shiloni's patience began to wear even thinner. He felt like mentioning there was a possibility some innocent worshippers might be killed in an attempted attack, without revealing the details of the Shimshon Plan. Then he figured the loss of a few lives for 'the cause' wouldn't make a difference in Abu Alim's decision.

"Well, Mr. Prime Minister," said Abu Alim confidently. "I expect you'll find a way to let me safely visit *Al Aksa*. It will mean a lot to my people. And remember, the world is watching you." Abu Alim returned the handset to its cradle, not allowing his nemesis to have the last word. He winked once more at Nasser Rajoub who nodded back proudly at his leader. The President leaned back in his chair, put his feet back on the desk and punched a button activating the volume of the BBC monitor. Spain was playing Italy in a World Cup match.

Thirty

After the attempted terror attack at the Haas Promenade, Rachel suggested she and Marc go back to Leah's house to settle their nerves. What Rachel really needed right now was a hug from her own mother to help her calm down from the nightmare she had just experienced. But her mother was six thousand miles away, and the last thing Rachel wanted to do was call her Mom about a terror attack. Mrs. Stein had been devastated by her future son-in-law's murder that came so close to the wedding. She was depressed for the better part of a year. When Rachel made the announcement that she was planning to come back to Israel, her mother was the lone voice of opposition. She couldn't stand the thought of living so far away from her daughter when there were more terrorist attacks than ever before. No, Rachel couldn't call her mother, but Leah would understand. She would make everything better.

Rachel and Marc were both surprised to find that Leah wasn't home at four o'clock in the afternoon. She usually reserved that time to make phone calls for an upcoming demonstration or to arrange meetings. Itzik, one of *Kol Ha'am's* chief activists met them at the door and let them in.

He told them about Meir's arrest. Leah had gone to Ma'alot Yair to lend moral support to Shoshana and help her with the children. She called about a half an hour ago, saying she was on her way back to Jerusalem. She had instructed Itzik to call the leadership of *Kol Ha'am* and organize an emergency meeting at her home that evening for 8:00 p.m. Itzik was on the phone making calls when Rachel and Marc arrived.

Rachel walked to the kitchen and filled the kettle with water. She pressed the electric starter on the gas stove and the flame burst into life on the element. The heat from the flame grazed her hand and she jerked it back, almost dropping the kettle. 'How fragile life is,' she thought. 'It's a miracle any of us makes it to adulthood.' What was happening to her world? Ari was dead. Meir was in jail. Leah was fighting her own government. Rachel had been injured at the demonstration, had her tires slashed, and then came the terror attack at the Haas Promenade. She felt numb. She couldn't bring herself to ask about the details of Meir's arrest, let alone tell Itzik about the attempted knifing that afternoon. Rachel felt like crying. She had come back to Israel to rebuild her life. After one week it seemed as if everything was falling apart. But then, there was Marc...

"Who would like a hot drink?" she called out. "I'm making myself some chamomile tea." Normally she wouldn't help herself to food or drink in someone else's home, but Leah had given her explicit instructions 'to be one of the family.' That thought helped calm her down more than the chamomile tea would.

"I'd love a cup of coffee," said Itzik, punching a phone number with his right thumb on the cordless handset. "I've been running on adrenaline since nine this morning when Leah called telling me about Meir. I can use a booster shot of caffeine."

Marc was standing in the dining room, staring at a photograph mounted in a silver frame. It sat on a shelf behind the glass doors of the china cabinet. Although he had never met Ari, he felt a bond with him. He gazed at the man frozen in time by the photograph, saddened that he couldn't share his feelings and thoughts with him. Marc wondered why God had chosen to let the murderer's knife find its target and take Ari's life, yet spare Marc's own life today. Had the terrorist not decided to run toward the old lady, and instead had directed his wrath on Marc who was only a few steps away, Marc's picture would have found its place here next to Ari's. He wanted Ari to talk to him. To talk to him about the world of souls. To share with him the meaning of life. To help him understand his role in the world and why the Almighty kept throwing him over cliffs and catching him. Most of all he wanted to talk to Ari about Rachel. To ask his permission.

"Marc? Would you like a cup of coffee too?" called out Rachel again from the kitchen.

Marc snapped out of his daydream at the mention of his name. "Uh, yes, sure. I'd love some." He turned away from the photograph and walked toward the kitchen to join Rachel.

Just as the kettle began to whistle, a key turned in the lock of the front door and Leah walked in, visibly agitated. She hung her keys on the brass key rack beside the front door, turned and noticed Marc standing in the living room. "Oh, I'm so glad you're here," she said to Marc, "what a nightmare this day has been."

Rachel, anticipating Leah's feelings, quickly poured a cup of tea for Leah and brought it to the living room. She left the tea bag floating on the surface of the boiling water, allowing it to steep in the cup. "Here," said Rachel coming out of the kitchen and placing the cup and saucer on the coffee table, "have some chamomile tea. It will help you relax. Itzik told us about Meir. How's he doing?"

Leah plopped herself down onto the sofa and picked up the tea cup. She stirred the water and the tea bag together, and squeezed the bag against the side of the cup with her spoon to hurry up the process. "Thank you sweetheart," she said taking a sip of the tea even before it was really ready. "I imagine Meir is okay, but I haven't been able to speak to him. No one has. I called our lawyer, but he hasn't been able to make any headway with the army. Don't forget, Ma'alot Yair is in that sliver of land that still lies between the '67 borders and Palestine. Israeli law, and Israeli civil rights don't apply there. They can keep him under military detention for quite a while before we'll be able to speak with him."

"How are Shoshana and the kids doing?" asked Marc.

"Shoshana is holding up pretty well. I actually think it helped that she was picked up and interrogated with Meir. At least she saw where he was and how he was being treated. As for the kids, all I can say is thank God that they were asleep and didn't see the soldiers come and take their parents away."

Rachel shuddered at the image of little Sarah and Yoni seeing their parents dragged away in the middle of the night. For the first time she could really identify with how her grandmother must have felt when the German soldiers took away Rachel's grandfather. An image of the gold watch flashed into her head, and then the photo of Abu Alim's bodyguard. "Let me get the rest of the hot drinks," she said as she got up to go to the kitchen trying to distract herself from her thoughts. She returned in an instant, handed the coffees to the men and sat down with her own tea. "What can we do to help get Meir out of jail?" she asked.

"Well, after making sure that Shoshana was all right, a group of us drove over to the army base where Meir is being held. We held a small spontaneous demonstration outside the gate. *Kol Yisrael* radio was there as well as the TV. We got a lot of coverage because it's a good human interest story. Now, if the story stays in the media, and we're demonstrating about the lack of democracy and human rights, it will embarrass the government into acting. There's a good chance that could happen. After all, a husband and a wife don't get picked up on suspicion of murder everyday you know."

"They're a regular Bonnie and Clyde those two," said Itzik. "All Meir needs is a black fedora instead of his knitted *kipah*. Maybe we can pick one up for him in Me'a She'arim." They all laughed which helped relieve some of the tension in the room.

"So let's activate the *Kol Ha'am* network and put a siege on the place," suggested Marc.

"That's exactly why I called the executive meeting for tonight. I want to make sure that my own personal agenda doesn't get in the way of the goals we set out for ourselves as a group. Don't forget, the *Mercaz HaMa'avak* has decided to devote this week to putting pressure on the government to not allow Abu Alim into Jerusalem on Friday. Also there are the demonstrations against the recent spate of terror attacks originating from Palestinian territory. If we decide to focus our energies on freeing Meir, I want the group to decide. But first, let's have something to eat before everyone starts arriving." Leah got up from the sofa and walked to the kitchen to pull out some leftovers from *Shabbat*. "Who would like a cold turkey sandwich?" She had slipped back into grandmother mode.

Thirty One

Yigal Ramon sat behind his desk at *Shabak* Jerusalem headquarters and massaged his eyes, making wide circular motions with the heels of the palms of his hands. He had returned to his office to quietly review the files on Meir Tal, Rachel and the Shimshon Plan after his meeting with the Prime Minister. He thought best when his eyes were closed. After a few moments he pulled his hands away from his face, clasped them together on his desk and considered the agent standing opposite him. Another annoying detail he didn't want to deal with. He felt like simply getting up and going home to his family for dinner. Instead, he reached for his phone and punched in a three-digit programmed rapid dial number.

"The *Mafkal* please. This is Yigal Ramon." Yigal paused to glance again at the agent, while he waited for Aryeh Levi, the national Chief of Police, to answer.

"Hello, Yigal? What can I do for you?" said an impatient but confident voice on the other end. "We're swamped over here. There were two attempted terror attacks today that haven't hit the radio yet, in addition to what happened at the Promenade. But, I always have time for you, *Motek*." They often used the nicknames that the soldiers in their paratroop brigade had given to each other thirty years earlier. No one dreamed at the time that the quiet obedient kid from Beer-sheba whom they labeled "Sweetie," would grow up to be a tough senior officer in the *Shabak*. Not only the defense establishment, but business, and especially Israeli politics spun around 'old boys' networks that were forged during three year army stints that began at age seventeen and continued throughout their lives in reserve duty. This was one of the main reasons it was so difficult for women and immigrants to break into the Israeli establishment. And also one of the main reasons political parties were filled with a disproportionate number of mediocre candidates. Positions were allocated to the 'old boys' based on loyalty and not necessarily on merit.

Yigal empathized with his old friend. "I can imagine what you must be going through over there, Aryeh" he said tiredly into the phone. "Actually, I don't need anything right now except for a quiet dinner with my wife and kids. I'm calling to help you. Are you still hunting for the good citizen who brought down the terrorist this afternoon at the *Taye-let?*"

"Are you kidding me? The mayor's been hounding me all afternoon to find that guy. He wants to give him a medal. I've got half a dozen of my best men out there looking for him."

Yigal paused for effect. "You can call them off their hunt. I've got the guy right here with me in my office."

The Chief of Police was caught off guard momentarily, thinking it might be one of Yigal's practical jokes. "For real? The guy's a national hero, not an enemy of the State. What are you holding him for?"

"I'm not holding him. He's one of my agents. He happened to be at the right place at the right time. He took off after the incident in order to avoid any unpleasant encounters with the press. Sorry, but I hope you understand. I'm sure you'll be able to come up with some explanation for the media."

Yigal could feel a sparkle in Levi's eyes over the telephone line. "Now that you mention it, it did seem kind of suspicious that all three shots hit a bulls-eye on a moving target. Listen, I owe you one. Had anyone been killed, I'd have more than just the mayor breathing down my neck. The whole country is panicking about the deterioration of the security situation. Especially in Jerusalem. Speaking of the security situation, I've got to run. Thanks a lot."

"You'd do the same for me," said Yigal hanging up the phone. He winked at the agent still standing across from him waiting for his instructions. He picked up the file folders on his desk and thought about his discussion earlier with the Prime Minister. Yigal sensed that Yossi Shiloni would ultimately give in to Abu Alim's demand to visit the Temple Mount. Shiloni loved making messes as long as he didn't have to clean them up. Yigal really hated cleaning up after other peoples. He knew it was going to be a long week. A lot of innocent people were going to have to be picked up as a preventive measure.

Yigal stood up and put on his jacket, signaling the meeting was ending. He decided to review the files at home. He put his arm around his agent and said, "Double up the coverage on Rachel Stein, Marc Goodman, and Leah Tal. Then put a man on anyone they come in contact with in the next forty-eight hours who even blinks the wrong way."

Thirty Two

Leah Tal's living room was buzzing with chatter. The dining room table was pushed into the corner of the room to make way for a large circle of high-backed upholstered dining room chairs and extra folding chairs that had been brought out for the meeting. A small group argued animatedly by the large coffee urn that was filling the room with the nutty aroma of fresh perked coffee. Marc squeezed past the group and pressed the black plastic tap to fill his cup with the rich, dark brew. He hesitated for a moment at the table, and decided to drop a chamomile tea bag into an empty cup and saucer and filled it with hot water. Marc maneuvered through the crowd, balancing the cup and saucer in his right hand and holding his coffee mug in his left. He sat down next to Rachel who was recounting their adventures that morning at the *Jerusalem Press* and the Haas Promenade to Devorah Eisenstadt. After waiting for Rachel to finish her sentence, he handed her the unordered cup of tea. Rachel's smile, in reaction to the tea, made Devorah feel a little uncomfortable. Devorah shifted in her chair trying not to intrude on the interchange between Marc and Rachel.

"Could everyone please help yourself to a drink if you haven't already done so, and try to find a chair? We'd like to begin." Leah was standing next to the kitchen, straining to make her voice heard above the crowd.

There was a slight decrease in volume as a few people turned to look at Leah and some even took their seats. Most continued their heated conversations, waiting for everyone else to sit down first. Leah spoke again, louder this time. She had become an expert at getting a meeting of Israelis started, more or less on time. "I'm sure many of you are tired after a long day's work, and I know a number have to get home early because of baby-sitters. We have a lot to talk about, so please let's get started." That's enough warning, thought Leah. She sat down in her chair in the circle and began right in with her introductory remarks. She began in a quiet voice that could only be heard if no one else in the room was talking. This was a traditional Talmudic public speaking technique. Immediately people began hushing each other, straining to hear what she was saying. The group by the coffee urn moved to the circle of chairs and sat down. Within five seconds the room was quiet.

"As you all probably know by now, Meir and Shoshana were picked up last night in connection with the shooting incident near the Ma'alot Yair road. Thank God, they released Shoshana after an initial interrogation, but Meir is still in custody. I was out at the settlement today and spoke with Shoshana. I'll brief you on that later." Leah paused to look down at the handwritten notes she had made for herself. Normally she was cool and confident at these meetings. Meir's arrest had flustered her. "What most of you probably don't know is that Marc and Rachel happened to be at the Haas Promenade today during the foiled terror attack. Rachel also woke up this morning to find the tires of her car slashed." A buzz shot through the room as people murmured comments to those sitting in the next chair. "We have information that there have been other foiled attacks the media haven't reported, in addition to the recent dramatic increase in terror attacks against Jews within the Green Line. Then, we have the rash of police brutality at recent demonstrations to contend with, and finally there's the issue of Abu Alim coming to Jerusalem."

Leah looked around the room at the inner circle of *Kol Ha'am* and saw the weight of the issues she had presented show expression on her friends' faces. Many looked overwhelmed and exhausted from the struggle they had been fighting for years. For most of the participants the battle was fought during hours after they had put in a full day's work at their regular jobs, when they should have been with their families. If they hadn't perceived a direct physical threat to their own families, many of them wouldn't have stuck it out. Leah knew this, and in her motherly way she wanted to take away some of their pain. She decided to lighten some of the burden she had thrown at them. "I'm not intending to deal with all of these issues tonight. In fact each one of these issues deserves an organization of it's own. What I want to do however, in light of these recent developments, is to reconfirm our strategy, or revise it. We all recognize that our group can't do it all. We have to choose our battles in the overall struggle. I want to be careful that my own biases don't pull all of us into a direction that isn't best for the group."

Ephraim Cohen, the head of the Psychology Department at Hebrew University was the first to respond to Leah's comments. "Our ability to produce ad hoc demonstrations against government leaders and our phone campaigns are unique and have been effective in embarrassing the government. We have caused them to lose credibility among many of their own supporters. What have you told us tonight that should cause us to re-evaluate our strategy?"

Rachel recognized the famous psychologist. She had even read some of his books. She slowly surveyed the people around the circle to see if there was anyone else she could identify. Rachel was surprised that she actually knew who a few were. Alexander Katsof, one of the original leaders of the Russian refuseniks in the '70s who was currently the editor of a Russian-language daily based in Jerusalem sat two seats away from Rachel. Aaron Silinsky, the millionaire retired American mortgage banker sat to Leah's right. Helene Shapiro, a former head of the San Francisco Jewish Federation sat to Marc's left. The majority of the group consisted of English-speaking immigrants, and the remainder was made up of Israeli academics and business people. Rachel suddenly came to realize this was not a Bnei Akiva youth group planning a noisy demonstration to free Soviet Jewry. These were very serious people. She took a sip of her tea and the tea bag that was still in the cup bumped into her noise. Rachel felt silly, like she didn't fit in with these 'adults.' She couldn't even drink her tea properly, let alone topple a government. As inconspicuously as she could, she lowered the cup and slipped the bag out of the cup and onto the saucer with her right index finger.

Leah took a deep breath, and focused her attention on Professor Cohen, although she was addressing the whole group. "The Jewish human rights issue is rapidly becoming as important, if not more important in the short term, than the security issue."

Rachel slumped farther in her seat feeling a mixture of pride and astonishment. This wasn't an elderly sculptress having tea with her Yemin Moshe neighbors. It was Golda Meir addressing her 'kitchen Cabinet,' the group of inner government ministers who came to the former Prime Minister's home to discuss urgent matters of national security in the early 1970's.

Leah continued her explanation sitting straight in the high-back dining room chair. "It's not just that my son and daughter-in-law have been picked up without charges and that Meir can be held almost indefinitely, but based on what Shoshana told me, they weren't really after them concerning last night's shooting of those Arabs. The proof is, why did they let Shoshana go if they really suspected them? What the government is really afraid of is a new Jewish underground. They think one has already formed, and that's who was responsible for the attack. They suspect Meir is either part of the underground, or at least will be able to give them the names of the members. If that's true, we all could be picked up for questioning."

"There might even be a *Shabak* spy among us right now!" said Alexander Katsof trying to throw in some humor. He couldn't believe that his own Jewish government would ever resort to what he had experienced at the hands of the KGB in the former Soviet Union. Not many people in the room took his statement as joke, especially the native Israelis.

"If they arrest all of us, who would be left to carry out our demonstrations and phone campaigns?" asked Aaron Silinsky sipping at his trademark Sprite with ice. This time everyone laughed.

The laughter had broken open a crack in the dam maintaining the decorum in the room and the comments burst out from all sides of the circle at once.

"They'd never arrest all of us. They idolize democracy. It would make them look stupid and not in control."

"What are you talking about, they outlawed *Kach* and *Kahane Chai*."

"But those organizations were actually involved in incidents with guns. We're just a bunch of professors, business people and grandmothers waving some posters!"

"Most of us are American citizens anyway, it would create an international incident."

"They hate us American immigrants more than they hate the Rumanians."

"That's right. To the Israeli left, anyone raised in the streets of Brooklyn is a suspected Jewish Defense League terrorist unless proven otherwise. Especially if you're orthodox."

"What do you mean we only wave placards? Meir had two guns in his car with him. We're all guilty by association."

"We all have to stop using our personal phones for *Kol Ha'am* business. And certainly don't mention anyone's name."

"Hey, wait a minute. You're all talking like there already is some kind of underground. How do we know there really is one?"

Leah stood up and raised an arm trying to bring the pandemonium under control. In a few moments there only remained two men shouting at each other. When they realized everyone was watching them, they too fell silent. David Moscowitz, the ranking lawyer in the room calmly broke the silence, "I think what Leah is suggesting, is that if we are not prepared with a solid strategy of how to deal with the possibility of a large number of us being arrested, then there is every likelihood it will happen. Perhaps we should take some preventive measures to make sure they don't try it."

"Like what?" asked Aaron Silinsky.

"Well, we've already discussed a few ideas this afternoon. First, we can create a mass demonstration demanding Meir's release. There is a lot of human interest in the story because of the involvement of his wife and kids. Since he has dual Israeli/American citizenship we can play it up into an international media circus. The focus will be to show how the 'Liberal' Israeli government is trampling on civil rights and democratic freedoms. All very 'un-American' indeed. And we all know how 'American' Yossi Shiloni would really like to be. If they feel the same thing will happen any time they make a similar arrest, they won't go near any of us. "

"I like it. What other ideas have you got?" pressed Silinsky. He was still a deal maker at heart and he liked taking charge and hearing all of his options.

"We haven't got the luxury to deal with potential threats," interrupted Helene Shapiro. "I'm very sorry that Meir's in jail, Leah, but sooner or later they'll either determine that he's innocent or guilty. The ballistics testing will determine that. As for us being arrested, I say we should deal with that when the time comes, if it ever does. In the meantime we shouldn't waste mental energy on the problem."

"Helene's right," said a middle-aged man whom Rachel didn't recognize. "The immediate problem facing us today, is Abu Alim's planned visit to Jerusalem on Friday. If all the groups cooperate with the *Merkaz HaMa'avak* on this one, we might be able to do something about it."

"There's every reason to believe that on Friday, while standing on the Temple Mount and speaking to the whole world live via satellite, Abu Alim will call upon the United Nations to internationalize Jerusalem," added Harry Shapiro, Helene's husband. "The Pope is pushing for it, and Yossi Shiloni might give in on it as well if there's enough pressure from the Americans."

"I shudder to think of the consequences of voluntarily giving up the Temple Mount to the Arabs. Not only will we have to deal with a demoralized population, but how will the Almighty treat the Jewish people for abdicating their responsibility to the site of his Holy House that He entrusted to the Jews, and to the Jews only?" The rhetorical question was posed by Moshe Dubinsky, an Old City shopkeeper, and the leader of another action committee. At that point, people started to murmur with each other again. Most, but not all the people present were observant Jews in one form or another, and they began arguing the merits of focusing on the issue of Jerusalem or human rights. In Judaism, both were religious issues.

Marc stood up to gain control of the room. The people fell silent, one-by-one as they began noticing Leah's 'vice-president' waiting to speak. He looked around the circle and gathered his thoughts. He wasn't as learned in Torah as some of the people in the room, and he was younger than most. Yet he was confident about what he was about to say. The issues were life and death. He felt somewhat unworthy of voicing an opinion, not being the head of a family himself. No one's life depended on him personally. Then his eyes caught hold of Rachel's and he felt his heartbeat speed up. Marc cleared his throat to speak.

"We must be careful to be clear about our priorities," he began slowly. "Every issue mentioned here this evening is important, and worthy of our attention, but what are we really fighting for?" Marc paused to let the people think. "The Land of Israel? Human rights? Religious principles? Or are we fighting terrorism and the threat of war?" Marc looked at the men and women sitting around the circle. Some had bowed their heads, others were staring intently at him, grateful at being giving the opportunity to ask themselves these questions.

Marc slipped his hands in his blazer pockets and looked down at his shoes. "Sometimes I'm so busy phoning, organizing and demonstrating that I forget there must be an enemy out there somewhere who we're fighting. Is it the Palestinians or the whole Arab world? Perhaps it's just the Islamic fundamentalists. When I look at Leah's face and imagine Meir sitting innocently in jail, I think that perhaps the enemy is our own government. Bolshevism? And what is it that would allow a Jewish Prime Minister to consider giving up the Temple Mount to terrorists? Is he the enemy, or is the enemy ignorance of Judaism and Jewish values?"

As he spoke he looked around at the people who had grown silent and sat expectantly waiting for him to answer his own questions. Marc swallowed, as he tried to sort through the issues himself. He felt that he was again being thrown over a cliff along with his whole country. What was the message? What was the lesson?

Rachel thought about Marc's questions, and images flashed through her head —The terrorist gripping his own hand who escaped after murdering Ari. Abu Alim's face on the television screen. The policeman who had shoved and threatened her. Meir and Shoshana being dragged out of their home in the middle of the night; The woman in the short-cropped hair in the black tee shirt who had called her a Nazi. Her head began to spin. Who was the enemy? Whose opinion was she trying to change? Rachel was confused, but looking at Marc she knew that she wanted him to be the one to help her make sense of this nightmare.

Thirty Three

Amiram Barr got out of bed after a sleepless night. His tossing and turning had come to no avail so he gave up and headed for the shower hoping it would clear his head enough to face the day. Standing in his bathrobe he gazed into the bathroom mirror as if sizing up the man in the reflection. He found it hard looking at himself in the face since he heard Rachel Stein was back in Israel. Amiram shook his head partially in an attempt to wake himself up, and partially in an attempt to shake out the secret that had haunted his sleep the whole last week. It was a secret that not even Udi and Yigal were aware of, that he had kept to himself since Ari's death.

Amiram stroked the sides of his face, measuring his morning stubble and reached for the black Philips cordless shaver resting on its caddie on the wall. He preferred to shave with the electric shaver before his shower. The steamy hot water was great for preparing a beard for a regular razor, but his dry skin, stripped of its natural oils by the shower, needed electric shaving lotion to keep the shaver from pulling at his skin. Amiram hated the scent of the lotion. Besides it made him noticeable in a crowd, and that was taboo for a *Shabak* agent.

As he sized up his face, planning his course of attack with the Philip's triple-heads, his image dissolved into that of another agent, at another time and another place.

Ari Tal stood at the sink of their room in the Marina Hotel in Eilat. He was wearing the white crew-necked T- shirt and blue sweat pants he had slept in. A Toronto Blue Jays baseball cap perched backwards on his head. The Jays had won the World Series that year, and he had picked one up at a gift shop on Dizengoff Street in Tel-Aviv. He liked the colors. The sky blue matched his sweat pants, and it suited his cover as an American tourist. Yigal oftened used Ari when an "American" was needed on an assignment because English was his mother tongue.

"Hurry up, Ari, I need the shower," called out Amiram, appearing in the bathroom doorway. Amiram smiled at his partner's Blue Jay's cap. He admired Ari's ingenuity at always being able to find some kind of discreet headcovering to wear in place of his kipah.

"I'll be finished in a minute," said Ari running the electric shaver in circles over his smooth olive skin.

Amiram leaned on the doorpost and folded his arms across his chest watching his friend. "Why do you use an electric shaver, I thought they were for married men, and grandfathers with shakey hands. We Shabak *agents have to keep up our Macho image you know, even amongst ourselves."*

Ari glanced at Amiram in the reflection of the mirror while massaging his neck with the shaver. "First of all, it's much faster than a blade and shaving cream, saving a Shabak *agent precious time.*

Second, there's no worry about nicks, saving a Shabak agent precious blood."

Amiram smiled. He liked his partner's dry sense of humor.

"And thirdly, it saves an observant Shabak agent from transgressing Jewish Law," said Ari with a flourish, finishing the job and snapping off the shaver. He rinsed his hands and face, grabbed a face towel from the chrome rack and turned to face Amiram. "You can have the shower, I'm done." Ari tweeked Amiram's cheek as he squeezed past him in the doorway and headed into the room.

Amiram's puzzled gaze followed Ari into the hotel room. "What do you mean transgressing Jewish Law?"

"The Torah forbids us from shaving the 'corners of our face.' It was a pagan custom to shave the face with a blade. They even cut themselves as part of cult rituals," explained Ari, toweling himself dry. "The Torah forbids us from following the customs of idolaters. This is one of them. Some are very strict about it and grow their sidelocks very long."

"If you're so religious, how come you don't keep the law and have long curly sidelocks?" challenged Amiram.

"I do keep the law. The prohibition is not to touch a 'knife' to your face. That includes razor blades. Scissors are permitted. The technology used by my Philips shaver is 'scissor like' and therefore it's kosher. The blades don't come in contact with the skin. Some electric shavers use a dfferent action and therefore can't be used."

"*Hmmm...,*" *said Amiram as he picked up his can of shaving cream. As a* Shabak *agent he appreciated the many fine details of Jewish law. The Talmudic fences around the law that helped prevent a major Torah transgression were like many of rules in the* Shabak *handbook. 'When exiting a building, always look to the left, right and at any parked vehicles on both sides of the street.' The rules to ensure an agent wasn't being followed could fill a book on their own. As an agent, Amiram looked at those regulations not as a nuisance, but as tools that allowed him to live life at the edge without the fear of taking unecessary risks that could lead to self destruction. That was part of the thrill of being in* Shabak. *Ari had shown him that that what was Torah law was really about as well. It gave one the ability to live life to it's maximum without going over the edge. But that required laws and details in all areas; eating, working, sexual relationships, and yes, even shaving.*

Amiram enjoyed learning about Jewish topics with Ari. It helped fill in the gaps in his own Jewish education that he lacked, growing up in the secular Israeli school system. He never felt threatened or judged. Ari always had a way of making things seem rational. Amiram liked to insist that Ari was 'different' than those other ultra-orthodox Jews, but Ari would always protest claiming he observed the same laws as every observant Jew. It was just the externals which might seem different. He had more in common with the black-hatted Jews of Mea She'arim than he did with the Shabak *agent he was sharing a hotel bathroom with.*

"Using an electric razor is an easy mitzvah and it counts in your favor in the World to Come, just in case there's a resting place for Shabak agents in the sky. You have to shave anyway, and nobody has to know you're doing it. It's not like giving up shrimp or staying away from pubs on Friday night."

Amiram hefted the Philips shaver that he had received as a Chanukah present from Ari right after their assignment in Eilat that year. Because it was a gift, he didn't have to explain to anyone why he had switched from blades to electric. Amiram had given Ari a Yankee's baseball cap for his collection that same Chanukah.

As he switched on the shaver, the buzz startled him, and he shut the bathroom door not wanting the noise to awaken his wife and two sons so early in the morning. The thought of his wife and sons, contrasted with the image of Ari's brutal death and Rachel's return made him take a deep breath and let out a sigh. A feeling of guilt overwhelmed him as he thought about his friend who never had the opportunity to know what it was like to be married or give his giggling son a shoulder ride. He swiped the shaver across his face with a few quick strokes and left the bathroom giving up on the shower. It wouldn't help wash away the dirtiness he felt inside anyway. That cleansing would only come through action. He quickly dressed and left the apartment, ignoring the red light on the coffee-maker signaling the brew was ready.

This early in the morning there was no traffic in the streets except for delivery vehicles and the few souls who began work early. Amiram loved Jerusalem at this time of day. The black night sky was just starting to show a hint of blue. Soon the first glimpse of sunlight would cast a golden glow on the pinkish Jerusalem stone that faced all the buildings in the city. He pressed the button on the handrest to lower the window and breathed in the moisture of the autumn air. Amiram negotiated the familiar streets and drove to his office on 'autopilot' leaving him with his thoughts and clenched fists on the steering wheel. There had to be a way to fix things without endangering himself. He thought about his sleeping wife and sons.

The security guard gave a sleepy nod of acknowledgment as the familiar white Ford Sierra drove up to the gate of *Shabak* Jerusalem headquarters. Amiram pulled into his designated parking spot and got out of the car without locking it. No strangers could be found in the secure compound who might steal or sabotage his vehicle. He took the front steps two at a time and nodded hello to the guard at the front door who buzzed him into the building. He strode quickly to his office, not too certain why he was in such a hurry.

Amiram sat down in his armchair and pressed his weight back against the spring controlling the tension in the chair. The blinking light on the fax machine he shared with Udi caught his attention indicating that one or more faxes came in during the night. He got up, walked to the machine and picked up the few sheets of paper from the 'in tray.' The first one was only a few sentences in a handwritten scribble for Udi from his informant Devorah Eisenstadt. Amiram scanned the lines, crumpled the page and stuffed it in his pocket. He hurried out of the room and back out of the building. He had some business to take care of before he would show the fax to his partner.

Thirty Four

The ABC anchorman read the headlines of the eleven o'clock evening news summary. The lead topics were domestic American affairs and some unrest in South Africa. Jibril Abu Alim grunted and punched the button for the NBC report. He hated it when there was no mention of the State of Palestine on the foreign news reports. Abu Alim got up early every day to watch the late night east-coast American news reports. There was a six hour time-zone difference between Jericho and New York City. Abu Alim thrived on being the center of attention and if there was no mention of him on the news programs he felt as if he wasted his time getting up early. He enjoyed the thrill of watching the news live. It was sort of like holding a lottery ticket and watching the television host picking out the ping pong balls with the winning numbers. Every time they mentioned his name, 'Abu Alim' on television, he felt the thrill of victory.

The Americans weren't interested in the Palestinian President's sense of self importance tonight, and the hatred welled up in Abu Alim's face as he surfed through the channels. His visit to Jerusalem was not only of international importance, it would be an historic event. Not just for his own people but for the world. How could these American infidels ignore him?

There was a sharp knock at the door, and the visitor waited to be invited inside. It was Rajai Ahmed, the Minister of Defense. The uniformed general entered the room and saluted Abu Alim who, as the President, was also the supreme commander of the Palestine Defense Forces. "Mr. President," he said slowly, "There has been another drive-by shooting in the occupied territories." Ahmed hated using the word 'Israel.' "A Palestinian has been seriously wounded. He has been evacuated to a Zionist hospital."

Abu Alim hit the mute button on his remote control. "Where was the attack." He didn't seem surprised.

"Near Bethlehem. A few minutes ago. When Palestinian day laborers were driving to Jerusalem. Our people have started rioting in Bethlehem." Ahmed didn't make the artificial distinction between Arabs living in Palestine, the occupied territories, Israel or even Jordan and Syria. They were all 'our people' to him, which was also consistent with Palestinian foreign policy.

Abu Alim reached for his small cup of Turkish coffee resting on a large circular brass tray on his desk next to an intricately designed brass coffee pitcher. The traditional Arab coffee set seemed out of place in the President's westernized high-tech office. He took a sip of the sweet mixture, being careful not to stir up the sludge that had settled to the bottom of the cup. "Who is the man who was injured?"

"A twenty-two-year-old Christian from Bethlehem."

A faint smile, unnoticed by Ahmed crossed Abu Alim's lips as he sipped the coffee. "Were there any witnesses?"

"No, your Excellency, although we have already contacted the Zionist Foreign Minister demanding an investigation."

"Good," said Abu Alim perfunctorily. "Keep me posted if there are any further developments. You may go."

Rajai Ahmed assumed that Abu Alim's 'good' was a compliment on his quick action in contacting the Zionists and demanding an investigation. He turned and left the office with a spring in his gait.

Abu Alim looked up at the set of ten round clocks hanging on the wall above the television monitors, each with the name of a major world capital written below it. He sighed in frustration as he realized it was too early to call Rome. The Pontiff did not like to be disturbed by phone calls before 8:00 a.m. That call would have to wait a few hours. But now that it was a Christian who had been shot, Abu Alim was certain the Pope would make an appeal to the Israeli Prime Minister to let him visit Jerusalem. After all, the Holy City was holy to the three major world religions. The Pope would not allow the Jews to prevent a Moslem from praying at *Al Aksa*.

Abu Alim smiled a mischievous boyish smile as he looked at the Washington DC clock. He reached for the red phone on his desk next to the green one. Eleven fifteen in the evening was not too late to call his friend the President of the United States. As a good Protestant he certainly would agree to Abu Alim's request to make a phone call on his behalf to Yossi Shiloni.

Thirty Five

Rachel came out of the *Makolet* carrying a plastic bag full of fresh rolls still warm from the delivery truck. In another bag she had cottage cheese and fruit yogurts. A copy of the *Jerusalem Press* was tucked under her arm. Her handbag bumped against her hip as she hurried home down the sidewalk. She wanted to have everything ready before Marc arrived. They had arranged the previous evening for him to stop by at seven for breakfast, and they would both continue on to the *Jerusalem Press* to pick up the photographs after arranging for her car to be repaired.

Rachel's thoughts were on making sure everything would be perfect for breakfast. The coffee was brewing in her apartment, and the sliced oranges were on the counter warming up from the chill of the refrigerator. The flavor of the juice is always more fruity when it's not so cold. Rachel was so engrossed in her plans, she didn't notice the car that had been following her from the *Makolet* pull up to the curb behind her. The driver slid across the bench seat and got out of the passenger side of the car leaving the door open. Just at that moment, the newspaper slipped against the shiny leather of Rachel's bag and fell to the sidewalk. She squatted down to pick up the paper.

Without warning, she felt a large hand grab her arm. She began to scream but another hand clamped down on her mouth silencing her. Rachel was so surprised that her body didn't know in which direction to struggle. Before she could gather her wits, her attacker began pulling her backwards toward the street. The plastic bags fell from her hands and her handbag slipped from under her arm to the asphalt. 'My gun!' she thought to herself.

Her assailant backed himself into the open passenger door and yanked Rachel in behind him. He slid backwards along the bench seat dragging her farther into the car until her feet cleared the doorway. With his right hand firmly grasped to her mouth, forcing her look out the open door-way, he leaned forward around her and slammed the door shut with his left hand. At this hour of the morning, there were no witnesses to Rachel's abduction.

Rachel still hadn't been able to see her assailant. As she struggled against the power of the man sitting beside her, she realized she was no match for his strength. Some self-defense advice that Ari had given her years ago leapt into her head. If you can't beat him, go limp and save your strength. It will put the attacker off balance, and that might give you some time to escape, or poke his eyes or smash the heel of a hand to the underside of his nose. As soon as she relaxed her body, she calmed down enough to realize what to do next. Rachel spoke quietly and confidently, but her words were unintelligible, muffled by the large hand pressed against her lips.

"I'm not going to hurt you," said a deep voice in English. "Don't scream or you'll attract attention. I just want to talk to you for a few minutes." Rachel's quiet murmuring made him confident that if he released his hand, she wouldn't scream. "Go ahead, what are you trying to say?" he said gently pulling his hand from her mouth.

"Shema Yisrael, HaShem Elokeinu, HaShem Echad." Hearing her own words out loud, made Rachel feel even calmer. 'Hear O Israel, the Lord, Our God, the Lord is One.' It was the testament of Monotheism that the Jewish People had brought to humanity. The phrase at the cornerstone of Judaism. In prayers each day, morning and night, and again at bedtime, Jews all over the world uttered the verse, accepting upon themselves the Sovereignty of the Almighty, and a commitment to dedicating their lives to bringing the world to an understanding of the Oneness of God. It was the wish of every traditional Jew to die with these words on his lips. As Rachel quietly repeated the phrase, she imagined her grandfather proudly saying those words as he was forced into a gas chamber. Her trust was implicit. She was ready to join her grandfather if God deemed it time.

Rachel's attacker was stunned by her recital of the *'Shema.'* Even though he was secular, he understood it's significance. Rachel felt her life was in imminent danger. A shiver ran up his spine. "I said I wasn't going to hurt you!" he protested. "I'm a friend of Ari's!"

Rachel stiffened at the mention of Ari's name. Who was this man who knew Ari? And if he was a friend, why didn't he just telephone, or walk up to her and introduce himself on the sidewalk?

"I don't want you to look at me. For both of our sakes. And I can't tell you who I am. But I'm here to help you. I owe it to Ari. Do you agree not to turn around?" He had both of his hands pressed firmly against her temples, focusing her gaze out the passenger window.

If he really was out to harm her, he never would have let her arms free. Rachel could imagine herself swinging her right hand around and catching the man under the nose in one swift motion. Ari had always told her to paint a picture of her attack in her mind. Your body responded to mental images. This man knew what he was doing. He was letting down his guard on purpose, to show Rachel he wasn't an enemy. Besides, if he really intended to harm her, he wouldn't have abducted her on a main street, especially without a driver to help with the getaway. She silently nodded her head indicating she would agree to his terms.

"The *Shabak* is searching for a Jewish underground. That is the real reason why Meir Tal was picked up. Your relationship to him and his family makes you a suspect. You may be picked up for questioning. The fact that you have been snooping around the *Jerusalem Press* for photographs of Abu Alim doesn't help matters any."

Rachel gulped hard weighing the man's words. Why was he telling her this? Did he expect her to give him information? Confirm or deny Meir's involvement in an underground? She decided to remain silent.

"I don't think you or Meir are involved in this. But I suggest you be careful this next week. You are being watched. I believe I know who is behind the recent terror attacks, but I need some evidence to prove it. That will take some time which we have precious little of. In the meantime I'll try to protect you." The man put his left hand over Rachel's eyes and reached past her to open the passenger door with his right hand. "Go now, but don't turn around until you count to ten. You won't turn to a pillar of salt, but it's very important for your sake, and mine, that you not to be able to identify me in case things go wrong."

Rachel got out of the car and heard the door slam behind her. The engine roared to life and the car screeched off. Rachel stood like a pillar of salt in the middle of the sidewalk for ten seconds and then burst into tears.

Thirty Six

Marc Goodman paced angrily in front of Rachel's apartment building. He buzzed her apartment for the third time and still no answer. She couldn't be sleeping. He had spoken to her just half an hour ago on the telephone. Where could she be? Marc wasn't angry with Rachel, but with what he had discovered a few moments before.

He had arrived early and decided to check Rachel's car in the parking lot. The Mitsubishi looked pathetically lifeless with its four flat tires. He had decided to inspect it a little more closely to make sure there wasn't any other damage since they had discovered the slashing. This was the first time in the past frantic twenty four hours that they had time to call the towing company. 'It seems like a week, not a day, since we were out here last in the parking lot,' Marc mumbled to himself.

As he had rounded the back of the car to inspect it from the other side, he noticed the trunk was open. He lifted the lid to see if anything had been stolen. The lock was broken, but inside he found a jack, a toolbox and a plastic bag with some shoes waiting to be taken to a shoemaker. Everything seemed in order. Why would anyone want to break into Rachel's trunk? As he continued his survey of the car he peered into the rear passenger window and noticed an official look-ing yellow sheet of paper lying on the back seat. He tried the handle and the door opened. Curious, he thought. They had locked the car after showing it to the police.

Marc then had reached into the car to retrieve the yel-low form. He noticed the official Police emblem at the top of the page. He scanned down the page at the scrawled hand-written report on the body of the form. Reading scrawled Hebrew was twice as difficult as English, but Marc managed to make out the gist of the message. The car had seemed suspicious, perhaps a car bomb. Therefore they had no choice but to break the trunk lock and force their way into the car to inspect it.

The blood rushed to Marc's face as he clenched the page in his fist. Those incompetent idiots! Why didn't they just check the license plates? The registration address was the same building the car was parked outside of! Marc un-crumbled the sheet to check the time of the report. Sunday evening 11:00 p.m. The very same police had inspected this car for the tire slashing fourteen hours before they came back to break into it. How could one hand not know what the other was doing? Unless...

Marc had stuffed the report into his pocket and rushed to the front door of Rachel's building. A sense of dread and fear filled his chest. He had buzzed, and buzzed, and buzzed. Still no answer. He was pacing back and forth in front of the building when he noticed Rachel's figure hurrying up the sidewalk crying.

Marc's mixed emotions of rage and horror melted into concern for Rachel. "What's wrong?" he asked.

"Inside," she sobbed, fumbling for her keys in her handbag. She fished them out and unlocked the door. They walked up the single flight of steps that led to her apartment.

She unlocked that door. Marc walked in behind her and turned to close the door. He left it slightly ajar according to Jewish law. It was a safeguard proscribed by the Talmud. A single man and woman shouldn't be in a locked room together alone. The thought that someone could walk into the room at any moment was assumed to be enough to keep a couple from doing anything inappropriate. Marc appreciated the wisdom of the Talmud. He felt particularly vulnerable around crying women.

Marc walked toward Rachel who was fussing with the yogurts in the plastic bag. "So tell me what happened? Are you all right?"

"A man just..." Rachel searched for exactly the right word to describe what had just happened, yet not give Marc the wrong impression. She couldn't think of any, so she stopped and began again. "I was coming out of the *Makolet* with breakfast when suddenly I felt someone grab my arm. Then he put a hand over my mouth and dragged me into his car." Rachel looked up at Marc and saw the shock in his eyes. She continued before he had time to react. "I didn't get a chance to see what he looked like, but he wasn't a rapist or a terrorist. He just wanted to talk to me."

"That's an awfully unorthodox way to strike up a conversation with a strange woman," said Marc impatiently.

"Well, ... you're right. But, it seems he wasn't such a stranger. He said he was a friend of Ari's." Rachel shuddered in confusion, rethinking how strange it was for a friend of Ari's to approach her that way. She walked to the counter and poured a coffee for Marc and herself from the coffee-maker that had been waiting for them to arrive.

"What did he say?" asked Marc, also a little confused.

"He told me the *Shabak* are searching for a Jewish underground, and that's the real reason why Meir was picked up. He said they suspect me also, as well as people who know Meir." She looked at Marc with concern in her eyes. Rachel realized his activities with *Kol Ha'am* and his personal wealth made him more of a suspect than she. That last thing she wanted was for Marc to be in jail too.

"That's it?" asked Marc.

"He also warned me to stop snooping around the *Jerusalem Press*. He said he thought he knew who was committing the terror attacks, and didn't believe I was involved, although he warned me to be careful. He said we are being watched, and that he would try to protect me." Rachel had stopped crying and her heartbeat was back to normal. By recounting her story, she realized her attacker wasn't really anyone to be afraid of. But why such cloak and dagger behavior?

"It sounds like he was a *Shabak* agent," said Marc dryly.

"What should we do?" asked Rachel, wanting Marc to take away the confusion.

Marc walked over to the telephone table beside the front door and pulled open the Yellow page section of the phone book. He dialed the number of the tow truck company with the biggest advertisement assuming they would be able to arrive the quickest. After replacing the telephone hand set he turned to face Rachel with a smile. "Do you still have that card with the phone numbers that the young policeman gave to you in the hospital?"

"Sure, I think so," said Rachel. She unzipped her purse, poked around the bottom of the bag and found the card. She handed it to Marc asking, "What do you want this for?"

"It has the name and number of the police officer that shoved you at the demonstration. The young cop's boss," he said as he dialed the number on the card. "*Shalom,* Sergeant Alon please." Marc looked up at Rachel as he waited for the secretary to transfer the call. Marc continued when a deep voice picked up the phone at the other end, "I represent Rachel Stein. She was injured at the demonstration outside the Renaissance Hotel on Saturday night. I just wanted to let you know personally, that we have no intention of filing charges."

The sergeant didn't seem surprised by Marc's call. He thanked Marc, and hung up without giving Marc a chance to respond.

As Marc put down the phone, Rachel asked, "What was that all about?"

Marc got up from the seat beside the phone table and walked toward Rachel. He wanted to tell her, but then again, his concern for her helped him hold his tongue. No, it was better not to burden her with the fact that her car had probably been broken into by the police. He would take care of the damage with a phone call to the garage that would be repairing the slashed tires. Marc also decided it was better not to share with her his suspicions of who had slashed her tires. If the Sergeant, or one of his underlings had done it for him, in order to intimidate her into not pressing charges, this phone call should have taken care of it. He looked into Rachel's eyes and with a smile said, "We have to pick our battles. We have enough real enemies. There's no need to fight the police. I just wanted to tie up a loose end."

The puzzled look on Rachel's face gave Marc the impression that she wasn't really convinced, so he decided to change the subject. "Come, let's have some of this delicious looking yogurt and coffee. The tow truck will be here any minute, and I want to take you to meet someone before we go to the *Press* to pick up the pictures."

Thirty Seven

The doorbell snapped Leah Tal out of her day dream. She was thinking about a summer long ago in upstate New York, when she and her husband Irving had taken their small sons to visit her parents at their summer cottage. Those were carefree days, between 1967 and 1973. Their two little *Sabras* splashing in the lake were the talk of the bungalow colony. To be Israeli meant to be a hero. She used to love watching the adults sit in rapt attention as Irving recounted around the campfire, tales of life in Israel. How she wished he was here now.

The abrupt sound of the doorbell reminded her of the harshness of life without Irving and Ari. And now Meir was in jail. She slowly got up from the chair at the dining room table, and absently put down the mug of coffee she had forgotten that she had poured for herself. She looked through the peephole and was surprised to see David Moscowitz, *Kol Ha'am's* unofficial legal counsel pressing the bell.

"David, what are you doing here so early?" she said, opening the door.

Moscowitz plodded into the room, almost dragging his black attaché case that Israelis liked to call a *'tik James*

Bond.' His mop of unkempt gray hair and sluggishness made him look older than his fifty nine years. He smiled an exhausted smile at Leah, and plunked his briefcase down on the dining room table. "Early?" he complained, "I've been up since five o'clock. I've already been halfway across the country and back this morning. How about a cup of coffee?"

Leah hurried to the kitchen to fetch him a cup and when she returned, he was fussing with some papers in his briefcase that lay propped open on the table. "So where have you been?" she asked.

"Well, ever since Meir was picked up on *Motzai Shabbat*, I haven't been able to sleep so well. Since I was awake anyway, I decided to do something constructive instead of stewing in bed. I drove down to the army base near Ma'alot Yair to see what I could do about getting him out of there."

Leah looked at him hopefully, waiting for him to continue.

"The new military laws for the territories say they can keep him under detention for two weeks, but I tried to persuade them to let him out after forty eight hours which is the law inside Israel. After all, he's an Israeli citizen." Moscowitz reached for the plastic yellow container shaped like an oversized mushroom sitting on a wooden tray in the middle of the table. He snapped off the lid and tapped a small white tablet of artificial sweetener into the palm of his hand and then promptly dropped it into his mug. "I threatened to file a petition in the Supreme Court for the army to show cause why Meir should be kept longer than that without any charges laid against him. They laughed at me. There have been numerous precedents of the Supreme Court not wanting to mix in to the Military Court's territory. Do you think we should file anyway?" he asked.

"Do you think there's any chance it might shorten his stay?" asked Leah, responding to his question with a question.

"Not really, it's probably a waste of the filing fee," he said glumly. It was understood that he would do the legal work of preparing the papers for free as part of his volunteer work for *Kol Ha'am.* "I was thinking we might send a fax to the Prime Minister, threatening to go to the US Ambassador in Israel for assistance, and have our friends in AIPAC bring up the issue with the White House that it's an American Citizen being held under detention without cause."

Leah shook her head slowly back and forth, indicating her disapproval of the idea. "You'll have to ask Meir about that, but I'm against it. It's an embarrassment to have to run to the Americans to help us against the Israeli government. We have to keep this battle within the 'Jewish' family." She paused for a moment, and then added, "As much as I hate the idea of Meir being held behind bars, his life isn't in danger. If it was, I'd even go to Jericho and beg Abu Alim for help."

Moscowitz took a sip of the freshly brewed coffee anticipating the effect of the caffeine to perk him up. He was tired. Instead, the loud ringing of the cordless phone resting on the table in front of him gave him a surprise jolt.

Leah reached forward to pick up the phone and switched it to 'on.' *"Hallo?"* she said, using the popular Israeli pronunciation of the English greeting. *"Ken, medaberet,"* said Leah acknowledging to the caller that he was speaking to the person he was looking for. Moscowitz listened to Leah's one-word Hebrew responses, curious to know who the caller was. Almost everyone who called her were English speakers, and the conversation had gone on too long for it to be a wrong number.

"Rak rega," she told the caller to wait a moment, and put her palm over the mouthpiece. "It's Aryeh Levi, the

Chief of Police. My Hebrew isn't so good, but he seems to be saying the police are conducting a major investigation, and they'd like to invite me to the Russian compound for a conversation. They think I might be able to help them."

The rush of adrenaline, resulting from his anger, woke Moscowitz up better than twenty cups of coffee could. "Here let me take that," he said, "I can't believe they think we're that naive. It's obvious they really want to interrogate *you,* but they don't have enough evidence to issue a warrant. And why is he making you break your teeth on the Hebrew? He speaks English fluently."

Leah passed the phone to Moscowitz who sat up straight in his chair and switched to lawyer mode. He spoke crisply into the phone in English. Israelis always went on the defensive when spoken to in English. It made it easy to get the upper hand in negotiations, thought Moscowitz as he chose his words carefully to intimidate the Police Chief. "This is David Moscowitz, Mrs. Tal's attorney speaking. She is a very busy woman, and therefore, unless you have a warrant for her arrest, she won't be joining you for any conversations. Thank you for calling." Moscowitz flicked off the phone before the Chief of Police could respond.

Aryeh Levi hadn't expected a lawyer to be at Leah Tal's house at 8:30 in the morning. He thought that by calling himself, instead of assigning an officer, he could persuade the Tal woman to come down for the investigation. He felt bad he wouldn't be able to so easily return the favor to his friend Yigal Ramon this time.

Thirty Eight

Marc backed the Volvo into the small space at the curb left by the car that had pulled away just as they had arrived in the Jewish Quarter of the Old City of Jerusalem. It was a tight squeeze, and at times like these Marc wished he had chosen a smaller Japanese car over his Swedish behemoth. The public parking lot was full. It was almost impossible to find a parking place at this time of day on Monday. It was a day the Torah was read during the morning services, and therefore a day when many families chose to celebrate the *Bar Mitzvah* of their son at the Western Wall.

Rachel got out of the car and took in the breathtaking view. The cool morning autumn air lifted the haze over the Jordan Valley just to the East, providing a rare crystal-clear vista of the Moab mountains rising on the other side of the Jordan River. It was from those mountains that Moses gazed at the Promised Land he was destined never to enter. He had surveyed the land that the Children of Israel would divide amongst the tribes under the leadership of Joshua. It was from there that Joshua led the entry into the Land. God's promise to His children was first fulfilled with the miraculous taking of Jericho.

Rachel instinctively stretched up on her toes to catch a glimpse of the ancient city, even though it was impossible from this vantage point. Jericho lay only twenty minutes away by car, but it was hidden by the brown barren foothills of the Judean desert stretching down into the valley before her. The city was also blocked by the Palestinian border somewhere between the Old City walls and Jericho. 'How could we have given this Land away to our enemies, after all the miracles God performed throughout history in order to give it to us?' The question haunted Rachel. She also wondered how much of the view in front of her lay inside the borders of the new State of Palestine. The breakfast yogurt churned in her stomach.

To Rachel's left, just on the other side of the Old City walls, standing testimony to over three thousand years of Jewish history in Jerusalem, was the Mount of Olives. The myriads of tombstones on the hill, marking the resting places of Prophets, Sages and simple Jews, made the mountain look almost white. The dates on the monuments reflected an unbroken Jewish presence in the area except for the nineteen year period between 1948 and 1967 when east Jerusalem was under Jordanian occupation. During that short time, after the Jordanians had killed or exiled all of the Jews under their rule, they embarked on a systematic destruction of synagogues in the Old City of Jerusalem and a desecration of the graves on the Mount of Olives. In the early sixties, they bulldozed the top of the cemetery to build a hotel, some broken tombstones were used in the construction of the building, a gruesome fact unknown to most visitors to the hotel.

"Come on, let's go! We can go sightseeing later," said Marc locking the driver's door. Rachel turned and they walked past the guard at the entrance to the Jewish Quarter residents' parking lot. Opposite them stood the four restored Sephardic Synagogues. The largest, the Synagogue of Rabbi Yochanan ben Zakai, was from the period of the destruction of the Second Temple, almost two thousand years ago. Here the Sage of the Mishna taught his students. The pinkish Jerusalem stone used to restore the ancient structure sparkling in the morning sunlight gave Rachel reason to hope. Her People had prevailed thus far, and would continue to endure until they had fulfilled their mission in history.

"This way," said Marc, indicating to Rachel to turn right into an arched passageway before they reached the synagogues. The passage narrowed like a funnel and near it's exit they had to squeeze past some residents walking in the opposite direction to the parking lot. Except for the ring road they had entered by, the Old City streets were closed to traffic except for morning commercial deliveries and disabled residents and tourists. Exiting the 'tunnel,' Marc made a quick left and jogged right under an archway into a large square. They crossed the square diagonally past some *kippah*-clad boys laughing and playing soccer. Rachel noticed a Hebrew inscription engraved on a stone plaque mounted in a wall to the left. It was a quotation from the Prophet Zechariah promising that at the end of the long exile, "... the city will be filled with boys and girls playing in the streets." Rachel's heart warmed as she realized that just as this prophecy had come true, so would others promising a brighter future.

They passed an olive tree at the corner of the square and slipped through another archway leading to a small courtyard bordered by the doorways of some residential apartments. The quiet enclosure was decorated with large flower boxes filled with pink and red geraniums providing a dazzling contrast to the pleasant monotony of the Jerusalem stone. Marc zigzagged through a passageway at the opposite end of the courtyard, and Rachel hurried to keep up. She had lost her sense of direction meandering through the narrow stone-lined 'streets' and passages of the Old City. "You have to be half rodent to find your way through this maze," she commented with a laugh.

"It's not so bad when you get used to it. Sort of like driving a bicycle. After a while you just 'home in' from point 'A' to 'B.' But don't ask me any of the street names," he called out to Rachel who was behind him admiring the geraniums. "Hurry up, we're already late," he said, making a circular motion with his hands encouraging her to catch up to him.

In another minute they mounted a staircase and entered a door that looked to Rachel like the entrance to a private apartment. Inside, Rachel was surprised to see a secretary with a phone to her ear, sitting behind a worn brown melamine desk. Marc waited for the secretary to transfer the incoming call before introducing himself.

The secretary smiled, "Yes, Rabbi Steinberg has been expecting you. Go right in."

Thirty Nine

Monday, 9:05 a.m.

Rabbi Yaakov Steinberg sprang from his chair and came around his desk to give Marc a big hug. *"Tzaddik! What brings you into my office so early in the morning? You're usually in the *Beis Midrash* learning at this time of day, aren't you?"* The Rabbi released Marc from his grip, looked at Rachel and raised his eyebrows animatedly, "This young fellow will be a Rabbi before you know it, he's already teaching an introductory class in philosophy." Rabbi Steinberg poked his thick index finger into Marc's belly and sealed his prediction with a wink. "Come my children, please have a seat."

Rachel was at once relaxed and awestruck. She was surprised by how big Rabbi Steinberg was. She had been expecting a smaller, slighter man. The spring in his gait made him seem much younger than she had imagined as well. His strong Brooklyn-accented English reminded her of her Uncle Harry. Rachel sank into a brown upholstered office armchair next to Marc.

"*Rosh Yeshiva*, this is my friend Rachel Stein. She and I are working together at *Kol Ha'am*. Rachel just arrived from Toronto last week." Marc spoke to Rabbi Steinberg in the third person, addressing him as the head of the Yeshiva. Rachel was usually intimidated by authority figures, especially great rabbis. Yet Rabbi Steinberg made her feel comfortable, like a little girl being taken care of. So much so, that the formal address seemed a bit incongruous.

"*Brucha HaBa'ah*, welcome to Jerusalem!" said the Rabbi with a huge smile that melted any last traces of discomfort that Rachel had brought with her into the room. He leaned forward on his desk and said quietly, "You must be a pretty tough lady to come to Israel at a time like this. Most Jews are staying away in droves. Either that, or you really have a lot of trust in the Almighty."

Rachel flushed at becoming the center of attention. She had expected the conversation to take place between the Rabbi and Marc. Rachel considered Rabbi Steinberg cautiously, trying to anticipate how she was expected to respond. She glanced at Marc for a hint, but none was forthcoming. She then leaned forward and spoke quietly, reflecting Rabbi Steinberg's tone. "I like to think I have a bit of both — trust and toughness."

Rabbi Steinberg leaned back in his seat, "Hmmm. Very good." He nodded his approval. Rachel felt her face getting warmer.

Marc jumped to Rachel's rescue by changing the subject. "We've come to speak with the *Rosh Yeshiva* to get his advice in a number of crucial areas," said Marc solemnly as if calling a court of law to order. "The first issue has to do with the general direction *Kol Ha'am* should be taking."

Rabbi Steinberg nodded and began listening attentively to every word Marc was saying. If his advice was being requested, it was his duty was not only to take in the information in Marc's words, but in his tone, inflection and body language as well.

Mare continued deliberately. "There are three areas in which we can proceed with our struggle; the government violations of human rights, the deteriorating security situation, and preventing the Palestinians from making anymore political gains." Marc looked at Rabbi Steinberg's eyes that had narrowed and were focused intently on him. Long ago Marc had learned that meant the Rabbi wanted concrete examples. He much preferred tangible problems to general abstract ideas. Marc cleared his throat, which provided him with a moment to choose his cases. "First, Meir Tal has been arrested in connection with the drive-by killing of those Palestinians last *Motzei Shabbat*. We have every indication that the authorities will begin picking up many more innocent people shortly and hold them indefinitely for questioning unless something is done to pre-empt the government's plans to do so."

Marc paused to give time for Rabbi Steinberg to consider the problem. Sometimes Marc would have to hold back the urge to ask the Rabbi what thinking processes he was going through when he sat in quiet thought. After receiving a nod from the Rosh Yeshiva indicating he was ready, Marc continued. "Second, I don't have to remind you that there has been a threefold increase in fatal terror attacks in the last two months. The Palestinians are totally ignoring Islamic terrorists who flee over to their side of the border, making it open season on Jews. Finally, Abu Alim is planning to come to the Temple Mount on Friday. There are those who say we should focus all our energies to prevent that from happening." Marc finished his presentation and leaned back in his chair without asking his question. It was understood.

Rachel was fascinated as she watched Rabbi Steinberg lower his eyes to help focus his attention on what Marc had just said. From her vantage point Rachel couldn't tell if his eyes were open or closed. She felt honored to be in the presence of such a great sage as he processed his thoughts against the Torah scroll and myriad of books that lay inscribed in his memory. When you asked a great scholar for an opinion, you weren't looking for the Rabbi's personal opinion. It was the opinion of the Torah that you were seeking. The Sage was simply more qualified to search through the sea of Torah wisdom and extract the information.

After a few moments, Rabbi Steinberg folded his hands together and rested them on the desk. He lifted his eyes, leaned forward and spoke in a calm soothing voice. "The Almighty is our Father is Heaven. He alone is true perfection. As the source of all perfection He loves us with perfect love. And that's why He gave us the greatest gift there is. Do you know what that gift is, Rachel?"

Rachel, unsure of what the Rabbi was looking for answered hesitatingly, "Life?"

"Something far more precious than life. He gave us the greatest good there is. The intrinsic good that is in God Himself. He wanted us to derive pleasure from that true good to the greatest degree possible for us."

Rachel couldn't figure out what all this had to do with what *Kol Ha'am* should be doing this week, but she was spellbound by the Rabbi. "How exactly do we derive pleasure from that good?" she asked.

"A wonderful question. You see the only thing we can really know *about* God is that He is perfect in every imaginable way. Therefore, to appreciate and derive pleasure from God, is to appreciate and derive pleasure from perfection in all its forms. To have an intimate relationship with God, means one must have an intimate relationship with perfection."

Rachel looked at Marc, unsure if it was appropriate for her to be asking all the questions. He smiled and nodded for her to continue. This was Rabbi Steinberg's mission in life

— to help people understand God and develop a relationship with Him. Rachel straightened up in her seat and asked a question that had bothered her since she was a little girl. Not until today did she feel comfortable enough to ask it and feel she might get a satisfying answer. She had stifled the question many times, assuming it was something to be accepted on faith. "If God wants us to have perfection, and relate to perfection, why did He create such an imperfect world and fill it with such imperfect people?" She thought of all the suffering she and her family had endured at the hands of evil people.

"That, my child, is something that will become clearer to you when you become a mother, God willing. If we were all created perfect, and never made any mistakes, we'd be zombies. Life would have no meaning. When a parent showers a child with gifts, does her homework for her, takes care of everything without any connection to the child's actions, then the child feels worthless and empty. All the good that the child has, really belongs to her mother. It's not her own at all. The Almighty wants us to have a perfect world, but He wants us to earn it through our own efforts."

"So that's why free will is so important to us?" asked Rachel.

"Exactly. God created a world, and human beings, with the potential for perfection or deficiency, and gave us the ability to freely choose either. When we choose to perfect ourselves and the world, our existence takes on meaning. The Jewish People are supposed to set an example for the rest of the world of what a perfect society can be. That way, the rest of the nations can choose to be good societies. To force values on society isn't Godlike. We are to be a 'Light Unto Nations.' If we show, that in practice, God's values work better than man-made values, then the rest of the world will beat a path to our door."

An image flashed into Rachel's head that she decided to share with the Rabbi. "I remember when growing up as a child in Toronto, that frequently delegations would arrive from different countries to observe our public transportation system. It was one of the best in the world."

"And I'm sure the Canadian government didn't advertise that fact in the Swedish newspapers. If you've got something great, people will find out about it." Rabbi Steinberg gave one of his Brooklyn winks to seal his point.

Marc began to see how the Rabbi's response was connected to his question about how *Kol Ha'am* should proceed, but he was still unclear. "I understand that to build the Jewish 'Light Unto Nations,' we need the People of Israel living together on the Land of Israel according to God's value system as presented in the Torah. It's obvious that we are lacking in all three areas right now. What should our priority be in the present situation? Avoid giving more land to the Palestinians? Security? Teaching Torah values?"

Rabbi Steinberg paused to give Marc and Rachel time to think. As an educator, he preferred to give his students the tools to answer their own questions. It made the answers much more meaningful for them. As a Rabbi, it was a much more God-like way to teach, than to force the answers upon them. "If you have to sacrifice one of the three in the short term, which would you give up — the People, the Land or the Torah?"

The answer seemed obvious to Marc. "We survived as a distinct people for two thousand years in exile without a land. As long as we have the Torah to live by, we remain the Jewish people. Without the Torah, we assimilate into the foreign culture and disappear within two or three generations. If I were forced to make a choice, I would give up the Land temporarily."

"Good," said Rabbi Steinberg, stroking his white beard. "Our goal is to develop a perfected society. The Land is a tool, a necessary tool, a *holy* tool — yet it is still just a means to an end. The same can be said of the Torah. The word Torah means 'instructions,' instructions for living. The Torah is our lifeline as a people. We can't survive without it. Yet when we are faced with life threatening situations, most Torah laws are suspended. We break the Sabbath to drive a woman to a hospital who is about to deliver a baby. We administer non-kosher medicine if it is necessary to save a life. The preservation of life should be our prime focus. If there is no one alive, who will be around to perfect the world?"

"But don't some people say that we should be willing to sacrifice our lives rather than give away the Land? They say the Land isn't ours to give away, it belongs to God." asked Rachel a little confused.

Rabbi Steinberg leaned forward in his chair, and lowered his voice almost to a whisper, "Might I remind you, that our lives are not ours to give away either, they have also been entrusted to us by the Almighty. So why would people say such a thing?" He paused for this idea to sink in, and waited patiently for Rachel to respond. The Rabbi had given her all the tools she needed to come up with an answer.

"Well," she began slowly, "they must feel that by giving up the Land, Jewish lives will be lost as a result. More so than if the Land would not be given away."

Rabbi Steinberg leaned back almost triumphantly in his chair. His student had succeeded. "That, my child is precisely what the majority of the Rabbinical leadership feel. There are indeed, a few who have turned the holding onto every inch of soil into an end in, and of itself, but they are a small minority. The secular government would like the country to believe that the religious population is interested in holding onto Land at the expense of loss of life, while the secular left is interested in saving lives by bringing peace. In fact the exact opposite is true. The government keeps referring to the loss of Jewish lives to terror as 'sacrifices' for 'peace.'

"But aren't there Rabbis who still support the continued negotiations with the Palestinians?" asked Rachel.

"In the beginning of the process, there were those who accepted the military experts' opinions that the result of giving the Palestinians autonomy would be a decrease in terror attacks. In that case, we would be obliged to trade land for peace. But as the negotiations continued, and the facts overcame the theories, we saw that the whole process led to more terror, and more loss of life than ever before. Now, among the Rabbinical leadership, there is virtually unanimous consensus that we must make no more concessions to the Palestinians. It will only strengthen the hands of those who wish to kill us. We must fight to keep the Land, not so much because it belongs to us, but to prevent the loss of life."

Rabbi Steinberg shifted his gaze from Rachel to Marc. He could sense that Marc felt energized by his words yet he still saw some confusion concerning the practical application of these principles to *Kol Ha'am's* dilemma. It was time to summarize. "Concerning the abuse of human rights, and the arrest of Meir Tal and possibly others in the future; as long as their lives are not in danger, I suggest you don't expend main efforts in that area. What the government is doing is only showing how worried it is that it is losing the battle to implement its own policies. As for Abu Alim's visit, that is an immediate danger as it involves the battle for Jerusalem. You must protest it, but show how it would lead to the loss of Jewish lives. You must protest on all fronts as long as there is a threat to life, and make it clear that you are struggling for security for the people. Never give the impression you want land for its own sake, or political gains for their own sake. Does that help you?"

Marc nodded. The process Rabbi Steinberg had taken them through was even more valuable than the answer. "If the *Rosh Yeshiva* has a few more moments, can I trouble him with another related but more personal matter?" asked Marc.

Rabbi Steinberg answered, "Certainly, go ahead."

"Well," said Marc grasping for the right words, "I've been helping Rachel gather information to track down a terrorist who murdered a very close friend of hers a few years ago. We think we might know who it was. Today, she was snatched into a car by a *Shabak* agent who warned her not to continue. It seems they are following her, err, that is they're following us. Do you think we should go to the police with the information about the terrorist?"

The Rabbi was a little surprised by the question, "You certainly are coming up with some interesting questions since you've gotten involved in this political activism. And they're a lot tougher to answer than deciding whether a chicken is kosher or not." Marc smiled as the Rabbi thought about the question before continuing. "Are you certain about the identity of the murderer?"

"Not one hundred percent," answered Rachel.

"Then don't go to the authorities yet. When you have more information, come back to me. In the meantime, try to gather the information you need through the help of others if you can do so safely." Rabbi Steinberg looked up at the large clock opposite his desk on the wall. He stood up, indicating the time was up. His next appointment had already been kept waiting for five minutes. He put his arm around Marc's shoulder and walked them to the door.

"Rachel," said Marc, "do you mind waiting outside while I ask the *Rosh Yeshiva* one last quick question?" Rachel was surprised that he asked her permission to speak to Rabbi Steinberg, but appreciated his politeness. She quickly exited the room and shut the door behind her.

In a hushed voice, so that no one in the waiting room outside could hear him, Marc asked, *"Nu,* so what do you think, Reb Yaakov?"

Rabbi Steinberg narrowed his eyes on Marc trying to decipher his question, and then burst into a smile still holding onto his shoulder. "I like her," he said giving Marc's arm a squeeze, "what took you so long to find her?"

Forty

"Udi, hurry up. We're late. Yigal's uptight enough as it is already." Amiram glanced at his digital watch. They were only three minutes late, but when Yigal was in 'operational mode' he measured time in '*ketanot.*' 'Little ones,' was the code word the IDF used over field radios for 'minutes.'

"Okay, Okay, I just want to grab this incoming fax. It might have some information relevant to the meeting." Udi was holding the facsimile of the hand-scrawled piece of paper, trying to read it as it jerked and spit its way out of the machine. A few seconds later there was the loud beep signaling the end of transmission and the built in paper cutter sliced Udi's message, separating it from the roll of paper inside the machine.

Amiram held the door open to the office that he shared with Udi. As Udi dashed out of the room still deciphering the fax, Amiram shut the door and hurried down the hallway behind his partner to Yigal's office.

That Udi and Amiram were two of the best agents in the General Security Services didn't impress Yigal. He expected his men to be the best. As they knocked on the door, and walked sheepishly into his office, he glanced at his watch and frowned. He didn't need to say anything and they knew enough not to apologize for being late. Lives were saved and lost over a few *ketanot*. There also was no need for a reprimand, it was understood.

Yigal continued to leaf through the papers on his desk as he waited for them to silently sit down in the two empty office chairs facing him. "Meir Tal," he said solemnly, announcing the first item of the agenda that Yigal had prepared only moments before in his mind.

Udi shifted in his seat, understanding that Yigal's mention of Tal's name was a request for an update on the interrogation. "We've got the results back on the ballistics check. The shots didn't come from his guns. We won't release the official results for another week or two which will give us some more time to interrogate him."

"Has he given you any leads?" asked Yigal rubbing his eyes. Yigal really had hoped Meir was the terrorist. It would have made his life a lot simpler and help his headache go away.

"He hasn't mentioned any names, and there's little chance of him giving us any, but during the initial investigation he mentioned being cut off by a couple who turned onto the Ma'alot Yair road. We thought Meir was trying to send us on a wild goose chase, but we checked it out with his wife, and she corroborated the story."

"Do you have a description of the couple?" asked Yigal.

"Meir refused to give us one, which would lead me to believe they probably looked like settlers. He would never turn in one of his own people," answered Udi confidently, thinking back to the sermon he had to suffer through during Meir's interrogation.

"Have someone track down that couple," snapped Yigal getting up from his chair. He walked over to the credenza to fill his coffee mug. Part of the reason he felt so tense was that this was his fourth cup this morning. "Just because Tal wasn't responsible for the drive-by shooting, doesn't mean he's not part of the underground planning to carry out the Shimshon Plan. There's no reason for us to assume the two groups are connected. There could even be a third, independently planning Abu Alim's assassination."

Amiram squirmed in his seat, listening to the dialogue between Yigal and Udi. He felt nauseous hearing Yigal trying to pin some kind of guilt on Meir. A voice deep inside urged him to speak up and reveal his secret about who he really suspected authored the fax about the Shimshon Plan, but that information wouldn't change things yet. He decided to listen and not talk. Meir wasn't in danger. Amiram just needed a little more time.

"Yigal," cautioned Udi, "this is Ari's brother you're talking about. They came out of the same womb. I had a hard time believing he had anything to do with the murder of those Arabs, and now that he's passed the ballistics test, I really don't think there's reason to suspect him of being in the underground. He was weaned on centrist Zionism. Their way is to change things through government, not violence. That's why his family is so involved with this *Kol Ha'am* thing."

Yigal took a deep breath, trying to control his temper and then spoke through gritted teeth. "I realize he is your dead friend's brother, but never, never let your emotions affect your judgment. We both know good agents who are dead precisely because they let their emotions keep them from doing their job, as cruel as that job might be at times." Yigal paused to measure Udi's reaction to his words. "And it's precisely because he *is* Ari's brother that makes him a suspect. Rational people have been known to act irrationally when their brother is bludgeoned to death a week before his wedding. Have you ever heard of revenge, agent Harel? And speaking of revenge, what has our Ms. Stein been up to?" Yigal was heeding his own advice and switched to surnames to help separate himself emotionally from the people involved in the case.

Udi fingered the handwritten fax, and hesitated about revealing its contents to Yigal. He had no choice, if he delayed, it would only backfire on him later. "I just received this fax from my informer as we were leaving our office for this meeting. That's why we were a few minutes late." Udi was glad to have an opportunity to slip in a good excuse for not being on time.

"Nu?" said Yigal taking a swig of the coffee in his mug.

Udi skipped the first sentence referring to the fax about Rachel that Devorah had sent him the previous night. There weren't any faxes from Devorah waiting for him in his 'in basket' when he arrived that morning, and he didn't want to have to defend himself when Yigal demanded an explanation for the missing fax. It was probably just some technical error.

Udi began paraphrasing from the fax, "Rachel thinks she knows who murdered Ari. She asked my informer to do her a favor and pick up the photographs Rachel ordered yesterday at the *Jerusalem Press* and put them in a taxi to the Old City where someone would be waiting to pick them up. Rachel needs the photographs to help identify the murderer. All the cloak and dagger stuff is because Rachel believes the *Shabak* are following her."

Yigal glared at Amiram, "That's your department. How did she find out she was being followed?"

Amiram squirmed in his seat as his mind raced to come up with an answer other than the truth. From the way he had snatched Rachel from the sidewalk and spoken to her in his car, it would have taken an imbecile not to figure out Amiram was a *Shabak* agent. He cleared his throat and sat up in his chair to give an air of confidence, "Do you know anyone active in right-wing causes today who doesn't think they're being shadowed and bugged by us? We've become the national boogie men." All three men laughed. It helped diffuse some of the tension in the room. "But more likely, she and that Goodman fellow probably put two and two together concerning the attempted stabbing at the Haas Promenade yesterday. 'What happened to the mysterious citizen who gunned down the terrorist?' 'How was he able to pump three bullets into the heart of a moving target from behind?' 'What was he doing there in the first place?' 'Wouldn't the *Shabak* have a reason to be following anyone closely connected to Meir Tal while he was under investigation?'" He saw Yigal and Udi both begin nodding. Amiram then asked, "Get it?" when he was certain they had already 'gotten it.'

Yigal reacted impatiently, "Listen, Udi, I want you to take over concerning the Stein woman. She might have used the story about finding the murderer of Ari as a smoke-screen when they really are after Abu Alim. I want an answer by tomorrow morning."

The phone on Yigal's desk rang and he snapped it up to his ear. Udi and Amiram sat silently while Yigal took the call. "Yes, Mr. Prime Minister," he said as formally as he could. He didn't want to call Shiloni, 'Yossi' in front of his agents. "Yes... Yes... Fine, I'll be right over." Yigal literally dropped the receiver back onto the telephone base and ran both hands through his disheveled hair. He felt like pulling a few clumps of it out.

"What did he want?" asked Udi cautiously.

"It looks like I lost. He's going to let Abu Alim come to Jerusalem after all. The Pope, and the President of the United States have already called him this morning pressing him to do it and it's not even noon yet! And don't we know our Prime Minister? He melts like butter on the beach in Eilat whenever the 'big boys' put on the heat."

Forty One

"Hey *Motek!* Fancy meeting you here." Aryeh Levi, the big burly Chief of Police, startled Yigal who had been silently pacing the cold stone floor outside the Prime Minister's private office. Yigal had been focusing all his attention trying to decipher the shouting that was coming from the other side of the wooden door separating him from Yossi Shiloni. Levi grabbed Yigal's right hand and clamped his left hand down on top of it in a power handshake. "Looks like we're going to let that unholy SOB, Abu Alim, into the Holy City after all."

Some angry muffled shouts escaped through the closed door into the waiting area where the two men were standing. "I hope not," said Yigal. "And it looks like we have an ally in the Mayor in trying to put a stop to this nonsense. It sounds like he's threatening to shut down all city services and personally lead a mass demonstration to prevent Abu Alim from coming into Jerusalem. Shiloni's been screaming at him over the phone for the last five minutes."

Aryeh Levi raised his eyebrows as if to say 'not bad!' Everyone involved in the security services was dead-set against allowing any Arab leaders into the city no matter who they were. It was always a security nightmare. In the case of Abu Alim in particular, there was a serious chance of violence breaking out, especially if the Mayor was planning to bring a few hundred thousand demonstrators into Jerusalem at the same time. Moments later, the IDF Chief of Staff came striding down the wide hallway leading to the Prime Minister's office flanked by the Defense and Police Ministers. They were animatedly discussing the tactics of handling Abu Alim's visit assuming it was foregone conclusion.

The shouting from Shiloni's office stopped and the door opened. A somber looking Yisrael Eitan, Director General of the Prime Minister's office, came out into the hallway. He breathed a deep sigh and then addressed the group of five men, "Please come in, gentlemen."

Yigal fell into line at the back of the others in an unspoken pecking order. First went in the Ministers, Defense followed by Police, then the Chief of Staff, and the Chief of Police. Yigal wondered why he was there and not his boss, the Head of the General Security Services. Perhaps it had to do with the missing copy of the Shimshon File. Yigal's boss was still unaware of its existence, and from Shiloni's perspective, it was going to play a key role in the decision-making process concerning Abu Alim's visit. Yigal balked at the acrid smell of stale cigar smoke that filled the room as he took his place in the small semi-circle of chairs arranged opposite Shiloni's desk.

The Prime Minister was impatiently tapping an unlit cigar on the edge of his desk. He pursed his lips tightly together. "As if Abu Alim isn't a handful already, I need the Mayor of Jerusalem to contend with as well?" he complained sarcastically. He stopped rapping the cigar against the desk and pointed it at the Chief of Police, "Can't you have the Mayor arrested and put somebody from the Labor party at the head of City Hall instead?"

A burst of laughter filled the room. Shiloni had realized he looked out of control and that was the last impression he wanted to give this group of men. He used the humor to give the illusion that he considered the Mayor more of a nuisance than a real threat. Inside, he feared the damage the right-wing Mayor could cause the government if he chose to. As the chuckles subsided, Shiloni sat up straight in his large chair and carefully placed the unlit cigar in an oversized crystal ash tray next to the remains of two butts he had smoked earlier in the day. He clasped his hands together, placed them firmly on the desk and leaned forward in a 'take charge' motion. "I've decided, for a number of reasons, to allow Abu Alim to visit Jerusalem. You have all been invited here to help develop a strategy to ensure maximum security and a minimum of disturbances while he is here. When the formal announcement is made about the impending visit, we'll have much more than an angry mayor to contend with."

No one in the room responded to Shiloni's comments. Yigal glanced at the other men in the chairs to his right. They all had learned long ago that you do not speak when this Prime Minister is leading a meeting unless he specifically asks for your input. Being in control was of prime importance to Shiloni. One to one, the Prime Minister was fairly relaxed, but if anyone ever got the upper hand over him in a group meeting, he would lash out at them.

Shiloni directed his attention to Shaika Oren, his Chief of Staff, "What do you anticipate the response will be to Alim's visit from the Palestinians in what's left of the territories, Shaika?"

"They love him. Look at him as sort of a Messiah figure," said the old army man dryly. "They like his *chutzpah* and fully expect him to liberate them along with the Arabs in Israel as well. The fact that he stood up against the previous Palestinian government and is coming to pray at the mosques puts him in a good position with even the most extreme of the Islamic fundamentalists among the population." He looked around the room to address everyone, "I expect there to be tens of thousands of them coming out to shower the guy with flowers, unless we put them under curfew."

"Curfews are out of the question," snapped Shiloni, "part of this exercise is to show the world how tolerant we are." He was sorry he mentioned world opinion, he wanted to downplay his need to respond to the pressures being put on him by the Pope and the American President. It was important for Shiloni to let his own people feel this was purely an internal Israeli affair. His Achilles' heel in the press was his bowing to international pressure. More than once he had been depicted in editorial cartoons as a poodle being pulled on a leash by Uncle Sam. Shiloni quickly changed the subject. "Have we ever had a demonstration of Arabs that large before, Chaim?"

Chaim Azriel sat up, surprised by the question. As Minister of Defense, he had little personal experience with demonstrations inside the Green Line. He assumed the Prime Minister had asked him because they were old friends and Shiloni trusted him. "I don't recall any that big. What do you say Aryeh?" He redirected the question to its rightful owner, the Police Chief.

"We've had up to twenty thousand Moslem worshippers on the Temple Mount on Fridays during *Ramadan*, that have gotten out of hand. There were about that many Palestinians on the Temple Mount when they rioted and began pelting rocks on the Jewish worshippers at the Western Wall during *Sukkoth* a few years back. That's the maximum." After furnishing the statistics, he addressed the Chief of Staff, "I just want to say, that even if they all come out carrying roses to throw at the feet of Abu Alim as his procession approaches the city, I wouldn't count on it ending up anything like the Americans' Rose Bowl Parade." Thanks to cable TV, the Israelis had become experts at American sports.

"I'm not so worried about what the Palestinians will do on their own. The question is what will happen when settlers, in their myriads, incite the Palestinians to violence." Moshe Porat, the Police Minister, wasn't afraid to speak without being asked. "Remember that a group of settlers violently attacked my car Saturday night outside the Renaissance Hotel. If they would do that to me, imagine what they might do to Abu Alim!"

An image of Moshe Porat cowering in fear from the innocuous Rachel Stein leaped to Yigal's head and he strained to hold back his laughter. Yigal disliked Porat as much as he disliked Shiloni. They were both whining hysterics prone to exaggeration. It was difficult to do your job properly if you weren't presented with the proper facts.

Shiloni picked up the cigar from the ashtray and began to finger it. It was a nervous habit. "It's obvious we have to have the minimum number of Arabs and Jews out in the streets when Abu Alim is in town. The question is how do we do that without curfews and arrests? Any ideas Yigal?"

Yigal Ramon cleared his throat. He had been thinking about this problem for the past two days. "The *Mercaz HaMa'avak* and the Mayor are definite powers to contend with. They are masters of logistics and organization. If you give them enough time, they'll bring hundreds of busloads of demonstrators to the city. They'll assign settlements and neighborhood groups particular intersections to block with their cars. It will be no different than a military campaign. If we are to defend ourselves from their tactics without forcing a confrontation, the key will be surprise."

Yigal had captured Shiloni's attention. As much as Shiloni detested Yigal, he respected him as a thinker. He struck a match and lit the cigar. For some reason he found it easier to assimilate ideas when he was enveloped by the blue plumes of cigar smoke. Shiloni leaned back in the chair and drew on the cigar. He motioned for Yigal to continue.

"Time is also a crucial element for them. It takes a lot of time to order buses and move people around the country. People also need time to arrange to take off work to come to demonstrations," explained Yigal.

"Not if the Mayor shuts down the city," interrupted Porat.

Yigal ignored the Police Minister and continued, "I suggest we announce to the press tomorrow that we have agreed to allow Abu Alim to come to the Temple Mount to pray on Friday. That will send the *Mercaz HaMa'avak* and the Mayor's supporters into a frenzy ordering buses and making plans. In the meantime we will play hardball with Abu Alim. We get him to agree, that for his own safety we will allow him to come to the Temple Mount on Wednesday morning, the day after tomorrow, instead of Friday. On Wednesday morning, an hour before he arrives, we announce to the press that the time of the visit has been changed. It will be impossible for the demonstrators to switch gears that fast. The Palestinians will all be at work, and won't be able to react that quickly either. At most we'll have a couple of thousand of demonstrators to contend with, and we'll have at least that many police and security forces already out on the streets."

"Brilliant," said Moshe Porat with some cynicism in his voice, "but do you really expect Abu Alim to go along with that? He thinks he's gotten the upper hand already. He has the Pope and the President of the United States on his side. If he wants to come on Friday, he'll be here on Friday."

Yossi Shiloni shifted in his seat. He liked Yigal's plan and wanted to develop it. Porat's jumping in and trying to squelch it was irritating. Shiloni puffed a cloud of smoke in the direction of his Police Minister. "Thank you for your wonderful insight, *Moisheleh*," said Shiloni, using the nickname that Porat hated. "Why don't you let me and Yigal work out that problem. Gentlemen, thank you for your input. You're dismissed. I will keep you informed of events as they develop during the course of the day. Yigal, would you please stay after the others leave?"

Forty Two

Marc turned the key in the driver side door and all four locks of the Volvo made a distinctive "thunk" as they opened. Rachel quickly slipped into the passenger seat from her side of the car, but Marc first paused to pick up a brown manila envelope occupying the driver's seat. It was exactly where his friend Gidon said he had left it when he returned the keys to Marc at Rabbi Steinberg's office.

Marc smiled as he passed the sealed envelope to Rachel, and he started the car. If anyone was following, there was no way for them to know that Marc and Rachel had the photos from the *Jerusalem Press*. Devorah Eisenstadt had picked them up from the newspaper offices and put them in a taxi to the Old City. Marc had given his car keys to Gidon, his learning partner at the yeshiva, who waited for the cab at the bus stop near the Jewish Quarter parking lot. Upon receiving the envelope, Gidon quickly crossed the street and discreetly opened the driver's side door and dropped the envelope on the seat. He then proceeded back to Rabbi Steinberg's office to return the keys to Marc.

"Where to now?" asked Rachel, clutching the envelope. Her heart was racing. She felt like ripping open the envelope to examine the photographs, but at the same time she was afraid of uncovering what information they might hold. She was afraid they might positively identify the murderer and then she would have to deal with the horror of having to follow up that information with the police and the government whom she had grown to distrust. On the other hand she was afraid her suspicions would be unfounded and she would have to deal with the frustration and disappointment of having to continue her search for Ari's murderer. She decided to wait before opening the envelope and suppress the adrenaline pumping through her body.

"I thought we might go to Independence Park," said Marc, glancing into the rear-view mirror and pulling out from the curb. "We can park the car and walk far out onto the grass. It should be a nice place to examine the contents of your parcel, and we'll be far enough away from the road and other people to be able to see if we're being followed. And even if we are, they won't be able to tell that we're looking at the pictures from the *Press*."

Rachel frowned. She hated the idea of being hounded, and reflected back to the encounter she had with the *Shabak* agent earlier in the morning. She felt like letting out a big sigh, but decided not to dump her depression on Marc. Rachel perked herself up and said as cheerily as she could, "Great, I love that park."

They began the descent along the road that hugged the Old City walls to their right. Some tourists were trekking along the ramparts that were still there from the 16th century Ottoman period. On the left they passed two yeshivas, and then the Western Wall appeared in front of them. Marc detoured around two cars festively decorated with pink ribbon and dozens of crepe-paper carnations. A video camera operator and a still photographer were backing into the narrow street in front of Marc as they photographed a bride and groom who had come to the *Kotel* to have their pictures taken before their wedding.

Rachel looked at the bride in her white gown and her heart was filled with a surge of joy, happy that this young woman was about to embark on a new life. The bride nervously lifted up her gown a few inches so as not to trip on the curb, but as she looked over at her groom, the anxiety in her eyes melted away into a warm, trusting glow. Rachel imagined herself wearing the lovely dress, and surprised herself by how different she was reacting today, to this bride, than she had the previous week at Mrs. Klein's granddaughter's wedding. Was it really only four days ago?

As Marc steered the Volvo to the right and navigated the tourists walking in the road in front of them, Rachel began sorting her feelings out. She had purposely ignored her outburst of tears upon seeing the bride at the King David wedding. She hadn't understood what button deep inside of her had been pushed. She thought it was that her marriage to Ari never took place. What had changed between last Thursday and today?

"These tourists are great for the economy, but horrible for the transportation system," said Marc, squeezing through Dung Gate, with a river of white- and orange-hatted tourists flowing past both sides of his car to their bus parked just outside the Old City walls. The gate was wide enough for only one vehicle to pass, and the driver of the "Number 2" bus began honking impatiently as he waited for Marc to exit, so he could enter the gate and deliver his passengers to the Western Wall bus stop. Rachel turned to look at Marc confidently steering the car, not allowing anyone, or anything to get to him - not the angry bus driver, thoughtless tourists, rude Arab pushcart owners, or even the smelly camel to their right waiting for some tourist to pay a few shekels for a ride.

As Marc turned right, at the direction of a traffic cop, and swung around two parked tour buses, the answer finally came to Rachel. She had been upset at the King David wedding, not because she hadn't married Ari. She had come to terms with Ari's death over a year ago. Had that *not* been the case, she never would have been able to come back to Israel. She had been upset by the fact that she wasn't yet married, and she was afraid she would never find anyone as wonderful as Ari to love. The only thing to change between Thursday and today was... Marc?

The Volvo continued along the road that hugged the steep slope of Mount Zion on their right. To their left was the sheer drop into the rocky *Ben Hinnom* valley. It was called *Gai ben hinnom* in Hebrew. Here the ancient Moabites passed their children through the fires of *Molech* as human sacrifices to their idol to help ensure a better material life. Rachel shuddered at the thought as she realized the Hebrew word *Gehinnom*, a euphemism for 'hell,' was derived from this place. 'Child sacrifices for 'peace,'' she murmured to herself.

Marc stopped at the traffic light opposite the Sultan's pool, and then turned right, continuing along the road ringing the walls of the Old City toward Jaffa Gate. At the next light he turned left onto Mamilla road which bisects the David's Village neighborhood. The white concrete domes of the luxury condominiums sparkled in the mid-day sunshine. The neatly tailored public park, and private gardens gave the project a gentrified air that stood in sharp contrast to the four-hundred-year-old stone walls of the Old City. A valiant attempt had been made by the architects to use arches and domes to make this project express the unique personality of Jerusalem.

From Rachel's point of view, the unique personality of Jerusalem came from an inner glow, not a surface shine. For her it was difficult to distinguish David's Village from any other luxury development of condominiums and boutiques anywhere else in the world. On the surface, and perhaps only on the surface, it seemed to represent the ultimate in western values, exactly what she had decided to leave behind. Ever since she met Marc, and found out he lived here, she had been bothered. It had created an unspoken barrier to her being totally comfortable with him. It seemed out of character for Marc to choose this of all neighborhoods. Did it reflect something about his inner character? Was he enamored by the surface beauty or was there some other deeper explanation?

Rachel had been taught as a child to 'judge everyone favorably,' and as a result she had buried her discomfort about the David's Village aspect of Marc's life. Therefore she hadn't asked Marc, 'Why David's Village?' for two reasons: one, because it really wasn't any of her business, and two, she was afraid she might be disappointed with his answer. Now she realized her emotions were quickly becoming entangled with the man sitting next to her, and that it was best to bring it out into the open. Rachel swallowed hard and asked a very innocuous question which might have a very great impact on her future. "Isn't this where you live?" It was more of a quiet statement than a question.

"Third garden on the left," said Marc nodding in the direction of his apartment.

Rachel craned her neck to catch a glimpse of the apartment, but they were already past it. She settled herself back in the bucket seat. "How did you pick David's Village?" she asked, trying to sound like she was only making small talk.

"Well, it really wasn't my first choice," admitted Marc. "When I first arrived, I wanted to be in the Old City near the Yeshiva since I was planning on spending a major part of my day studying. That way I would waste as little time as possible in transit."

"Sounds very practical," said Rachel.

"That's true, but to be honest, I didn't come to live in Israel for practical reasons. I came because of what Israel had to offer in terms of spiritual opportunities. And if you're going to be in Israel for those reasons, how can you not live in Jerusalem if it's possible?"

"Sounds very reasonable to me."

"And if you're going to be in Jerusalem, why not in the Old City, near the Western Wall and the Temple Mount? After all, isn't that what Jerusalem is all about? It's not the Jerusalem stone on the buildings that makes Jerusalem unique, it's what's behind those stones."

"So why aren't you in the Old City?" asked Rachel. She didn't want to add, 'obviously you can afford it.' That was understood and she felt uncomfortable talking about money.

"Well, when I got here, there was nothing available in the Jewish Quarter, neither for sale or for rent, so I had to look at other neighborhoods," explained Marc.

"How did you decide which neighborhood?" Rachel was thinking that if you wanted a spiritual environment, there are a lot better choices in the city.

"As a single man, it was actually quite simple. I realized wherever I picked was only temporary until I got married." Marc pulled to a stop at the red traffic light at King David Street that was the end of David's Village. He took the opportunity to glance over at Rachel who looked puzzled. He decided to explain himself better. "You see," he added, "the Rosh Yeshiva suggested, and virtually all my happily married friends concur, that a man should give tremendous weight to his wife's opinion when they are picking a community to live in. The Talmud says that the woman is called a man's home. The wood, bricks, concrete and glass are the house, it's the inner spiritual glow that is the home — and the woman in her spiritual relationship with her husband has a unique ability to develop and nurture that feeling together with him in their marriage... so they tell me."

Rachel smiled.

"So if I'm going to be seriously dependent on my wife to provide the spiritual foundation for our home, then I had best let her use her judgment to find the environment that she feels has the necessary spiritual raw materials for us as a couple to draw from." Marc glanced over at Rachel a little uncomfortably. On an official 'date' it was common for people to discuss serious life choices and how they viewed married life. In this community unmarried people only dated when they were seriously contemplating marriage. Therefore it was natural to talk about their feelings about marriage. But this wasn't really a 'date,' at least officially.

The light changed and he turned his attention back to the road. Rachel was quiet, her heart beating a little faster. "So," said Marc matter of factly, "if my wife wants David's Village, we'll stay. If she wants Mea She'arim, Mea She'arim it is!" He glanced over at Rachel and then lowered his voice as if sharing a secret in confidence, "but between you and me, David's Village is no place to raise a troop of little kiddies, and I probably wouldn't marry someone who wanted to live here. It's convenient for now because it's near the Old City and it makes a good impression on business associates, but most of the owners are foreigners who use their place as a vacation home. It's basically a ghost town most of the year."

The Volvo cruised past the United States consulate on their left and Marc turned right at the next street into Independence Park. On the sidewalk to the right a female consulate security guard was inspecting the underside of a car parked opposite the consulate by looking into a mirror attached to a long broomstick. Marc slowed down to navigate a speed bump and cautiously passed a few pedestrians strolling along the side of the road through the park. A few moments later he pulled into a parking lot to the right and took a ticket from the guard sitting in a booth at the lot entrance.

As she got out of the car, Rachel felt like throwing off her shoes and running through the grass. She knew she should have trusted her intuition all along about Marc. The irritation of not knowing had been totally unnecessary. 'Next time,' she resolved silently to herself, 'confront the situation head on when it arises, and trust in the Almighty that everything will work out for the best.' Then she remembered the manila envelope tucked under her arm and her heart began thumping involuntarily. What would its contents reveal?

At first glance, Marc and Rachel looked like a handful of other couples enjoying the relative privacy of the park on an autumn Monday morning. As they walked back along the road under the watchful eye of the twenty story Plaza Hotel standing sentry over the green manicured lawns and shade trees, they blended into the scenery. Only the watchful eye of someone like the man parked in the white Ford by the side of the road would be able to pick them out of the crowd by a few tell-tale signs; they weren't walking arm in arm, Rachel's pleated skirt reached below her knees and the sleeves of her blouse came to her elbows.

Halfway along the road, they veered right onto the lawn and walked to the center of the open field. Nearby a young mother was supervising her two preschoolers scampering in the grass. Marc noticed a shade tree to the left which provided some cover from the noontime sun and he sat down on the grass, followed by Rachel.

"So," said Marc, "let's take a look at what's inside the envelope." He surprised Rachel who had already forgotten about the photographs, having been distracted by the little boy and girl squealing with laughter. The talk about neighborhoods and seeing the young mother playing with her children forced Rachel's attention on her future. She was quickly untying her emotional bonds with her past. She almost felt like giving Marc the envelope and not opening it at all.

With a sense of dread she nervously tore open the envelope and slipped out the small set of eight-by-ten-inch black and white glossy photographs. The last thing she wanted to do, to spoil her morning, was to look a bunch of close ups of a smiling Abu Alim. The first three photos only brought a sense of revulsion to her, like someone looking at a book of mug shots. But the fourth photo filled her with horror. The man at the *Press* had done his job well. The cropped photo from the previous day's paper showed only the back of Abu Alim's head and the profile of his body guard pressing the earphone into his left ear. The octagonal shape, large roman numerals and gold mesh band of her grandfather's watch were unmistakable. The horror was provided by a thick scar on the man's left hand running from the watchband to his index finger. The kind that would have healed over the blood drenched hand of Ari's murderer. Rachel felt like screaming, but was stopped by the sour yogurt rising up from her stomach into her throat. She dropped the photos, jumped up and ran to the nearby bushes to throw up her breakfast.

Forty Three

The Bell Helicopter swung wide out over the Mediterranean. From high above, the noontime sun made the sea sparkle like a blue-white diamond set in a gold setting of the sands of the Gazan beach. Abu Alim beamed as he surveyed his jewel, but was sobered as the helicopter headed back towards the coastline and brought the squalor of the still over-populated Palestinian refugee camps into view. For the President of Palestine, those camps, and the poverty they represented, were both a curse and a blessing. They were a blessing, because they were the key to receiving hundreds of millions of dollars of handouts from the West. After all, what country would give foreign aid to a state where everyone owned a villa and went to work in a suit and tie? Since no viable economic structure had yet been developed in Palestine, Abu Alim was dependent on foreign aid and therefore he had a vested interest in keeping his population in poverty as long as possible.

On the other hand, the camps were a curse. The longer the people were kept in squalor and hunger, the more appealing Islamic Fundamentalism would become to them. And the greater would be the threat to him personally and to his

regime. Abu Alim represented secular Palestinian national-
ism, whose promise was a better material life. If he didn't
provide that to his people, they would look elsewhere for
leadership.

A number of housing projects had been started with
American and Japanese grants, but these were too few to
affect the mood of the local population. They only fueled
hatred against those family members and friends of the government ministers and assistants who 'won' the lotteries for
the rights to purchase the newly constructed apartments.

Each day it became more important for Abu Alim to
win over the growing religious community in Palestine. That
is why he was making such a big event out of this afternoon's ground-breaking ceremony of the fifteen million
dollar mosque in the center of Gaza City, being donated by
the Saudi Royal family.

As the helicopter moved over the city, its shadow cut a
sharp line in the merciless desert sunshine. A few thousand
well wishers were gathered around a large outdoor platform
that had been erected for the ceremony. The crowd began
shouting and waving when the black, red and green helicopter came into view. Abu Alim ordered the pilot to circle the
crowd a few times so he could wave back at them, and allow
each person an opportunity to see him riding his mechanical
steed high in the heavens. His heart thumped excitedly as he
compared himself to the prophet Mohammed making his
mystical night-time ride from Saudi Arabia to *Al Aksa* on his
trusted steed *Al Buraq*. For this reason he used the Bell helicopter, which he nicknamed *'Al Buraq,'* as much as possible.
He liked the idea of his people looking up into the sky and
watching their leader descending from the heavens.

The ringing of the cellular telephone in the breast
pocket of the security guard at the back of the helicopter was
barely audible under the roar of the aircraft's thundering

rotors. The guard didn't bother to answer it since he wouldn't be able to hear anything. Besides, the helicopter was making its final descent, and in a few seconds the engine would be silent. The sand kicked up as the spinning blades hovered momentarily a few dozen meters above the ground so the pilot could finesse the machine into position for a perfect landing.

With the engine stopped, and only the loud swish of the spinning blades to contend with, the security man reached into his pocket and answered the phone before the doors of the helicopter were opened. As the pre-positioned Palestine Security Services agents surrounded the helicopter, the guard in the rear of the aircraft reached forward and handed the phone to Abu Alim.

"Yes, good afternoon Yossi," said the President of Palestine to his counterpart in Israel. "Are you watching me live on Palestine Television?" he added cynically. "I would be happy to relay your greetings to my honored guests gathered here today for this historic ceremony."

Yossi Shiloni let out an inaudible grunt on the other end of the line from his office in Jerusalem. He didn't have a clue what ceremony Abu Alim was referring to. He hated being put on the defensive, and decided to ignore Abu Alim's comments. "I would like to talk to you about your requested visit to Jerusalem," he said trying to take charge of the conversation.

"Can it wait an hour? I have a few thousand people here waiting for me to turn the first shovel in the ground-breaking ceremony of the new mosque. You wouldn't want to further harm the religious sensibilities of my people — especially when the Saudi royal family are the patrons of the project." Abu Alim enjoyed this 'parrying' with his Jewish opponent.

Yossi Shiloni looked across the desk at Yigal Ramon with whom he had worked out the strategy for this call. They anticipated Abu Alim would want to stall and had prepared the response. Shiloni spoke slowly and icily, "We must talk now. If not, without the necessary time to prepare, I will have to refuse your request to visit Jerusalem. It is your choice."

Abu Alim was taken aback by the finality in the Prime Minister's voice. The Palestinians had become accustomed to the weak spine of the Israelis bending over backwards to keep the 'peace process' going forward at all costs. Every time the Palestinians had pushed the Israelis, by making minor violations of the agreements, the Israelis always responded by saying, "If this happens again, there will be serious repercussions on the peace process." In fact, the Israelis never did anything about their threats. Abu Alim had come to despise them as yapping Chihuahuas with no bite. Yet this time there was something foreboding in the Prime Minister's voice that was unnerving. Abu Alim waved his security man and the pilot out of the helicopter and signaled to the Security Services officer on the ground to stall for time.

"Yossi," said Abu Alim as placatingly as possible, "if you feel it is so important, of course I will talk with you. What is bothering you, Yossi?"

Shiloni gritted his teeth and felt like spitting into the phone, hoping some of the saliva would ricochet off the satellite transmitter and into Alim's face. But he composed himself before responding. "There is nothing bothering me. I am only trying to help you." He was lying. He was under tremendous pressure from the Americans and the Pope to find a solution to this problem. "You see, our intelligence services are informing us that there is too much risk in a Friday visit. Since you say your visit is purely for religious reasons, we want to help you come in and out of Jerusalem as quietly as possible, but still giving the visit the honor befitting your office."

"Yes, go on," said Abu Alim. He enjoyed listening to the Jews cower before him.

"So what I am suggesting is this: We make a formal announcement that you will be visiting the *Al Aksa* mosque on Friday morning. That will send the right-wing elements on our side into a frenzy trying to organize a protest. It will also be a smoke-screen for any potential assassination plots. The media will hype up the event as a formal state visit, even though we announce it as a personal religious pilgrimage. That will make my life a little easier in the Knesset."

"I see," said Alim quietly into the phone.

"Then, early Wednesday morning, meaning the day after tomorrow, you make an announcement that due to personal reasons you have asked me to allow you to come that same day, two days early. I will then respond positively to your request, since it is really only a private religious visit anyway. You fly your helicopter onto the Temple Mount an hour or two after the announcement, and you leave a half-hour later from *Al Aksa* like the prophet Mohammed ascending to heaven." Shiloni stopped abruptly, letting Abu Alim fill in the details. It was also an attempt to put the Palestinian President off balance. The permission to land a helicopter on the Temple Mount and the reference to Mohammed were designed to appeal to Alim's ego.

Abu Alim paused to think about the repercussions of Shiloni's proposal. From Alim's point of view, all he required was a visit to *Al Aksa* and a reasonable-sized crowd of a few thousand well wishers. That could be accomplished on half an hour's notice with a few strategically placed phone calls. Yet Yossi Shiloni didn't know that. Abu Alim decided to use the fact that Shiloni's plan would mean there wouldn't be twenty thousand Arabs welcoming him as a bargaining chip. "Since this is a private religious visit, I don't want any Israeli security forces on the Temple Mount while I am there. Soldiers and Policemen with guns are not appropriate at a place of worship. My private security personnel will protect me." Uniformed Israelis were an embarrassment to Alim's claim to Palestinian sovereignty over the Islamic holy places. If Alim could appear on the Temple Mount without any Israelis visible, it would create a tremendous boost to his stature in the Moslem world.

Yossi Shiloni was surprised by Abu Alim's quick implicit acceptance of the plan. He covered the phone to relay to Yigal Ramon, Alim's request for the absence of Israeli Security forces on the Temple Mount. A decision had to be made quickly before the President changed his mind. He was famous for his flip-flopping on issues.

"Tell him, that we won't have any *uniformed* personnel on the Mount while he is there," advised Yigal. "That doesn't mean we won't have soldiers stationed on every high building around the site. But he doesn't have to know that. Also tell him he can't have any of his goons in camouflaged uniforms prancing around up there either. We'll have our people up there protecting him, but they'll all be plain-clothes *Shabakniks*."

Shiloni gave his head a slight twitch trying to absorb Yigal's advice and then think of a way to translate it into more diplomatic language. "Mr. President," he said, "I appreciate your desire not to have military people near the mosques while you are praying. But we must at least have our plain-clothes security personnel there to protect you. There will be no need to have your people there to assist us."

"But I must have some of my own people," insisted Abu Alim.

He needs to maintain his honor, thought Shiloni. "All right, you may have some of your own people, but only twenty of them, and they must also be in plain clothes." Shiloni momentarily imagined twenty unidentifiable armed Palestinian agents moving about the Temple Mount and quickly added, "And we will assign one of our men to accompany each one of your men. One-to-one."

"Fifty," answered Alim.

"Thirty."

"Done. It's a pleasure doing business with you Yossi. Our staffs will work out the details. I must go, my people are waiting," said a victorious Abu Alim into the phone.

Yossi Shiloni, a little shell-shocked by this 'bazaar' diplomacy, hung up the phone thinking it was he who had bargained the better deal, not Abu Alim. So why was his adversary so happy with the results?

Abu Alim stepped out of the helicopter and moved through a double line of armed security personnel toward the stage where an announcer had been making a speech praising the guest of honor. The President of Palestine took a spade that was handed to him by the mayor of Gaza City and plunged it into the hard desert ground to the cheers of the crowd. When the clicking of the cameras subsided, he mounted the stage and took the microphone into his hand.

"My dear Palestinian brothers," he roared into the microphone, "today is the beginning of a new era for the Moslem people. It is my hope, that in the near future we will all pray together in this wonderful mosque presented to the Palestinian people by our Saudi brethren. But on this happy occasion I have more news for you. I have just spoken with Yossi Shiloni, and I have arranged to pray at *Al Aksa* on Friday morning." A murmur rushed through the crowd as Abu Alim continued. "And I solemnly promise to you that the day is not far off, when all of us here today will go up to *Al Quds* and pray together at *Al Aksa*."

The crowd broke into a wild frenzy and began chanting. At first it was difficult for the foreign press to understand what they were saying, but as the chant became louder and louder until it sounded like a battle cry, the familiar words became recognizable to all. *"B'roch, b'dam, nifde et Al Quds."*— 'With spirit and with blood we will redeem Jerusalem.'

Jibril Abu Alim raised his fist high into the air and at first joined in with the chant. But then through the force of his personality and to the delight of those present he began to lead the rhythmic chanting. 'Let the Chihuahuas yap,' he thought to himself, 'today the people are mine.'

Forty Four

Rachel was a jumble of emotions as she turned the key to enter her apartment. From Independence Park, Marc had taken her straight to Leah's house in Yemin Moshe. There they had shown the photograph to Leah which for all intents and purposes brought her face to face with her son's murderer. Unlike Rachel, who had become physically sick over the revelation, Leah took the news more stoically. They spent the first hour after Marc and Rachel arrived discussing all the possible options they might take, and the pros and cons of each. Should they go to the police? Perhaps the *Shabak*? Find an attorney? What about the media?

Marc left with all the possible scenarios to get some input from Rabbi Steinberg who had asked them to come back if they made a positive identification. While Marc was gone, the announcement of Abu Alim's impending visit to Jerusalem came over the radio on the three o'clock news. That's when things erupted at Leah's house. The incoming phone line didn't stop ringing the rest of the afternoon. Rachel helped by taking the calls while Leah was on the other line speaking to bus companies and printers, putting into action the plans that had been readied for the day Abu Alim would make his inevitable visit to the Temple Mount.

The excitement helped distract Rachel from her own problems, but by six o'clock she was feeling faint. She had thrown up her breakfast, and she and Marc had forgotten to eat their lunch at Independence Park. Rachel just wanted to go home, have a shower and climb into bed. Leah insisted that Rachel eat something, knowing that Rachel, in her state of mind, wouldn't bother with dinner before going to bed.

By late afternoon there was already a flood of volunteers buzzing around Leah's apartment. When Rachel was ready to go home, Itzik gave her a ride in the *Kol Ha'am* van.

As Rachel opened the door to her apartment, the cool quiet of a single person's home wafted out into the hallway and engulfed her. She placed her bag and manila envelope of photographs on the telephone table behind the door. She decided not to disturb the calm of the apartment by switching on the light. The fluorescent fixture under the upper kitchen cabinets that she left on twenty four hours a day provided enough glow to make her way around her familiar sanctum even though it had been years since she had lived here.

Rachel took a glass tumbler from the dish rack beside the sink and opened the refrigerator to look for a bottle of mineral water when there was a quick double rap at the door. "Just a minute," she called out, placing the glass and the plastic bottle on the kitchen work island.

Suddenly, the front door opened and a man poked his head into the apartment. "Did you say come in?" he said with a smile in his voice.

A little startled by the strange man, Rachel answered cautiously, "Actually, I said, 'just a minute.' Who are you?"

The man flicked on the light beside the door, wanting to relax Rachel as much as possible. He purposely 'misheard' her, using it as an opportunity to enter the apartment. Had he remained on the other side of the door, she might never have let him in. He smiled as warmly as he could and said apologetically, "If you want me to go outside so we can start again, I would be very happy..."

"Just tell me who you are, and what you're doing here," said Rachel still a little nervously realizing her gun was in her bag on the table next to where the strange man was standing.

"Actually, I'm part of the team investigating Meir Tal. My name's Yoram. You must be Ms. Stein," said Udi walking toward Rachel to shake her hand.

Rachel picked up the glass and the bottle of water to occupy her hands so she wouldn't have to shake this man's hand. Aside from considerations of Jewish law, she was repulsed by the thought of having someone who was involved in keeping Meir locked up, touching her. "Do you have a warrant for my arrest? Because if you don't, I have nothing to say to you, and you may leave the same way you came in. As you know, the door's unlocked."

Udi stopped in his tracks. In the initial moments of meeting Rachel face to face, he was experiencing first hand the combination of strength and vulnerability that his friend Ari had so proudly described about his fiancée. Udi understood how Ari's attraction to this woman involved more than her beauty.

"I'm not here to harm you in any way. I just want to talk for a few minutes. Perhaps I can even help you," said Udi soothingly, sitting down into a sofa chair. He was trying to make his presence a fact, and buy a little time to win over Rachel's trust.

"You sound just like your friend did this morning. I don't need your kind of help," said Rachel defiantly. A puzzled look crossed Udi's face, and Rachel realized she had made a mistake assuming her abductor this morning and this man were working together. She decided to change the subject quickly. "Besides, I'm not feeling well and I need to go to sleep. Why don't you just leave." Rachel held her physical line of defense, not budging from behind the work island.

"I don't think Meir was involved in the drive-by shooting. But we think he might be a link to a new Jewish underground plotting to assassinate Abu Alim."

"If you know he's innocent, why don't you let him go? He has a wife and two small children," protested Rachel.

"These are difficult times, Ms. Stein."

"You're telling me?"

"Can you help me in any way track down who is really involved in the underground? If you can, we'll be able to release Meir immediately," said Udi trying to bait Rachel. He assumed that since Meir was Ari's brother, Rachel's emotional connection to the family might overshadow her loyalty to the cause.

"Even if I knew, I wouldn't tell you," she snapped. "You'd only use it against me. Against all of us."

Udi realized he was getting nowhere. Time was running out. He needed a breakthrough. After Abu Alim's visit was announced, dozens of phone calls were monitored coming in and out of Leah Tal's house — most of them using some kind of code words — to and from every major right-wing group and faction. Rachel had been there all afternoon. If anyone had access to the information Udi needed, it was Rachel. He decided to bend the *Shabak* rules once again, and said quietly, "I wouldn't use it against you. You see Rachel, I used to work with Ari. I owe it to him to help you, not to harm you."

Twice in one day? This was a little too 'coincidental.' They must both be lying, trying to gain her trust. Rachel decided to test this 'Yoram.' "Then you must know Udi as well?"

Udi let out a chuckle, "Indeed, I do. We're good friends. I'm even closer to him than I was to Ari."

Rachel narrowed her eyes, "Who is Udi's boss?"

Udi smiled. He now knew he could win her over, even though he would be risking a lot. "Yigal," he said dryly.

For the second time in the day, Rachel's head began spinning. The fact that this man knew Yigal was Udi's boss proved that he really did know Ari. But that he said he had worked with Ari, shook Rachel to her core. Ari had been a *Shabak* agent, and he had never told her. She started to sob uncontrollably.

Rachel's sobbing caught Udi off guard. He got up and started pacing the room, giving Rachel some time and space to gather herself. Udi always felt uncomfortable, and rather helpless around crying women. He noticed a box of facial tissues resting on the telephone table beside the door and brought it to the kitchen work island. Rachel popped three tissues out of the box, wiped the tears from her face and blew her nose. "What do you want from me?" she asked, still trying to catch her breath.

"I understand you've been gathering information and photographs related to Abu Alim's personal security system. If you can give me a good reason why you're doing the snooping, you'll be fine. If not, I can't call off the dogs. You're a prime suspect to be part of a group plotting an assassination. Your fiancé was murdered by a Palestinian terrorist, so you have the motive, and you are closely involved with right-wing extremists." Udi felt honesty might get her to admit her involvement, especially since she appeared to be so emotionally vulnerable right now.

Rachel walked silently to the telephone table and picked up the manila envelope. She brought it back to the work island where Udi was standing and dropped it on the white countertop. Udi opened the envelope and flipped through the photos. Confused, he asked, "What are these supposed to mean?"

"Not these," said Rachel, reaching for the close up of Ari's murderer, "this." She slapped the photograph down hard onto the Formica counter hoping the person in the picture would feel some pain as a result. "I wasn't looking for pictures of Abu Alim. I was looking for pictures of the terrorist who killed Ari. That's him. He's wearing my grandfather's watch Ari had with him at the time. He also has a scar on his hand. Ari's murderer fled, holding onto a bleeding left hand."

Udi whistled in astonishment. "Now it's starting to make sense," he said more to himself than to Rachel.

"And we're not trying to assassinate him either. We just want to bring him to justice..." said Rachel, starting to sob again, "and get my watch back."

Udi picked up the photograph and walked back to the sofa chair, his mind racing. "Can I have this photograph?" he asked.

"No, I need it. But if you want a picture of that animal, you can take that copy of Sunday's *Jerusalem Press*. What you're holding is a blowup of the picture on page three."

Udi put down the photograph and picked up the newspaper resting on the coffee table. He opened it, and found the photograph Rachel was talking about. The image was good enough to clearly identify Abu Alim's bodyguard. Udi got up and looked at Rachel. His heart reached out for his dead partner's fiancée who stood there looking so confused and helpless. "We'll get him Rachel. And we'll get the watch too. I promise."

Udi tucked the newspaper under his arm, and walked to the door, not expecting Rachel to answer. As he walked out, he twisted the doorknob open and silently closed the door as if there was a sleeping baby in the room. Rachel had been through enough. He didn't want to cause her any more suffering.

Forty Five

It was three hours since the last employee left the building. The security guard just finished his scheduled rounds of the empty offices. He walked over to the desk of the beautiful secretary with the red fingernails and long black hair. Between rounds he preferred sitting at her chair. Even hours after she left, the scent of her perfume lingered.

The beige upholstered secretarial chair groaned under the girth of the heavyset guard as he kicked up his feet to rest them on the desk beside the computer monitor. He leaned his head back to rest it against the wall, where a small greasy spot had developed on the white paint since he had discovered this haven a few weeks earlier. He closed his eyes to pick up his day dream where he had left off. But as he folded his arms across his chest, a sharp stabbing pain shot into his left bicep, interrupting his reverie.

He dropped his feet quickly to the floor, sat forward and looked down at his shirt pocket to see what was the source of his discomfort. Then he remembered the hard, three-and-a-half-inch floppy diskette his cousin had given to him earlier that day. His daydream could wait. What was

contained on that diskette would help him occupy the next
few hours.

The guard slipped the diskette out of his pocket and
gingerly slipped it into the computer built into a special slot
under the desk. He didn't have to turn on the machine since
it was already 'on.' In fact, he had been instructed by the
secretary a number of times to make sure that this particular
computer was left 'on' all night. It was used to send out international faxes in the middle of the night to save money on
long distance charges. He still had a few hours before the
machine woke itself up.

The guard then pulled out a piece of paper from his
wallet where his cousin had written down the exact instructions of how to activate the program on the diskette. He
hunted and pecked the letters on the unfamiliar English keyboard:

A: START

A small amber light flickered on the floppy disk drive,
and the drive began its rhythmic humming as the program
loaded into the system's memory. It seemed to take a long
time. The message at the bottom of the blank screen wasn't
much help as the guard didn't speak English.

Now loading. This may take a minute or two
depending on your system...

Suddenly the screen burst into a rainbow of colors accompanied by a tinny fanfare of synthesized music coming
over the PC's internal speaker. The bright gold logo of the
game cast a glow from the screen into the darkened room.
"Holy Stones!" At the bottom of the screen, another message

appeared as more chunks of the program were copied from
the floppy disk into memory:

This is a freeware game. Copy it as often as you
wish. The author's payment is the pleasure in the
knowledge that you are participating in some
small way in the Ultimate Battle.

The guard waited patiently for the game to begin. Even
though the graphics did not compare with the realistic 3-D
animation in state-of-the-art software, this was his favorite
computer game of all. It looked and sounded like a large-
screen color version of a 'Gameboy' game. His reflexes
weren't so great, so he could never reach scores like those of
his nine-year-old son, but that wasn't important. No matter
what score he achieved, he always felt good after playing this
game. The author, who was probably a 'brother' living in
America, was a genius.

A small figure looking a lot like a 'Mario Brother'
wrapped in a black and white checkered *kefiyah* appeared on
the screen against the backdrop of a pale blue sky. He began
floating down through fluffy white clouds, and then suddenly
came to an abrupt, bouncy stop on top of a large stone wall.

The guard placed the fingers of his right hand on the
'arrow' cursor keys, and rested his left thumb on the space
bar. He leaned forward getting ready for the action to begin.
The screen zoomed back, revealing a large golden dome in
the background to the left. Now you could see the small figure standing on top of a huge wall with dozens of similar
sized human figures bobbing back and forth on the ground
next to the wall. At the top right of the screen was a large
'zero' indicating the score, and beside it were four miniature
masked 'Marios' indicating how many 'warriors' were left

besides the one currently on the wall. When all five were used up, the game was over.

The guard tested all the cursor keys to make sure they were working properly. He held down the 'right arrow' and the figure sidestepped in a little dance along the wall to the right. 'Left arrow', left shuffle. 'Up arrow,' jump. 'Down arrow,' duck. He carefully positioned his warrior and pressed the space bar. A large stone fell from the warrior's hand and splattered on a man standing below wearing a round fur hat and a black and white striped prayer shawl. Ten points registered on the score board. The guard's chubby index finger pressed the 'left arrow' and he held down the space bar at the same time. Three stones fell, dropping in an arc and splattered on three more Jews praying at the Western Wall. The guard smiled as twenty points registered for the two Hassidim and fifty-points for the one settler. The settlers were the real enemy and deserved the most points. If you hit a tourist without a *kippah*, five points were deducted.

Suddenly a green-uniformed soldier appeared at the side of the screen and fired a shot. The guard pressed the up arrow, and little "Ahmed," as the guard had nicknamed his hero, easily jumped over the approaching bullet. He quickly dropped five more stones, scoring eighty points. Then a helicopter appeared in the sky and began shooting. He ducked the first round of bullets, but was struck down when another soldier fired from the left of the screen. Five hundred bonus points were added to the score for dying a martyr's death. The guard leaned back in his chair and sighed. Only six hundred and sixty points with his first 'Ahmed.' Oh well, the night was young, and things would get better as his fingers warmed up.

For quite some time, the empty office was filled with the clatter of the guard's fingers attacking the keyboard, and the simulated pinging of bullets and crunching of skulls. After about an hour of frenzied action and three hundred and forty thousand points later, the guard collapsed in exhaustion. He removed the diskette from the computer and placed it back in his shirt pocket, and then pressed the 'escape' key to exit the game. He folded his arms on the desk, and leaned forward placing his forehead on his right arm. As he closed his eyes, a satisfied smirk crossed his face as he tried to calculate how many 'virtual infidel Jews' he had eliminated from his Holy land tonight. Within minutes he was snoring contentedly, dreaming no longer about 'warriors' and 'infidels,' but about the woman whose perfume was tickling the bushy hairs in his nostrils as he slept.

An hour later, a high-pitched beeping roused him from his slumber as the computer began dialing a phone call. He opened his eyes momentarily when the squeal of the two computers 'handshaking' was echoed over the speaker. The guard closed his eyes, remembering that this computer did this every night. What did seem a little strange was that the computer appeared to spend much longer transmitting its information tonight than usual. He fell asleep as the computer was dumping its thirtieth megabyte of information over the telephone line to another computer only a few kilometers away. The heavy-set man fell so soundly asleep that he didn't even budge when the computer began its regularly scheduled sequence of fax calls about an hour and a half later that night.

Forty Six

For the second night in a row, Amiram had not slept. He was so exhausted this morning that he left home without showering or shaving. His knuckles glowed white as he mindlessly clenched the steering wheel with both hands. There were just over twenty-four hours to go before Abu Alim arrived in Jerusalem and all hell would break loose. Amiram's secret churned in his stomach. There had to be a way to positively identify the source of the "Shimshon" fax.

He sped down the empty streets of Jerusalem and screeched to a halt in his parking spot. He ran up the stairs into *Shabak* Jerusalem headquarters, but instead of turning right down the hallway to his office, he took the main staircase opposite the front doors down to the basement level. At the bottom of the staircase he turned left and at the end of the hall he knocked loudly on a door marked 'Information Systems and Communications.' Not only was this room protected by sixteen-inch-thick reinforced concrete that allowed it to double as a bomb shelter, but it also had an electronic lock. Every visitor first had to be visually identified by a small video camera mounted above the door frame and then 'buzzed' in.

Amiram was surprised, but pleased to see that it was Motti Nir, the Department Chief, who buzzed him in. "What brings you into the office so early in the morning?" asked Nir.

"I was about to ask you the same thing. I thought they let you old guys sleep in and made the young bucks handle the midnight to dawn shift," said Amiram walking into the cool, climate-controlled room. At this time of the morning there was no real need for air-conditioning, but some of the high-tech equipment was very sensitive to fluctuations in humidity.

"Normally, I'm not into the office until eight or eight thirty, but we've had an avalanche of information coming in lately that needs to be processed. We're backlogged by over a week," said Nir pointing to a desk behind him stacked high with computer printouts. "It seems I've created a monster," he added with a grin.

Amiram walked over to the desk and sat down in one of the two old wooden armchairs next to it. There was virtually an unlimited budget for electronic gadgetry, but the furniture was never replaced down here until it literally fell apart. Amiram was itching to get down to business, but he needed Nir's expertise and cooperation. These kinds of geniuses need to be humored he thought. And if you compliment them on a great idea, they'll do anything for you.

"Vot kind ov monster did you create, Doktor?" asked Amiram in his best Hungarian accent, "and speaking of monsters, do you happen to have any coffee in this dungeon? I feel like I'm one of the walking dead at this hour of the morning."

Nir walked over to a bookcase and took a large thermos from the shelf. He never kept liquids near the equipment. He opened it up and poured some coffee, pre-mixed with milk and sugar, into a Styrofoam cup. "Here," he said handing the cup to Amiram, "I brought this thermos with me from home last night. It's not steaming, but it should still hit the spot."

Amiram took a gulp of the warm brew. "*Nu?* So tell me about your monster already. Have you given it Abu Alim's address and phone number yet?"

"Not exactly, but some of Abu Alim's friends have already given their addresses and phone numbers to my monster," answered the communications genius with a smirk on his face.

"What are you talking about?" said Amiram shaking his head, trying to clear it of some cobwebs.

Nir sat down in the empty seat next to Amiram. As an inventor, he took most pleasure in the accomplishments of his mind. But in this business there were precious few people to talk to about his inventions. Since Amiram had the highest level of security, Nir jumped at the chance to describe his new 'baby' to him. "Well you see, about six months ago a new guy named Ilan joined the team down here. After he finished the army, he went to America for a while and worked as a computer programmer for one of the giant software houses. He's a genius in all areas of computing, but he developed an expertise in graphics and animation. Since he arrived, we racked our brains trying to come up with a way to take advantage of his talents."

Nir reached forward and flicked on the PC sitting on the desk in front of them. "Then we came up with it," he added as the machine booted up and the initial screen of *'Holy Stones!'* flashed on in brilliant color, "a computer game!"

Amiram looked at Nir as if he were a mad doctor who had actually gone mad. "What the heck does a computer game have to do with the spy business?"

"Exactly our point! No one would suspect it," said Nir triumphantly. "First we had to come up with a game that would be so anti-Semitic, and so controversial, that it would spread like wildfire." Nir started to play the game, and Amiram winced as he watched the rocks crashing down on the Jews praying at the Western Wall.

"I could imagine how some of our Arab neighbors might want to play the game and give a copy to their friends. But I'm sure there are a lot of Arabs who would be just as disgusted by this game as any Jew would be," added Amiram.

"Of course there are," said Nir acknowledging the obvious. "Only our enemies who want to terrorize us would play this game, and give it to their friends who hate us as well. It's a self selecting process. But that's exactly who we want the game to get to. And it's spread faster and wider through the Arab world than any known computer virus ever has."

"Why do you want the enemies of Jews to play a computer game that kills Jews. You really want to give them an opportunity to practice?" asked Amiram naively.

Nir shut off the computer and pulled out the floppy diskette. "Of course not, but you see there's more on this little floppy than the computer game. While the game is loading, a special communications program is loaded into memory if it detects some kind of modem in the system. The program stays in memory even after the game is finished and the diskette is removed, as long as the machine isn't turned off. Then at two o'clock in the morning, local time, the communications program wakes up and dials one of our trusty little computers in this 'dungeon.' After their machine links up with ours, it proceeds to dump the contents of its entire hard disk across the phone lines to us."

Amiram's jaw dropped as he considered the implications of what Nir had just explained. "It's simply brilliant.

But won't they catch on pretty quickly? Can't they trace you by the unexplained call on their phone bill?"

"First of all, after the program shuts down it erases itself from memory, so there is no trace of it. Also the program can't be discovered on the floppy disk, because it is embedded in the game itself. Next, the program will only operate on a computer which is left on all night that has a modem built into it. That means it won't be suspicious for the computer to make a call in the middle of the night, even if someone happens to be around in the room at the time." Nir stood up triumphantly on hearing himself explain the genius of the program. "And the phone number they're calling is a fake Arab business, registered in East Jerusalem. They'll have a heck of a time tracking it to us. If it does get discovered, they'll think it's some kind of corporate espionage and never let anyone know that their computer security has been breached. Arabs don't like being embarrassed.

Amiram whistled.

"Our only problem is storage capacity. In the last week alone we've been flooded with over forty gigabytes of data from all over the world, ranging from a car dealership in Pakistan, to the Iranian Embassy in London." Nir gave a self-satisfied grin like a kid who had sneaked some candy away from the neighborhood bully. What gave him more satisfaction was Amiram's astonishment. "So what can I do for you this morning?"

Amiram was so entranced by Nir's monster that he had almost forgotten why he had come. He took a sip of coffee from the Styrofoam cup and cleared his throat. "It's about the Shimshon fax. I need to know who sent it. We only have today to find out. Tomorrow will be too late." Amiram didn't have to add, 'it's a matter of life and death.' In this building that was understood.

Motti Nir's face flushed. In the excitement of the calls coming in from all over the Arab world, and the intelligence opportunities that presented, he and his staff had forgotten the cryptic fax. "We still haven't discovered the source," he said quietly, being careful not to lie about forgetting it, 'but with all this new data flooding us, we might be able to find some new clues." Nir looked at his watch. It was time to go home. The next shift would be arriving shortly. The exhilaration he felt inside due to the success of his brainchild, contrasted with the desperation in Amiram's face made him decide to stay and help his friend. "Come," he said to Amiram, "I'll make some fresh coffee and we'll do some data surfing together to see what we can find."

Forty Seven

"There simply isn't enough time. This whole plan is absurd," said Moshe Porat dismissing with a flip of his hand the copy of the briefing paper that had been placed in front of each of the men sitting at the large conference table. He removed his reading glasses, indicating he had seen enough, and sat back in the brown leather armchair that was a clone of the other eleven chairs in the room. Only six other chairs were occupied.

The Police Minister's words broke Yigal Ramon's concentration and he looked up from his copy of the paper he had stayed up all night preparing. He frowned at Porat. His smug arrogance was irritating. The Police Minister constantly tried to prop himself up by putting everyone else down — especially his own Police Commissioner. The Police Minister was a political appointment and knew little about security matters. Aryeh Levi, the Police Commissioner was a career professional who rose through the ranks of the police force. There was no love lost between them.

The other men in the room had, with experience, learned to ignore Porat's remarks and were still reading the brief. Yigal surveyed the room that was populated by the same group that had met yesterday in the Prime Minister's office with two exceptions; Yossi Shiloni's absence, and the presence of Yigal's own boss, Dov Zehavi the head of *Shabak*. Shiloni decided to remain in his office, waiting for the group's decision so as not to arouse suspicion among the media that something serious was happening. They monitored the Prime Minister's schedule daily.

Yigal shifted his glance to his friend Aryeh Levi, the Police Commissioner, who under normal circumstances would be the one to head this operation. Due to the sensitive nature of the visit and the requirement to keep a large part of the security undercover, the Prime Minister had decided to put the campaign under the control of the *Shabak*. Since it was a Jerusalem-based issue, it was reasonable for Yigal to be given the reigns, rather than his boss Zehavi. Besides, the Prime Minister wanted it that way. The new head of *Shabak* had only been in office for less than a year and was still an unknown entity to the Prime Minister. Even though Shiloni despised Yigal, he at least knew with whom he was conducting business.

"You seem to have covered every contingency, Yigal," said Shaika Oren, the Chief of Staff. He closed his black plastic folder containing the brief and glared at Porat as if to say, 'you're an idiot.' Yigal smiled.

"It's seems like the best we could hope for under the circumstances, but we definitely have to move fast," said Aryeh Levi, the Police Commissioner. "As a matter of fact, if we're going to meet tomorrow morning's deadline, we have to send a bus down to Gaza immediately to pick up the Palestinian security men and get them to Jerusalem for a briefing this afternoon."

Yigal breathed a sigh of relief. The two most important professional security men in the plan, the head of the Police and the head of the Armed Forces were on his side. The rest was politics. "The bus is already there, and I have a team going over the list of names of the security officers the Palestinians want to bring along with Abu Alim to the Temple Mount."

Yisrael Eitan, Director General of the Prime Minister's office, jumped into the conversation. "Before we get caught up in details, now that we've all had a chance to go over the brief, why don't we let Yigal review the key points for us." Eitan didn't trust Moshe Porat's reading comprehension abilities.

Yigal took the nod from Eitan and stood up. He felt it gave him more authority, and would help minimize the amount of dissension to his plan. There really wasn't any time left to change it anyway. He cleared his throat and began.

"At 2:00 p.m. this afternoon, the busload of thirty Palestinian security personnel will depart from Gaza. They will travel directly to our Police Headquarters Training Facility in Jerusalem. There, they will be briefed directly by you Aryeh, about their deployment on the Temple Mount. We don't want any second level people involved in this until the latest possible moment.

"At 4:30 p.m. we will have gathered together in this building our thirty men who will be 'one-on-oneing' the Palestinians and begin our briefing of them. After dinner, our men will be brought to the Police Training Facility to meet and be assigned to their counterparts.

"Also, beginning at 2:00 p.m., the Police, in conjunction with the Border Police and other Army personnel will be briefed with the plan to secure the Temple Mount giving the illusion we will be doing it on Friday, and not tomorrow. I understand that the order to move vehicles and other riot control equipment has already been given. Isn't that so Shaika?"

The Chief of Staff nodded.

Yigal looked around the room to ensure they were still with him before continuing. "The beauty of this whole plan is that Abu Alim will be arriving and leaving directly to and from the Temple Mount by helicopter. Since the area is self contained, we only have to secure it for the twenty minutes he will be there to *daven* at the *Al Aksa* mosque." The men in the room laughed at Yigal's use of the Yiddish word for prayer.

Yigal waited for the laughter to subside. "There will be no speeches or statements. No press to contend with. No re-routing of traffic to protect any official motorcades. We simply arrive at 6:00 a.m. to deploy our personnel along with the Palestinian security men. At seven, we have local Jerusalem police seal off all the gates leading into the Old City and the Temple Mount. Abu Alim's helicopter lands at 7:45 accompanied by two of our IDF choppers, while most of Israel is on their way to work. At 8:15 he flies off into the wild blue yonder. Then we pack up and go home, before anyone opposed to the visit realizes what happened."

"I don't trust Abu Alim," said Shaika Oren, "how do we know he won't start mouthing off up there and then demand to tour other Moslem sites in the city."

"Remember," answered Yigal, "there are no press people up there. Also, he has no access to any vehicle, and all the gates are locked. Besides, part of the agreement is that Abu Alim announce he will be holding a press conference in Gaza at 9:00 a.m. tomorrow to make a major announcement. It's part of the smoke screen, but it also guarantees he will be on the Mount for the minimum amount of time. There is no way he will be late for an opportunity to speak live to all the major networks. His public image in the West is very important to him."

Yisrael Eitan glanced down at his watch. "As a matter of fact, Alim should be announcing the press conference right about now. We wanted him to wait a few hours, but he insisted on giving the network technicians twenty-four hours to set up all their satellite equipment."

"Disinformation is crucial in this whole exercise," said Zehavi, the head of *Shabak*. "Without the element of surprise, we'll need a full military campaign to control all the people who are against this visit."

"On both sides," added Chaim Azriel, the Minister of Defense. "Yisrael, you are going to play a critical role over the next few hours. As Director General of the Prime Minister's office, what you say about Friday's visit, and whether the public believes you or not could make or break the whole operation."

Everyone except Yigal began folding up their papers. As experienced military men, they knew when everything that needed to be said had been said. Anything more would be redundant for the planning stages. Now it was time to put the plan into action. As they began to get up from their seats, the red phone on the conference table rang out, stopping everyone in their tracks. It was the direct link to the Prime Minister's office.

Yigal picked up the receiver and put it to his ear. All eyes in the room watched his face go white as he listened silently to the voice on the other end of the line for about thirty seconds. He replaced the hand set and ran both his hands through his hair, buying time to control his anger.

"Yisrael," he began slowly and quietly, "that was your assistant. The Prime Minister asked him to call us. Apparently Abu Alim not only announced over the radio that there will be a press conference in Gaza at 9:00 tomorrow morning, but that the topic of discussion will be his visit to the

Temple Mount we have asked him to make tomorrow morning at 7:45 a.m. instead of Friday morning."

The men in the room stood in shocked silence.

"Shiloni doesn't want to talk to us. I guess he's afraid we'll try to convince him to cancel the visit. He gave strict instructions that we go ahead at all costs," continued Yigal through gritted teeth.

"Looks like we're going to have a long day, and that military campaign after all," said the Chief of Staff dropping his files back on the table and taking his seat.

Forty Eight

"Hey kids, look who's here!" called out Shoshana Tal as she opened the door, inviting her unexpected guests inside.

Sarah looked up from the Lego city she was making for her little brother on the living room floor. "Uncle Marc!" she shouted.

"MUK!" chimed in Yoni as he got up. The two year old ran to Marc and gave his left leg a big bear hug.

"And what about saying *Shalom* to Auntie Rachel?" asked Shoshana cocking an eye at her eight-year-old daughter. Inviting guests and making them feel comfortable was a major *mitzvah* in the Tal home. Shoshana gave Sarah an encouraging nod, understanding that Rachel was for all intents and purposes a new person in her life. The years that had passed had erased all recognition of Rachel from Sarah's memory.

Sarah got up and walked over to Rachel to help her with the plastic bags she was carrying. "*Shalom*... Auntie Rachel," she said very politely, but a still a little uncomfortable calling this woman with whom she had only spent one *Shabbat*, 'Auntie.'

"Hi Sarah, shouldn't you be in school at this time of the morning?" asked Rachel, trying to make eight-year-old small talk, but realizing it was the wrong thing to say as soon as she said it.

Sarah blushed, not wanting to tell Rachel the real reason she was home. She was afraid the soldiers might come and take away her mother while she was at school. Sarah didn't want to tell her mother the truth either, so she had complained of a bad stomach ache this morning. Shoshana not knowing the exact source of her daughter's pain, let her stay home under the circumstances.

The lack of response from Sarah to her question made Rachel uncomfortable. She looked to Marc for help who was already down on the stone tile floor giving Yoni a horsy ride.

Sensing Rachel's discomfort, Sarah said, "I had a tummy ache this morning, so I stayed home from school today."

"In that case, I don't know if the Barbecue-flavored *Bisli* we brought is going to hurt or help," said Rachel handing some of the plastic bags to the little girl.

As they walked to the kitchen to put the bags down on the kitchen table, Sarah looked up at Rachel and asked, "If *you're* Auntie Rachel, and *he's* Uncle Marc, does that mean you're married?"

Now it was Rachel's turn to blush. She was glad Marc hadn't heard the question, otherwise she would have become beet red. Rachel smiled at Sarah and tried to come up with a quick answer to get out of the situation. "Well," began Rachel, "I'm not really your Aunt. In fact I'm nobody's *real* aunt. And Marc isn't your *real* Uncle either. So I guess it doesn't make sense that we would *really* be married either."

Sarah gave her one of those eight-year-old looks as if to say, 'what do you mean, it doesn't make sense that you would be married, it's a perfectly reasonable assumption.'

Then she looked at the parcels on the table and pulled out a package of potato chips. "Do you think it would be okay if I had this?" she asked.

"If your Imma says its all right, it's fine by me," smiled Rachel, understanding that Sarah's aches weren't really sourced in her tummy.

Sarah started to skip toward the kitchen door but paused to look at Rachel. "You know, we really *looooove* Uncle Marc. And you're pretty nice too," she said looking down at the bag of chips. "Why don't you get married? You look really nice together."

"Sarah!" scolded Shoshana, "I think it's time for you to go play with Yoni and Uncle Marc in the other room. You can share your potato chips with them." Shoshana gave her daughter a pat on the back of the head, shooing her out of the kitchen. When she was out of earshot, Shoshana said quietly to Rachel, "But she was right about you two looking really nice together."

Rachel blushed again, and decided to change the subject. "We came to see if we could take care of Yoni... and I guess Sarah too, so that you could go and visit Meir for a few hours. How is he doing?"

"That's so sweet of you," said Shoshana giving Rachel a hug.

"Actually it was Marc's idea," added Rachel, "Sarah's right about him being very special."

Shoshana gave a knowing nod as if to say, 'Aha, I see Sarah wasn't too far off in her prognosis.' Then she said, "I really don't know how Meir is doing. They won't let me see him. But they do let me bring him food, as long as I don't bake any metal files into the apple cake."

Both women laughed, and Rachel gave Shoshana a hug this time. She was inspired by how well Shoshana was taking the fact that her husband was locked up in jail. Shoshana put her arm around Rachel and they walked into the living room.

"Auntie Rachel says she and Uncle Marc came to baby-sit for a while so I can take some food to Abba. What do you say kids?" asked Shoshana, a little concerned about how Sarah would feel being left at home.

"*Yesh!*" shouted Sarah in the Israeli version of 'yippee.'

"MAWC! MAWC! Hossy!" laughed Yoni.

Rachel gazed at Marc wrestling with the two children on the floor in front of her, and looked forward to the opportunity of playing house for the next few hours.

Forty Nine

The morning bustle of activity at the Information Systems and Communications Center of the *Shabak* Jerusalem Bureau failed to penetrate Amiram's concentration as he stared at the computer screen. Motti Nir was busy discussing various projects in process with some of his men, but Amiram had been glued, trance-like to the screen for the last hour, hoping that the file search program would find something. He was mesmerized by the small animated icon of a set of file folders passing under a magnifying glass. This let the computer operator know the machine was working. The process was agonizingly slow.

The first search Nir had tried in finding a copy of the Shimshon Fax among the data that had come in via the 'Holy Stones' game was a based on file name. Nir guessed the author of the fax might have saved it on his system with a file name beginning with S-H-I-M. Amiram had often done similar searches on his home computer. What would have taken about 5 seconds to scan the 100 megabytes on Amiram's home PC took almost 25 minutes to scan 40 gigabytes this morning. Forty gigabytes was four hundred times the amount of data on Amiram's machine.

At 6:45 a.m., after the file name search had failed, Nir decided to try a much longer word search. To speed up the process, he asked the computer to look for files that contained the word 'Shimshon' that were less than 25 Kbytes in size. It was only a short note, and Nir hoped it wasn't saved as part of a larger document. But even with these restrictions designed to speed up the process, Nir still estimated the search might take up to five hours.

Amiram felt a sharp pang in his stomach which broke him out of his trance. He looked at his watch. Ten thirty. The program had been working for over three hours, and still nothing. On the table beside the computer he noticed the torn empty wrapper of a large package of chocolate-covered lemon wafers. That was the source of his stomach ache. He had absently eaten the whole package. The sugar from the lemon filling grated at his teeth.

Suddenly the computer screen popped to life and four file names appeared on the screen followed by a message at the bottom:

IRIGSYS.L01	21,424
IRIGSYS.L03	14,336
IRIGSYS.L05	12,272
IRIGSYS.L06	19,594

4 FILES FOUND, SEARCH COMPLETE.

Amiram jumped out of his seat excitedly and ran to find Nir. 'IRIGSYS,' he thought, 'I wonder what that means?' Motti Nir, walked back quickly to the computer terminal. He was exhausted after having been up all night. He sat down and his fingers danced on the keyboard activating a file viewer program to examine the contents of the four files. Amiram leaned annoyingly close over Nir's shoulder to watch the results. Within a few minutes the answer became clear. Amiram's English was just as good as Nir's and he understood the contents of the files. They were letters from an agricultural supply company in Cairo to a company called Irigsys in Beersheba that manufactured automated drip irrigation systems. Apparently the sales manager at Irigsys was named Shimshon.

Amiram slumped down into the chair beside Nir and rested his head in the palms of his hands. 'The fax must be somewhere in that electronic haystack. I have to find it,' he thought. It was almost a prayer.

Nir leaned back in his chair and turned his attention away from the computer screen to the defeated looking agent next to him. He liked Amiram, and wanted to console his colleague. "Listen Amiram," he said. "I don't understand why you're so upset about not finding that Shimshon fax in this pile of data. Why should we think a message threatening to kill Abu Alim and a bunch of innocent Moslems at one of Islam's holiest sites would come from an Arab computer?"

A butterfly fluttered through the churning lemon wafers inside Amiram's stomach. He composed himself and looked at Nir in an attempt to hide the fact that that's exactly what he suspected. Amiram spoke slowly and coldly, "There are less than twenty four hours before Abu Alim is up on the Temple Mount. So far we've reached a dead end. *Shabak* agents are trained to think 'sideways.' We have to consider every possibility." Amiram stood up and stretched his back. He moved to Nir who was still sitting, and squeezed his shoulder. "Thanks for your help. I've got to get moving. See if you can find someone with a fresh mind to try some other kind of search. I still have a hunch that our fax is buried in there somewhere."

An over-tired Motti Nir looked up at Amiram and gave him a half-hearted smile of encouragement as he walked out the door.

Fifty

"*Bisli, Bisli!*" whined Yoni.

Rachel leaned over and spoke as sympathetically as she could to the two year old, "I'm sorry Yoni, the *Bisli* are all finished. You and Sarah ate them all an hour ago."

Yoni paused to think, the way two year olds do. He looked up at Rachel, and with a sparkle in his eye and a big smile on his open mouth he asked hopefully, "Chips?"

Rachel pursed her lips to keep from laughing. Yoni was just too cute. The world was so simple from a two year old vantage point. "Sorry, Yoni, we finished those too..."

A loud wail pierced the relative calm of the house as Yoni dropped to the floor and began his tantrum. Marc ran into the house followed by Sarah. He looked at Yoni huddled into a ball on the floor screaming 'Chips, Chips, *CHIPS!*' Rachel was sitting patiently on the living-room sofa next to him. Marc looked at her and they both broke into laughter.

"I think he's hungry," she said in an understatement.

"It's probably time to start thinking about lunch." Marc looked at his watch. "Who wants some French toast?" he asked. It was more of an announcement.

"Me!" said Sarah, hopping on both feet. She loved Marc's French toast.

Yoni abruptly stopped his crying. He jumped up and shouted with a big smile, "ME!"

"Okay," said Marc, breathing a sigh of relief, "Sarah, you and Yoni go outside and pick up all the toys while Rachel and I make the toast."

The children ran outside and Rachel followed Marc to the kitchen. "You're really great with the kids," she said.

"It's easy when you're dealing with really great kids," he answered, taking half a dozen eggs out of the fridge. "Can you please see if there's any bread in the breadbox over there on the counter, otherwise I'll take some out of the freezer." Marc was uncomfortable talking about his domestic side.

"There's almost a full loaf here," she said, bringing it over to the work island where Marc was cracking and checking the eggs. "And don't be so humble. It's rare to see someone who's not married, so comfortable around kids. Most of the men I dated in Toronto who were successful in their careers were usually intimidated by little children." Rachel felt it was time to start making 'date' conversation.

"That's understandable," he said beating the eggs with fork. "Guys in their thirties who are single and successful, are competent in most areas of their lives. They feel in control, and they like to be in control. It's very difficult to be a high-powered professional pleading with a two-year old to put on his pajamas." They both laughed.

"So how do *you* do it so comfortably?" she asked.

"Before I answer your question, I'm going to show you how to make perfect French toast. First you add a tablespoon of water to the scrambled eggs. Then," he said reaching into a cupboard above the counter, "you add two drops of vanilla extract and beat it all together. Now if you could get the milk out of the fridge and pour a cup of it into that stainless steel bowl in the dish rack, I'll show you the secret."

Rachel followed his instructions, fascinated by discovering this new side of Marc.

"And speaking of secrets," added Marc, beginning to answer Rachel's question, "my secret to being comfortable around kids is to focus on the difference between competence and control. A lot of guys like me feel competent in their business lives, and therefore mistakenly feel in control as well. In truth, I'm not in control of the results I achieve in life, God is. I'm only in control of my actions. Usually if you are competent in your actions, the result is success... but not always. Once I learned I wasn't expected to achieve results, but was only expected to act responsibly I could relax around kids. I'm not expected to get Yoni to stop crying, I'm only expected to deal with him responsibly. Make my best effort."

Rachel poured the milk into the bowl, drinking up Marc's thoughts.

"Now as I was saying, here's the real secret to great French toast. We're going to soak the slices of bread in the milk before we dip them in the vanilla-flavored egg batter." Marc placed the bowl with the batter next to the bowl with the milk and undid the twist-tie opening the bag of bread. "I'm sure there must have been a lot of good guys in Toronto you were set up with— you couldn't find one who was appropriate?" It was obvious Marc was fishing for a description of what Rachel was looking for in a husband, to see if he himself fit the bill.

"Well," said Rachel, "to be honest, I want to marry a real hero."

Marc dunked a slice of bread into the milk, lifted it out of the bowl and let the excess liquid drip out before he dipped it into the egg batter and placed it on a plate. "A hero? That's a tall order. There aren't too many of those around today."

Rachel opened a drawer marked 'dairy' beside the stove looking for a frying pan. "Well it all depends on your definition of 'hero.' Before I came back to Israel I was working as an administrator of a rehabilitation center for stroke victims. Every day dozens of volunteers would come into the center to help formerly competent adults relearn how to communicate and live a normal life. I don't know who impressed me more, the volunteers or the patients struggling to achieve their potential. A hero is someone worth emulating. Today in America that means the strongest, wealthiest, most beautiful or most entertaining. My hero is not the one who entertains his fellow man, but someone who takes care of his fellow man."

Marc pressed the electric starter on the gas range and a blue flame popped to life. "Maimonides teaches us that the highest form of charity is when one gives another human being the ability to help himself," he said giving support to Rachel's insights.

"I'm into fulfilling my career potential just as much as the next person," she said taking over the dunking of the bread as Marc began frying the first slices of toast. "But I want to use my career as a tool to help people. That's what I'm looking for in a husband. And if my goal is to help people, then I never want my career to interfere with my ability to help my own husband and children from fulfilling their potential first."

Except for the sizzling of the frying pan, an uncomfortable silence filled the kitchen as Marc considered if he could live up to Rachel's expectations.

Unknown to Marc, Rachel had already decided that through his actions of coming to Israel at the peak of his career, helping Leah start *Kol Ha'am*, teaching at the Yeshiva, and finally taking the care to make lunch for Sarah and Yoni, he had already become one of her heroes. Rachel noticed the puzzled expression on Marc's face turn almost to resignation indicating he was accepting the fact that perhaps he wasn't the one for Rachel. Rachel's heart began to pound. No, no that's not what she meant to do. She was trying to show how different he was from the other men she had dated. She felt like yelling out, 'It's okay Marc. You're my hero, you are my hero!' But she held herself back. She didn't want to embarrass him. She would find another way to tell him how she felt.

"What smells so great?" asked Shoshana Tal as she came into the kitchen with Sarah and Yoni trailing behind.

"Marc's frying up a batch of the world's greatest French toast," answered Rachel.

Marc blushed. "How's Meir?" he asked, changing the subject.

"They still wouldn't let me see him, but they took the food," answered Shoshana trying to hide her disappointment. "I hope he gets to eat it. But I also spoke to my mother-in-law on the car phone on the way home," she added, also trying to change the subject. "It's pandemonium over there. You'd better get to her house right after lunch. They're in a rush to organize tomorrow morning's demonstration against Abu Alim's visit."

Sarah looked at her mother and then at Marc and Rachel. "Do you really have to go?" she asked. "Don't you see that none of these demonstrations will work until the Jewish people do *teshuva*?"

The adults fell silent. The little girl in her innocence had uttered something very profound. Sarah was only echoing what she learned in school every day from the books of Moses and the Prophets. Whenever anything bad happened to the Jewish people as a nation, it was an indication for them to do *teshuva*, to change the self destructive path they were on and return to one that would help them achieve their potential. They had a role to play as a light unto nations, and if they didn't set the highest standard of morality for other nations to see, then problems befell them throughout history. Sarah assumed the current situation that had taken her father away from her was no different.

Rachel kneeled down and took Sarah's hands. "Let's assume somebody wakes up one morning and opens up his front door, only to find a lion sitting on the porch."

Sarah's eyes widened as she imagined the scene.

"Certainly, *HaShem* is trying to get that person's attention. And when he figures out the message, and changes his ways, the lion will go away. But it makes sense that *HaShem* would want him to shut the door so the lion couldn't come inside while he was trying to figure out the message and do *teshuva*."

Sarah nodded.

"So *Saraleh*, our demonstrations are like shutting the door on the lion. They give us more time so we can work on helping the Jewish people become the best they can be." Rachel didn't want Sarah to see the tears welling in her eyes, so she gave the little girl a hug.

It was clear to Marc what Rachel meant when she spoke of heroes.

Fifty One

Amiram Barr stared blankly at the computer screen on his office desk as the Reuters news clippings scrolled by. He didn't know what he was looking for, but anything was better than wasting time trailing Rachel Stein and Marc Goodman. He had requested a search of all news items that quoted Abu Alim from the last two weeks. Perhaps there was an incriminating hint hidden in something he said in a recent article. If Motti Nir couldn't come up with any leads, Amiram had to find some other way to link the Shimshon fax back to the President of Palestine.

If only Amiram hadn't printed out that copy of the Shimshon file from Ari's terminal, none of this would be happening. Amiram was reeling with guilt. If he hadn't taken things into his own hands, his friend Ari might be alive today. Amiram thought of Rachel and slammed his fist down on the desk as he quickly got to his feet. His office chair rolled backwards a few feet, almost as if to get out of his way. He walked to the window to look out at the city and gather his thoughts, but the view was blocked by a large eucalyptus tree. He felt closed in. He wanted to run away from this nightmare but he couldn't. Now there were even more lives at stake, and he was the only one who held the key to stopping the innocent deaths.

Everyone assumed it was Ari who had printed out the copy of the Shimshon file as an insurance policy. It was reasonable that anyone leaving *Shabak* because of a moral argument would take with him some incriminating information against the organization as protection. No information could have been more incriminating than the Shimshon file — a government plot to kill innocent Palestinians on the Temple Mount. All Ari would have had to do was deposit a sealed copy with a lawyer with instructions to open it in the event of his death. In fact it was so obvious, that Yigal had never thought it necessary to get a blackmail letter from Ari. That the file was printed from Ari's terminal after he quit said it all.

Yet this wasn't what happened at all. It was Amiram who printed out the fateful file. He thought he was doing his friend Ari a favor by foiling the Shimshon plan. Amiram had been almost as outraged as Ari was when he first heard about Shiloni's idea for giving the Temple Mount to the Palestinians. When he found out Ari had quit over it, and he lost the best partner an agent could have, he decided to do something concrete about the outrage. He also wanted to do something to guarantee the plan would never be carried out.

Amiram thought continuously for two days considering all the options. If he leaked it to the Israeli press, they would be smart enough to link it back to *Shabak* and cause a national scandal. If he put it in the hands of the opposition political parties, they would have used it to bring down the government and take control of the country. Neither option appealed to Amiram. There had to be a third option that would get the job done, yet cause the least amount of interference. Then it came to him. The safest thing to do was send the Shimshon file anonymously to the PLO. He assumed they would leak it immediately and take credit for breaking Israeli security. Naively the Palestinians would think they would be able to capitalize on the ensuing international sympathy generated from the revelation of the Israeli government plot. In fact, no one would have taken them seriously. The western world would assume that the plan was a fabrication of the Palestinians themselves to gain sympathy. The crisis in Israel would be averted, and there would be no way for Shiloni to carry out the plan anymore, now that it had been revealed to the world.

Amiram's plan was simple and brilliant. The only problem was it didn't work out that way. For some reason the Palestinians decided not to reveal the Shimshon file. Instead, a few days later Ari was murdered in a terror attack.

In the ensuing two month investigation, Amiram, Udi and a *Shabak* team assigned to them worked around the clock tracking Ari's murderer. They pulled out all stops and cashed in all outstanding favors with their informants. Finally they determined his identity. It was Ahmed Abdo, a senior body guard to Jibril Abu Alim, who at that time was a rising star in the PLO.

Amiram had proudly presented the information to his boss Yigal, and waited patiently for a response. Instead of receiving the anticipated order to eliminate Abdo, Amiram and the rest of the team were shocked and furious when they received instructions from the Prime Minister, by way of Yigal to 'do nothing.'

Amiram's intuition told him that there was a connection between the Shimshon file that he had leaked to the PLO and Ari's murder, but he couldn't talk about it. It was a secret that had eaten away at his soul for years.

When the Prime Minister confronted the PLO leadership with the fact that one of their senior *Fatah* people had committed the terrorist murder which was a direct violation of the Oslo Declaration of Principles, they responded by saying that Abdo acted alone. The PLO indicated that Abdo's cousin, an Islamic terrorist had been killed by *Shabak* agents the previous week. Ari's murder was simply a private act of revenge due to temporary insanity.

The Israeli government bought the story and agreed with the PLO to drop the affair. That a senior PLO member carried out the terror attack could cause serious damage to the peace process if the public became aware of it — and the peace process had to advance at all costs, before the Islamic fundamentalists became too powerful.

Amiram felt nauseous watching Abu Alim's name scroll up his computer screen as the Reuters's stories flew by. Abu Alim had somehow been behind Ari's murder, thought Amiram, and he must somehow be involved with the Shimshon plan as well. Alim had been acting with a lot more *chutzpah* lately than usual.

The office door opened abruptly, startling Amiram. "Sorry," said Udi hurrying in the room, "I didn't expect anyone to be here, I thought you were supposed to be out chasing Rachel." Udi walked over to his desk and opened the bottom of three drawers on the right. He pulled out a clean shirt that he kept there for emergencies and tore open the wrapping from the dry cleaners.

"You know it's a waste of time to follow her, she's got nothing to do with this," said Amiram sitting up in his chair. He began to actually read some of the words rolling by on the screen.

"I know," said Udi unbuttoning the soiled shirt he was wearing, "she's only back to bring Ari's murderer to justice. And it seems she's found him." Udi reached into his attaché case and tossed the *Jerusalem Press* he had taken from Rachel's apartment to Amiram. It was open to page three and folded back so that the photograph of Abu Alim and his bodyguard Ahmed Abdo was on top.

The two agents looked at each other, blushed and burst out laughing in an unspoken admission that they both had spoken to Rachel Stein since she was back. The details of those encounters were better left unsaid.

Amiram swiveled his chair to face his partner who was already doing up the freshly starched shirt. "My intuition tells me that Abu Alim was behind Ari's murder," Amiram paused to think before making the next admission, "and I think that somehow he's behind the Shimshon fax as well."

"What did you just say?" said Udi temporarily suspending the buttoning of his shirt.

"You heard me. Motti Nir is downstairs trying to track down the source of the fax right now, and I'm scanning some news stories to see if I can find a connection."

Udi narrowed his eyes at his partner. He trusted Amiram implicitly. Reading his face, he knew it was better not to quiz Amiram about the source of his suspicions. If he stated them aloud, there were firm grounds for his hunches. "If that's true, then our whole plan of defense in this operation has to be turned upside down." Udi's mind raced in an attempt to catch up with Amiram's information. "If it's not the settlers planning the attack on the Temple Mount, and instead it's Abu Alim's own people..." Udi shook his head trying to come up with some logic behind Amiram's claim. "Does Yigal know?" he asked, changing the subject and thereby giving himself some time to think about what Amiram was implying.

"I'm not going to confront Yigal with this until I have some hard evidence," answered Amiram. "Who could believe that Abu Alim would consider such a diabolical act? What could possibly be going on in Alim's head?"

"Well," answered Udi, "I can ask him for you. Yigal's elected me to be the one to accompany the President of Palestine tomorrow morning in his private helicopter. That's why I'm in such a hurry, I'm on my way down to Gaza right now." Udi finished buttoning the cuffs on his shirt. "And I sure would appreciate it if you could find that information quickly, because I'll be standing right next to Abu Alim tomorrow morning on the Temple Mount when the fireworks start." Udi took a deep breath, grabbed his briefcase and overnight bag and started toward the door. He turned back to look at Amiram, "Unless of course you can stop whoever it is from lighting the fuse."

Fifty Two

"It's all right. They don't need beds or mattresses," explained Itzik hurriedly into the phone, "They'll bring their own sleeping bags. How many can you fit on your living room floor?" Itzik smiled as he received the answer, thanked the family on the other end of the line and hung up the phone. "The Charlap's have room for eight," he called out to David Moscowitz who, because he was visiting Leah's house at the time, had been drafted to consolidate the list of host families living in the Old City of Jerusalem.

Leah came out of the kitchen to make an announcement to the assembled volunteers who were frantically making phone calls and compiling lists just as Marc and Rachel walked in the door. "Everyone get ready to pack up," she shouted over the din, "we're going to move everything to the Old City. The Community Center in the Jewish Quarter is going to take over as headquarters for the demonstration."

Marc and Rachel walked towards Leah. "What's happening? Shoshana told us things were a little crazy here."

Leah sighed. "We're trying to organize a demonstration for tomorrow morning against Abu Alim's visit to the Temple Mount. The problem is we're in a race against the clock as well as the army and the police."

"What does that mean?"

"I just got off the phone with the head of the Civil Guard in the Jewish Quarter," explained Leah. "He told me the police informed him that the Old City gates will be closed starting at 5:00 p.m. to vehicular traffic other than Jewish Quarter residents. At 8:00 p.m. no more cars will be let in at all, and only pedestrians who have documentation proving they live in the Old City will be allowed in."

"A closure of the Old City?" said Marc incredulously, "It's a tourist site!"

"That's not all," continued Leah, "it gets better. After 9:00 p.m. no one will be allowed in the streets of the Old City except for security personnel until 9:00 a.m. tomorrow morning, after Abu Alim's visit is over."

"A curfew?!" shrieked Rachel. "That's outrageous."

"That's Yossi Shiloni," said David Moscowitz cynically, folding up his papers.

Leah pursed her lips before continuing. She too couldn't believe this was happening in the 'only democracy in the middle east.' "The way they figure it," she explained, "if there are no people to demonstrate, there's no demonstration. Simple. What we're trying to do is get as many people into the Old City before they shut it down. Somehow tomorrow morning we'll find a way for them to get out into the streets to demonstrate. I've been on the phone with various yeshivas around town to see how many of their boys they can send to the Old City with sleeping bags. In the meantime we've also been calling families living in the Jewish Quarter to see how many people they can host. Because time's running out, we're moving to the Old City. They already have people walking through the streets with megaphones asking residents to come down to the Community Center to inform us how many demonstrators they can host."

Rachel looked at Leah, and then at Marc. "Is it really worth all the effort? Nothing's going to stop Shiloni or Abu Alim even if we manage to break the curfew and have a few hundred people shouting slogans and waving placards."

Marc watched the reasonableness of Rachel's words weigh heavy on Leah's shoulders. Was it really worth it? Marc turned to Rachel and spoke loudly so that he was directing his words not just at Rachel but to Leah and everyone else in the room as well. "This 'visit' of an arch enemy and murderer of the Jewish people to our holiest of sites is a message from the Almighty. That a Jewish government is forcing us to accept this moral outrage is also a message. Throughout our history, the response of the Torah community to a spiritual attack was a physical one. That's the lesson of Chanukah. When the Greeks threatened the Jewish people with assimilation, by outlawing Torah study, circumcision and Temple worship, the Maccabis struck back like a hammer to defend our values. Who would have expected a band of renegade ultra-orthodox Jews to defeat the might of the Greek army? No one. But because they took action, God let the miracle happen."

Marc focused his attention squarely on Rachel. "No one expects us to bring down the government through waving some signs and shouting some words. But if we make an effort and show that we really care about what the Jewish people stand for by focusing our prayers to the Almighty as well, then miracles can and will happen."

"Come everybody, *Mi Lashem Elai*" shouted Itzik using the Maccabi's 2,500 year old rallying cry, "let's go to the Wall!"

Fifty Three

Two huge maps of Jerusalem stood on easels next to the conference table of the operations room in *Shabak* Jerusalem headquarters; one of the walled Old City, and one of the entire metropolitan area. Yigal Ramon sat at the head of the round table listening to an update from the field over a cellular telephone. He was flanked on the left and right by senior assistants to the Police Commissioner and the Border Patrol respectively. Each had his own cellular phone tied to his boss over a secure, scrambled line. Aryeh Levi directed his part of the operation from his own office at Police Headquarters, and Shaika Oren had joined the head of the Border Patrol at temporary headquarters set up in the Old City.

"I don't care if the traffic is backed up Jaffa Road all the way to Jaffa port on the Mediterranean," he yelled into the phone, "only residents are to be allowed into the Old City, and only if they have a parking lot sticker. Any car that doesn't have a sticker doesn't get in, even if a resident of the Old City is driving." Yigal looked down at his untouched coffee and grunted. Someone rushed up from behind him and placed another cellular phone into his left hand that he immediately placed against his left ear. "And remember, no vehicles at all allowed in after 8:00 p.m."

Realizing the person on the end of the phone in his left hand must be confused, he put down the phone in his right hand without signing off and spoke into the phone still in his left hand. "Sorry, who is this?" he said. It was a struggle to maintain civility. Yigal listened patiently to Yisrael Eitan relay a message from his boss Yossi Shiloni. It was hard to hear above the pandemonium in the operations room. Virtually everyone in the room had their own secure cellular phones, and about half of them were being used.

Yigal put down the phone when Eitan had finished speaking and paused to consider the Prime Minister's relayed request. Yigal was ultimately responsible for the security of this operation, but he would have to have an extremely good reason to go against a direct suggestion from the Prime Minister. He decided to give in to Shiloni on this one. It wasn't worth the fight. Yigal turned to the Police Sergeant on his left and said, "The Prime Minister wants us to round up all leaders of right wing activist groups who live in Jerusalem for questioning and keep them in custody until 9:00 a.m. tomorrow. If you happen to see any demonstrating publicly, pick them up. Otherwise don't bother going to their houses. Also, anyone breaking the curfew in the Old City tonight, is to be arrested immediately, no questions asked."

The Sergeant emotionlessly relayed the message over the open line to the Police Commissioner's office.

Amiram slowly entered the operations room unnoticed in the commotion. He felt more like he was on the trading floor of the Tel Aviv Stock Exchange than in *Shabak* Jerusalem headquarters. He walked past the giant Old City map as an agent with a telephone to his ear used his free hand to shuffle some magnets around the map indicating updated personnel positions. Amiram eyed Yigal speaking simultaneously over two phones, and took a deep breath readying himself to confront his boss with his suspicions about the source of the Shimshon fax. Time had run out. He had to make the information known. Innocent lives were at stake. Once again the life of his partner was at risk, only this time it was Udi and not Ari. If it meant he would lose his job by having to admit that he himself had sent the copy of the Shimshon file to the PLO, Amiram was ready to do that. He was tired of living with guilt.

As Amiram took a step toward Yigal, who still hadn't noticed him, he felt a tap on the shoulder. Amiram turned to encounter a beaming but exhausted Motti Nir.

"I found it," said Nir with a twinkle in his eye. "I beat my own monster."

Amiram felt his heart thump in his chest. Thank God he thought. "How? Who sent it?" He grabbed Nir by both shoulders, not wanting him to escape before he revealed the information.

"Well, when we didn't find anything with the text search, I figured there was nothing to find. Obviously, either our game didn't reach the computer of the sender of the fax, or the sender had deleted the file, or had never saved it on his word processor in the first place."

Amiram folded his arms, restraining himself from saying, '*Nu*, get to the point already!' He let Nir savor his own brilliance.

"But then I recalled that when a message is sent from a wordprocessor over a built-in fax, the program first rasterizes the information," explained Nir.

"What does rasterize mean? It sounds like a disinfectant to get rid of bugs in the program," said Amiram.

"Not exactly," laughed Nir, "the program scans the text like a fax machine, and basically turns it into one big picture. Just a bunch of black and white dots. Then it sends the rasterized file over the phone lines to the fax machine on the other end of the line as a series of dots. Most computers save the rasterized file in a 'send log' in case it needs to be resent at a later date. So even though the text file might have been deleted, if the computer operator forgot to delete the rasterized file, it might still be there."

'I'm beginning to understand,' thought Amiram to himself, 'but just tell me who sent it already.'

Sensing the impatience in Amiram's face, Nir hurried up his explanation. "I looked for all files with an extension beginning with the letters .FXS which is the most common extension for a 'sent fax' in rasterized format. We came up with a few dozen files, but since they couldn't be scanned for text, I began looking at them one at a time with the fax viewer module of our own fax program. After fifteen minutes I found it. Bingo," said Nir handing Amiram a copy of the fax proving he had found the needle in the 40 gigabyte haystack.

Finally, Amiram could ask his question, "That's amazing. You're a genius Motti. But who sent it?"

"Interestingly enough, it was a local east Jerusalem number. It came from the Palestinian Center for History and Culture," announced Nir triumphantly.

"That's a front for carrying out a lot of illegal political activity in Jerusalem isn't it?"

"You got it," confirmed Nir. "Either one of Abu Alim's illegal agents or a secretary of their's sent the Shimshon Fax from the office computer. I imagine some janitor or security guard played the 'Holy Stones' game on the same computer after everyone had gone home and infected it with our 'virus program.'" Nir patted Amiram on the shoulder, "And now I gotta go home. Good luck."

Amiram watched his colleague walk out of the room. He looked down at the fax and turned to confidently face Yigal. His secret could remain intact.

Fifty Four

The honking of the cars and trucks lined up Jaffa Road was beginning to make the two police officers edgy. They were directing traffic at the traffic light located at the intersection at the bottom of the ramp leading up to Jaffa Gate. Marc glanced at his watch. He had been stuck in this jam for fifteen minutes. Each driver in the line up in front of him had argued loudly with the policemen, pleading with them to let them in. It hadn't helped. Orders were orders. Since 5:00 p.m. only vehicles with Jewish Quarter parking stickers were let in. All others had been waved past.

"Maybe I should get out of this line and turn right at Mamilla and park in the David's Village parking lot," said Marc to Rachel and his three passengers in the back seat. "It's only a ten minute walk anyway to the Old City community center from there, and they're still letting pedestrians in."

"Come on Marc, let's go for it," said one of the yeshiva students, "when they see us here in our army uniforms and our kit bags, they'll assume we're part of the security forces here. There hasn't been enough time for an orderly deployment. I'm sure some guys from the units who were on leave are finding their own way to the Old City."

As Marc's Volvo reached the head of the line, he kept his window rolled up, smiled at the policeman at his left and pointed with his thumb at the three soldiers crammed into the back seat. The officer smiled, and waved them through.

Marc made the sharp left turn to make the ascent to Jaffa Gate, maneuvering past a number of blue Ford Transit police vans and green army Jeeps. Entering Jaffa Gate and passing the Kishle police station he was taken aback by the sheer numbers of military people milling around drinking coffees out of Styrofoam cups.

"I can't believe that guy let us in," said the student sitting in the seat next to the left window.

"It's obvious why it happened," answered his friend beside him, "we're on our way to do a *mitzvah*. And God clears a path for those running to do good deeds."

Fifty Five

Amiram held the fax in his hand for a full minute before approaching Yigal. The din in the room faded from his ears as he lost himself deep in thought. If Nir had taken just one minute more before getting the fax to him, Amiram's would have admitted to Yigal what he had done, and his career would have been over. Coincidence? Amiram thought for a moment how Ari had pointed out to him on many missions how the Hand of Providence played a role in their success. He filed the thought away, pulled himself together and stepped toward Yigal.

"We discovered the source of the Shimshon fax," he said coolly, placing the page on the table in front of Yigal.

Yigal looked down at the fax and then up at Amiram. "I'll get back to you," he said into both telephones and lay them down on the table. He picked up the fax, got to his feet and said quietly, "Come."

Yigal walked away from the conference table and entered a small meeting room adjacent to the large operations room followed by Amiram who closed the door behind them. Yigal sat down. "So?" he said to Amiram who was still standing.

"The Palestinian Center for History and Culture," answered Amiram.

"What?"

"The Palestinian Center for History and Culture."

Yigal planted his elbows on the table and placed his palms over his eyes. He felt like he had just been told he was adopted as a baby and his mother was not really his mother. His first reaction was, 'how could a settler have gotten into that place to send the fax?' Then his denial melted into a realization of the more probable scenario. The author of the fax was a Palestinian. But why? Yigal got to his feet, placed his hands in his pants pockets and began pacing.

"You know it's Abu Alim's 'unofficial' office in Jerusalem," said Amiram hammering home the truth to Yigal.

Yigal continued to pace. How did Abu Alim get a hold of the Shimshon file? Could Ari Tal really have given it to him? Why would Abu Alim want to kill his own people?

Amiram who already had a few days to digest these questions sensed what was going on in Yigal's mind. He offered some unsolicited help, "However Abu Alim got the Shimshon file, he must have liked the plan. He probably figured we would never have the guts to carry it out. So why not dress up some Palestinians like settlers and blame the Jews for the massacre? And just as in the original plan, in the ensuing world outcry, we would be forced to divide Jerusalem and give at least a piece of it to them."

Yigal stopped pacing and faced Amiram. "The drive-by shootings and the target practice on Abu Alim's portrait were probably diversions carried out by Palestinians masquerading as Jews. They were designed as a wild goose chase to put us in the frame of mind that it was a Jewish underground preparing to carry out the Shimshon plan."

"Probably," said Amiram who had come to the same conclusion. "What do we do now? The Army, the Police and

Shabak are all wasting their time hunting down Jews when we should be looking for Palestinians."

Yigal sat down and ran his fingers through his unkempt hair a few times.

"Why don't we just have Yossi Shiloni confront Abu Alim with the fact that we've got his number, and call the whole visit off?" asked Amiram. "There's still time for that." He was thinking about Udi being up on the Temple Mount when the shooting would start.

Yigal paused to think about the implications before responding. He studied the noise coming from the operations room on the other side of the door. "No, we can't tell Shiloni," he said dryly. "What if he likes the idea that Abu Alim is prepared to do the dirty work in carrying out the Shimshon Plan? If we tell Shiloni, he could give us explicit orders not to act. He could demand more concrete proof tying the fax directly to Abu Alim as a stalling tactic. That could take days, or even weeks." Yigal stood up to pace some more. "We can't let Shiloni or Abu Alim know that we suspect Abu Alim is behind all of this. It will be too easy for both of them to deny it and still carry out the plan. The only losers will be us."

Amiram watched the seriousness of the situation weigh on Yigal's shoulders. "But we have to do something," said Amiram.

"I'll get the word out to the Police and the Army to be on the lookout for Islamic fundamentalists, dressed as settlers, plotting an assassination attempt against Abu Alim. But we have to be very careful to give the impression that we think it's settlers who are behind the Shimshon plan. Abu Alim assumes we think it's settlers behind it and therefore he is anticipating our moves in a certain way. His plan is taking that into consideration. In the meantime I want you to try and figure out what his plan is. I have to continue the operation letting him think we are after the settlers. That will give you some room to operate and use the element of surprise."

Amiram saw the logic in Yigal's approach of keeping the information secret. He just didn't like the feeling of having to work alone. It would require a miracle for one *Shabak* agent to stop the attack.

"The chances of you stopping them are slim," added Yigal, "but if you fail, and the attack occurs, we'll leak the Shimshon fax to the press and pin the massacre back on the Palestinians. If Abu Alim throws it back on Shiloni, that will be Shiloni's problem."

Amiram sighed a half-sigh of relief. It wasn't all riding on him. There was a fall back position. But what about Udi?

Fifty Six

Ahmed Abdo absently massaged the scar on the back of his left hand as he waited to be admitted to Abu Alim's office in the Presidential residence in Gaza City. The quick drop in temperature in the late November Mediterranean evening caused the scar tissue in the muscles under his skin to tingle. Suddenly the large wooden door opened and the Palestinian Minister of Police and Foreign Minister exited. Apparently they had been discussing last minute details for tomorrow morning's visit and press conference. Nasser Rajoub, the Foreign Minister, signaled for Abdo to go inside. He knew that Abdo had requested a private meeting.

Abu Alim's office in his residence was much more ornate and Arabesque than the high-tech facility in Jericho. Like his predecessor, he had a number of residences and frequently changed the place he would sleep as a security measure.

As Abdo walked toward a vacant high-backed chair in front of Alim's gold and marble desk, the President used the few moments to scan the channels on the television monitor on his desk. The President seemed unusually calm to Abdo as he took his seat.

"So, Ahmed, are you ready for our historic flight to-morrow morning?" asked Abu Alim still gazing at the screen and not at Abdo.

Abdo fidgeted in the upholstered seat, cleared his throat and responded, "Yes, your Excellency, but there is one minor detail that concerns me." Although Ahmed Abdo had been Alim's private bodyguard from the days even before he was President, he still chose to address the President in the third person. Abdo felt it was more professional that way.

"What detail is that?" asked Abu Alim fiddling with the remote control.

Abdo shifted again in his seat, "It concerns the *Shabak* agent who will be accompanying us in the helicopter."

"Yes, what about him?"

"Well," continued Abdo, "his name is Udi Harel. Our Intelligence informs me that he used to work on assignments with Ari Tal." He rubbed the scar on his hand with his right thumb a little more intensely.

"So?" asked Abu Alim, shifting his gaze from the television to his old friend, recognizing the genuine concern in his voice.

"Well, I just thought that there might be a chance he would use the opportunity in the helicopter or standing next to me at Al Aksa to... ," Abdo paused to find the right words, "... to perhaps settle a personal account."

Abu Alim laughed, "Don't worry. Nothing will happen tomorrow. Besides, I look at the *Shabak* agent as an insurance policy. Consider him your personal hostage." Abu Alim was careful not to even hint that the Shimshon plan was to be carried out tomorrow morning. No one knew except for the lone gunman. The secret had even been hidden from the woman and her assistant who had helped the gunman carry out the 'target practice' and the drive-by shootings to divert the attention of the Israelis.

Alim had been waiting for the right moment to execute the Shimshon plan since he received the copy years ago. He assumed it came from a disgruntled Ari Tal and he had his trusted bodyguard eliminate Tal before the Israelis found out the PLO had a copy of the file. Alim could then put his plan into action as if it were being carried out by right-wing Jewish settlers.

Abu Alim was confident he was doing the right thing. Even though some of his brethren would have to die, he would get Jerusalem for the Arab people. Had not Assad in Syria killed 30,000 of his own people for less? Saddam Hussein dropped poison-gas bombs on his own Kurdish citizens to maintain control of Iraq, hadn't he? Even King Hussein rid himself of the PLO in the 1970's in a bloody expulsion.

But in spite of his confidence, secrecy was necessary for success. The world had to assume it was a Jew responsible for the massacre. Abu Alim's visit was the perfect alibi. How could anyone assume the President of Palestine was behind the plot when he himself would be on the Temple Mount when the shooting began? Although this presented a small risk Abu Alim wasn't worried about his personal safety. The gunman was not just a gunman, he was a marksman. And the plan for his escape was infallible. The Israelis suspected nothing.

Fifty Seven

"I hope nobody here feels claustrophobic," said Saul Greenberg placing down a tray full with teas and coffees. "The curfew has started. We're locked in for the night."

"Don't worry," said Marc, "I couldn't imagine a more comfortable place to spend the curfew."

"Or a nicer group of people to spend it with," added Leah Tal.

Rachel picked up a cup of tea from the tray and glanced around the sunken living room observing all the nick-nacks and artifacts accumulated over a lifetime. Saul was a semi-retired lawyer from Philadelphia. He and his wife Harriet had moved to Israel a decade ago fulfilling a lifelong Zionist dream. In addition to his charitable work, he spent much of his time studying at the Yeshiva with Marc.

The Greenberg home played host to a constant stream of guests. Saul would bring home some tourists he met at Friday evening services at the Western Wall for Shabbat dinner. Old friends from America would always drop by when visiting Israel. They considered it a privilege to own a large three-bedroom apartment in the Jewish Quarter of the Old City, and felt it a responsibility to share it with others. That is why when Marc called to ask if they could host some people for the demonstration, they immediately said 'yes.' Leah and Rachel would share one of the bedrooms, Marc had the other, and three Yeshiva students would crash in sleeping bags on the living room floor.

Harriet had seized the opportunity to whip up a giant pot of spaghetti and meat sauce for dinner. Now over tea and cookies for desert, the business of planning tomorrow's demonstration was to begin.

Harriet and the guests sat in a beige set of overstuffed couches arranged in a 'U' around a large square oak coffee table. Saul sat down in his large 'lazyboy' lounger.

"You know, with this curfew on, I still can't figure out how you're going to have a demonstration tomorrow morning. The police have orders to arrest anyone the minute they appear on the street," said Saul taking a sip of her tea.

"I haven't seen this many security personnel in the Old City since President Clinton came to Jerusalem," added his wife Harriet.

"If we all wear army uniforms," said one of the eighteen year old Yeshiva students, "they'll never notice us."

"Shimmie, that's dumb," said his friend sitting beside him elbowing him in the side, "they'll never notice the demonstration either because we'll blend into the crowd of soldiers outside."

"Besides," chimed in the third student, "there probably aren't more than fifty uniforms in the whole Old City. What kind of a demonstration can you make with fifty people?"

Leah had to control herself from laughing and spitting out her mouthful of tea. These Yeshiva boys were so delightful. The sad thing was that in the prime of their youth, they were being forced to spend half their time in the army. They were part of a *Hesder* program where they alternated between studying in Yeshiva and serving in the army every six months for five years.

"Marc, how many people do we have available for the demonstration anyway?" asked Leah.

Marc pulled out a small orange notebook from his shirt pocket and flipped it open to some handwritten notes he had made earlier. "There are about four hundred families living in the Jewish Quarter with about one hundred children over the age of sixteen. Assuming most of the teenagers come and one of the parents - somebody has to stay home with the little kids - that makes about three hundred and fifty. We've placed an average of five demonstrators in two hundred and fifty of the homes. That brings the total to sixteen hundred. If we get permission from the various institutions in the Old City, there are probably an additional four hundred Yeshiva students dorming in the Jewish Quarter who can join us. That makes about two thousand in total."

"That's an impressive number," said Saul, "but how are you going to get them out to demonstrate without being arrested?"

"What's so bad about getting arrested?" asked Shimmie, "if we don't resist, and let them arrest all of us, it will make the government look totally out of control."

Marc got up from the couch to walk to the living room picture window. The Greenberg's were one of the few fortunate families to own an apartment facing the Western Wall. Down below on the large plaza paved with Jerusalem stone, he noticed about twenty parked police Ford transits. There were five military buses that had brought in soldiers from all parts of the country as reinforcements, in addition to a dozen Jeeps and six ambulances. Soldiers milled all around the vehicles as well as at the entrances to the Western Wall plaza and the Dung Gate leading out of the Old City.

Rachel stood and followed Marc to the window. The view was breathtaking. She looked down at the military vehicles. A lump formed in her throat as she shifted her gaze to the Western Wall itself. At this time of night, there would normally be from one- to two hundred worshippers. Tonight she could make out one lone soldier praying at the Kotel. Rachel's temples began to pulse as he became filled with outrage. Could it really be true that an Israeli government was preventing Jews from pouring out their hearts to their Creator, in order ensure a safe visit of a murderer of Jews to the holiest site of the Jewish people? Something had to be done. The enthusiasm and determination of Leah and Marc had penetrated a chord deep inside of her. Rabbi Steinberg's words echoed in her head. What does God want from us, she thought.

Nervously Rachel turned to look at the small group assembled in the Greenberg home. She paused for a moment to decide if it was really her place to speak up. She glanced back at the Wall just to make sure that what she felt inside was right. The plan was clear to her. Rachel spoke slowly, taking the people in the room a little by surprise. "We are not going to demonstrate tomorrow morning. No amount of shouting slogans and waving placards will move the government. We are simply going to fulfill our obligation to pray at the Western Wall. We must show the Almighty that our relationship with him is more important to us than anything else. He will take care of the rest. There is a time to fight and a time to pray. This is a time to fight with our prayers."

The room was silent as Rachel spoke. Tears began to fill Marc's eyes.

"But how will we get past all the soldiers to the Wall?" asked Shimmie quietly, trying not to disturb the mood in the room.

Rachel looked at Shimmie and spoke confidently. "There are two thousand of us. If we all walk out of our apartments at exactly the same moment with the men dressed in *tallis* and *tefillin*, the police and soldiers will be taken by surprise. There won't be enough of them to be everywhere at once. At least half of us will get through to the Wall."

The Yeshiva students nodded in agreement.

"Rachel, you're brilliant," said Marc. In his excitement for the plan he felt like hugging her, but held himself back. "Harriet, do you have a Jewish Quarter phone directory?" asked Marc. "We have to start calling every home in the Old City and let them know to leave their homes at exactly 7:15 a.m. tomorrow morning for a mass prayer service at the Kotel."

Rachel turned to the Yeshiva students, "Shimmie, you, Rueven and Levy put on your uniforms and get to as many Yeshiva dorms as possible and let them know about the plan. Dressed as soldiers, no one should pay any attention to you wandering through the streets tonight."

Leah watched Marc and Rachel work and realizing what a great team they made she said, 'If you keep this up, Rachel, I'll be able to retire from *Kol Ha'am* sooner than I thought."

Fifty Eight

The black night sky to the east behind the Mount of Olives had already softened to a navy blue. From his unique vantage point standing on top of the Western Wall, Amiram could sense the pink, orange and even yellow light pushing its way ahead of the approaching sun. He zipped up his paratrooper bomber jacket to cut the chill of dawn. The cold he felt was not only from the night air, it was mixed with the kind of cold one feels from staying up all night.

Except for a half hour cat nap at 3:30 a.m. Amiram had spent all of the previous evening and night at his desk pouring over the text of the original Shimshon file. He read, and re-read every word of the fifteen page document including the three pages of maps and diagrams of the Temple Mount and the secret tunnels below it.

In the original plan, *Shabak* agents were to dress up as settlers and enter the Temple Mount through a secret passage discovered during the excavations of the Western Wall tunnels. During the 1970's and 80's a long tunnel the length of the Western Wall had been dug out underneath the Moslem Quarter buildings butting up against the Wall. They would arrive at the Golden Dome of the Rock via a system of passages and tunnels that were constructed for the Jewish priests at the time of Solomon. After appearing momentarily, and firing their automatic weapons at the unsuspecting worshippers standing to the south at the entrance of the Al Aksa Mosque, they would disappear down through the same passage under the Dome of the Rock. They would find their escape through a different series of tunnels discovered by the Wakf. Over the years, in their effort to hide and destroy any archeological evidence linking the Temple Mount to the Jewish people, the Moslem religious council had discovered many other secret tunnels unknown to the Jewish archeologists, but were revealed to Shabak via informants. This 'unknown' set of tunnels exited into the basement of the Madrasa school, butted against the northern retaining wall of the Temple Mount, on the site of the Antonia Fortress from Roman times. From there the 'terrorists' would change clothes, leave the building, and disappear into the Moslem Quarter, far from the site of the attack.

Would Alim's assassin's use the same tunnels outlined in the original plan? Wouldn't that be the first place the Shabak would look for the attackers? Were there other secret tunnels known to Alim, and not to the Shabak? The questions rolled over and over in Amiram's head all night making him dizzy. After a nap, he decided to come to the Old City to see if looking at the site first hand would give him some new insights. He donned his Colonel's paratroop uniform, figuring it would give him the easiest access through the security in the Old City, and strapped his Uzi automatic handgun to his hip.

Amiram stomped his burgundy-colored leather paratroop boots against the hard stone in an attempt to warm his toes. He hadn't expected it to be so cold. Gazing out over the gray dome of Al Aksa and the open plaza between it and the blue-tiled Dome of the Rock, Amiram counted only a few dozen security personnel patrolling the site. The full deployment of security people was only to begin at 6:00 a.m. He turned 180 degrees to survey the Western Wall plaza below him. A few lit up picture windows of the apartments facing the Wall caught his attention. The citizens are up early this morning, he thought. On the roofs of the apartments and the Yeshiva buildings adjacent to them stood about half a dozen armed border police. Below him and to the right of the plaza next to some public water fountains was the entrance to the Western Wall tunnel excavations. During the day it was operated as a guided tourist attraction.

Amiram rubbed his hands together hoping to warm up his fingers. His mind raced trying to out-think Abu Alim. There was not enough time, nor the help to follow up all the possibilities. He was going to have to 'hit a homerun on his first swing' as Ari used to say. Ari used to explain everything either through baseball or Torah. Amiram walked to the small police outpost to his right, built on top of the roof of a building in the Moslem Quarter at the level of the top of the Wall. Inside sat a policeman speaking to someone over a wireless radio. Amiram ignored the upside-down stack of Styrofoam cups and picked up a plastic cup meant for cold drinks. He filled it with some boiling hot water from the aluminum electric hot water urn, and squeezed the plastic cup between his two palms. After warming his hands for a moment, he dumped a spoonful of Turkish coffee powder into the cup and stirred it. A few swigs of caffeine were just what he needed to get through the next few hours.

Amiram put the half full cup down on the table, nodded to the policeman and walked out of the building and down the stairs to street level to make his second tour of the Old City this morning. He walked north through the Moslem Quarter meandering through the narrow streets along the length of the Western Wall. Most of the run down stone residential buildings were from the Turkish period. The streets were empty except for the occasional pair of Israeli soldiers on foot patrol.

As he reached the northern limit of the Temple Mount platform he turned left in front of the El Malakiya school. A kippah-clad Israeli soldier was opening up the front door of the school.

"*Shalom Aleichem*," said Amiram greeting the soldier.

"*Shalom Aleichem*," answered the soldier as he disappeared into the building.

Amiram smiled as he thought about Abu Alim's request to have only plain-clothes servicemen on the Temple Mount during his visit so as not to have any evidence of Israeli military control of the site. Little did he know that the top of the Western Wall and the roofs of all the buildings surrounding the Mount would be crawling with Israeli soldiers in their khaki uniforms.

Amiram continued his walk all the way to the Lion's Gate on the eastern side of the Old City. This was the gate stormed by Israeli paratroops in 1967 during the Six Day War. He paused to reflect about those heady days in Israel history and contrasted them to the depression he was feeling this morning.

Amiram walked back through the Moslem Quarter along the Street of the Chain, through part of the Arab market and then made a left turn in the direction of the Jewish Quarter. Moments later he exited a tunnel into the Western Wall Plaza. He walked silently toward the Wall along the smooth hard slabs of Jerusalem stone. He was alone standing in front of the giant stones looming above him. Amiram reached out and touched the cold face of the stone. He closed his eyes and searched deep inside of himself struggling to find the words to ask for help.

Fifty Nine

"There must be a couple of thousand Palestinians lined up here," reported the sergeant in charge of the unit assigned to Lion's Gate. He was speaking to Yigal over a cellular phone, who was troubleshooting as well as directing the campaign from the operations room a few miles away. "They're starting to chant slogans. If we don't do something soon, I'm afraid the mob will take on a life of its own."

"Are all the plainclothes people deployed on the Temple Mount?" asked Yigal.

"Everybody arrived right on time at 6:00 a.m. It's like summer camp up there. They've each got a buddy. A Palestinian with one of our boys. It's really cute. They're all wearing blue blazers and gray pants. It looks like an IBM convention."

If the situation wasn't so serious, Yigal would have laughed. He couldn't let a thousand fired-up Palestinians onto the Temple mount with only sixty 'computer salesmen' to keep them under control. The only secure approach was a highly visible show of force.

"Are you still there?" asked the sergeant. Yigal was thinking.

"We only promised Abu Alim that there wouldn't be any uniformed personnel around while he was up there. We can clear them out just before the helicopter lands. In the meantime, send up fifty border police with tear gas launchers to help back up the blue blazers. Once they're in place, start letting in some of the Palestinians... but only if they're forty years or older."

"Yes sir," said the sergeant, relieved that he could release some of the steam in this pressure cooker.

Even though there was a curfew on the Old City itself. People were allowed free movement in the New City. Hundreds of police and soldiers were stationed at each of the gates around the Old City. Access was limited to Lion's Gate, and then only to Palestinian well wishers.

At Jaffa Gate a crowd of a few thousand Israeli protesters were shouting anti-government and anti-Abu Alim slogans. The police had formed a human barrier behind the blue metal barricades that had been set up to keep even pedestrians out of the Old City. As the mob became noisier and more boisterous, frantic clipped conversations were taking place between the police on the front lines holding back the demonstrators and the local headquarters in the Kishle police station inside Jaffa Gate. Moments later the large red metal bar was lifted from the entrance to the Kishle station and the first of ten huge horses stepped out into the street, proudly bearing their confident masters carrying shields and riot sticks.

As the horses exited Jaffa gate, a loud jeer roared through the crowd and people began whistling in indignation. The horses stopped. The mounted force had been given strict instructions from Yigal not to act. They were to be a visual deterrent only. He didn't want to be accused of unfair treatment of the Jewish population. It was bad enough that Yossi Shiloni had ordered him to allow the Arabs on the

Temple Mount while the Jews were to be kept out of the Old City, and those residents inside the City were forced to stay in their homes.

Sixty

Udi Harel looked like a tourist hurrying through the white lobby of the Hotel Palestine. The black strap of his overnight bag was slung over the right shoulder of his blue blazer. His orders also specified gray slacks and a white shirt. Udi ignored the clerk at the cashier wicket and he pushed through the glass revolving entrance door with his left hand. He wasn't sure who was going to pay for his room, but certainly it wasn't him.

Even though the sun was still casting long shadows in the Gazan sand this early in the morning, Udi slipped on his dark sunglasses. On assignments like this, he preferred others not being able to see what he was looking at. He quickly glanced left and right without moving his head as he ducked into the back seat of the black Mercedes waiting for him with the engine running.

Abu Alim's personal security force were not happy about a Shabak agent joining the President in the helicopter with him, but it was the only way Shiloni would allow them to come to Jerusalem without an Israel air force helicopter as an escort. Indignantly the Palestinian Secret Service had isolated Udi at the hotel until the last possible moment. As the limousine sped through the few short blocks to the Presidential residence, Udi gazed out the tinted glass window. He was taken aback by the contrast between the pristine luxury of the Hotel Palestine and the filth of the narrow Gazan streets.

Moments later the Mercedes moved through an open metal gate operated by a uniformed security guard into the Presidential compound. It was a much smaller estate than Udi had imagined. The limousine came to an abrupt stop at the side entrance of the villa. The loud roar of rotors could be heard inside the car. Udi looked out at the neatly manicured lawn and gardens to the right and thought 'where's the helicopter?'

A secret service man opened the door for Udi while another took him by the right elbow to help him out. Udi felt like saying, "keep your paws off of me," but he held his tongue. The two men led him into the villa and up three flights of marble stairs with ornate stone banisters to the exit to the roof. Another secret service agent stood guard at the door with a Kalachnikov machine gun. Udi's hosts nodded to the agent and opened the steel door. A gust of wind from the powerful blades blasted Udi in the face as he was led across the flat roof of the villa to the helipad.

Waiting for Udi at the opened passenger door to the helicopter was still another Palestinian secret service man. As Udi approached him under the deafening roar of the rotors, he felt he was looking in the mirror. The anonymous Palestinian was also wearing a blue blazer, open white shirt, gray slacks and dark sunglasses. It was going to hard to tell the good guys from the bad guys today, thought Udi.

The Palestinian made a movement with his right arm, indicating for Udi to get into the helicopter. Out of instinct Udi shifted his eyes in the direction of the cabin without moving his head. The pilot sat alone in the front. The back seats were empty. Udi stepped up into the helicopter and in an unnoticeable motion put his hand on the small weapon under his blazer they had allowed him to bring, making sure it was still there as he bent himself behind the front seats. He shuffled his body across to the far side of the helicopter and the Palestinian immediately followed Udi inside, taking up the place to Udi's right in the back seat. Only then did Abu Alim appear at the roof exit surrounded by half a dozen agents. The group moved as a single wave towards the helicopter. Udi strained to see if he could pick out Ahmed Abdo, the President's private bodyguard, and Ari's murderer, from among the circle. In an instant Abu Alim was placed in the front passenger seat and the door was closed.

The pilot increased the throttle and the rotors roared even louder as the helicopter lifted into the desert air. Udi felt a queasiness in his stomach but he quickly realized it wasn't from the sudden acceleration of the aircraft. Surrounded by these Palestinians, at their mercy, he felt helpless. Udi thought of Amiram. Where was he right now? Had he already apprehended the enemy?

Udi wished he was with Amiram actually doing something, and not sitting here as window dressing for Abu Alim's visit. Then Udi caught himself. Stop thinking, he thought. Get your mind out of the clouds and into the here and now. Once you began an operation, it was suicide to use your brain for anything else other than monitoring what your eyes were seeing, your ears were hearing and your nose was smelling. Daydreams were deadly.

Listening to the engine roar, Udi shifted his eyes from the Palestinian beside him, to Abu Alim, to the pilot, and then to the beauty of the rocky desert whisking below them. His anonymous Palestinian 'buddy' reached into his inside right blazer pocket and pulled out a piece of paper and handed it to Udi.

Udi unfolded it. It was a set of instructions in Hebrew the Palestinians expected Udi to follow while they were on the Temple Mount. '*Chutzpah*,' thought Udi, 'I'll do whatever I feel like doing up there.'

Udi realized something had caught his attention and glanced back at his 'buddy's' left hand. The one that had presented him with the sheet of instructions. There was a huge scar from the index finger to the bracelet of his watch. Udi looked up at the face hiding behind the dark glasses. It was Ahmed Abdo.

Sixty One

Amiram gazed through the large black military binoculars to get a closer look at what was taking place up on the
Temple Mount. He was standing beside some Israeli soldiers
who were stationed on the roof of a Yeshiva building set on
top of a natural cliff facing the Western Wall. This was one
of the few vantage points in the Jewish Quarter that one
could see onto the plaza between the Al Aksa mosque and
the Dome of the Rock. Consequently the army used the private roof as a security lookout during high-risk events.

Even though some trees planted on the Mount partially
blocked his view, Amiram guessed there were five hundred
to a thousand Palestinians milling about the plaza waiting for
the President of Palestine to arrive. Through the binoculars
he could make out about half a dozen of the pairs of plain-
clothes security men in their blazers ringing the crowd.

After a whole night of thinking and wandering through
the Old City, Amiram still had come up with nothing. How
could the Shimshon plan be carried out? Shabak agents were
everywhere. All the gates of the City had been sealed. The
Old City residents were under curfew. Police and army personnel were patrolling every stone-lined street and alleyway

in all four Quarters of Old Jerusalem. Even if they carried out the attack, how could the murderers escape?

Two voices shouting from somewhere directly below Amiram caught his attention. He put down the binoculars and leaned forward over the metal protective barrier. Amiram expected to see a couple of people arguing, but what he saw took him completely by surprise. Four stories below him was a small security check point with electronic metal detectors on a large landing on the main staircase leading up from the Western Wall plaza into the Jewish Quarter. A man wrapped in a white prayer shawl was being led down the staircase by a soldier toward one of the Police vans. Behind him six other soldiers held back a silent crowd at the checkpoint. Filling the twelve-foot-wide stone staircase up to the right were hundreds of people. The men were all wrapped in their prayer shawls giving the appearance of a white woolen blanket covering the giant staircase. The Jewish worshippers waited silently and proudly to be let through to the Wall.

Amiram pulled back from the railing. Where the heck did they come from? Instinctively, he ran down the staircase through the Yeshiva building and out the front door. A group that size, cramped into that little space won't stay quiet for long, he thought. He rushed past some soldiers stationed on the front terrace of the building and then out the metal gate to a second smaller staircase leading down to the same checkpoint. Amiram had to squeeze past dozens of worshippers crammed onto this staircase. As he pushed his way down the stairs no one protested. They were all reading quietly from prayer books.

"Let them through," commanded Amiram to the soldier in charge at the checkpoint. As he arrived, another two men in prayer shawls were being led down the staircase.

"You'll have a riot on your hands in a minute if you keep arresting these people." There was fire in Amiram's eyes.

The soldier stood his ground, "I have strict orders to arrest anyone who breaks the curfew. We'll lock 'em all up if we have to."

Amiram looked up at the people waiting on the stairs. Some men and women standing next to him looked at him hopefully and with relief. Finally someone understood them and what they were doing. One elderly woman had tears in her eyes.

Amiram turned back to the soldier, beginning to lose his patience. "I'm a Colonel, and I say let them through! Now!"

The soldier remained calm and shrugged his shoulders. He held up a cellular phone and pointed at it indicating where the authority came from. "Orders," said the soldier.

Amiram grabbed the phone and punched in some numbers. After two rings there was an answer. "Yigal," Amiram impatiently, "it's Amiram. I'm down here by the *Kotel*, and there are a few hundred Jews dressed for synagogue waiting patiently to get to the Western Wall. I have no idea how so many of them got here, but the officer in charge is arresting them wholesale. If he keeps it up there'll be a riot down here."

The soldier watched closely as Amiram listened to Yigal's response.

"I'll take full responsibility for what happens," said Amiram. "All these people want to do is pray. There aren't any placards. All they have are prayer books. There's no way they can get to the Temple Mount. The place is crawling with security. Stop the arrests and let them go."

After hearing Yigal's response, Amiram handed the phone to the soldier. Amiram couldn't hear what Yigal told him, but in a few seconds the soldier waved his men back and the people began filing through the metal detectors.

As the men and women walked past him on their way down the stairs, many of them paused to say *'Shalom'* and 'thank you.' Amiram smiled back at them realizing that what had motivated him to act was not so much the prevention of a riot, but rather the thought of having to explain to his grandchildren one day how he, as a Jew, had helped prevent his people from praying at the Western Wall.

Suddenly, a familiar face in the crowd caught his eye. Something inside made him respond. "Rachel!" he called.

As she exited the metal detector, Rachel paused to look at the strange man in the dark glasses and the paratrooper uniform. She didn't know any Colonels.

Amiram crossed in front of Rachel to the opposite side of the landing where it was a little quieter. Intrigued, she walked toward him, followed by Marc who had passed through the detector behind her.

"I'm Ari's friend," said Amiram uneasily.

Rachel shuddered. Although she had not seen him, she recognized the deep voice of her abductor from two days earlier. It was the *Shabak* agent who had warned her about snooping around the *Jerusalem Press.*

"I found the evidence I needed. You and Meir are off the hook. Now all I have to do is find the bad guys," revealed Amiram. In spite of the tension he felt, with only half an hour to go before Abu Alim's helicopter arrived, Amiram felt some relief in being able to do a few deeds.

"How about my friend Marc here," asked Rachel a little cynically, "is he off the hook too?"

Marc, feeling somewhat disoriented reached out and shook Amiram's hand. *"Shalom Aleichem,"* said Marc formally.

Amiram was taken aback by having someone wearing *tefillin* shake his hand. The last time that happened was in synagogue the morning of his *bar mitzvah* almost twenty five years ago. Amiram thought of Ari who over the years had answered all his etiquette questions about synagogue behavior. He searched his memory for the appropriate response to Marc's greeting. For some reason he wanted to get it right. Then it came to him. "*Aleichem Shalom*," said Amiram, returning the handshake. "*Behatzlacha*," he added, wishing them success.

"I hope you're successful too," responded Marc, "but I have to tell you, your security around here is pretty sloppy. We got into the Old City last night after the general public couldn't enter anymore simply because we had a few guys in army uniforms in the back seat. Nobody bothered to check if they were supposed to be here or not."

"You must have not looked too threatening," said Amiram.

Rachel and Marc continued on their way down the stairs. After a few steps, Rachel stopped and turned to look back at Amiram. It was too much of a coincidence that they ran into him. There must have been a reason for it. "Is there anything we can do for you?" she asked.

Amiram smiled. What could she possibly do for him. He was about to say, 'Nothing, thanks,' when an image of Ari flashed into his head. Then he thought about Udi only a few minutes away in the helicopter with Abu Alim. He needed a miracle.

Something about the sincerity in Rachel's eyes broke into Amiram's soul. He spoke slowly, "How about a prayer?"

Sixty Two

The pilot pressed on in the direction of the yellow sun rising over the hills in front of him to the east. The helicopter had traversed the entire coastal plain and now was increasing altitude as it approached the foothills leading to Jerusalem.

Looking down out of his window, Udi had watched the desert sands and squalor of Gaza meld into the rocky desert of the Negev. As the aircraft continued to the north and east he watched the desert bloom into a patchwork of fields belonging to a series of *Kibbutz* and *Moshav* farms.

Now the fields had melded into tree covered hills. From high above, Udi found it hard to imagine that virtually every mature tree in the carpet of green below him had been lovingly planted by a worker of the Jewish National Fund over the last seventy five years.

Udi wondered what those early Zionist pioneers would think of Israel today. Where had all the idealism gone? Where was the self sacrifice? What were we trying to build here anyway? What would those who fell in the wars to liberate the Jewish homeland think of Udi Harel, a *Shabak* agent, escorting Jibril Abu Alim to the Temple Mount?

Udi looked momentarily at Ahmed Abdo sitting beside him. He was looking out the right passenger window picking at his teeth with the back of a wooden matchstick. In the front passenger seat, Abu Alim sat staring straight out the window, fixated on his goal that lay before him only a few minutes away. In spite of the roar of the rotors, there was a cold silence in the cabin. For a brief moment Udi imagined himself pulling his gun out from under his blazer and empty-ing its contents into the back of Abu Alim's head.

* * *

For the second time this morning Amiram finished traversing the Western Wall tunnel. This was one of the es-cape routes recommended in the original Shimshon plan. The six and a half foot high horizontal shaft stretched all the way from the Western Wall enclosed prayer area northward under the city for a length of 300 meters along the Wall. Cross tunnels perpendicular to the main tunnel extended under the Temple Mount near the location of the First and Second Jewish Temples.

An exit to the north into the Moslem quarter, and the entrances to the cross tunnels were closed to the public. Since these escape routes were explicitly mentioned in the Shimshon plan, Amiram doubted that Abu Alim's men would use them. It was too obvious. But just in case, Ami-ram had requisitioned some soldiers and had stationed them at each one of the exits. Even if he couldn't stop the attack, Amiram felt that if Abu Alim's men could be captured af-terwards, the *Shabak* couldn't be accused and Israel's claim to maintain control of the Temple Mount would be strength-ened.

Stepping out of the entrance to the tunnel into the fresh morning air of the Western Wall plaza, Amiram heard the dull clacking of the approaching helicopter to the west. He couldn't see it yet. Apparently Abu Alim was arriving at a low altitude to give the Arab citizens of the villages of Abu Tor and Silwan a chance to see their leader arriving.

Amiram looked up into the crisp blue morning sky and thought of Udi riding in the helicopter. His stomach muscles tensed. It's not enough to capture them after the attack. I have to stop them.

* * *

Inside the storage room the man wearing the knitted kippah and green khaki army uniform worked swiftly but silently. He moved a glass cutter skillfully along the window in front of him marking a square thirty centimeters by thirty centimeters. That was large enough for him to cover eighty percent of the area between him and the Dome of the Rock. As he worked he could hear some soldiers laughing in the classroom behind the locked door to his right. Behind him some more soldiers patrolled the hallway on the other side of another locked door.

The marksman placed a suction cup against the window, and carefully lifted out the square of glass. A billow of cool November air brushed across his face providing some relief from the stuffiness of the dusty storage room. Now that there was a hole in the window, he could hear the approaching helicopter. Below, he could see the security men take up their positions for the landing. The uniformed Israeli border patrols were being herded off the Temple Mount through a gate below him and to the left. The chanting of the crowd began to get louder as he mounted his M-16 rifle on a metal tripod that he had hidden behind some bookshelves earlier in the week.

When the rifle was in place, he loaded it with a regulation army issue clip of thirty bullets. They had considered using specially made extended clips, but then it would have looked like a professional job. It was important to give the impression that the ammunition was stolen from the army by Jewish soldiers. The marksman placed three more clips on the window sill. He doubted he would need them. Based on the density of the crowd waiting for the helicopter to land on the northern section of the Temple Mount only sixty meters in front of him, he estimated one clip would kill five or six and seriously wound another ten. In addition to the two people he had killed in the drive-by shooting, that should be enough to create the world outcry that Abu Alim wanted.

Now it was time to wait, but only for a few minutes. He picked up a small plastic switch with a red button, attached to a long white wire. This too he had prepared when he had hidden the tripod. The wire ran across the window ledge to the wall on his left. Then it was hidden behind the bookshelves continuing along the wall toward the door behind him. It followed the top of the door frame and passed out into the hallway through a small gap between the top of the door and the frame. The white wire continued a few meters down the hall way at that level until it disappeared behind the large red bell of an old style fire alarm. There it was attached to the alarm's electrical source as well as a moderate amount of plastic explosive.

When the time was right, he would press the button detonating the charge in the hallway on the other side of the door behind him. All the soldiers in the classroom on the other side of the second storeroom door to his right would run back into the hallway away from their positions next to the classroom windows. In the pandemonium, he would fire his M-16 into the crowd below, unlock the door to the classroom on the right and lock the door behind him. In the confusion he would walk out into the hallway melding into the crowd of other soldiers trying to figure out what happened. Then unnoticed because of his uniform, he would simply walk out the front door.

* * *

Standing in front of the entrance to the Western Wall tunnels, Amiram could watch the people praying at the Western Wall to his left. He wondered what they were saying. What were they asking for?

Some more men walked past him wrapped in their prayer shawls on their way to join the service. One old man with a long white beard being escorted by two younger men nodded at Amiram and said, "*Shalom Aleichem.*"

"*Aleichem Shalom,*" said Amiram, nodding back. '*Aleichem Shalom,*' thought Amiram. Ari taught him that a religious Jew always responds '*Aleichem Shalom*' when greeted first by '*Shalom Aleichem.*' But that religious soldier entering the Arab school this morning answered back, '*Shalom Aleichem,*' and not '*Aleichem Shalom.*' And what was he doing alone? All soldiers had been deployed in pairs.

Marc's words from earlier that morning reverberated in Amiram's head...

"but I have to tell you, your security around here is pretty sloppy. We got into the Old City last night after the general public couldn't enter anymore simply because we had a few guys in army uniforms in the back seat. Nobody bothered to check if they were supposed to be here or not."

The clack of the approaching helicopter grew louder. Amiram turned to his right and started to run. He disappeared into an archway leading to the Moslem Quarter.

There were only a few minutes left to reach the school building.

* * *

The pilot had circled around Jerusalem and was approaching the Old City from the south. Abu Alim asked him to slow down his approach and drop lower so that the people could see him waving. The helicopter hovered about two hundred meters above the walls of the Old City slowly approaching the Al Aksa mosque which was the first building on the southern side of the Temple Mount.

As they slowly inched their way from the black dome of Al Aksa to the golden Dome of the Rock two hundred meters to the north, Udi did not like what he saw below. There are too many citizens and not enough security, he thought. One hundred meters north of the golden dome about twenty men in blue blazers formed a human wall keeping the area behind them clear for the helicopter to land.

The pilot dropped altitude and Udi could see the crowd of about five hundred waving their fists in the air in rhythm. He wondered what they were saying. To the left, on the other side of the Western Wall he noticed about an equal number of Jewish worshippers praying down below. How did they get there? I thought there was a curfew. I hope there aren't any more surprises waiting for us down there.

Abu Alim turned and smiled at Ahmed Abdo. A few moments later the helicopter gently touched down on the Temple Mount and the pilot cut the engine. A group of blue blazers surrounded the aircraft and Abu Alim stepped out of the open door, hidden from view of the crowd. Ahmed Abdo got out next followed closely by Udi who hurried up next to him.

As the noise of the rotors died down, Udi could make out the rhythmic chant of the crowd to which the President of Palestine had joined in.

"B'roch! B'dam! Nifde et Falastin!"

Exactly which Palestine did the President plan on *'liberating with spirit and with blood?,'* thought Udi.

* * *

Amiram burst past the soldiers standing at the entrance to the Arab school. They had never seen someone with brass *'felafels'* on the epaulets of his jacket, signifying such a high rank, running that fast. They shrugged their shoulders and held their post, assuming that if he needed them he would have ordered them to follow.

Amiram leapt up the staircase two steps at a time to the second floor. The 'soldier' would have to be on the second floor inside the building to have a good enough vantage point. He ran into the open door of the first classroom opposite the stairs. Four soldiers standing at the window watching Abu Alim turned to see who came into the room.

No time to explain. Amiram turned and left. The murderer would probably be alone. His heart pounded in his chest. He was out of breath from his dash from the Western Wall. His temples were throbbing from the blood pumping through his body.

Four soldiers were stationed in the second classroom. Down the hallway, the third door was closed. Amiram tried the handle with his left hand. He held his cocked Uzi in his right. He pushed open the door. Four more soldiers.

By this time a few soldiers had come out of the classrooms to find out what Amiram was doing. "Hey!" called out the sergeant in charge of the deployment in the school, "what's going on?"

Amiram ignored the sergeant, as well as the open door of the fourth classroom. More of the same.

The wall at the end of the hallway stopped Amiram's momentum. To his right was one last door... 'Please God,' he thought, as he reached out to try the handle. It was locked.

* * *

The jiggle of the door handle behind him startled the marksman. No, it is too soon, he thought. Abu Alim is too close to the crowd.

He squeezed the red button detonating the charge in the hallway, just as Amiram kicked in the door. A blast much stronger than he had anticipated ripped through the hall taking down the soldiers trying to catch up to Amiram.

The force of the blast forced it's way through the open door of the storeroom knocking down Amiram and slightly shifting the tripod.

The marksman rose to his feet. There was no choice. He grabbed the M-16 fumbling for the trigger.

* * *

The sound of the explosion coming from the school building behind the Presidential party startled all the security personnel surrounding Abu Alim. The security men, including Udi, instinctively turned their attention from the crowd in front of them to see where the noise had come from.

Only Ahmed Abdo didn't look behind. He leapt forward onto the back of Abu Alim, shielding his beloved President's body with his own.

* * *

The marksman had no time to aim his weapon at the crowd beyond Abu Alim. Amiram lying prone on the floor, regained his bearings after having been thrown to the floor of the storeroom from the explosion in the hallway. He looked up in front of him and breathed deeply as he lifted his right hand that amazingly still gripped the Uzi. There was no time to aim at the 'soldier' holding onto the M-16. Amiram squeezed the trigger.

A burst of gunfire from the Uzi ripped through the back of the 'soldier' just as he pulled the trigger on the M-16. Only a few rounds managed to leave the M-16 before the 'soldier' dropped to the ground. The marksman died, never to know if he had accomplished his mission.

* * *

There was so much shouting on the Temple Mount that no one heard the momentary crackle from the window of the school building.

Five bullets ricocheted in a line off of the large stones that paved the Temple Mount behind Udi. The sixth bullet whizzed by Udi's right elbow into the back of Ahmed Abdo who was lying on top of Abu Alim.

Pandemonium broke out as Palestinian security people crushed towards Abu Alim to protect their President. Udi was knocked onto Abdo in the confusion, and another agent fell on top of him.

Udi found it heard to breathe. Because of the mass of bodies, he couldn't move his limbs. He felt helpless.

After what seemed like an eternity, when it became clear that there were no more shots being fired, the pile of bodies began unraveling itself. Someone yanked Udi and then Abdo's limp body from off of Abu Alim.

Everyone's attention focused on the President of Palestine, except for Udi. Udi knelt down beside Ahmed Abdo and unnoticed by anyone, picked up his left wrist and checked his pulse. Although Jibril Abu Alim escaped the attack without a scratch, his trusted bodyguard was dead.

Sixty Three

Isaac Abramson, head of the *Jerusalem Press* photo archive, switched off the radio on his desk. There was no new information on the identity of the assassin on the five o'clock news. Even though he worked at the *Jerusalem Press*, ever since the shots were fired on the Temple Mount that morning the only way he could get coherent information was from the radio. The *Press* offices had been a mob scene all day — reporters rushing in and out, phones ringing, fax machines beeping, people shouting.

All day Abramson had been haunted by the memory of that nice young couple he had prepared the photographs of Abu Alim for earlier in the week. Could they have been involved in the assassination attempt? Israel radio had initially reported that the assassin was an Israeli soldier and that he had been apparently killed by another soldier. The American was a tourist. It couldn't have been him. But did he help the assassin with information in the photographs?

Since nine o'clock no further information was reported about the assassin on Israel radio. Had they not been able to identify him? Did they need time to inform his family? Were the Israeli security forces keeping his identity secret to buy time to round up other suspects who might have been involved in a conspiracy?

At 10:00 a.m. Abu Alim held the press conference in Gaza that had been delayed because of the shooting on the Temple Mount. He virulently attacked the Israeli Government for conspiring to assassinate him. He called for an emergency meeting of the United Nations Security Council to condemn Israel and begin proceedings to discuss transferring east Jerusalem to Palestine.

CNN interviewed the Secretary General of the United Nations in New York who expressed sympathy and understanding for the President of Palestine's request. The Security Council was to convene later that morning. He strongly condemned the Israelis for the serious breach in security around the Temple Mount.

At 3:00 p.m. Palestine Television broadcast a photograph and some archive footage of the Palestinian bodyguard who had been killed in the attack. It was Ahmed Abdo; former terrorist and long-time assistant to Abu Alim. Abu Alim mourned the loss of this trusted friend and loyal guard who sacrificed his own life for the sake of his people. The President of Palestine would not let the crime go unpunished.

Isaac Abramson fingered the copies of the photographs he had produced for the couple from *Kol Ha'am*. After the announcement on Palestine Television he had retrieved the *Kol Ha'am* invoice and pulled the original photos from the files. Each one of them had an image of Abu Alim *and* Ahmed Abdo in it. Was Abdo the real target?

Strangely, the Israeli Government had been silent all day. The spokesman of the Prime Minister's office was the only official talking and he was giving no information. "The matter is under investigation." "We will have more information soon." "The Prime Minister is consulting with the Security Cabinet." "No, we have no information concerning the identity of the assassin."

Abramson stood, put on his overcoat that was hanging on a hook attached to the wall and picked up the photos. He walked out of the relative calm of his office into the pandemonium of the newsroom and crossed it toward the office of the Editor-in-Chief. Behind the glass door he saw the Editor, Akiva Singer in an animated discussion with a couple of reporters. Abramson hesitated before knocking on the door. Should he tell them about the couple who had ordered the photographs? If they really were part of an assassination conspiracy, Abramson would be responsible for the scoop of the day. If they were innocent, their lives would become a nightmare for at least the next month due to interrogations by reporters, police and army. Was the scoop that important? He would be retiring in a few months anyway.

The elderly newspaperman turned the handle on the door to the Editor's office. They wouldn't have heard him knock over the shouting anyway. Abramson walked between the noisy reporters and dropped the photos on Akiva Singer's desk.

Singer picked up the small pile of pictures and looked up at Abramson with a puzzled look on his face. "What the heck are these?"

Abramson cleared his throat while buttoning up his overcoat. "They're the photos of Ahmed Abdo you asked me to find in the archives." He decided not to add that they happened to be exactly the same photos that the couple from *Kol Ha'am* ordered only three days earlier. It could wait for twenty four hours until the truth came out.

"Oh yeah. I forgot," said Singer, "Good work. We'll use one of them on the front page. If we don't have a picture of the assassin, at least we have one of the victim."

Sixty Four

The oversized open command car slipped off the main road to the east of the Ma'alot Yair settlement onto the hard-packed military patrol road. The jolt of the vehicle dropping from the asphalt to the dirt road caused the Belgian machine gun to momentarily bounce out of the grip of the helmeted gunner sitting high on a bench in back of the car. As the command car moved slowly toward the fence, marking the boundary between Israel and Palestine, two smaller enclosed jeeps slipped off the main road behind it and fell into line.

The convoy proceeded northward keeping about ten meters from the metal chain-link fence. An Israeli Bedouin scout sitting in the front left passenger seat flashed a hand-held search light on the finely raked sand lying between the road they were traveling on and the nearby fence. He was looking for foot prints of Palestinian terrorists who may have infiltrated the border. Even though this was not a regular patrol, they were simply providing an escort for the jeeps behind them, the Bedouin scanned the *tishtush* for tracks out of habit.

The three military vehicles proceeded along the bumpy path for about fifteen minutes, and at a marking labeled

'129' they came to a halt. The driver of the lead command car flashed his headlights three times. From the darkness on the other side of the fence, the headlights from an unseen vehicle flashed three times in response.

The 'officers' jeep pulled out from its position in the middle of the convoy and passed the lead command car. It advanced about fifty meters and came to a stop. The driver left the engine running. A high ranking officer got out of the passenger side of the jeep and stepped carefully across the raked dirt toward the fence. He had his hands stuffed into his bomber jacket pockets to keep them warm. As he arrived at the fence, he could make out another single uniformed figure approaching alone from the other side of the fence.

"Jibril"

"Yossi"

"I am sorry your body guard had to die today," said Yossi Shiloni quietly through the fence.

"He was more than a body guard. Ahmed was a trusted friend since childhood," answered Abu Alim, coldly. "But I'm sure he could not have found a better way to die. He went to heaven serving his People the best way he knew how... protecting his President."

Shiloni tried to look into Abu Alim's eyes but it was difficult in the darkness of the Judean desert. "We also determined the identity of your other man who died," baited Shiloni.

"My other man?"

"Yes, your man from the Palestinian Center for History and Culture, dressed up as a religious IDF soldier," said Shiloni coolly. "We also traced the faxed threat to carry out the Shimshon plan to the same office. It's just a matter of time before we link the whole thing back to you, so you can stop this game of blaming us for an assassination conspiracy."

Abu Alim let out a loud cackling laugh which startled even the soldiers waiting patiently in the command car sixty meters away. "Yossi, remember, I'm the one who has a copy of the original Shimshon plan which mentions your name explicitly as well as the *Shabak*."

"Of course I realize that," admitted Shiloni, "it's a stalemate. That's why I wanted to talk to you out here alone. No one must know about this. I don't even trust the Green phone. It's in neither of our interests to let the truth out. It would mean the end of both of our careers, and the end of the peace process for the foreseeable future as well."

Abu Alim's reaction was lost in the darkness.

"We must come up with a joint explanation for the 'assassination' attempt to release to the media before too many rumors start circulating," said Shiloni nervously.

Abu Alim looked down at the ground and kicked at a stone as he considered Shiloni's proposal. In a moment, now used to the darkness, he lifted his eyes to meet Shiloni's. "The assassin was a recent returnee to Islamic fundamentalism. He had infiltrated our ranks. Because you and the world have not come up with the financial aid we need, Islam has swept its way through the hearts of our poverty stricken people."

Sure, thought Shiloni, blame everyone except yourselves for your problems.

"If there were Palestinian elections today," admitted Abu Alim, "the Moslem extremists would take over."

"I don't know who would be worse off if that happened," said Shiloni, "you or us." Even though Shiloni recognized that Alim wanted to destroy Israel just as much as the fundamentalists did, Abu Alim's party was the lesser of two evils. Shiloni saw no defense against radical terrorism and suicide bombers. However there was a chance to cut

Israel's losses with the political approach of Alim's secular faction.

"The main obstacle to an Islamic fundamentalist take-over is me," continued Alim. "The only way there could be a minor backlash against the extremists, is if it was one of them who assassinated me. Many of their own people still appreciate what I have accomplished for them. How shrewd for the assassin to dress as a religious Jewish soldier, so it could be blamed on the Israelis. Those very same Israelis that I am being accused of cooperating with."

"That's what this is all about isn't it?" said Shiloni. "This isn't an Arab/Israeli conflict. It's really an Is-lam/Judaism conflict. You must hate the Islamic fundamen-talists as much as I hate the ultra-orthodox Jews and the re-ligious settlers."

Abu Alim looked away, back at his waiting jeep and ig-nored Shiloni's questions. He didn't really hate the funda-mentalists. They had the same goals, only different tactics. After a moment he turned back to Shiloni, "It is decided. You will announce that the assassin was a recent returnee to fundamentalism. He acted alone to eliminate me as a traitor to Islam. As long as he is not attached to any political group, it will be impossible to disprove the claim."

Yossi Shiloni stared at Abu Alim in amazement. He couldn't tell if the story was true or if Alim was making it up on the spot.

Sensing the meeting was over, Yossi Shiloni turned to leave, but Abu Alim called out to him.

"Yossi."

"Yes?"

"This 'peace business' makes strange bedfellows doesn't it?"

Sixty Five

Rachel switched off the radio on her living room wall unit. She was suffering from information overload and the news reports were only upsetting her. There had been a constant barrage all day of live updates discussing this morning's assassination attempt. Miraculously only one Palestinian security guard had been killed and the assassin. The soldiers in the school building escaped with light to moderate injuries. As the day wore on, the government blackout of information started to weaken. Even though it appeared it was one assassin acting alone, some Knesset members jumped at the opportunity to denounce the entire settler movement and the right wing political parties. A government minister on the radical left had just suggested on the news that all religious soldiers from the territories undergo lie-detector tests to test their loyalty since the assassin was a soldier wearing a *kippah*.

Enough, thought Rachel. She scanned the metal rack of CDs beside the tuner, picked out a favorite guitar concerto and slipped it into the machine. Instantly, the soothing chords of the classical guitar wrapped in the harmonies of the violins, violas and cellos filled the room. Rachel felt her shoulders relax. She walked to her bedroom, picked up a pillow from her bed and brought it back to the living room. After placing it on the sofa chair, she walked back to her bedroom to get the book on her night table. Rachel had started it on the plane, but still hadn't finished it. The week had been hectic to say the least.

Rachel just felt like losing herself in a book and a mug of hot chocolate. An emergency meeting was still going on at Leah's house to decide on a response to the attack on the Temple Mount. There was total confusion. Leah was worried about Meir. Marc was worried there would be more arrests of members of *Kol Ha'am*. At 9:00 p.m. Rachel left the meeting, as much as she hated to leave Marc. She simply couldn't keep up with their pace. After all, Rachel had only been at this business for less than a week.

She kicked off her shoes and plopped herself down on the sofa chair. After finding her page in the book, she reached for the mug of hot chocolate waiting on the coffee table. Rachel took a deep relaxing breath looking forward to thinking about the challenges facing the characters in her book for an hour or so, instead of her own.

Just as she nestled her body into the exact right spot between the pillow and the arm of the sofa chair, there was a sharp knock at the door. It figures, she thought. Rachel considered ignoring the intrusion and pretend she wasn't home, but there was a second louder and more deliberate knock.

"Okay, okay. Just a minute!" she called out. Rachel slipped on her shoes and got out of the chair. She walked toward the door, leaned forward and put her eye to the peephole.

Rachel gasped when she recognized both men standing in the stairwell outside. Had they come to arrest her? She paused for a moment to gather her wits. Thinking about the encounter on the stairwell leading to the Western Wall that morning, she decided to open the door. After all the one on the left had given the orders to allow them to pray at the Wall. How bad could he be? And the other one had promised to help find Ari's murderer.

"I realize it's late, but is it all right if we come in for a few minutes?" asked Udi. "We've got some important information to share with you."

The two *Shabak* agents were dressed in civilian clothes. "Nice music," commented Amiram, "Segovia?"

"Actually, it's a Julian Bream concert," smiled Rachel, impressed that the tough Israeli even knew who the great master Andres Segovia was. She motioned for the men to take a seat on the couch. "Can I offer you something hot to drink, these November evenings can get pretty cold." For some reason Rachel felt relaxed now that these two were together in the same room wearing blue jeans and wind breakers.

Udi leaned forward and put his fore-arms on his knees. "No thanks. Actually we planned on only staying a few minutes. We've had a long day, and I'm sure you have too." He didn't want to reveal to Rachel that both he and Amiram had been in debriefing sessions for the last nine hours.

"We have some important facts that haven't hit the news yet. We decided we owe it to you to tell you about it," added Amiram.

It was obvious these two were partners. Rachel picked up her mug of hot chocolate with both hands and sat back in the sofa chair waiting for them to continue. She didn't know what to say.

Udi cleared his throat. "Can you keep a secret?" Amiram and Udi had already decided they could live with the consequences if Rachel revealed the information they were about to share with her, but secrecy would be best for everyone involved.

Rachel nodded and took a sip of the hot chocolate.

"Well, now that that's settled," continued Udi, "as Ari the eternal optimist used to say, would you like the good news or the good news first?"

"Get on with it already," pressed Amiram with a laugh. He could see Rachel was getting a little impatient with the small talk.

"Okay," agreed Udi. "First of all, the politicians are in a frenzy about revealing the identity of the assassin. They haven't determined his exact identity yet, but we know that he was a Palestinian impersonating a religious settler in an IDF uniform."

Rachel shook her head in disbelief. "Then why are they letting the media blame..."

"Don't ask any questions. That's all we can say right now," said Amiram cutting her off. He looked over at Udi and continued their rehearsed script. "But it will all come out in the next few days. What's important is that it means Meir Tal will be released shortly and you don't have to worry about you or any more of your friends being arrested... at least in the short term."

"And now for the good news," said Udi.

"You mean it gets better?" asked Rachel. "When I saw you guys through the peephole I was ready to pack up a toothbrush and overnight bag to take to prison."

Udi laughed. "It really does get better. For some strange reason I got elected to accompany Abu Alim on his visit. I was standing right next to him when the shooting started. It's a miracle only one person was injured in that mass of bodies. The bullet missed me by inches. It's also a miracle it was Ahmed Abdo who was killed."

"Ahmed Abdo?" said Rachel. She heard the name broadcast on the news, but it meant nothing to her.

Udi bent up his left arm resting on his knee as if lifting a barbell and pointed at his left hand with his right index finger. "He had a scar from his left index finger across the back of his hand to his wrist."

"What?" gasped Rachel.

"That's right," said Udi, "the one in the newspaper you gave me. Ari's murderer."

"*Baruch HaShem*," she said.

Udi stood up and nodded for Amiram to do the same. "I was the first one to the body. He died on the spot." Udi reached into his right pant pocket, "This 'happened' to fall off his wrist while I was checking for a pulse." He gently placed the gold watch on the coffee table in front of Rachel. Tears filled her eyes. She was speechless.

"I figured no one would be interested in it at the office," said Udi awkwardly filling the silence, "so I didn't tell anyone about it. It's our secret." Udi nodded at Amiram. It was time to leave, and he headed for the door.

"Why don't you go on ahead," said Amiram to Udi. "I have another couple of stops to make before I go home. I'll take a cab"

Rachel leaned forward and put her mug down. She delicately picked up the gold watch and squeezed it between her hands. "*Baruch HaShem*," she said, "it's amazing how God manipulated all the pieces of the puzzle so the impossible could be done."

Udi opened the door. "I'm not so sure about the God part," he said, "but I have to admit it was pretty amazing. *Behatzlacha*." He disappeared into the hallway.

"Rachel," said Amiram trying to get her attention away from the watch. "I want to thank you for your prayer. I think it might have helped."

Rachel smiled behind her tears.

"And one last thing," he said searching uncomfortably for the words, "since Ari died I've had no one to ask my questions about religion. He always had great answers. I'd like to talk to someone like him about providence, miracles, prayer... that sort of thing. Maybe you can suggest someone appropriate at the Yeshiva."

Rachel brought the gold watch to her lips and felt the soothing coolness of the metal against her skin. "How about Marc?" she said softly. Rachel wasn't answering Amiram. She was speaking to herself.

Sixty Six

"Where did you say you got this?" asked David Moscowitz leafing through the pages of the black plastic file folder.

"I told you already," said Leah sitting down at the table beside Moscowitz with two mugs of coffee. "This strange fellow knocked at my door last night around eleven thirty and handed it to me."

Moscowitz again didn't listen to her answer. He was too caught up scanning the pages of the document entitled, "Shimshon File." His heart started beating faster, and it wasn't from the caffeine this time. "Listen, either this is a hoax, or it came out of a government computer. And if it's real, there's no way Yossi Shiloni will politically survive the scandal." He looked up from the pages and looked at Leah. "Who did you say gave it to you?"

"David," complained Leah, "that's the third time you asked me the same question!"

"Okay, okay, I'm sorry. Now I'm listening. Tell me everything exactly as it happened."

Leah sat up straight in the chair, folded her hands on the table and closed her eyes to help gather her thoughts. She reopened her eyes and spoke slowly making sure to get all the details correct. "Around eleven thirty a man about thirty-five-years-old knocked at my door. He was wearing blue jeans and a navy windbreaker. I wasn't going to let him. Then he told me he was an old friend of Ari's and that he had something to give me. For some reason my intuition told me to trust him even though I didn't recognize him. He came in, sat down at the table here, unzipped his windbreaker and pulled out a large manila envelope that held the black folder you're holding."

"What did he say when he gave you the envelope?"

"He said there was important information in the envelope related to the shooting on the Temple Mount. It was information that could bring down Shiloni and his government and force new elections."

Moscowitz took a sip of his coffee and gave a puzzled look at Leah. "Why would he bring the envelope to you? Why not go straight to the media, or at least to one of the right-wing political parties?"

"I asked him the same question," answered Leah. "He said he came to me because he owed it to Ari. He wouldn't explain the details, only that if not for Ari's death, he wouldn't be leaking this secret information. That's why he came to me, as Ari's mother, and not someone else."

"Hmmm..." Moscowitz's mind was rapidly processing the facts before him. It sounded like a legitimate leak. He leafed through the file once more in amazement. First there was a copy of Yossi Shiloni's memo to Yigal Ramon requesting *Shabak* to produce a scenario to commit a massacre on the Temple Mount using agents disguised as settlers, in order to deliver Jerusalem to the Palestinians. Second there was Yigal's detailed Shimshon Plan on how to execute the operation successfully. Third there was a copy of the 'Shimshon' fax threatening Yigal with an attached note saying it was received by *Shabak* from the offices of the Palestinian Center for History and Culture. Finally, there was a note stating Abu Alim had a copy of the Shimshon Plan, unknown to the Israelis since before Ari's death implying Abu Alim was behind the shooting on the Temple Mount that morning.

"What should we do with it David? Should we send a copy to Shiloni and ask him to resign?" asked Leah.

"No, by doing that, we are defacto showing we assume the information is true. Using it that way would be an illegal use of stolen government information. This material is so unbelievable that it's reasonable for us to consider it a hoax. We'll make a few copies and deliver them anonymously to all the major newspapers. Let them have a field day with it. After they establish that these documents are authentic, it will be only a matter of days before Shiloni resigns and has to call for new elections."

"...and they have to release Meir from prison." Leah finished Moscowitz' sentence. "When they discover it was the Palestinians behind the attack, they'll realize there never was a new Jewish underground."

Moscowitz took a deep breath. "I never thought it would be this easy. No signs, no demonstrations, no phone calls. One little black file folder and the nightmare is over."

Leah slowly put down her mug of coffee. "It's not over yet, David", she said solemnly. "We may be able to stop the handing over of land to the Palestinians for a non-existent peace for a while, but there are many more challenges ahead of us. Somehow we have to get the spiritual needs of the Jewish people taken seriously by whichever government comes to power next. In the scramble to be fair to all our neighbors, we've neglected to develop a sensitivity within our people to each other, our land and our Torah. We can't expect any government to represent the Jewish nation successfully until we're all clear about what the Jewish nation represents."

"At least this is a beginning," David said raising the black folder in the air as he stood preparing to leave. " It took a lot of courage for that young man to come forward with it. Come on. Let's go to my office and make some copies of this "Shimshon File," there are a lot of newspaper editors who are going to love to see it."

Gathering up her own papers Leah thought about Ari and the mystery linking him with the man who had brought the Shimshon file to her last night. 'So many things we'll never know my son,' she thought. 'So many things.'

Turning out the lights and locking the door behind her, she followed David outside leaving the headquarters of *Kol Ha'am* peaceful and quiet for the moment.

Sixty Seven

The sounds of singing filled the dining hall overlooking the Western Wall. The guests had come not only from all over Jerusalem, but from North America as well. White table cloths decked with freshly cut spring flowers covered the long tables normally used to serve up the Yeshiva lunch. The celebration transformed the normally staid room into a banquet hall.

"Can I please see Auntie Rachel's baby?" asked Yoni reaching up on his tip toes to peer at the newborn sleeping in the baby carriage. Yoni's ability to talk had grown just as much as his body over the last fifteen months. Rachel beamed at Yoni as she jiggled the handle of the baby carriage.

"Stop dropping crumbs on him," said Shoshana grabbing the piece of chocolate cake out of his hand.

"He's only eight days old Yoni," added Sarah imitating her mother, "he can't eat cake yet."

Meir Tal reached over, scooped up Yoni and plopped him down on his lap. "Shh," he said, "Uncle Marc is about to start his speech."

A small head table had been set up in front of the wall of windows looking out at the *Kotel*. Marc sat next to Rabbi Steinberg along with three other rabbis who taught at the Yeshiva. Marc, as father of the newborn baby, was the last to speak. As he rose from his chair, someone clanked his fork against a water tumbler encouraging everyone present to stop singing and give the host of the *simcha* a chance to speak.

"Rosh Yeshiva, distinguished rabbis, relatives and guests. I want to thank you all for joining us at my son Shalom's *bris milah* in the Yeshiva earlier this morning," Marc paused and looked over at Rachel, "that is to say, *our* son Shalom's *bris.* Rachel had something to do with it as well."

Laughter filled the room.

"And thank you all for joining in this festive meal celebrating his circumcision. We are especially blessed to have Rachel's and my parents here with us today. Our only regret is that Rachel's grandmother was too frail to make the trip from Toronto.

"It's traditional at a bris for the father to speak about the baby's name. 'Shalom' means peace. Many of you thought we named him that as a sign for better days to come. In fact, he is named after Rachel's grandfather who perished in the Holocaust.

"The Sages tell us that a name reflects the true essence of a person. At eight days old, it's impossible for most of us to peer into the inner soul of the baby. So our tradition explains that the parents receive a kind of Divine Inspiration to pick the exact right name. In this case, there must be something about our son Shalom's character that he shares with his great grandfather. There must also be something in his soul that reflects the Torah concept of *Shalom*. I would like to speak for a few minutes about both, so we can better understand who this brand new member of the covenant of Abraham, and the family of Israel really is.

"The word *shalom*, is related to the concepts of completeness and perfection. A person is on the path to human perfection when they eliminate character flaws by using free will to choose good and avoid evil.

"From the stories Rachel's father has told me, her grandfather Shalom was such a man. Even though he was a working man in Austria, he found time every evening to learn Torah. Whenever he discovered a new truth, he would immediately put it into practice. He used to say, 'a believer is someone who puts into practice what he knows to be true. If you are not doing, you don't really believe. You don't believe because you don't know. Go and study some more.'

"The world is on a path to global perfection when societies eliminate war, poverty and disease by choosing good and conquering evil. That's a huge task many of us might be tempted to say is impossible. What difference can any one individual make? But the Torah teaches us that each human being is a world in him or herself. We must realize that a society is just a group of individuals. If we all only strive as individuals to achieve the greatness of Zaidie Shalom, and show our families and neighbors in ever growing circles how to do the same we would eventually see evil disappear from our midst. Who would be left to steal? Who would be left to build the ovens at Aushwitz? Who would be left to commit suicide terror attacks against innocent women and children?

"In his own way, Rachel's grandfather fought his own battle with evil and won. First, in developing a sterling character. Second, in facing the Gestapo to the very end with dignity, pride and trust in the Almighty... the ultimate source of perfection. The evil Nazi regime may have conquered land and armies, but they could never conquer Zaidie Shalom's soul.

"This gold watch that I am wearing today, belonged to him. It symbolizes him in a very profound way. When you take raw gold ore, and smelt it down removing all flaws and impurities, you are left with a shining gem that brightens peoples hearts with an untarnished glow for eternity.

"Today, Zaidie Shalom's eternal memory lives on not only with the watch, but through his namesake as well. My blessing for our son Shalom is that he follow in his great-grandfather's ways. That he strive to achieve his potential through a life full of Torah values. That he inspire others to greatness. And that with the Almighty's help, he play his role as a member of the Jewish people in helping the world live in a perfect state of *Shalom*."

Marc sat down and the guests burst into song and shouts of Mazel Tov. Rachel looked at her husband with tearful eyes. She thought about how proud her grandmother would have been to hear Marc's speech. It had been a long and bumpy road, but in the end her grandmother's blessing had come true. Her husband wore her grandfather's watch, and her son bore Zaidie Shalom's name. Rachel looked out the window at the Western Wall. She felt her grandfather's presence in the room with her. Looking over at the new life that she had been blessed to bring into the world, Rachel was filled with hope for a brighter future filled with peace for her son Shalom.

Author's Note:

This book was written between April 1994 and December 1994, during the peak of the negotiations for implementing the Oslo Accords between the Government of the State of Israel and the Palestinian Authority.

Although it is a work of fiction based in the future, many of the events have already occurred. To the best of my knowledge, the Shimshon Plan does not exist. Yet, on December 23, 1994, the day this manuscript was finished, the Voice of Israel reported a massive police exercise on the Temple Mount and in the Old City of Jerusalem. Two thousand top police officers were brought in from around the country to see how quickly they could be deployed in case of an emergency. The current police commissioner justified the unprecedented maneuver by saying, "The Temple Mount is the most sensitive spot in the country. We must be prepared for any eventuality."

Acknowledgments:

Thank you to my dear friend and fellow author Pinchas Winston and to Yonah Yaffe for convincing me to write this book. Marc and Batya Friedman, Yocheved Barzel, Shelly Dunn, John Tamerin and Bob Benia gave me early encouragement which kept me going. The insightful comments of Moshe Kempinsky, Richard Senturia, Shalom and Sima Menora, and P.C. Frieberg helped fine tune the characters and the plot. I am very much indebted to Estie Cooper whose professional touch helped tie up all the loose ends and put a final polish on the finished product. Thank you to Sharon Friedman whose initial feedback helped me double my convictions that the book must be written. John and Tabby Corre provided the final push.

Even though the characters in this story, with obvious exceptions are fictitious, I am indebted to the following people and organizations for providing the inspiration for many of the characters and events in the book: Rabbi Noah Weinberg, Jack Kaminker, Ruth and Nadia Matar, Ruth Gregor, Bob Lang, Meir Indor, Dan Polisar, Dr. Martin and Ruchie Seiden, R. Tom Meyer, Mordechai Haller, Moshe Smith, Moshe and Dov Kempinsky, Dr. Eli Pollack, *Nashim Lema'an Machar, Moetzet Yesha, Mate HaMa'amatz, Mate Ha'Ma'avak, Shalom LeDorot, Tzedek Tzedek, Mabat LeShalom, Va'ad Lema'an Tzion* and Aish HaTorah.

Without the constant support and encouragement of my wife Chanah, I never could have completed this book as quickly as I did. She is at the same time my best fan and best critic.

Finally, thank you to the One whose invisible hand helped me find the strength and words to write this book.

About the Author

Charles Samuel is a former management consultant from Toronto Canada. In 1983, he and his wife moved to Israel where he writes and lectures internationally in Jewish thought and philosophy. Charles is the author of *Missiles, Masks and Miracles,* an astonishing true account of the Gulf War in Israel.